Also by Lolita Files

Scenes from a Sistah

GETTING TO THE GOOD PART

GETTING TO THE GOOD PART
LOLITA FILES

WARNER BOOKS

A Time Warner Company

Warner Books, Inc., 1271 Avenue of the Americas, New York, NY 10020

 A Time Warner Company

Printed in the United States of America
First Printing: January 1999
10 9 8 7 6 5 4 3 2 1

Library of Congress Cataloging-in-Publication Data

Files, Lolita.
   Getting to the good part / Lolita Files.
     p.   cm.
   ISBN 0-446-52420-4
   1. Afro-Americans—New York (State)—New York—Fiction. I. Title.
PS3556.I4257G48   1999
813'.54—dc21

98-22549
CIP

This book is dedicated to my goddaughter,
Courtney Rolle
for being such a beautiful and inspiring ray of sunshine in my
life . . . even from a distance.

ACKNOWLEDGMENTS

First of all, I say "Thank God" for blessing me with the opportunity to realize my own possibilities, and, therefore, so many of my dreams.

Secondly, to all those wonderful people who have always been in my corner, to those who recently discovered my corner and parked themselves there to cheer for me, and to those who root from the sidelines . . . I give you love up front. Just in case I fail to mention you by name, know that I have infinite appreciation for all you have done for me.

Special thanks to:

Cecil D. Rolle—for all the initial enthusiasm and support that helped get me on my way.

Jackie Jacob at Warner Books—a multi-talented wonder who was there for me from the very beginning. I'm glad I can call you my friend.

Jacquatte Rolle—for bearing with me on this journey of self-discovery; for staying fixed and ever-present.

Michael Cory Davis—the coolest discovery I've had in 1998 (okay . . . so it was actually the end of 1997, but I'm rounding up). Thanks for being the a^2 to my b^2. As a result, we're creating a whole lotta c^2's. Here's to more screenwriting together, to making movies, to more Falmouths and Ft. Lees, to sitcoms and big budgets, to cross-countries and El Segundo-ing. For being my creative match.

Maxwell—'nuf said 'bout you, so "don't ever wonder." You already know I think you're THE BOMB on a grand scale. You be inspiring people to write books and stuff. Keep making that fantastic music . . . I just might squeeze out a few books more!!

Lillie & Arthur Files, Sr., Arthur Files, Jr., Eric A. Brackett, the Brackett and the Files clans, Carolyn Brackett (the most positive-minded person I know), Mary and Willie Davis (and the whole Atlanta clan), Sharlyn Simon (Big Up, Doug!!!), the Rolle Clan (Dr. Cecil & Annie Rolle, Gary & Katrina and family, Angie & Tony and family, and Jenifer, Melanie, Justin and my Goddie, Courtney), Jenean Amber (*'zup girlfriend!!*), The Davis Family in Brooklyn, Lisa "Brownie" Brown, Kim and Cody, Bryan Keith Ayer, Suzette Webb, Jonathan and Julian, Antoine Coffer and my "Live Twin" Teresa Coffer of Afrocentric Books in St. Louis, Cheryl, Doris, Michelle, Taura, and Cassandra at Warner Books, Clara Villarosa for taking me under your wing the way you have, Marty & Monique Fleming-Berg of BCA Books (& Dinky), Shonda Cheekes and the rest of the clan—Moms, Calina and Ramzari (my babeez), and Warren, R. Malcolm Jones and family.

E. Lynn Harris—for being a Godfather to us all, and all my author friends—Eric Jerome Dickey (twin), Omar Tyree, Victoria Christopher Murray (my girl), LaJoyce Brookshire (my Libra sistah . . . *'zup, Gus and Tony!!*), Franklin White, Blair S. Walker (you nut!!), Kimberla Lawson Roby, Van Whitfield, David Haynes, Lisa Saxton, Sheneska Jackson, and Sharony Andrews—for this great bond that we have created amongst us. We all have each other's backs. This is the way it's supposed to be.

Jill Tracey, Karla Greene, Troy & Rejeana Mathis, Eric Saunders, Rod Crouther, Lee Eric Smith, Rodney & Johnika Lee, Brenda Alexander & Family, Frank Jenkins and Family, Harry C. Douglas, Jr. and the Douglas clan (Pamela, Willie Mae, and Harry, Sr. and Rachel), Sherlina, Brenda, Vernette, Rhonda and Michael Ware, Mommy German, the Brown Family, the Mayweathers, The Williams, Bernadette Andrews and family, Andrea and Patrick, and all the old crews, Dr. Joseph Marshall, Jr., Christine Saunders, Carol Ozemhoya, Kim Bondy, Bo Griffin, Yvette Miley, Olive Salih and Alison Tomlinson, Pamela Crockett, KathyAnn Saleem (where are you?), Leroy Baylor, Michel

Marriott, Kevin Cowan, Darryl "Double D" Davis, Louis Oliver, Abdul Giwa, Jr. M.D., Bruce McCrear & the B'ham Crew, Bryonn Rolly Bains, Dedan Baylor and the whole Baylor clan at *Make My Cake.*

The Florida Connection—Janet Mosley of Tenaj Books, Jackie Perkins at Montsho, Felecia Wintons at Books for Thought, Naseem Barron at Nefertiti, D.C. at Afro-n-Books-n-Things, and Akbar at Pyramid Books.

Shondalon and Sundyata Ramin of RaMin Books in New Brunswick, N.J., Shelly and David Jones of Mirror Images Books and Toys in Charleston, S.C., Faye Williams and Cassandra Burton of Sisterspace & Books, Kiki Henson.

My editor Caryn Karmatz Rudy, Nancy Coffey, my Warner publicist—Anita Diggs, Larry Kirshbaum for all the love and support, Pat Houser, Yvette Hayward, The Sorors of Alpha Kappa Alpha Sorority, Inc., and all the book clubs that have supported me, and continue to do so every day.

CONTENTS

GETTING TO THE GOOD PART

I LIKE THE WAY YOU WORK IT

"*Check baby, check baby, one-two-three-four! Check baby, check baby, one-two-three!*"

My heart was percolating like my grandma's raggedy old coffeepot as I chanted the words to Wreckx-N-Effect song "Rump-shaker." It was booming all around me, pouring from the speaker system.

The sound echoed throughout the empty theater, blending with the crazed patter of dancing feet moving with synchronized rhythm across the much-scuffed wood floor of the stage.

There weren't a lot of frills in the Nexus Theater. Nestled on West Twentieth Street between Fifth and Sixth Avenues, it was a tiny little thing that was a far cry from the glitz and glimmer I'd anticipated.

There were none of the dramatic red velvet curtains and elegant balconies I envisioned would serve as backdrops for my grand stage debut. The place was hollow and naked.

Strictly utilitarian. About as bottom-line as you could get.

Plain wooden seats, a stage, a no-nonsense curtain that was just a few threads shy of being deemed burlap, some random fixtures here and there, and the obligatory backstage area.

It was all prop and circumstance. If circumstances called for props, then that's when you got 'em. Otherwise, the place was as scaled-down and threadbare as they came. Just a few steps above the size and status of a high school auditorium.

(Okay, maybe it was a *little* bit bigger. But *damn,* not a whole lot.)

I glanced out in the direction of the empty audience seats as I made my moves. All I could see were the shadows of three men. Who were they, and what were they thinking?

I didn't care. My adrenaline was blowing up.

I boogied across the stage. Sweat trickled down my body, streaming over my teeny-weeny deep blue tank top and working its way down the small of my back. My spandex shorts clung to every curve of my perfectly tight booty, and I was waving it 'round for all the world to see. My clothes were discreetly, provocatively, sweaty in all the right places.

I couldn't have planned it any better.

I wanted to get the part in this production bad. Real bad. If I got it, it meant a whole new life change for me. I was going to try my hand at dancing for the stage, maybe even Broadway.

What was I talking about? Bump *maybe . . . definitely* Broadway!! Why would I stop at just a small-scale production? *Hell,* I'm *Reesy.* Everything I do is *over-the-top.*

And if I was going to try my hand at this, it was going to be over-the-top, or not at all.

Not that this was going to be a small-scale gig. I mean, if I got the part, it was going to be a pretty big deal.

But it wasn't Broadway. That was still a *loooong* ways away.

There were two parts up for grabs, and there were six other women dancing alongside me, all of us shaking our asses like our lives depended on it. But, as far as I was concerned, those heffahs weren't even there.

It was all about *me.* I was gonna get one of these roles, dammit, if it was the last thing I ever did.

Still singing in my head, I zooma-zoomed in the poon-poon.

I worked my hips and wiggled my butt as I gyrated across the stage, adding my own little flava (The Reesy Special, I like to call it) to the routine the choreographer had taught us to do to the music. I had this way of letting my body go, as flexible as an overcooked noodle, while I got into the groove. This shit was a workout, but I was getting a helluva rush out of it.

I had my back bent, leaning forward, slanging my braids all around my head. Right on cue, I spun around booty-forward, back still bent, and began to wiggle again.

Buttcheeks for dayz.

And from watching the body language of the shadowy male figures that sat in the audience grading our performances, I could see that it was working.

Considering the way one of them had been crossing and uncrossing his legs, something sure as hell had to be going on.

And *yes,* it *was* me causing the effect. I had no doubt about that. Sure, those other girls were bad, but wasn't nobody up there working it quite like me. I could feel it.

No telling what they had been scribbling on their lethal pads with those loaded pens. But whether they liked me or not, I was gonna make damn sure I got a rise out of their asses.

My endorphins doing the bump. I felt like I was about to spontaneously combust.

"That'll be it, number three."

I worked my shoulders downward, ass jiggling like Jell-O in the mold.

"Number three, thank you."

I zooma-zoomed on, singing away in my head.

"Number three, you can *go* now!"

The girl to my left elbowed me discreetly.

"They're talking to you," she smirked.

Sneaky heffah. She was just trying to distract me and make me mess up. I ignored her and kept dancing.

I did my thang, sliding to the side along to the music, my arms waving around over my head in a hula-like dance that had me adding way more hip than the choreographer had planned.

"NUMBER THREE!!"

I sang on under my breath, wiggling my behind.

I was still grooving when the music came to a sudden stop. I was dancing hard, in the zone. I didn't notice right away that I was the only one moving on stage. My body was racing ahead so fast, that it took all my brain could muster to send it the message to stop. I leaned forward, my hands on my thighs, panting heavily.

The girl who had elbowed me was standing there next to me, staring. She had her hand on her hip. Her mouth was now wide open in a mocking grin. Beside her, the other girls huddled, some of them shaking their heads. A couple of them were laughing.

"Number three?" a heavy voice boomed from the shadows of the theater seats.

I looked down at the piece of white paper stuck to my tank top. A big *3*, scrawled in black Magic Marker, stared back up at me.

Oh shit! I thought. *They want me!*

"Yes?!" I panted excitedly.

"That's enough," the voice said dismissively. "Thank you for coming."

His words didn't register at first.

"Thank you," he repeated.

"That's *it*?" I gasped, barely able to breathe from the energy rush I had created. My heart was thumping like it was about to explode.

"We'll call you," he said, sounding as empty as I did when I told my random lies to used-up lovers on the phone.

Now ain't this some shit?!!?!! I thought.

Let me tell you something . . . I ain't *nevah* been dismissed from nothing. *I* was the one who did the dismissing.

Even when I left Burch Financial, my last job, where I worked as an administrative assistant for my best friend, Misty Fine, it was *my* decision. I wasn't fired.

But enough about *that*. We'll talk about *that* later.

Standing there on that stage, giving the audition of my life, hoping to find some new direction as a dancer in the theater, I was now *mortified*. How the *hell* were they gon' single me out from everybody else and tell me to get the hell out?

Those other bitches stood over there, smirks on their faces, just staring at me.

I started to cuss 'em out, but, *lucky for them,* I was so out of breath, I was barely able to speak.

I rushed over to the side of the stage, grabbed my duffel bag, and fled.

On my way out, I saw the guy who had asked me to come to

the audition. He had invited me because he liked the way I danced at the audition for *Bubbling Brown Sugar,* the first audition I'd gone to after leaving the corporate world.

He was *definitely* the last person I wanted to see.

"Thanks for coming out," he said with a smile, his hand touching my back as I passed.

"Yeah," I replied shortly.

"Don't look so sad," he said. "It's all good."

"Whatever," I snapped, just trying to get past him and out of the place.

I shoved open the heavy steel back door that led out of the Nexus. In my hurry to get out, the strap of my duffel bag got caught on the outside door handle.

As I struggled to free it, my eyes gravitated upward to the white flyer taped to the door.

Black Barry's Pie Auditions.

I managed to get my bag free and hurried out onto Twentieth Street. I didn't even want to acknowledge what just went on in there.

I walked across Twentieth toward Sixth Avenue, barely aware of what was going on around me or the people that I passed.

Damn!! What made me even think I was good enough to be picked?

Misty was right. I was *crazy* for thinking I could jump my ass into a theatrical production, just like that. With no experience. Who the hell did I think I was, anyway?

Misty was the career girl. She was the one who got all the breaks. I must have been outta my mind to think that something like this was just going to happen for me.

I kept walking. I was humiliated, sweaty and stank. I could smell every orifice of my funky, sticky body.

I frantically waved for a cab, heading uptown on Sixth Avenue.

One slowed down and was about to pull up alongside the curb.

The man took one long look at me, standing there like a two-dollar hoe in my sweaty clothes, and kept on going.

Shit.

This was *not* my day.

• • •

Finally, one guy pulled over and picked my sorry ass up.

His cab reeked of curry, and his black turban was so wide and so tall that, once I got in the car, it blocked my entire view of the left side of the street ahead.

The turban was wrapped tightly, and just kind of teetered and tilted, as if, at any given moment, it was going to topple over and take his head right along with it.

"Wearrr-do?" he grumbled in an Indian accent, rolling his tongue thickly over his *r*'s.

"West Seventy-fifth and Amsterdam," I sighed, sinking back into the torn-up seats of his funky cab. "The Milano building."

The cabbie zapped the meter and sped off from the curb.

His cab was so raggedy on the inside, it's a wonder I was even able to sit on the seats without getting a shredded ass from the cut-up leather.

He turned up the radio and began singing this wack-ass Hindu song. *Loud.* Like he was *crazy.* Like I wasn't *eeemuch* in the car.

He weaved and bobbed through the heavy traffic, working his head and the Tower-of-Pisa turban to the music.

I leaned forward and looked at his reflection in the rearview mirror. Around his neck, he wore a Star of David.

What the . . . ?!

Surprised, I quickly glanced at his ID, which was openly displayed on the visor of the passenger side of the front seat.

Mustafa Klein, it read.

"Damn!" I squealed, laughing out loud for the first time that day. "New York is *sooooooo* fucked up!!"

He continued to ignore me, happily singing and bobbing away.

I collapsed back on the seat again, a smile still lingering on my lips.

Not for long, though. As the cab raced its way uptown, I sat there trying to block out the details of my embarrassing audition. Most unsuccessfully.

I kept seeing the look on the face of the chick who tried to get me to stop dancing, skinning and grinning at me as I made a fool of myself on stage.

Dang!! A chill ran through me and my skin flushed.

Nothing . . . well, *almost* nothing . . . embarrassed me. But this was bad. I couldn't block it out.

I kept seeing that heffah's jeering expression.

"Shit! Shit! Shit!" I muttered. *"Damn!* If Tyrene only knew how I messed *this* one up!"

Tyrene is my mom.

And, check this out: my dad's name is *Tyrone.*

I know, I know . . . that's about as goofy as it gets, but I don't even try to understand it. It's one of those situations where you figure two people were just made for each other, from their names on down.

They were two vulgarly rich, black-as-they-wanna-be attorneys who ruled the world (and the law firm their thrones sat at the helm of) with an iron fist.

Between their two names, they came up with mine . . . Teresa.

I know—the obvious, ghetto thang for them to have done was name me Tyreoné (with an accent . . . *gots* to have the accent at the end).

But my folks ain't never had no parts of the ghetto in 'em.

I was their only child. The one they tried to mold into their image. The one they threw money at with both hands, in the hopes that I would conform to their ways of thinking.

The one on whose shoulders they rested the fate of Western civilization as they knew it.

I called my parents by their first names to let them know they could not rule me or force me to carry the weight of the world on my back. Calling them Tyrone and Tyrene was a habit I established long ago, which they indulged at first.

They actually thought it was quite cute, coming from their outspoken little yellow-faced daughter, running around in her dashiki with her head full of braids. The two of them always smiled when I referred to them in my strong, but tiny, little voice, as Tyrone and Tyrene in front of company.

After a while, as I grew older (and more rebellious), they began to be annoyed by it, and that mess got old. But, by then, it was too late to make me change. We were officially on a first-name basis.

At this stage of their lives, and mine, I could truly say they hated me addressing them that way with a passion.

Yeah. If Tyrene knew about my attempt, and failure, to make my mark in the Big Apple, she would be right up here, giving me an earful. Handing me a check. Demanding that I come back home to Fort Lauderdale.

Telling me to stop being so foolish and do something meaningful with my life.

Damn!! Maybe she was right. Perhaps I *did* need to get a grip and move on to something normal.

I closed my eyes, taking deep breaths to try to relax myself and clear my head. That *diddle-diddle-diddle-diddle-ding-ding* music piping through the car didn't help me at all. Neither did all the squawking coming from the kosher swami in front of me as he tried to sing along.

What I *needed* was some Maxwell.

I could just see him now, looking all sexy on the back of his first CD—my favorite, with that crazy head of tangled hair, turning me on with one of his sexy tunes.

It would be even better if I could actually throw down with Maxwell while he was crooning to me. *Yeah.* Wouldn't *that* just make everything all right?

So what, every hot-blooded sistah in America was probably jonesin' for him, just like me? A girl can dream, can't she?

Misty didn't feel it when I got into my Maxwell mode, but she was weird anyway.

She obsessed over Denzel.

Pleeeeez.

Denzel ain't have *nuthin'* on the Blackarican Lover.

Misty said Maxwell was too young for me (another giveaway that she was *way* too conservative for my tastes sometimes).

Too young? Please. Youth was insurance that the sex would be even more thorough. Besides, all the books said that men reached their sexual peak way earlier than women. The way I saw it, me and Maxwell (sexually speaking, that is) were perfectly matched.

Just thinking about Maxwell made the ol' Bermuda Triangle itch a little. Which, in turn, made me unconsciously rub my thighs together. Which, in turn, made me aware that my shorts were kinda sweaty in the front.

Which, *of course,* reminded me of that fiasco of an audition.

"Great," I mumbled, my eyes still closed. "There's just no escaping this."

The car hit something, a bump in the road, or the curb for all I knew, as it careened recklessly through traffic. My eyes popped open just as we were passing Forty-ninth Street and the neon red lights of Radio City Music Hall.

I thought about the Rockettes. As a kid, I'd always wanted to be a black Rockette. Have my fast ass up there on that stage, flashing my tight, toned gams at the world as I kicked 'em high for all to see.

Guess *that* dream was a long ways off.

I sighed, and leaned back against the seat, closing my eyes once more.

The simultaneous sound of smacking and the smell of something rank made me abruptly open them again.

Homie drove using one hand and ate furiously with the other. We weaved and bobbed, barely missing other cabs and cars struggling to get through traffic.

"Excuuuuuse me!" I shouted. "What *is* that you're eating?"

"Wdut?!"

"What are you eating?! Whatever it is, it's making me sick!"

"This?" he asked, waving his hand in the air.

"Get that *out* my face!"

"You ask. I show. Is gefilte fish. Is good. You want try?"

"*No!* Just get me the hell home!"

Swami Klein turned back around, tossing the piece of fish into his mouth.

I was thrilled as hell when we finally pulled up in front of my building.

"Five seventy-five," the Swami declared, announcing the total, not even turning around to look at me.

"I'm gonna need my change back," I said flatly, handing him a ten.

"Sure," Mustafa said happily, finally turning around. He smiled, taking the ten out of my hand with his gefilte fish fingers.

He grabbed another piece of fish and quickly tossed it into his mouth. Then he reached into a zippered bag he had on the seat beside him. The smile still plastered on his face, he offered me four one-dollar bills and a quarter. I looked down at the money.

The bills were wet with gefilte fish from his fingers, and so was the change.

That *muthafucka*. Ol' slick-ass Mustafa.

"Just keep it," I grumbled, wondering how my day could get any worse. Was the whole world determined to screw me?

I exited the cab in a digusted huff. I was barely out of the car before Mustafa sped off, in search of another fool.

Len, the doorman, was standing there in front of the apartment building, cheesing at me like a hungry rat.

"Having a good day so far, Miss Snowden?"

I was so annoyed, I didn't even bother to answer.

I swept past him, into the lobby, and rushed on to the elevators.

I pressed the Up button, hoping that it wouldn't be too long of a wait.

To my relief, the elevator doors opened immediately.

I quickly stepped inside.

The doors squeezed shut, and the elevator whisked me away.

I found myself wishing I could be like Charlie Puckett, in that scene from *Willie Wonka and the Chocolate Factory,* where he and Willie sped up in the elevator, bust through the glass roof, and shot off, clean out into the stratosphere.

As wack as my day had been, I wouldn't have minded being shot out into space. Not one little bit.

I knew Misty wasn't home, but I really needed to talk to her.

She was a corporate bigwig. Misty worked every day of the week, and half the night sometimes.

Or so she *said*. Of late, I'd been having my doubts about what she was doing with her nights. Something about the way she'd been behaving smacked of being a little bit more involved than just working late.

Tired and frustrated, I stepped off the elevator and trudged down the tiled art deco corridor, groping in my bag for my keys. By the time I reached the door to our apartment, I was mentally deflated and in desperate need of a place to just fold up and hide.

I fumbled with the lock for a second or two, then lazily pushed against the door with all my body weight.

I tossed my duffel bag to the side as I walked through the pale beige marble foyer. It was old marble in an old building, but it was elegant nonetheless.

I beat a path across the room. I knew exactly what I needed, and made a beeline for it straightaway.

Our living room was a series of warm browns and russets, rusts and golds. The floor was an endless, sprawling expanse of deep rich hardwood. And we had a view of Central Park, that was, *baby*, simply to die for.

The walls were the color of butter. It was such a welcoming tone that it immediately set your mood when you walked into the room.

There was a big cushy armchair made from a soft and velvety rust-colored material. It was Misty's personal favorite.

The matching sofa was my spot. Made from the same fabric, it was all pillows and comfort, and had served as a bed for me on many a night I was just too damn lazy to crawl to my room.

Our black art covered every possible square inch of wall space. It was like a gallery in there, with her Frank Fraziers and Art Bacons dominating the east wall, and my Varnette Honeywoods and Leroy Campbells dominating the west.

The works of Charles Bibbs, beautiful, colorful, engaging pieces of long-limbed people swathed in stunning regalia, populated the foyer. And the hall leading to the bedroom was a collage of African masks that were, at once, both magical and frightening.

Misty's treasured collection of Senegalese African villagers was showcased on a small round table in the southeasternmost corner of the room. The table was covered with kente cloth and the villagers were gathered proudly in a huddle on its surface.

In addition to the sofa and the armchair, we had found a couple of cute, eccentrically flavored chairs in the shapes of open hands. We'd gotten them from Ikea, a store I loved for its quirkiness and flair and, most of all, for the fact that you could get some really cool furniture there for really, really cheap.

On the squat, mahogany coffee table in front of the sofa was a funky blue vase made out of cracked glass. And in the middle of our living room was a massive fixture that housed the TV and all the other audiovisual equipment. If it hadn't been carved from such a beautiful pickled wood, we would have literally considered it the armoire from hell, and had the thing moved outta there on the day we moved in.

Instead, the armoire's beauty was its saving grace. But it was a lumbering thing that gave us much grief, with its popping panels and creaking shelves. Its doors often ricocheted open unexpectedly, damn near hitting you in the face when you passed. Sometimes, the TV shut off for no reason, right in the middle of the best part of a movie or a show. CDs often skipped at will.

Mind you, the same equipment was totally operational when we removed it from the armoire's housing. Bizarre stuff only happened when we put it back inside.

Misty thought the thing was possessed. Sometimes, I swear, I thought so, too.

I found the electric blue CD, sitting faceup on the middle shelf, on top of the audio equipment. I pressed the Eject button on the CD player, the tray slid out, and I very gingerly placed the disc inside.

I pressed the button again, and the tray retracted.

I pressed the Skip button, fast-forwarding to cut number two.

Home at last, I thought, as the soothing sounds of "Welcome" by Maxwell began to pour from the speakers.

Finally, I could relax and allow myself to forget about all the crazy shit that had happened to me.

The heavy beats of the music came thumping out of the speakers.

I stood there for a second, swaying to the beat, and then made my way over to the couch. I flopped down, lying back against its velvety cushions.

With the heel of my right foot, I pushed the sneaker off my left foot. When the shoe came off, I did the same with the other one.

I lay there, my left arm across my forehead, eyes closed, and breathed in and out, in and out. Trying to calm my frazzled nerves. The music was like medicine. It was slowly but surely taking me away.

". . . make yourself at home, 'cause you're welcome . . ."

By the time the song was halfway through, a physically exhausted and psychologically battered version of me had drifted off to sleep.

I found myself basking in the glow of a peaceful dream of me and Maxwell, him rubbing my sore muscles, making everything feel better.

As for me . . . in the dream, my fingers curled happily around one of his tangly locks, as I prepared to take his young and tender ass on the ride of his life.

I was awakened by the phone ringing.

I sat up on the couch, groggy, looking around.

There *was* no Maxwell, musically or otherwise.

How could he just dip on a sistah after that nice-nasty little session we just had?

Well . . . so much for *that*.

I rubbed my eyes and reached for the phone on the coffee table. "Hello?"

"Well, *hellooooo,* Miss Reesy!"

I blinked a few times, trying to get myself to fully wake up.

"Uh-huh. Who's this?" I mumbled.

"It's Hudson," the deep, seductive voice went on.

"Hudson *who?*" I asked, not moved in the slightest.

"Reesy," he reprimanded, "it's me, Hudson Webb. We've got a lunch date today, in case you forgot. You didn't forget, did you?"

Lunch date? *Hudson Webb?* Who the *hell* was this . . .

Ohhhhhhhhh!!!!

Suddenly, I remembered.

"Hey, Hudson!" I chirped, trying to clear my throat. "How are you?"

"I'm fine, baby. You sound a little tired."

"No, I'm straight. I was just taking a quick nap. My morning was kinda busted."

"I'm sorry to hear that," he said. "I hope I didn't wake you."

"Well yeah, you did. But I needed to get up anyway."

"Are we still on for lunch?"

"Yeah," I replied. "Lunch is still fine for me. Can we make it a late one, though? Maybe around one? I need to shower and change."

"One is fine. How about China Grill?"

"China Grill is good. Fifty-third and Sixth, right?"

"Exactly. The reservation will be under my name."

I stretched, drinking in his soothing voice. Perhaps Hudson had *other* things that were just as soothing. I could use some soothing right about now.

"All right. I'll be there at one."

"Okay, gorgeous. See you when I see you."

I hung up the phone.

I had forgotten all about Hudson Webb. How could I forget about him, and that lunch date we had planned well over a week ago?

Hudson was a tall, buff, cafe-au-lait brother with deep, deep dimples. Very handsome. He was a Wall Street broker, but he wasn't one of those tight asses, like so many of them were. He had flair and flash about him.

I actually met him in the Village, at a hip, retro clothing store called Antique Boutique. He was hunting down an eclectic jacket. Something that would make him stand out at the firm where he worked.

Well . . . *that's* what he said. He loved being different.

I was looking for a pair of funky shoes.

He asked my advice on a jacket, and I picked one out that I thought best matched his demeanor.

We swapped numbers and talked a few times on the phone. He wasn't exactly the type I usually went for, but brother was too fine to let go by.

Going to lunch with him would *definitely* be a good move.

Besides, I needed something to change my disposition. After that horrible audition, a nice meal in the presence of a good-looking man just might do the trick.

I ran my tongue around the insides of my mouth. It was very cottony, very dry.

And I stank. I still had on the same clothes I'd been in all morning.

"I *needs* to get my funky behind in the shower," I mumbled.

I got up from the couch and stretched again. A long, feline stretch.

Then, right there, in the middle of the living room, I very carefully took off my tank top, peeled out of my shorts, and stepped out of the thong I'd been wearing.

I didn't have on anything else. The windows were not covered. The view was wide open for all the world to see. But that was straight me and my exhibitionistic streak.

The way I saw it, if some freak was out there, desperate enough to be looking through a telescope, trolling through the views inside people's apartments, trying to get his peep on, then he deserved a look at my black ass.

Okay, *yellow* ass. You had to be determined like a mug to be able to catch somebody standing naked in their apartment, on one of the highest floors of a building, in the middle of a Monday morning. *That* was no small feat. *That* took talent.

I stooped down, gathered up my clothes, and walked into the kitchen. Butt-nekked.

I opened the refrigerator and pulled out a bottle of Evian. I stood there in the doorway, the clothes now tucked under my arm, arctic bursts of air blasting over me and my naked funk, screwed the cap off the water bottle, and drank straight from the container. That water was delicious. I just let it course down my throat and cool my palate.

"*Mmmmm*. This tastes *sooooo* good. I really needed it."

(I talked to myself a lot. It was the way I blew a lot of my frustration off. That, and meditation.)

I took another long sip, then screwed the cap back on. I closed the refrigerator door and leaned back against the counter, stretching my legs.

"Let me get my butt in the shower." The smell of my own rank body was beginning to get to me.

On my way to the bathroom, I tossed the clothes I had been holding into the laundry basket. *Misty will be proud of me for that,* I thought to myself, smiling. I wasn't the neatest child on the planet, I knew. As she so often reminded me.

I stepped into the bathroom, pulled back the shower curtain, and turned on the hot water.

I let it run for a little bit, while I stood in front of the mirror in the vanity area, studying my body.

I looked at my tight figure, thinking back to the audition that morning. I had been damn good. I knew it. I moved well, and I had the best presentation of all those heffahs out there.

The thought of it all still made me mad.

And made me feel a little sorry for myself.

I put both my hands up to my head and grabbed my braids. I stared at my reflection. I looked like Medusa, with all those snaky plaits stretched out like that. My yellow face had a slightly red flush. It seemed beat and tired, and my eyes had a curious slant, like what they needed most were a decent night of sleep. I looked pitiful.

My saving grace, thank goodness, was the fact that I looked a lot younger than most people thought I was. I was often confused for being anywhere from twenty-three to twenty-seven, when I was really thirty-two. That was mad cool, especially when it came to pulling cuties.

From the way I looked right now, though, I couldn't pull a cutie with a ten-ton truck.

"*Uuuuuuuuugggghhhhhhh!!*" I screamed, holding the braids in my hands tightly away from my head. "I have to shake this!! Things have to get better!! They just *have* to!"

I was determined to have a good time at lunch. That's just all there was to it.

I grabbed a couple of hairpins, wound my braids together into a ball, and pinned them up.

I pulled back the curtain, stood under the steamy water for a few seconds, then took a long, hot lingering shower. With each drop that pelted my body, I could feel the tension of the morning rinse away.

I oiled and perfumed my body, slipped on my robe, and dipped down the hall to my bedroom.

I grabbed a bone-colored crochet halter dress. It was always an attention-getter and even though it was only the end of March, we were in the midst of one of those "el Niño hot spells" so I figured I could get away with it. I picked out a pair of my favorite sandals, the brown leather Via Spigas, and snatched a black thong from my underwear dresser.

I was dressed in no time flat. I freed my braids from the pins and peeped the total results as I passed by the full-length mirror in the corner of my room. My legs were nice and golden, lean and muscular. The dress showed off the tight curves of my calves and fell over my booty just the way I liked.

"Not bad, not bad."

I scooped up my purse and headed out the door.

On my way out of the building, Len greeted me again.

"Doing better, Miss Snowden?" he asked.

"Much better, Len. Much better."

"Do you need a cab?" he asked. "I can hail you one."

"No thanks. I can do it myself."

I stepped out to the curb and stuck my finger up.

A cab pulled over immediately, and I jumped my butt in.

"China Grill. Corner of Fifty-third and Sixth."

The African brother nodded as he pulled away from the curb.

"And could you step on it? I'm running a little late."

As usual, the lunch crowd at China Grill was pretty thick.

Located in the bottom of the CBS building, it was a very popular spot.

A few heads turned my way. I was dressed pretty funky considering how most of the crowd was attired. It was mostly the midtown set, people coming from nearby offices to power lunch and flex.

The young woman at the front podium greeted me. "May I help you?"

"Yes. I'm meeting someone here. Hudson Webb."

"You must be Miss Snowden."

"Yes," I smiled, suddenly feeling a little important.

She spoke to one of the hostesses, who was standing beside her.

"Right this way," the hostess smiled, leading me past the bar and toward the back.

I followed her, feeling a number of eyes following me.

There was Hudson, fine as ever, sitting at a corner table, staring out the window. He had on the jacket he'd bought from Antique Boutique. It *did* make him stand out.

In a very good way.

He stood up when he saw me approaching.

"Damn," he whispered, kissing me on the cheek. "Mama, you look *hot, hot hot*!!!"

"Thank you," I beamed. "You're not looking too shabby, either."

"Well . . . um . . . you know," he joked, rubbing his chin in a pimpish manner, "I kinda had a li'l *hep.*"

When he kissed me, he left a little moist spot on the side of my face.

Brother's got a wet mouth, I thought. *Hmmmm.*

That could be a good thing. *Or* a bad thing. Wet kisses walked a fine line between being real nice, or just plain nasty.

He held out my chair so that I could sit down.

I did, and he followed suit.

I picked up the menu and began to sift through it.

"You're looking pretty tasty there, mama," he said. "For someone who had a busted morning, you sure as hell clean up real good."

"Thank you," I smiled sweetly. "But do me a favor. Let's not talk about my morning. Let's just order some food, 'cause a sis-tah's a little hungry, ya know?"

"Whatever you want," he beamed. "Just say the word."

"I think I'll have some of their dumplings as an appetizer," I mused. "But no, *wait* . . . these lamb ribs sound real good, too."

"Why don't we get one of their sampler platters, to start?" he said. "It has a bunch of different things on it that you can nib-ble from."

"Okay."

Hudson signaled to our waiter as he passed.

The man came and scribbled down our order. For my meal, I got the grilled chicken salad.

"What would you like to drink?" the waiter asked.

Hudson looked at me.

"A glass of merlot? A cocktail?"

"No," I said, shaking my head. "It's too early in the day." I looked up at the waiter. "Just let me have a glass of Pellegrino."

"Fine, ma'am. I'll bring a whole bottle."

He took our menus and disappeared.

Hudson leaned back in his chair and sighed.

"So, mama! Let's talk. Play catch-up with me. It's good to fi-nally see you again after our brief, chance encounter."

I leaned back in my chair and smiled.

Coming to lunch was *definitely* a good idea. Already, I was digging him.

Thoughts of my dreadful morning were fading far, far away.

● ● ●

The sampler platter arrived in a flash.

There were all types of assorted little goodies, but the lamb ribs caught my eye from jump.

I speared one and put it on my plate.

Then I tried to be cute and cut it with my knife.

Hudson laughed.

"Now, you *know* you want to pick that up and eat it with your fingers!!"

"*Uh-huh,*" I chuckled.

"Then *do* it!"

I glanced furtively around the room.

"What you looking around for?" he quipped. "These crackers don't know you, do they?"

"No, they don't."

"And *so* what if they did!" he added.

I laughed again, and thought about Misty. She would balk if she saw me right now.

But that was the difference between me and her. Sometimes, I plain just didn't *give* a shit.

I picked up the lamb rib and began to get down.

It was *delicious*. It had a nice, subtle gamy taste, and the sauce was in*cred*ible.

There were three more left on the platter. I eyed them, hoping he didn't like lamb nearly as much as I did.

"You can have them," he answered, reading my mind. "I'll just nibble on this other stuff while you get your grub on."

"Thank you," I grinned.

The ribs were so good, I didn't have any conversation with him as I ate them. I just picked them up, one after the other, and gnawed my way around the bones.

I was feeling so relaxed, I could have just floated away.

My fingers were a mess.

I reached for the napkin on my lap.

"*Uh-uh,*" Hudson said, and caught my hand.

He pulled it toward him, turning it over and looking at it.

I watched him, totally taken by surprise.

He pulled my hand toward his mouth.

My brow rose in confusion. I tried to pull my hand away.

But Hudson was determined (and pretty damn strong!). Apparently excited by my resistance, he tugged harder, and, once again, my hand continued its trajectory toward his mouth.

He parted his lips, and I watched in horror as, *one by one,* he began to *suck the sauce* right off my fingers. He pulled each one through his lips, long and slow.

It took me a second for it all to register.

I stared at my hand in his mouth.

My stomach lurched in horror as his sloppy spit was slathered all over my hand.

The people at the table next to us snapped their heads our way.

I was thoroughly appalled.

"What the *fuck* are you doing?!!" I shrieked, snatching my hand away. "Are you out of your *fucking* mind?!!"

Hudson was as surprised as I was.

"But, *baby,* I was just trying to help clean you up!"

"You nasty *bastard*!" I screamed, picking up the Pellegrino and flinging it in his face.

Gasps flew all around the room.

Hudson sat there, shocked and sputtering.

I pushed up from the table, wiping his nasty spit off my hand.

"What made you think you could suck my damn fingers?! Did I *ask* you to do that *shit*?! Spitting all over me like some kind of fool!"

Everyone was staring. All of China Grill, the back part anyway, was now my stage.

"Reesy, *sit* down!!" he pleaded, water dripping off his face. "*What* are you doing?"

"Getting away from *your* sick behind! What kind of *shit* is that? Sucking my fingers!! You don't even *know* me!!"

I snatched up my purse and rushed over to the bathroom. It was down a flight of stairs.

I burst inside and ran straight over to one of the sinks. I turned on the hot water and pumped out handful of soap, frantically washing my hands in an effort to remove his foul spit from my fingers.

I felt like I wanted to throw up.

I should have *known* Hudson's ass was too good to be true.

The bathroom attendant offered me a paper towel.

In my haste, I snatched it from her, rubbed my hands till the skin was raw, and flung it in the trash.

Hudson was standing at the top of the stairs when I came out of the bathroom.

"*Reesy, I . . .*"

"Get the *fuck* away from me, you *freak*!"

I rushed past him and all the staring diners, past the bar and out of the restaurant.

I raced across the concrete, up the stairs, and onto the curb.

"*Taxi!*" I screamed. "*Taxiiiiiiiiiiiiiiiii!!!!!*"

To my relief, the traffic light turned red, and a slew of taxis were trapped in front of me.

I hopped into the nearest one. I didn't even bother to check if it was empty or on duty.

"West Seventy-fifth Street," I snapped. "Just off Amsterdam."

The cabdriver didn't look too pleased to have me, but *dammit*, his ass was stuck.

I looked to my left.

Hudson was running out of the restaurant and up the stairs, toward me and the cab.

I looked at the light. It had changed to green.

"*Hurry up!*" I screamed at the cabdriver. "*Go on! Get outta here!*"

He glared at me through the rearview mirror.

"There are other cars ahead of me," he snarled.

"Just *drive* the cab, all right?!" I cried.

As Hudson reached for the door, the cabbie bolted away, leaving him standing there, looking like an idiot.

I slumped back in my seat, relieved. How could my day get any worse than this? I felt like that old Lenny Williams song. I wanted to just roll myself up in a big ol' ball and die.

I sat on the couch, miserable.

I knew I had to be miserable. You know why?

Because I wanted to call Tyrene.

I *never* wanted to call Tyrene.

I mean, I had already tried to call Misty, but I hadn't gotten a response.

First, I paged her, and got no answer.

Then I broke down and called her at Burch. And I *hated* calling Burch.

Ever since I had left my job there, I stayed away from the place like the plague.

So what, they discovered I used to be an exotic dancer? That wasn't necessarily the reason why I kept my distance.

It wasn't like I was embarrassed about *that*.

What *was* a little embarrassing for me, though, was the *way* I ended up leaving my job there.

Like I said, I used to be Misty's administrative assistant. In retrospect, it wasn't the smartest thing in the world for Misty and I to work together. Business and friendship don't always mix.

But we were doing just fine until this stupid ass, traitor-to-the-race piece-a negro (a *sexy* mutha, at that . . . that's what made it so bad) rolled up in the house and blew up my spot right in front of everybody, talkin' 'bout how he used to love to see me dance at the Magic City.

The Magic City was the strip club where I worked when Misty and I used to live in Atlanta. It was right before we came to New York.

In a three-year period, we had hopped from Fort Lauderdale (our hometown), to Atlanta, to here.

Running from men. *Misty's* men. Running to new jobs. *Misty's* jobs.

I was the official tag-along.

Misty was the new top gun at Burch, and, as a sistah, was already under a lot of scrutiny.

So, when brother blew my cover, it made her look bad as well as me.

I personally swore that if I ever saw his *tired* ass again, it was gon' be *on*.

Misty had already known about my stint as an exotic dancer. She found out about it in Atlanta. But she didn't care.

All right. Maybe she cared a *little* bit. But not enough to keep her from being my friend through thick and thin. It didn't stop her from giving me a job at Burch when I couldn't get one anywhere else on my own once we made the move to New York, after she got a promotion.

I had even done a little dancing at a spot in Times Square for a hot minute, but damn near got raped. I was hemmed up in a back alley with some greasy lout who roughed me up pretty good.

That scared me enough to make me bring that whole exotic dancing chapter of my life to a close.

But my exotic dancing was Misty's and my little secret, and she had been hoping like hell that nobody at Burch ever found out about it.

Wasn't shit I could say when it happened. I tried to play it off, but I was wide open. And even though things went down ugly, and the big boss, Rich Landey, came up from Atlanta to try to straighten everything out, I *still* got to decide whether I wanted to stay with the company or go.

It was *my* choice. Nobody else's. I was in total control.

I chose to leave. Who needed the hassle of all those white folks in my shit every day, making judgments about me? So it was my call, any way you looked at it.

But, because of all *that* stupid shit, I really didn't like going anywhere near Burch, and that included calling there. I only did it when it was absolutely necessary. And I always dialed Misty direct.

I usually hung up if I heard anyone's voice other than hers.

Like now. When I dialed her up, some perky white voice answered the phone.

Click.

I was *not* in the mood.

I tried my Grandma Tyler, but she wasn't at home.

So that left Tyrene.

Like I said, I had to be feeling *mighty* bad to go *that* route.

Right now, it would feel really good to hear my mother's strong, comforting voice taking control of the situation. She was good at taking control. It was her forte; she prided herself on her management skills, both on the job and in her—and everybody else's—personal life.

But, just as that would be a good thing, it would also be a bad thing, for the very same reason.

She would take complete control, say something crazy, like *Bring your foolish behind back home where you belong,* or she would offer me money and piss me slam off.

And, to me, that would be like pouring salt on an already gaping wound. I would end up madder than I had started out.

I blankly stared at the coffee table, trying to fix my attention on a dark spot on the wood until I could sink into it and forget all the shit of the day.

My hand *still* felt nasty. I couldn't get that image of Hudson sucking off that sauce outta my mind.

"Uuuuuuuuuuuuuugggggghhhhhh!!!!!!" I screamed, fighting against myself and my raging emotions.

When the tears began to fall, I knew I was losing the fight. I cleared my throat, hoping the tears would get the hint that they were *not* going to win.

Obviously, the tears didn't care. They dropped with renewed energy as I fell over sideways on the couch and grabbed hold of one of the pillows. I pushed my face into it, muting any sounds that were even considering escape.

I couldn't believe I was crying. It was just something I didn't do. No one *ever* saw me cry. My grandma had heard me do it on the phone, but those were rare moments that were few and far between.

I had to get this mess out of my system. The way I saw it, tears and Reesy Snowden were like oil and water. They just *didn't* mix.

I bit into the pillow, my eyes feeling puffier and wetter by the minute.

"I'm not gonna stay," I said, sobbing quietly into the fluffy cushion. "I gotta go back home. I'm gonna call Tyrene and tell her. I just need to get my butt outta here, 'cause New York is not for me."

I let myself consider that thought for a moment, resigning myself to it little by little.

By the time I reached for the phone, I was ready for whatever it was Tyrene had to say.

As long as she sent me a plane ticket home.

I could have used one of the stipends she and Tyrone sent me every quarter, but I just refused to go that route. Besides, no matter what anybody thought, the money was not sitting around somewhere, liquid, able to be accessed by me at will. I always invested it, immediately, and there were penalties and taxes that would come into play. So I couldn't do anything but leave it alone.

I sat on the couch, sniffling hard. I took a few deep breaths, and then I did it.

I picked up the phone.

I dialed Tyrene's number at work. Her direct line.

Within seconds, her keen voice pierced the airwaves, reminding me of the magnitude of what it was that I was doing.

"Tyrene," she piped, sounding like the black shark I knew her to be.

I paused a moment.

"Tyrene!" she snapped again.

"Hey, Tyrene," I finally surrendered.

"Well, *hello,* daughter!" she chimed. "A phone call from you in the middle of the day? There must be trouble, honey. Tell me what it is."

Boy, she didn't mess around. She cut right to the chase.

Just like I knew she would.

"There *is* trouble, isn't there."

She said this as a statement, not a question.

Before I could open my mouth to confess to her, the phone beeped.

"Hold on, Tyrene," I replied, relieved. "That's my other line."

I clicked over.

"Hello?" I asked.

"Yes. May I speak with Teresa Snowden, please?"

I instinctively frowned. It was probably some damn bill collector calling me up in the middle of the day. It wasn't like I was that late on my shit. *Damn.*

My natural instinct was to confront these jerks. I never pretended that I wasn't home. If you were bad enough to come after me for money, then I figured you had better be bad enough to put up with my shit when you asked me for it.

"Speaking!" I snarled with a mouthful of attitude.

"Great! Teresa, this is Gordon Stock. I'm calling about the audition this morning."

"Oh really?" I said flatly. "What do you want? No, let me guess. I didn't get the part. I knew that shit this morning."

"I see you speak like you dance," he chuckled.

"Look, *muthafucka,* I *got* the point. I didn't get the gig. But you don't call here telling me 'bout how I talk. I'll come right back down there and show you just how I do it."

"As a matter of fact, Teresa, that's just what we'd like you to do," he said, now laughing.

"What?! Come back down there for *what*?!"

"To claim the part," he chuckled. "You outdanced every woman in that room today. As you know, there were two spots open. One of them is *definitely* yours, if you'll take it."

I sat there, frustrated, eyes wet, confused, staring at the phone in disbelief.

"If I was so good, then how come y'all damn near threw me outta there this morning?"

"Because we knew you were right as soon as you started dancing," he said. "We wanted to let you go so we could concentrate on filling the other slot."

"Are you serious?" I asked.

"Oh, please!" he exclaimed. "You were making the other girls look sick! They couldn't hold a candle to you!"

A broad grin broke out across my face.

"Really?" I beamed.

"Really."

"Well, I'll be damned."

"As well you should be," he replied. "Could you be back down here by three this afternoon?"

"Sure, yeah, no problem!"

"All right, then. We'll see you at three."

"And I definitely got the part?"

My voice shook nervously as I asked this. It was just a little too freaking good to be true.

"The part's all yours," Gordon confirmed. "You just make sure you bring the same kind of energy this afternoon that you let loose on us this morning. Judging by the way you handled this phone call, I don't suppose that will be a problem."

"No, it won't!" I laughed.

"Good-bye, Teresa," he chuckled again, and hung up the phone.

I sat there, stupefied, the phone in my hands. I was grinning from ear to ear, braid to brow.

It took a minute for me to remember that I still had Tyrene on hold.

"Oh, snap!" I exclaimed, clicking over to the other line. *"Ma?!"*

"Ma?!" Tyrene exclaimed. "Oh, now I *know* something's wrong!! What are you doing, calling me *Ma?* And you know better than to leave a person on hold that long! We raised you better than that, Teresa Snowden! You won't get far in life handling your business like that!"

I sat there, the phone in my hand, just grinning, while Tyrene went on her tirade. I let her go off like that for a few more breaths.

"Tyrene, look, let me call you later."

"Later?!" she huffed. "What did you call me for in the first place? Something *must* be wrong!"

"Everything's great," I said happily. "See . . . look at you. Always expecting the worst. I was just calling to say *hello.*"

"Teresa," she warned, "don't you lie to me."

I wasn't going to let her get to me.

"I'll call you back, all right? Tell Tyrone that I said hi."

Before she could gather up a comeback, I hung up the phone.

I leaned back on the couch, drawing up my knees and hugging them close to my chest.

Hot damn! I just got myself a bona fide dancing gig!

I squeezed my knees so hard, it made me laugh out loud. I rolled free, onto the couch, lying on my back. I closed my eyes and began to sing. *Loud.*

"Start . . . spreading . . . the . . . news . . ."

I kicked my feet in the air rhythmically, à la Liza Minnelli.

". . . New York, New Yooooork!!"

GOOD NEWS TRAVELS LAST

*S*o *you got the gig?!"*

"Yeah," I replied flatly. "I got it."

"*So?!* Why you sound like that? You should be bouncing off the ceiling!!"

'Cause you're a day late and a dollar short, I thought to myself.

"Been there. Done that."

I was stretched out on the couch with the phone in my hand and my sock-covered feet perched high. I stared out the window into the pitch of the night and the shimmering skyline around Central Park.

"I left you a message at the office," I said accusingly. "It's probably sitting on your desk right now. You know, a small piece of pink paper with my name and the word *urgent* written on it. I also paged you. I never heard back."

"Girl," Misty sighed, "it's been crazy here today. This job is kickin' my behind."

"So you can't return a page?"

"The afternoon got away from me."

Her lying *azzzzzzz.*

She tried to keep her voice upbeat. Tried to keep me from going down a road I knew, and she knew, we were destined to travel.

"Well, it don't matter," Misty chirped happily. "Girl! I'm so *proud* of you!! You went out there with no experience, shook your booty like only you can, and claimed your space!!"

"I *have* experience."

As much as I wanted to let go and be giddy with my best friend, I couldn't. The moment for *that* had passed.

When I was running around the house, naked as a jaybird, dying to spread the news, she was nowhere to be found.

I tried to track her down and tell her. I wanted to share my joy with her. I wanted to tell her about that shit with Hudson-the-fingersucker at China Grill. I wanted to tell her *everything*.

After all, she *was* my favorite person in the whole wide world. But *no*. Sistah-girl was *ghost*.

But if it had been that nigga calling . . .

"I know you have experience, boo," she said quickly, trying her best to keep me cool. "That's not what I meant."

"Say what you mean then," I snapped.

Misty let out a heavy sigh.

"Look, I'm sorry I forgot to return your page. I was in meetings all day. Sometimes I just can't juggle it all."

"That's obvious. Tell it to the white folks, not to me. You're the one who wants everybody to think you're Superchick."

"I'm not Superchick, Reesy. I never said I was."

We let the silence hang between us for a minute before either of us spoke again.

"Awww," Misty cooed. "My baby's mad at me, ain't she?"

You know, it's one thing to dis me on the regular. It's another thing to insult my intelligence, to boot.

And what was with all this *baby* and *boo* shit? These days, I was always her *baby*. So was everybody else, probably. Now that she was all pushed-up with broham, she was doling out love to the world, *yes sir, yes sir,* three bags full.

I, *personally*, didn't appreciate that patronizing shit.

"You mad at me?" she pressed.

"You need to get your priorities straight."

"Oh *really?*" she snickered, catching me off guard with her own piece of attitude. "Well, I thought I was doing okay."

"Think again."

"Reesy. Just because I don't hop when you say so . . ."

"I never asked you to," I snarled, getting madder by the minute.

"Then don't cop an attitude with me because I'm not where you want me to be when you want me to be there. I *do* have a life, you know!"

"*Hmph!* For *your* sake, I'm glad you finally got one!"

Ooh. Reesy. Girl, that was kinda mean.

But inside, it felt damn good. And knowing Misty the way I do, I knew she took my statement to mean just what I meant by it.

"So you're saying that I think I have a life now, now that I'm seeing Rick?"

"Well? You certainly didn't seem to think you had one before him, even though you clearly did."

I could hear her breathing silently on her end. I knew the pace and pitch of her breathing well. From the way she sounded now, I could tell that her feelings were hurt.

Good, I thought.

Not that I got off on being mean to her, but she had been being pretty mean to me of late. Maybe *mean* was the wrong word. More like *selfish.* Misty was never there anymore when I needed her. She had practically dumped me for something that she felt was obviously better.

How would *you* feel, knowing that you had been a stand-in for years, just killing time, until Mr. Right came along and gave your best friend something worthwhile to do?

I didn't like being treated that way. I don't play second fiddle to anybody, and if someone tries to do me like that, I don't take that shit lying down.

"Why are we fighting?" she asked in a soft voice.

"Is that what we're doing?" I shot back sarcastically. "I thought we were just having a little chitchat. I talk to you so infrequently these days, I don't know what's what anymore."

"I don't wanna fight," Misty said. "Today is supposed to be a happy day for you. Reesy, come on. You just landed a gig in an off-Broadway show. Do you know how big a deal that is?"

"*I* know," I said, unrelenting. "The question is, do *you?* You didn't even care enough to return my pages. You even forgot that I had the audition today."

"You're not gonna let this go, are you?" she asked.

"I don't like being handled like this."

"I'm not trying to handle you, Reesy."

"Then act like a friend."

I was being hard. I knew it. But why did she have to kick me to the curb just because she was getting some dick on the regular?

"I'd like to celebrate this with you," she said.

"I have my doubts about *that*."

"You get off on this, don't you?"

"Get off on *what*?"

"Negative feelings. Bad energy. For all the damn *nam myoho renge kyo*ing you do, and the meditating and questing for personal growth, you sure know how to beat a dead horse and dwell on the dumb shit."

Her words knocked me for a loop. I couldn't say a thing.

"Tell you what," Misty said, her attitude backing off. "I'm going to pretend we didn't even have this conversation. We should be celebrating something really wonderful that just happened for you. Despite how long it took me to call you back, and regardless of how long you can hold a grudge."

I sat on my end, feeling smaller by the minute.

"I'm going to hang up the phone," she instructed, "and I want you to hang yours up, too. Then, I'm going to call you right back, and we're going to start this conversation all over again. Cool?"

I sat there, listening to her. She was taking charge, just like that, telling me how she wanted things to go. Like my feelings or opinion didn't count.

"I'm hanging up now," Misty said. "Hang up the phone, okay?"

I didn't respond. My grip on the grudge zone was too tight and too comfortable to shift in the slightest.

"Hang uuuuuuuuuup!!" I heard her singing, her voice growing fainter as she spoke to me while placing her receiver back in its cradle.

For a few fat seconds, I sat there with the receiver in my hand, feeling a mean streak coming on. I was determined not to have Miss Divine dictate the situation.

She's probably dialing right now, I thought.

Let her wait, my mean streak sneered.

Girl, stop tripping, my conscience broke in.

I placed the phone back on the hook.

Immediately, it began to ring again.

I listened to it ringing.

One ringy-dingy.

Two ringy-dingies.

Three ringy-dingies.

Make her ass wait.

Four ringy-dingies.

My phone was set to roll over to my service after four unanswered rings.

Just how mean was I? Just how crucial was this grudge?

"Hello?"

"*Heyyyyyy girl!!*" Misty sang. "Congratulations! I got your message! So you're gonna be in *Black Barry's Pie*! I'm so *proud* of you!"

"Thanks," I mumbled sheepishly. This was kinda weird.

"Does your mama know yet? Oh, who *cares*! All that matters is that we can share this moment! Girl, you know what?"

"What?" I asked quietly, feeling a tad bit silly going along with this ruse.

"I love you *soooooooo* much!" she gushed in an exaggerated tone. "You are my one and only sistah! You make me proud of you every time you turn around! You're so strong, so determined. There ain't *nuthin'* you can't do!"

Instantly, upon hearing those words, my attitude melted away. I felt my face splitting down the middle. Cheeks forming. Pucker in place. Turning into a genuine booty.

"You hear me?" Misty asked. "I love you, Reesy!! I'm so proud of you right now, I could break down and cry!"

"*Now* you're getting carried away," I giggled, all resistance gone. "You were going good there for a minute, but you got a little raggedy at the end."

"Yeah. You're right. Strike the part about crying. Girl, I'm so proud of you right now, I could take you out to dinner and get drunk over a few dozen Amaretto sours!"

"*That's* more like it!" I laughed. "I could deal with drunk tears. Just don't cry for me right now, Argentina."

"So where you wanna go for dinner?" she asked. "On me."

"*Of course* it's on you!" I exclaimed. "That goes without saying!! This is *my* good news, not yours!"

"True dat," she replied.

"*True dat?* When did you start dropping that phrase? Ain't that a little too hip for you?"

"Probably something I picked up from Rick," she said with a chuckle. "Mr. Homeboy-in-a-Suit."

"I can't even picture you saying it, let alone hearing it come out of your mouth!"

"Girl, you'd be surprised at the stuff I'm picking up," Misty laughed.

"I don't think I want to know," I giggled.

"So where we going for dinner?" Misty asked. "You wanna hit Justin's or the Shark Bar?"

"Mmmm," I moaned, thinking of the liver and grits at Justin's and that good ol' macaroni and cheese the Shark Bar had. "I've got an even better idea. Let's hit the Soul Cafe."

"That's a bet," she said. "Maybe we'll even catch a glimpse of Mr. Yoba."

"That wouldn't be so bad," I replied. "Last time I was there, I saw Bryce from Groove Theory. That's a fine mofo."

"Ain't he though?"

"What you doin' looking?!" I laughed. "You's off-limits now, girly. Ain't you got somebody?"

"I ain't blind," she said.

"I hear *that.*"

"Maybe we can go get our boogie on at Nell's when we finish dinner."

"Are you serious?" I asked, thoroughly surprised. "Tomorrow's a workday for you. You know when I go to Nell's, I make it an all-night thang."

"So?!" she quipped. "I can hang!"

"What's your man gonna say?"

"*See ya tomorrow,* probably," Misty returned.

"Gon', Miss Divine! Sistah-girl jumpin' bad on a negro!"

"Rick doesn't own me, Reesy. He's secure and encouraging. That's why I'm diggin' him so much."

"*Diggin'?*" I grinned. "Girl, *shut up* with these hip phrases. I don't know how much more of them I can take from you!"

"So where we meetin'?" she said, trying to change the subject.

"In front of the restaurant."

"Okay. Forty-second between Ninth and Tenth, right?"

"Choo got it, man!" I said in a chica-chica voice.

"Thirty minutes," Misty said.

"Twenty-five," I challenged.

"It's *on*," she replied.

"Bye, fool!"

I hung up the phone, laughing. She was a mess, but she was my best friend.

Still it was hard adjusting to this new Misty.

It was bad enough that she wasn't around much these days. On top of that, she was picking up all manner of freaky phrases along the way.

Rick was really leaving an impression on her. She wasn't one to just start dropping street lingo like that. We'd been friends since the second grade, and were going into our third decade together. And you can best believe we'd been running our mouths with each other the whole time, gabbing it up every day that had passed since that first moment on the playground.

Yet, for all that crazy stuff she'd heard me saying over the years, our diction still remained as separate and as different as could be.

I smiled to myself as I got up from the couch and went rummaging for my shoes.

Bump the shoes. Hell, I was going to Nell's later. I needed to funk up my whole look.

I rushed off to the bedroom, mentally picturing what I could slip into.

I had to get dressed and be in front of the Soul Cafe in a matter of minutes. I thought I'd let my braids hang down tonight.

A sistah was feeling a little footloose and fancy-free.

Exactly twenty-five minutes later, I stepped out of a cab in front of the Soul Cafe.

I stood there on the sidewalk with my back to the entrance. On time and ready to dis, I glanced around for Miss Divine, who was nowhere to be seen.

I turned to my left, looking for her to come walking up the street.

"*Mmmm-hmmm*," I muttered under my breath. I should have known that she wouldn't have her butt in place on time.

"*Mmmmm-hmmm,* what?" a voice behind me challenged.

I smiled, my back still turned. When I faced her, she scooped me up in a big ol' hug.

"*Hey, baby!*" she squealed.

Misty was all smiles and giggles, looking fresh and perky in a lime green mini-suit. It was her typical corporate-cum-sexy fare.

The suit was one of those numbers that could go from work mode to boogie, depending on how you accessorized and fixed your hair. Today, her hair was a tumble of loose curls falling all around her shoulders, framing her face and showing off the beauty mark on her upper left cheek.

Misty and I were about the same height—five-seven. She was the brown one, I was the redbone. (I really hated that term—it had been slung at me by brothers one time too many like it was a badge I should wear with pride.)

And while I had a true dancer's figure, all tight and firm, Misty was the voluptuous one, with curves galore. Now, don't get me wrong. She wasn't plump or full-figured by any stretch of the imagination. She was, actually, a perfect size seven, just like me.

But she had those breasts that men were always flipping over. Those things had gotten us into situations one time too many, and I really think she secretly got off on that mess. And while she was always complaining that she didn't have the high, round sistah booty I'd been strapped with, it apparently never stopped her from getting any play. The two of us always got our share of attention whenever we hung out together.

"*Hey girl!*" I grinned, hugging her tightly.

"I'm *soooo* proud of you!" she whispered, squeezing me back. "Let me look at you!"

She leaned away from me, still holding my hands, and studied my face.

I was beaming. It felt so good to be sharing this moment, at last, with my sistah. My braids were hanging loose, and I was feeling rather funkdafied in a short, kicky little slip dress and some strappy sandals. My dress was a dark shimmering blue that made my skin give off a glow.

"Girl . . . you look *good!*" Misty exclaimed.

"Look who's talking! You're knocking 'em dead in that lime green suit!"

She did a quick twirl.

"You likes?"

"I likes."

"Compliments of Vera Wang, baby."

"Girl, Vera Wang hooked you up!"

A couple of brothers walked into the restaurant, checking us out as they stepped inside. From the looks of things, they liked, too.

She grabbed me by the hand.

"C'mon! Let's get this party started right!"

Misty grabbed the big handle on the door, gave it a strong tug, and the two of us stepped inside the darkened restaurant.

There was a sistah at the entrance, standing sentinel behind a hostess stand. One of those exotic types that I'm sure brothers went for with a vengeance when they saw her at the door.

"Two for dinner?" she asked.

"Yes," Misty chimed.

The sistah gathered up two menus.

"Right this way, please."

We followed the hostess onto the raised dining area. The room had a warm, golden glow, with an interesting array of booths and tables, with beige slipcovered chairs, that really had a way of getting your mind in just the right mood to relax.

I loved the ambience of this place. Tonight, it was thick with people dining, but it still managed to feel intimate. The smooth sounds of Erykah Badu's first album, *Baduizm*, were pouring from the speakers. The song "No Love" was playing. It added to my bouncy upbeat feeling as we were led to our table.

I could feel the eyes of brothers and sistahs alike following us as we weaved through the room. The hostess seated us at a small table near the center.

"Your waiter will be right with you," the exotic sistah smiled.

"Thank you," Misty and I answered in unison.

We stared at each other foolishly, then burst into giggles.

"Let's get some champagne," Misty whispered, leaning forward. "We have so much to celebrate!"

"That's a great idea!"

Within seconds, the waiter materialized at our table.

He was a dreadheaded brother, fine as wine. He had hazel-colored eyes and was quite sexy. He looked like an actor I had seen somewhere before. Who was it?

"Can I start you ladies off with a cocktail?" brother cooed.

Misty took charge.

"Give us a bottle of Veuve Clicquot. Yellow label. Do you have that in stock?"

The brother smiled, opening the wine list and pointing it out to her.

"Great! Then we'll have that for starters."

The handsome dreadhead glided away.

"What happened to Perrier Jouet?" I asked in surprise. "I thought that was your favorite?"

Girlfriend had been drinking P.J. for years. Usually wouldn't *touch* nuthin' else.

"I've been trying something new these days. It's not half bad. Just trust me on it."

"It's your dollar, baby. Slang it as you will."

The sexy dread arrived with the champagne stuck inside one of those chilly ice bucket stands.

Who did he remind me of?

I eyed him closely. He cut his eyes back at me, smiling slyly as he worked on uncorking the bottle. It ceremoniously popped.

He glanced at me and grinned.

Talk about a freaking metaphor. Shit.

He poured a bit into a champagne flute and offered it to Misty.

She sampled it quietly and nodded her approval.

He filled our glasses halfway, then stuck the bottle back down in the bucket. He shot me another quick seductive glance as he walked away.

"Stop flirting."

"I'm not flirting."

"You're *such* a liar!" Misty laughed. "You're in mack-mama mode if ever I saw you!"

"Anyway . . . ," I replied.

"Anyway . . . ," she sang, mimicking me.

We giggled in unison.

Misty raised her glass.

"To you, girl."

"To *moi*," I grinned, raising mine.

We clinked and sipped. I licked my lips, savoring the taste.

"*Umph!* Not bad, not bad."

"Told ya."

Our sexy waiter returned with a basket of warm bread. I took a good, long look at him.

"*Shaza Zul!*" I exclaimed, remembering at last. He looked at me strangely, then smiled.

"Are you ready to order?" he asked.

"I am," Misty proclaimed. She looked over at me. "Go on, girl. Order first. It's *your* celebration."

I already knew what I wanted.

"Let me have the jerk chicken."

"What do you want as your sides?" sexy Shaza asked.

"I'll have the mixed greens and the candied yams."

"And you, miss?" he said, turning to Misty.

"I'll have the same thing," she replied, "except with macaroni and cheese instead of candied yams."

He jotted it down.

Erykah's music was still streaming through the speakers. "Drama." My favorite cut off her first CD.

Little did I know how prophetic the title of that song was about to be.

"Is that it?" the waiter asked.

"Bring us some lobster sausage as an appetizer," I added.

"Anything else to drink?"

"Two Amaretto sours," I replied.

His right eyebrow went up. He turned to Misty.

"And you'll be drinking?"

"One of the Amaretto sours is for her, fool," I interrupted.

He chuckled to himself. I smiled back sweetly in return.

"Of course," he grinned, shaking his head. "I'll be right back."

"Wit' yo' sexy azz," I mumbled.

He heard me. I know, because he was laughing and shaking his head as he walked away.

"You're a mess, girl," Misty chuckled.

"I'm just a red-blooded African-American female, is all."

"Translation . . . *hoe.*"

"*Hey, now! Watch that!*"

We laughed.

"So what did you mean about that *Shaza Zul* thing? What was that?"

"That's who he looks like!" I replied. "Remember the guy from the show *A Different World*? The one Freddie was dating? He had reddish-blond dreads and hazel eyes. He was in Janet Jackson's video "Again." The one where they get caught outside in the rain."

"Oh yeah," Misty said, nodding. "He does kinda look like him."

"*Mmmm-hmmm,*" I agreed. "He is a sexy mofo if I ever saw one!"

"You need to sit your little hot ass down," she said. "So tell me this . . . how can you order all that food and still have the figure you have? My body registers every little thing I consume. If I swallow a gulp of air, my thighs are wearing it the very next day."

"Gotta work it out, baby! I burn off everything that comes into my body. Exercise, exercise, exercise!"

"*Hmph!*" She snickered. "Maybe I need to join you for a few sessions of that. Fat's showing up on me in some strange places of late."

"What are you complaining about? You look great. I see that regular sex is just like milk."

"What do you mean?"

"Does a body good."

Misty clucked her tongue, at herself for falling for my stupid little comment.

Sexy Shaza came back with our Amaretto sours.

I didn't waste any time. Immediately, I raised mine in another toast. I waited for Misty to raise hers.

"To the opening of *Black Barry's Pie*," I piped. "You gon' be there for me, right?"

"Of course I am! Wouldn't miss it for the world! When is it?"

"We rehearse for three months. Then, it officially opens on June fifteenth."

She smiled, but I noticed something strange in her eyes, like she was unsure or a little concerned.

"What's with that look?"

"*What* look?"

"*That* look. I know you well. Something funny's going on in that head of yours. I can tell. Don't tell me you've got a work conflict or something like that! I'm giving you three months' advance notice!"

"I don't have a conflict," she insisted.

"You better *not*."

Now, all that time, I still had my drink raised. I lowered my glass. My arm was getting way too tired. I could have caught a cramp waiting for her to raise hers.

"Are your folks coming?" she asked.

"I didn't tell them about it," I said casually.

"*What?!*" she shrieked.

Heads in the restaurant snapped our way.

"Why the heck wouldn't you tell your parents about something this significant?!"

I sighed heavily. Misty knew me. And she knew Tyrone and Tyrene. Very well. I don't know why she was tripping so hard.

"Because," I said, "if they came, the pressure would be too much for me. I wouldn't even be able to concentrate during the show. Even if I couldn't see their faces, I'd feel them there, just staring at me. They'd be asking a million questions. Wondering why I even wanted to be doing something like this to begin with."

"*And? So?*" Misty persisted. "They'd still be proud of you."

"They'd critique me to death," I replied. "Tyrene would politely remind me that I have an MBA. I don't need that. I'm still feeling this whole thing out for myself. I don't need her mouth interjecting her two billion cents."

"Damn, Reesy," Misty said. "That's your mom."

"Don't try to give me a guilt trip, Misty," I sighed. "You know Tyrene is no ordinary mother. I'll have her and Tyrone up when I'm more comfortable with my role in the show. After I've gotten my part down pat, and know for sure that this is where I want to be."

Shaza Zul arrived with our lobster sausage.

I immediately forked a piece onto a saucer, and reached for a warm jalapeño roll from the basket of bread.

Besides, I wanted to change the subject from the issue of Tyrone and Tyrene.

"*Mmmm,*" I moaned, savoring the meat. "This is too good."

Misty watched me, unable to resist. She forked a piece, too.

"You know I don't need to be eating this," she said with a smile.

"Good," I mumbled, my mouth full. "More for me."

I buttered the roll and bit a large chunk out of it.

I needed to take a drink to wash the whole thing down. I raised my glass again, in an effort to renew my attempt at a toast. Misty finally followed suit.

"To my off-Broadway debut on June fifteenth," I said, talking around the lump of meat and bread in my mouth. "Be there or be axed!"

"To your off-Broadway debut," she repeated.

I took a quick sip of my Amaretto sour. While I was sipping, she continued the toast.

"And to me and Rick moving in together. Effective June fourteenth."

I almost spat my drink out.

"*Whaaaaaaaattt?!!!!!!!!*"

Misty visibly flinched.

I sat there, swallowing, gulping, semi-gagging, trying to choke the chunk of bread and sausage down.

I swallowed the whole lot and sat there for a few more stunned moments, frantically clearing my throat.

"*Ummmmmmmm!!*" I screeched, doing my best to open my clogged esophagus.

"Are you all right?" Misty whispered.

My eyes narrowed.

"*No!!*" I hissed loudly, my voice tinged with anger. "I am *not* all right. When did all *this* come about?"

"Keep your voice down, Reesy."

"Fuck *that*!! When did you decide all this?!!"

I locked my gaze onto her, trying to see if she would tell me the truth or give me her usual song and dance, do-si-do-ing around the issue.

Misty looked at me, but was unable to hold my stare. Her eyes began to wander around the restaurant, looking at everything but me. The backlit sconces in the shapes of mathematic symbols. The open warehouse-type ceiling. The waiters and the walls.

"We actually just decided to do it a couple of weeks ago," she mumbled. "Things seem to be going really well, and we'll both have a little time off around then. So we decided that's when we're gonna do it, if everything is still moving along like it is."

"You decided all this a couple of weeks ago?!" I shrieked. "And you didn't feel it was important enough to tell me about it? You used to tell me *everything*! This affects me, too, you know!"

Misty rubbed the back of her neck casually, trying to play the situation off. She looked around under-eyed to see if anyone was noticing our growing tiff. Of course they were, but I couldn't care less.

"So he's moving into the apartment with us?" I asked, wondering how in the hell it would be with three people, two of whom were a couple, pushed up, living there together.

Misty's eyes shifted rapidly around the room. She still wouldn't look at me directly.

"Actually," she said, her voice soft, "I'll be moving into his townhouse in Greenwich."

"You're moving to *Connecticut*?!" I said with alarm, panic rushing over me at what her statement really meant.

"It's a quick commute into the city," Misty interjected, as if that made any difference. "It's just like living in Jersey or on Long Island."

"Actually," I said flatly, "it's *not*."

I sat there, letting all of this wash over me. This whole thing was going to affect me way more than it would affect her.

For starters, I would have to move.

As I mentioned before, the apartment we were living in was paid for by Burch Financial. It was Misty's, rent-free, as a part of her compensation package with the company. At least for a limited amount of time. My name was not on the lease. If she left, I would definitely have to go.

And I knew she wasn't going to be inviting me to move up to Greenwich with her and her man.

I sat there, my mind going a mile a minute, wondering why she didn't give me more notice to try to find a place of my own. She'd known for two weeks. I could have been out there looking, or at least making preparations.

So what, I had three months to do it? I'd always heard that finding a place in the city was a nightmare. Definitely no easy task. And what if I wasn't able to afford it? Rents were pretty high in Manhattan. It's not like I was being paid a lot of money for my part in the show.

I was only getting fifty bucks a show. Off Broadway paid shit for money. At eight shows a week, that was only four hundred bucks. Sixteen hundred a month. What the *hell* could I get in Manhattan with *that* kind of income?

No way could I call Tyrone and Tyrene and ask them for money. And no way was I going to spend one of those stipends they sent. Those were for investment purposes only, as far as I was concerned. I was not going to have my parents thinking they were supporting me financially.

I felt Misty watching me furtively. It was as if she was sitting there reading my mind.

"You don't have to move out of the Milano," she said, reaching across the table for my hand. "You can stay there. Burch doesn't have to know that I moved out. In fact, I don't want them to know that Rick and I are living together just yet."

"Of course you don't! That wouldn't look too good, now would it? Boss and employee hooked up together like that, in a cozy little love nest? You'd lose the little bit of credibility you're barely hanging on to. You can't have much left these days as it is."

Misty's face twitched. I thought I saw her eyes fill a little.

I speared another piece of lobster sausage, and, apathetically, began munching away.

"Why aren't you happy for me?" she asked, her voice cracking a little. "Why do you always have to be so mean?"

I kept munching on the sausage. I was definitely not feeling her. I didn't even look at her.

She had her nerve, especially for calling me mean. She had no idea that what she was doing was making me just crumble on the inside. Here she was, just a few months into dating this guy, and she was ready to walk out on our friendship. Just raise up, take all her stuff out the crib, and go shack with him.

Leaving a sistah ass out.

I had no sympathy for her. For that, she got no love from me.

Misty's eyes were now fixed upon me, without wavering. But I had nothing to say. I didn't even want to see her face. She held on to my hand.

I nonchalantly pulled it away.

"Don't be mad at me, Reesy," she pleaded.

"I'm not mad at you," I lied. "Would you pass me the butter, please?"

Caught off guard, Misty looked around for it. It was sitting in a saucer, just to the left of her. She passed it my way.

I picked up my jalapeño roll, broke off a piece, slathered it down, and pitched it into my mouth.

"You are mad at me," Misty insisted. "Stop lying."

"*Mmh-mmh,*" I mumbled, shaking my head. My mouth was jam-packed full of bread. I stared absently at the door.

"Look at me, Reesy," she commanded.

I kept watching people come in and out of the restaurant. I had my gaze so locked, that it took me a second to register what I saw before me. I stared and stared, until my eyes came into focus, and I realized who it was that had just walked into the place.

It was Denzel Washington. I couldn't freaking believe it.

That's what I loved about New York and places like the Soul Cafe. Extraordinary people just walked right up on you and did the most ordinary things.

"*Ohhhhh shit!*" I mumbled, watching him as he sauntered up to the bar. He shook hands and gave a quick hug to a man that obviously knew him.

"What?" Misty probed, misreading my comment. "What's the matter, boo? C'mon . . . please don't be mad about this."

I wasn't stud'n her. *Please.* Denzel Washington was in the house.

Me and every sistah in there was politely checking him out. Misty was the only one who wasn't in the know. An audible buzz had taken over the room.

"Reesy."

She kept on trying to get through to me.

Now, let me tell you how mean I can be.

Misty Fine *loooooves* herself some Denzel. I mean, she loves him. So much so, that sometimes, I swear, she modeled the men in her life after his image.

Denzel was to Misty what Maxwell was to me. And if she knew he was in the room right now, she'd damn near faint. She wouldn't stop talking about it from now until the end of time. It would be one of the most memorable moments of her life.

I sat there, contemplating. Trying to decide if I should tell her about it or not. Since she claimed I was so mean and all.

"Reesy," she said again.

Her back was to the bar. She was facing the main part of the restaurant, not the front part, like I was.

I thought about it. I was pretty pissed at her regarding this moving situation. This would be a cool way to get even. I could just tell her about it later on tonight, and let her stew over the fact that I deliberately let her miss seeing Denzel.

She would really be upset, but it would show her that I'm *nots* to be fucked with.

But what would I really gain from doing it?

I thought about it. If Maxwell walked into the Soul Cafe, even if Misty was mad as hell at me, she would drop her anger, and go out of her way to point him out.

I let out a heavy sigh.

"Your man is up in here," I said in a reserved tone.

"Who?" she asked, visibly excited. "Rick? He knew it was girls' night out for us. He wouldn't come here unless it was an emergency."

"Not him."

Misty turned around in her seat, looking in all the wrong places.

I couldn't help but laugh.

"Why you playing with me, Reesy?" she asked sharply, turning back around. "What man are you talking about?!"

"Look over at the bar."

She turned around in her chair again, and glanced in the right direction this time.

She blinked once. She blinked twice.

All at once, the reality of it hit her.

"OH!!!!!!" she exclaimed, sucking in a breath of air so audible, Denzel himself snapped his head in her direction.

Her eyes locked onto his. He smiled politely, nodded, and resumed his conversation with the man at the bar.

Misty turned back around abruptly, facing me. She was seriously shaken. Girlfriend was rocked to her very core. Her hands were trembling as she held them in front of her.

Shaza Zul arrived with our dinner.

"I can't eat," she whispered nervously.

"Child *please!*" I laughed. "Denzel could care less about your azz. You'd better eat this food you're paying for!"

She turned around again and watched him openly.

"I've got butterflies," Misty said, mesmerized. "I can't believe I'm breathing the same air that he is."

I sank my fork into the mixed greens, then sank the fork into my mouth.

"Mmmmmm," I moaned, in ecstasy.

The Soul Cafe has the best greens I've ever eaten. Short of my grandma's.

"Eat, heffah," I chided. "That man's happily married with a house full of kids. And you *know* this, maaaan!"

I worked my neck as I did my best Chris Tucker imitation.

Misty didn't hear a word I was saying.

"He is the finest man on the planet," she whined.

"Get out!" I countered. "Have you seen my man Maxwell lately?"

Misty clucked her tongue.

"Please," she replied.

"Oh, don't even *go* there with me!" I warned.

"Maxwell looks good, but he ain't no Denzel," she had the nerve to say again.

"I told you . . . don't even *go* there with me. It's not just about Maxwell's looks. He sings like an angel. He makes me high. The fact that he's fine is just gravy, baby."

I speared a chunk of candied yams.

"Eat," I said with my mouth full.

"Can't," she repeated, still watching Denzel.

Thankfully, he finished talking to the man at the bar and quietly left the restaurant.

"You can turn around now," I chuckled.

Misty faced me again, her eyes starry and glazed.

"I can't believe that I actually saw him," she sighed.

"Well, for the record," I said nonchalantly, smacking my lips as I chomped away, "I'm pretty sure his shit does stank."

"Ew!" she exclaimed. "Now, why'd you have to go there? Why couldn't you just leave me with my lovely memory of him?"

"Because," I smiled, "we need to get back to the lecture at hand."

"Oh," Misty said and grinned sheepishly. "Me moving out?"

"Yeah, Miss Divine. You moving out."

I cut into my jerk chicken. I brought it to my lips, savoring the spicy aroma. I tasted it.

Ummmph, ummph, umph! That bad boy was *off* the hook!

"You're smiling at me," she said. "Does that mean you forgive me?"

"It means that I'm enjoying my food," I kidded. "You need to get into yours before I have to take over."

Misty tasted her greens. Like me, she began to smile.

"So when you moving in?" I asked.

"June fourteenth."

"You sure about this?"

"I love him. We want to see how it would be if we were together all the time."

"You guys are already together all the time," I said.

"You know what I mean."

I kept eating, nodding my head.

"You ain't scared of that *cow-free milk* thang?"

"What?"

"You know, the kind of stuff your mama always says. *Why buy the cow when the milk is for free?* What would his incentive be to marry you if you're willing to just shack up?"

Misty's eyes narrowed on the defensive.

"We're *not* shacking, Reesy."

"Hey, I ain't mad at cha. I'm just making a statement."

Misty dug into her macaroni and cheese.

"I'm with you," I said with way too much enthusiasm. "Like Wesley said in *Mo' Better Blues,* 'Black people in love . . . that's a beautiful thang.' "

She cut her eyes at me.

"Yeah, right. And you know how he meant it when he said it, too. You're judging me and you know it."

"I just want you to be careful," I replied. "The last live-in situation resulted in a black eye, some pissy sheets, and a restraining order. And I'm always your cleanup girl. I don't wanna go through *that* shit again."

"Reesy Snowden, the eternal optimist."

"I'm a *realist,* baby. I know how the game goes."

"What*ever*."

She began cutting into her chicken. So did I. We let the silence hang between us for a few bites.

"So . . . how's the sex?"

"What?!" Misty shrieked.

"You *heard* me," I replied in a flat tone. "Don't act so surprised. *How's the sex?* It must be *bangin'* if you're ready to live with this mug."

Misty stuffed a forkful of chicken into her mouth to keep from talking. I patiently waited.

I had all the time in the world.

(Besides . . . I felt like throwing a few crumbs her way, giving her a chance to talk about her little funky new relationship. I could tell she was chomping at the bit to share, but she was afraid to get me mad with all her excitement about it. This was supposed to be my night, to celebrate my achievement, but I was willing to share with her a little.)

Just a little, mind you. Not a lot.

Misty chewed slowly. Eventully, however, she gulped.

"Yes?" I persisted, staring piercingly into her face.

Misty looked around the room, embarrassed, her brown cheeks flushing a little red. She took a sip of water.

"What the hell are you blushing for?" I laughed. "Dayam! He must be poppin' that nana sumthin' fierce!"

She quickly looked down at her food. Just as quickly, she looked up at me and nodded her head.

"Girl, he's poppin' it like *corn!*" she whispered with a giggle.

I bucked my eyes. Rick? *Poppin' the nana?*

"True dat?"

"True dat!" She leaned in closer to me. "Girl, the other night, he, um, went south for almost a whole hour!"

I was now leaning toward her in my seat as well.

"A whole *hour?!*"

"Mmmm-hmmm. And, girl, he's a *toe sucker.* I ain't never had a toe sucker before!"

"Nice, ain't it?" I answered dryly, like that was old hat to me (which it *was*). "It's a whole 'nother sensation altogether."

"Shole is."

We were both silent for a moment, playing around with our food absently.

The image of Rick with Misty's toes in his mouth skitted through my brain. I shuddered, trying desperately to shoo the thought away.

Not that her toes were jacked up, or anything. But I didn't really need the visual while I was eating my dinner.

And, strange to say it, a part of me was a little, well, *jealous* of the fact that Misty had a man who ate her cat for an hour and was sucking her toes. I kinda felt like she was bragging about it, ya know? I even felt like she'd set me up a little, with her little innocent blushing act, then busting out and talking about how he was poppin' her corn.

Bitch.

I mean, she knew that I didn't have anybody in my life right now, and here she sat, across from me, gloating about her little sexual feats with Rick the Dickslanger.

I decided to change the subject. I was getting a little pissed. After all, wasn't this supposed to be *my* night?

"So you coming to my opening, heffah? It's the day after you move in, so you should have no problem being there."

Misty looked up at me, trying to feel me out.

"You sure you want me to come?"

"Of course I do, silly. You're my girl. Shackin' or no. I want you there in that audience when I make my debut on that stage."

"Really?" she asked, grinning.

"Really. And bring your raggedy ass man, too, if you wanna."

"Okay," she beamed.

We ate in silence again, a weird mixture of giddiness, camaraderie, and slight jealousy (on my part) hanging there between us.

"Hey, Reesy," Misty whispered, breaking the silence.

"What's up?" I said, looking up from my food.

She leaned in toward me, her eyes narrowed and glistening. She was cheesing like a Cheshire cat.

"We saw Denzel tonight," she giggled.

"I know." I smiled back.

"Girl, that's some monumental shit! Give me some dap on that."

I held out my fist and she gave me a pound. I gave her one back.

"What you know 'bout dap?" I laughed at last. "You're killing me, Miss Divine!"

Misty waved her hand at me dismissively.

"Bump *that*," she said. "All I know is, Denzel is one fine mofo!"

"True dat."

I reached for another jalapeño roll and the butter.

"But he still ain't no Maxwell!"

By the time we left the Soul Cafe, we were lit.

We had offed that bottle of champagne, downed a few more Amaretto sours, and some cosmopolitans, to boot.

We took a cab downtown to Nell's. It started out as a nice little pleasant cruise.

"So you ain't going back to Greenwich tonight?"

"Girl, naw! I'm too bent! After we get our boogie on, I'm gon' need to crawl my ass straight in the bed!"

"See, that couldn't be me."

"What do you mean?" Misty asked.

I laughed, scooching down in the seat, my head as light as a feather.

"Girl, whenever I get the slightest bit of alcohol in my body, my cat gets to itchin' for a scratch."

I noticed the cabdriver, a quiet brother with a Haitian-sounding name, stir at my comment.

Misty glanced over at me.

"So you tryna say you're horny now, heffah?"

"*Ummmm-hmmm*. Like a dog in heat!"

We both burst out laughing.

Misty attempted to shove me away from her.

"Stay over there, then! I don't do nuthin' but dicks!"

The cabbie cleared his throat.

"Dicks I know," she added.

I screamed with laughter.

"Girl, *hush*! I forgot how you get when your azz is drunk! You know damn well that I'm as heterosexual as they come. So don't even *play* like that!"

"I'm just saying it for the record. I bednot feel your yellow hand creepin' round my room tonight, you horny hoe!"

The cabbie was obviously disturbed. Brother had the hot foot. All of a sudden, the cab shot forward, bolting down the avenue in a mad rush to Fourteenth Street.

Misty slapped my thigh, her hand covering her mouth to keep from giggling out loud.

"Brother's probably got a stick of granite between his legs up there," I whispered. "We better quit talkin' 'bout dicks and shit 'fore he mess around and kill us!"

Misty was laughing so hard, tears were coming out of her eyes.

"Stop it!" she squealed. "I have to pee!"

I looked at her over there, squeezing her legs together, trying her best to keep her cool.

I burst out laughing again.

As the cab sped on, slinging us around the backseat like rag dolls every time he turned a corner, we laughed and laughed until our eyes were red.

When we finally got to Nell's, we were still squealing like fools.

We rolled up inside the club, all drunk and silly, and cut it up on the dance floor with every strange man who asked (and some who didn't), until the crack of the crack of dawn.

NEVER NO TIME TO PLAY

*H*igher! Higher! Come on, Reesy, kick it higher!"

The music was blaring, and I was dancing across the empty stage, side by side with the other dancers, sweating my ass off.

Julian screamed at me, his face all brown, beaded, and balled up. His mouth was so close to my head, I swear, I could see his tonsils, or uvula, or whatever the fuck that thing was, dangling down at the back of his throat.

"Show me some goddamn ass! Shake that shit! This ain't no damn Miss America pageant!"

"Grrrrrrr!" I snarled at him, wanting to snatch him out the frame for being in my face, screaming at me like that.

Julian was the show's choreographer, and, *goodness,* he sure didn't believe in cutting you any slack.

His reputation was as long as 125th Street, and he had danced with some of the best of the best. I knew it was an honor to be working with him, but right now, I was hating him with a passion that knew no bounds.

He wore one of those spandex bodysuits that was really a tank top connected to some shorts. You know. A *unitard,* I believe it's called. The kind that wrestlers and weight lifters wear. It grabbed his crotch vulgarly, in a manner that gave me *waaaay* more information than I was interested in receiving.

Especially from Julian. 'Cause, as fine as he was, he had absolutely *no* interest in sharing with a sistah none of what that spandex was clinging to.

He hovered around me like a mosquito in a blood bank. I wanted desperately to swat him away. My vengeance was the salty sweat that flew all over him from my overtaxed body. Every now and then, one of my braids would fly free and crack him in the face.

I glared at him. I was kicking as high as I could, and I knew for damn sure that I was, at the very least, up to par with what the other dancers were doing.

The muscles in my legs were screaming bloody murder. My heart was about to burst.

"Work it, you bitch! How'd you get in this show anyway? You must know somebody. Who'd you fuck?"

Oh, *hell no! That* was the last straw. I stopped and tried to catch my breath. I was gonna need all the wind I could muster to kick his natural ass.

"All right, everybody!" Julian shouted, moving away from me. "Enough!! Take five, and I mean *no more than five,* then have your asses back in place! *Gotta make moves!"*

I bent down, my hands resting on my knees. My breathing was so thick, I thought my chest was gonna explode.

Julian passed close to me, just enough so that only I could hear him.

"You need to get it right," he whispered, his tone harsh. *"The show starts in a few weeks."*

I angled my head up to look his way, my eyes piercing him like lasers.

"I'm giving you a thousand percent!" I hissed. "You can't get more than I got inside me!"

He stood there, his hand on his hip, covered from head to toe with a trough of my sweat.

"If that's all you got, then you can take that shit somewhere else. We don't half-step here. Either bring it on, or *take it off*!"

My heart skipped a beat, in a moment of panic.

"What do you mean, *take it off*? My *clothes*? Ain't nobody said nothing to me about having to do that!"

"That's not what I meant, Miss Thang. But I guess that's a phrase you're pretty used to hearing, huh?"

Julian stared me square in the eye, trying to make me uncomfortable. I gave him back the same stare. Did he know about my exotic dancing days?

"I meant *take it off our stage* and *out* the door. Either come correct, or get to steppin'!"

He snapped his finger, high over his head in the air, in a grand gesture of dismissal.

I glared at him, sizzling mad.

"What's it gon' be?" he challenged. "Can you bring it on?"

I stood up, got as close to his face as I could, enough to make him uncomfortable, and whispered,

"You just watch me."

I turned around abruptly, and located my bottle of Evian.

"Now, *that's* what I'm talkin' 'bout!!" I heard him utter behind me.

Gordon Stock, the brother who had called me up and told me I had gotten the job in the show, was sitting out in the audience watching the whole thing. He beckoned to me.

I guzzled the water and walked off the stage toward him.

He patted one of the seats next to him, gesturing for me to sit down.

I slid into the seat, relieved to get a moment of real rest.

"You looked fantastic up there," he said in that booming, chocolate-thick voice of his.

I looked into his face. A rich Hershey brown, it was a series of squares and blocks. Square eyes, square jaw, square nose, block head. But I saw genuine kindness and honesty there. Also a good dose of open admiration.

I sighed heavily, overjoyed to get a little praise from somebody, anybody.

"Thank you, Gordon. I needed to hear that. You'd never know it, from listening to Mr. Man up there."

I glanced toward the stage. Julian paced the floor, every now and then shooting an accusing look at me and Gordon.

"Do you know he had the nerve to ask me if I fucked my way onto the show?!"

Gordon chuckled that pea-soupy laugh of his.

"You think that's funny?" I asked.

"No, no!" he interjected quickly, shaking his head. "That's not why I'm laughing. I'm tickled because I love the way you just spit things out. There's a crudeness there that's so endearing."

"I am NOT crude!!"

"I didn't mean that in a negative way," he said, trying desperately to dig himself out of what he knew was a rapidly widening hole. "In fact, it was a compliment of the highest order."

"Oh."

"Stop being so defensive, Reesy."

"Can't help it around here," I replied, wiping my brow, noticing that the thumping in my heart was beginning to slow down a little.

Gordon smiled at me.

"I can't believe you haven't figured Julian out yet. It's been three months now. He's done this to you every day."

"I've figured him out, all right," I said. "He's a mean mutha-fucka with an ax to grind. And I'm the one he's laying it into."

"Then you *haven't* figured him out," Gordon said. "You haven't figured him out in the slightest."

I studied Gordon closely, trying to make sense out of his words.

"Five minutes up, everybody!" Julian shouted, clapping his hands together loudly. He was staring at me in particular. *"Let's get this show on the road! Gotta make mooooves!"*

"See what I mean?" I said. "He can't even let us get a good rest. An extra minute wouldn't have hurt nobody."

"He thinks you're the best," Gordon said matter-of-factly.

"Get the *fuck* outta here! He treats me like shit."

"That's how he treats the ones he has the most hope for. You see him doing what he's doing to you to anybody else?"

"Not nearly as much. I just thought the brother couldn't stand me."

"On stage, Miss Thang!" Julian demanded, snapping his fingers like I was a dog being called in for dinner. *"Now!!* Ain't no monkeys gon' stop my show!"

"Watch him," Gordon whispered, pushing me up and out of my seat. "You'll see what I mean. Everybody else is working hard, and you're doing much better than the whole lot. But still he dogs you. He sees your talent. He's just testing your mettle."

"Well, I hope he figures out what I'm made of, before I have to bust out and do a little ass-kickin' up in here. I'm'on get black on his ass the next time he calls me out my name."

"What'd he call you?" Gordon asked, amused.

"A bitch!" I replied, and scampered back up toward the stage.

"Oh *hell*!" Gordon laughed. "He *definitely* loves you, girl!"

The other dancers huddled on the stage, waiting for me. Reveling in the extra seconds of rest I was making it possible for them to take.

Julian stood there, staring at me, his leg cocked to the side, clapping his hands to the staccato rhythm of his voice.

"Chop . . . chop . . . chop, bitch! Gotta . . . make . . . mooooves!"

I rushed up on stage and took my place.

In typical fashion, he came alongside me and stood as close to me as he possibly could.

"No special favors," Julian hissed with venom. *"Five minutes up* means *five minutes up*! I will *not* have you standing in the way of my show!"

"I'm *back*, ain't I?" I sneered with just as much venom.

I saw his left brow raise in surprise.

Uncontrollably, the left corner of my lip curled up in a smile.

Julian studied me, amazed at the fact that I was giving him back some of what he was dishing out. His eyes flashed, and his lips pressed tightly together.

Slowly, he stepped out toward the front of me and the other dancers.

"All right! One more time! Let's take this shit from the top!"

He waved his hand in the air, beckoning for the music.

It began, and I started my boogie all over again.

Julian walked around the group of us, checking out the flow and the rhythm of our moves.

He stopped in front of me. I locked my eyes onto his, as I swayed my head and body to the music.

He stood there, tapping his feet in time, cutting his eyes at me.

I flashed him a wide-mouthed, toothy grin.

Slowly, reluctantly, his eyes began to soften.

And to my surprise, as he stood there, watching me, Julian's lips began to form into a smile.

I sat at my little section in the dressing area, my legs propped up on the makeup table.

The dressing area was very spartan, very bare. The makeup counter was a weather-beaten, cracked, and faded beige Formica, with bright bulbs lining a long horizontal mirror that ran all the way across the top.

I had magazine clippings of makeup tips stuck in my section of the mirror. I also had two little pictures stuck there—one of me and my grandma taken at my college graduation, and one of me and Misty from our high school grad night at Disney World.

I was sitting there, my eyes were closed, and I had a headset on, grooving to "The Lady Suite" on Maxwell's *Unplugged* CD.

"It's been so long since I've seen you," I sang, bobbing my head to the music.

My body was beginning to relax and wind down from that electrifying rehearsal. My man Maxy was strokin' my ears and soothing my spirit with his heavenly voice.

I felt a tap on my shoulder.

I opened my eyes.

I saw Julian standing over me, working his mouth.

I pulled down my headphones and hit pause on my Walkman.

"Not bad out there today," he said.

"Thanks," I replied flatly.

"I hope you don't think I'm being too hard on you."

Julian looked at me, resting his hand on the back of my chair.

"Well, you damn shole ain't makin' it easy," I smirked.

"And I *never* will," he said, kneeling down and moving closer to my face.

For the first time, I noticed the calibration of his voice. It was very masculine and strong. Not too deep, but not effeminate in any way. He was about five-ten, and his body was tight, lean, muscular mass.

"You *got* something, Miss Thang. It's in the early stages, but it's there. And I see it. I want to make sure you see it, too, and don't take it for granted. The time to bring it out is now."

"So you think by cutting me down and calling me a bitch, you're bringing it out?"

"Got your juices flowing and kept your ass moving, didn't it?" he grinned.

"You never lied about that," I mumbled.

"See!" He smiled, touching me on the shoulder. "Sometimes you can get more flies with salt than sugar."

"Hmph!"

Julian pushed up with his hand and stood.

"Keep up the good work," he said, patting me on the back. "When the show opens, I want to have the best possible of everything falling into place."

He walked away, just as quietly as he'd arrived.

Before he disappeared into the shadows backstage, I called out to him.

"Julian!"

"What's up?" he asked, turning around.

I tried not to look at that innocuous but eye-popping bulge between his legs. Wasn't nothing a sistah could do with it but show it to another man.

"Did Gordon talk to you?"

He shook his head.

"No. Why? What's up?"

"Nothing," I said, relieved.

I guess Julian was just being nice to me on his own. Maybe Gordon was right about him really liking me and my potential.

Julian's eyes narrowed, and his mouth broke into a bit of a grin.

"You *are* fucking him, aren't you?!"

I looked around abruptly to see who might have heard him. There were dancers and stagehands coming and going all around us.

Nobody seemed to notice.

"No!!" I hissed. "Stop *saying* that!"

"Well," he said, coming closer, "y'all are mighty chummy."

"He's just a cool person. We have a little theater chitchat every now and then."

"Mmmm-hmmm," Julian muttered suspiciously. "Well, you have to earn your breaks with me, Miss Thang. Can't fuck your way to the top in my camp. Not unless you grow a dick."

"Dannnnnng!" I exclaimed, both alarmed and impressed by his candor. "That is *soooo* nasty!"

"Just telling it like it is."

"All right," I laughed, putting up my hand.

"We finished?" he asked.

"I'm through."

"All right," he said, "I'm outta here. I'll check you tomorrow."

"Cool," I said, taking my Walkman off pause and getting ready to slip my headset back on.

"He's straight," Julian said, lingering, pointing at my CD case.

"Yeah," I replied. "He's my favorite."

"Mine, too," Julian smiled.

"For real?"

"For real."

He and I kind of just smiled at each other quietly for a moment. Then Julian turned, gave me a quick wave, and rushed away.

I guess he didn't hate me after all.

Maybe things weren't going to be as bad as I thought they might.

I put my headset back on, grinning to myself as I sang along to the music.

I couldn't believe Julian and I actually had something in common.

I put my feet up on the makeup table, closed my eyes, and let myself slip into a Maxwell reverie.

Three weeks later, I was sitting on stage, doing stretching exercises.

No one else was in the theater. I had deliberately come early just to give myself some time alone to tone.

I had my legs stretched apart, and my head was facedown on my left knee, my right hand gripping my left ankle.

"You know he's coming to Radio City in two weeks?" a happy voice broke out.

I knew who it was talking, and I knew what he was talking about.

"Yep," I breathed, not lifting up my head. "Can you believe it? He's actually coming here to New York! His own backyard, at last!"

"I already got tickets."

"Really?!" Now, that made me look up. "I couldn't get any! It was sold out in a matter of hours!"

Julian was standing there in gray tights, bulge a-bustin', right in front of my face. He was grinning like a kid.

"Wanna go?" he asked.

My heart did a double thump.

"What?!"

"What I said!" he replied, his hand on his hip in mock indignation. "Do you want to go? You can go with me."

"But I thought . . . ," I began.

"I didn't say as my *date*. We can go as fellow Maxheads. My friend Tonio has been tripping anyway. I think I'm gon' leave his tired ass at home."

"I'd love to go," I mumbled, completely astonished at this outrageous turn of events.

"All right," he said. "We'll talk about it."

"Cool," I replied.

Julian turned and walked away, waving at me over his shoulder without looking back.

"Later, Miss Thang. I'll holler."

"Peace out, Scout," I replied, still reeling from what had just occurred.

Hot damn! I thought to myself. *I'm going to see my Maxy!! Wait'll I tell Misty. Life don't get no better than this!!*

"Come on, shake that ass! Shake it, shake it, shake it!"

Julian was in his usual form, and all of us dancers were working it out on that stage.

I was shaking it fiercely, on *that* I couldn't lie.

But, let me tell you . . . a sistah was in a little pain while she was doing so.

See, um. It was that time of the month. And I was like crazy. I was miserable.

Anyway, I was trying my best to ignore the cramps, but I couldn't.

Besides that, rehearsal had been going on *waay* too long. We were well overdue for a break.

Every now and then, when we did a funky spin or a turn, I would stumble a little here and there. On the sly, so I thought.

One time, Julian caught me, and shot me a look that made me feel a little ridiculous.

"All right, take ten!" he announced at last.

Thank goodness!! Things were getting pretty hairy.

Julian stepped over to me.

"Go address yourself," he said in a low tone. "You obviously have issues."

"Why?!" I asked with alarm, clenching my legs tightly together. "Can you tell?! Is something showing?!"

"Reesy . . . I'm a choreographer. It's not like I haven't seen *that* move before."

I stood there, feeling silly.

"Now, get outta here, and handle your business. You've got ten minutes."

"Thanks," I whispered, grabbed my duffel bag, and rushed off to the bathroom.

There was someone in it when I got there.

I waited impatiently, hoping the person would come out before our time was up.

I heard the toilet flush.

After a second, the door came open.

It was the sistah who had elbowed me when I first auditioned for the show. The one who was smirking when the guys told me to leave.

She was the one who had gotten the other part that was up for grabs when we first auditioned.

She *hmmmphed* at me as she walked out.

Nasty heffah. Didn't even wash her hands.

I stepped into the bathroom and shut the door behind me.

I sat down, my head in my hands, moaning softly. After a few deep breaths, I reached into my bag and pulled out some Aleve.

The *only* thing that worked when I had cramps like this. I swallowed two of them. Dry. And prayed for quick relief.

I lingered in the bathroom a little while, then struggled my way up.

I slowly made my way out of the bathroom. There were two girls standing outside, waiting to use it.

"Our damn time is almost up," one of them snarled.

I ignored her and hobbled my way back over to Julian.

He was sitting on the edge of the stage, sipping on some Evian. His legs were cocked open. *Bulge a-plenty.*

"Why you walking like that?"

"I got a situation . . . ," I began.

"Oh, *here we go* . . . ," Julian said, rolling his eyes. "It's the cramp thang, huh? I never figured you to use that one for an out, Miss Thang."

"No," I whispered. "It's not like that. I can keep working through cramps. I've done that before. These are just real severe."

"So go on then," he said. "Get outta here."

"Okay. So you don't mind?"

"Of course, *I mind,* but it can't be helped!! Now *get* outta here so the rest of us can get back to work!!"

I could tell he was serious.

I had a windbreaker in my duffel bag. I took it out and tied it around my waist.

"See ya later," I said and waved as I walked awkwardly away.

"Go home and lie down" he said, standing up.

He gestured to the other dancers.

"All right, y'all! Let's shake it loose! Back to work! Gotta make moves!"

The next day, I once again arrived early for rehearsal.

But, since those cramps were still kicking my butt, I would be sitting out the day's activities, again.

Rowena was on stage, doing her thing. I stood there on the sidelines, watching her with fascination.

Rowena Shaw was the star of the show. She was amazing. A bundle of pure energy and talent.

She played the part of Mimosa Jones, a celebrated beauty

from the fifties who headlined a successful all-black Vegas-styled revue that toured across the country.

The role of Mimosa was central to the show. Practically every scene revolved around her. Mimosa was *Black Barry's Pie.*

Consequently, so was Rowena.

Rowena had been in ten other off-Broadway productions, and had worked with Gordon and Julian several times before.

Long-legged and limber, she was one hot mama. Now, *that* sistah could dance *and* sing! She breathed life into Mimosa and made the character excitingly real. I only *wished* I could move the way she did.

I came in early many a day and watched her rehearsing her part. I had come to know it well. Just to see her dance gave me something to aspire to.

One day, I often mused. *One day.*

That was gon' be *me* up there on that stage.

But for now, I had more pressing issues at hand. I had to make it through my very first show.

And now that the opening was rapidly approaching, the heat was on and the excitement had begun.

A STAR IS SCORNED

I waited backstage, my heart racing.

We were all dressed. The show was due to start in less than five minutes. There was a nervous electricity in the air that affected us all. People I had been rehearsing with who hadn't bothered to say two words to me for the past three months were now saying *hello* and *break a leg* left and right.

Every light backstage was on. The smell of greasepaint and freshly pressed costumes filled the air. All I could hear was rustling feet and endless chatter.

In the midst of it all, I stood there. Frantic. Excited. So keyed up I could have just popped.

I should have been sweating from all the heat and the energy, but, somehow, go figure, I managed to stay cool.

Julian rushed by, hurrying toward the stars' dressing rooms. He doubled back when he noticed me standing.

"Make me proud out there tonight, girlfriend," he whispered. "You know you're my *great black hope*. Don't make me take my Maxwell ticket back!"

I smiled nervously. Squeamish, and a little frightened, for once in my life.

I saw him disappear inside Rowena's dressing room.

Where was Misty?

We had been in rehearsals all weekend, along with everyone else involved with the show. We'd put finishing touches on the presentation, costume fittings, perfected moves, and made sure everything was as tight as it could get.

Julian was leaving absolutely *nothing* to chance.

I walked around in my fuchsia cocktail dress. All the female dancers wore cocktail dresses, but I thought mine was the prettiest color. It just jumped out at you, sorta like I did.

The flimsy material clung to my waist and the dangerous curves of my breasts and my butt. My calves were shapely and strong. The heels I wore had guided me flawlessly through many a dress rehearsal.

My braids were pulled up into a chignon, with a few tendrils falling gently, seductively, around my face. My nails were kissed with a soft fuchsia polish. My lips were a soft fuchsia gloss. The color was a beautiful complement to the hue of my skin.

"I could eat your yummy ass up," a deep voice very close to my ear murmured.

I turned around. It was Donovan. One of the male dancers.

He was one of the sexiest men I had seen since I'd been in New York, and I've seen some lovelies. I'd watched him many a time during reheasals, and had caught him watching me back.

But too many women were trying to give the brother play. And he was taking it, with two hands. That's not how I roll. I'm not one to go after what the huddled masses do.

He stood there in his tux, that rich cocoa-brown skin of his smooth like silk.

"Shouldn't you be full by now?" I replied, my expression dull and flat. "You've had your share of yummies over the past few months."

"I have *many* appetites," he growled. "Right now, I'm a little hungry for some *red* meat."

I stared into those deep brown eyes of his.

Any other time, I would have been in *fuck mode* for sure. I would have definitely left the brother deliberately hanging so that I could pick things up after the show was over.

This time, I wasn't in the mood. I had too many things going on in my head, and was way too excited and distracted. I was so keyed up, I could practically feel the entire path my blood took as it coursed through my veins.

But Donovan persisted. In a vulgar, kinda predatory way.

"Don't speak too soon," he cooed. "Why don't you catch me on the flip, and we can grab something to eat? Maybe later, we can check out the haps at my crib."

I didn't respond.

"I got a brass *wawtah*bed," he whispered seductively.

I looked at him, not believing he had the nerve to dredge up that old tired-ass Morris Day shit. He had to be trippin'.

"Step off!" I shot back with a laugh. "You don't know me from *Adam*!"

"It ain't like a nigga ain't tryin'," Donovan smiled, flashing his pearly grill.

In the theater, I heard our small band (we were calling it an "orchestra" for grand purposes only) begin to play.

"Places everybody!" Dreyfus, the stage manager, shouted.

I fell into line. Donovan took his place a few bodies down from me. He leaned forward, waiting for my response.

"No time right now," I mouthed.

"When?" he mouthed back.

A couple of sistahs that Donovan had obviously hit and quit cut their eyes at me.

"Catch me next lifetime," I said with a smile.

Thank you, Erykah Badu, I thought gleefully.

Donovan's smile faded. The dissed sistahs seemed to be quite pleased.

I didn't have time for this. Inside my head, all I could really hear was the roar of my own blood as the excitement mounted.

I was about to make my stage debut! In a matter of seconds, those curtains were gonna go up!

This little caterpillar was about to spread her brand-new wings.

"Turn it out, y'all!" Julian whispered from the sidelines.

The music got louder.

Dreyfus stood nearby and, using his fingers, gave us a countdown.

5 . . . 4 . . . 3 . . . 2 . . . 1 . . .

". . . SHOWTIME!!"

As the curtains rose, we began our groove. I worked my hips in a violent shimmy, grabbing the hand of the tuxedoed brother next to me. We danced around each other in a circle, then he spun me like a top and tossed me up in the air.

When the stage lights hit me, I was hooked. All fear had fled, and I was nothing but pure-dee, electrified adrenaline.

I peeked around the curtains during intermission, looking for Misty and Rick, but the crowd was so thick for this first night's show, all the faces were practically one big blur.

Gordon knew a lot of people, and had put on some pretty successful off-Broadway shows. Rowena needed no words, and everybody knew Julian's reputation. New York had been salivating, waiting for *Black Barry's Pie* to finally take off.

I knew my girl was sitting out there, prouder than Tyrene and Tyrone could have ever been.

The way I was cheesing when I got under those bright lights! It was like I'd found the place I was born to be!

I couldn't wait for us to celebrate. Me, her, and Rick. It didn't matter if I didn't have a date. Just being with my girl would be enough. I had *soooo* much to tell her. I was bursting with excitement, dying to describe how it felt to be out there, on that stage, a part of the whole musical machine.

I could hear the band/orchestra starting up.

"All right, everybody!" Dreyfus called. *"Take your places!"*

I was in my spot, lickety-split. Ready for it all to begin again. When the music started, I slid into my boogie, legs bent, arms waving down around my sides, as I wove out onto the stage.

One of the male dancers shimmied around me, and we made artful merry with each other as we danced. He grabbed my hand and led me into a high-steppin' jitterbug. I danced around him, twirling my fingers and shaking my shoulders with delirious vigor.

I was intoxicated.

It felt so wonderful, that I didn't want it to ever end.

I sat at my area in the dressing room, exhausted, exhilarated, ecstatic. People came by here and there, offering up pats on the back and words of approval.

"You were fantastic out there, girlfriend!"

"Girl, I'm scared-a you!"

"We still got time to hook up, tonight. My place. Brass *waw-tah*bed."

I couldn't help but giggle at that. I had to give it to Donovan for trying.

"You made me proud out there, girl," Julian smiled, giving me a kiss on the cheek. "You earned those Maxwell tickets tonight. If you don't ever perform up to par again—and you know that I won't allow that—just know that you showed up for the opening!"

I blushed. A rarity for me.

"Thanks, Julian," I beamed, reaching up and giving him a warm kiss on the cheek in return. He was really beginning to feel like a friend.

"I'll see you tomorrow morning," he smiled, waving his finger at me. "And we'll start this show all over again."

"Aye, aye, Cap'n!" I said with a salute.

I was so happy that I had finally found what felt like my niche. *Where was Misty?*

I needed to be sharing this with her. Any minute now, I knew I would see her pecan-tan face rounding the bend, arms outstretched for hugs.

We'd chatter like chipmunks with excitement. And she'd give me her rundown on my performance.

Hell, I might even go easy on ol' slick Rick and not dish out any sarcastic lip.

I was punch drunk with glee.

"Ooooooooooooooh weeeeeeeeeeeeeee!" I squealed. *"Hot damn, hot damn, hot damn!"*

I couldn't wait to tell her *every*thing!!

LET'S JUST DIS AND SAY GOODBYE

An hour later, I was *still* sitting in the dressing room, waiting for Misty and Rick to show.

Everyone was gone. From the stagehands on down. Even the janitor had bounced.

I just sat there, because I didn't want to move. Moving would mean accepting the fact that I had been duped. I'd gone for the *okey-doke*. Misty had not only failed to show, but probably had no intentions of doing so to begin with.

I had waited around for nothing. My so-called friend had given me the royal dis.

I felt like a fool.

My elation went through a series of mutations, turning into disappointment, then disbelief, and, finally, *fatally,* to rage. My eyes were wet, but I couldn't tell if it was from tears, or the steam that was forming inside every pore of my being.

She didn't call, leave a message, stick her face in, send over flowers . . . *nothing*.

I was fit to be tied. I wanted to *kill*.

Misty had pulled some stunts on me before, but this had to beat all. To me, her not showing up for me tonight was the equivalent of your parents missing your high school graduation.

That's just some unforgivable shit.

I changed into my jeans and a T-shirt. Right there in the middle of the backstage area. Wasn't nobody there to see me do it. Shit. Everybody else was long gone.

I wasn't about to let Miss Divine put me down and humiliate me like that for no nigga. She wasn't going to get off tonight without getting an earful from me.

I grabbed my duffel bag and headed for the door.

I ran through Grand Central Station and barely made the 1:07 A.M.

That's right. I was tracking her butt down in the middle of the night.

I sat there in the almost-empty train, eyes blazing. In my jeans pocket was a balled-up address.

I sat there now, my lip stuck out. I was mad, hurt, and determined. I talked to myself to keep my rage contained.

"I can't believe a woman can be *this* damn stupid over a man!" I said out loud.

There weren't a lot of folks on the train, but the handful that were there shot strange looks my way.

I stared out the window into nothingness until the train left the tunnel at Ninety-seventh Street.

When the train stopped at 125th Street, I watched the colored folks get on and off.

I wonder what it would be like to live in Harlem, I mused to myself.

That could be the answer. Maybe I could just disappear. Let Miss Divine go her separate way, and I could go mine. I could move uptown with my peeps, and get lost in the artsy, Afrocentric, cultural crowd.

Harlem World.

No one would ever have to know where I was, unless I wanted them to know. If I didn't want to, I would never have to see Misty's flaky ass again. Wouldn't have to worry about Tyrone and Tyrene all up in my Kool-Aid, either.

I could do it, no question. Black folks were the masters of disappearing at will, and not ever being found again.

I had a teacher once who just got tired of being bothered by his family. So he stepped. Was never seen *ever* again.

Could be, God knows, *anywhere* right now. Maybe even just down the street from his folks. No one even knew where to begin to look.

I tell you, if a negro wanted to get lost, she could do it. Be living right around the corner from your ass, and you'd never know.

Yep. Black folks could teach the Witness Protection Program a few things about falling off. Their people were always discovered and killed, all dressed up in disguises—wigs and fake beards—trying to pass for somebody else. But colored people had been perfecting the disappearing act for years. We could be walking right past your house every day, *au natural* and unchanged, and *still* you wouldn't know.

I sighed heavily. Falling off wasn't the answer. I'd miss my folks, even though they did get on my nerves sometimes.

The train rushed on, toward conflict and resolution.

Because, regardless of anything, I was going to resolve this situation tonight. I was having no more of it. My cup was full and had runneth over.

I sat there, chewing my bottom lip, not thinking about how things were gonna go down.

I preferred to let it unfold on its own. I worked best extemporaneously.

Let shit happen.

And let the chips fall where they may.

I rang the doorbell.

Lights were on inside, and I could hear raucous laughter.

Misty. Giggling *way* too hard and happy.

I stood on the porch, looking around at the nice, peaceful little buppified area. Rick's townhouse sat right on a lake. Ducks were sleeping on the surface of the water.

The porchlight came on, and the peephole went black.

"Who is it?" a man's voice asked.

"Open the door!" I demanded, my voice calm but firm.

There was a pause, and I thought I heard mumbling.

Nigga probably thought it was one of his women, 'bout to show out on his azz.

The lock clicked, and the door made a squeaky sound as it was pulled back on the hinges.

Rick Hodges peeked out cautiously. His wore a puzzled look on his brown face, and ran his hand across his freshly trimmed fade. He didn't have on a shirt.

Actually, for all I know, he could have been butt nekked behind that door.

"*Hey, girl!* What you doing here this time of night? Something wrong?"

"*Hmmmph!*" I snorted, and pushed my way past him, into the house.

When I got inside, he definitely wasn't butt nekked, but it took me a second for that to register.

The first thing I *did* notice was Miss Divine, laying all sprawled out on the couch in a bright red teddy, her legs cocked up, the remote in her hand.

I also saw things from our apartment. One of the hand chairs from Ikea. And the blue vase made of cracked glass. A stack of Frank Fraziers were leaned up against the living room wall.

"What are *you* doing here?!" Misty exclaimed, sitting up and sounding like Rick's broken record. "Hang on a second, let me go get my robe!"

She jumped up from the couch and scampered back to the bedroom. Without saying a word, I bodaciously followed her.

When she went into the room, I was right on her heels. I closed the door behind us and locked it.

Misty spun around.

"What's up?"

"*You* tell *me*!!" I snapped, my hands on my hip. I was in *let's throw down* mode. I hadn't had a good street fight in years.

"What do you mean?" Misty was genuinely puzzled. "Is everything all right? Did something happen at the theater toni—

"*Oh shit, Reesy!!*" Misty gasped, clasping her palms over her mouth. "*Oh shit, oh shit, oh shit!! I forgot all about it!!*"

She reached out for me with both arms.

I slapped upward with my hands, knocking her arms away.

"*Don't touch me, bitch!!*"

Her face crumbled at my words.

"*Wha . . . ?!*"

"You did this shit on purpose!" I screamed. "It's bad enough you don't half support what I do, but to promise me that you're gonna be there, and then don't even *come?*! That's some low-down, nasty shit, Misty! And I *don't* appreciate it!"

She reached out for me again, and I pushed her away.

Hard, this time.

She bounced back on the bed, looking foolish in that trampy-ass teddy.

"Stop acting so ghetto, Reesy," she said softly. "I don't wanna fight with you. That's not my style."

"Is *that* your style?" I replied sharply, pointing at her in that hoe-ish getup.

Misty sighed and reached for her robe. It was lying on the bed beside her.

I snatched it from her hands.

"Don't try to cover up now!" I shouted. "Let me see you in all your glory!"

"Don't be ridiculous," she mumbled, reaching out, trying to take the robe back.

"Noooo!" I sneered, holding it behind my back. "Be yourself! You felt comfortable enough to walk around Rick this way! Don't try to front with me!"

Misty got up from the bed and went to the closet.

"Don't . . . walk . . . away . . . from . . . me," I said through gritted teeth.

She spun around, her face hard and feisty.

"Look . . . what do you want me to do? *Huh?* I can't change things. What's done is done!"

I stood there, seething.

Her face softened.

"I forgot all about it," she whined, holding her palms out in a pleading gesture. "I'm sorry. I can't tell you how sorry I am. Rick and I played hooky from work and moved my stuff in here today."

Misty took a step toward me. I stepped back, breaking my silence.

"I don't give a *fuck* about you and Rick!" I screamed. "I would have never done this to you! *Never!!* Not in a million years!"

"I didn't *do* this to you!" Misty screamed back. "I made a *mis-*

take! I *forgot*! Why are you so freaking paranoid, like I did this to you on purpose?"

There was a knock at the bedroom door.

"What's going on in there?"

"Fuck off, muthafucka!" I screamed.

"It's all right, Rick," Misty yelled. "I got this."

"Oh?" I laughed, working my head. "You *got* this? So you think you handlin' me?"

I couldn't wait to throw down.

Misty sat down on the bed, refusing to give me the pleasure of fisticuffs. She sat there like the pathetic piece of crap that she was, and just gave in to the whole thing.

I kept on.

"How you can call yourself a friend? Anybody's friend? I've had pets more loyal than you!"

"I made a mistake," she whimpered, her head hanging down. "I don't know what you want me to do."

"You knew how much this meant to me," I said in a lowered tone, my teeth bared. "You're just so foolish, all you care about is that man. You always put a man before everything else."

"That's *not* true," Misty pleaded. "I love you! You're my sis-tah!"

"You don't *love* me!!" I screeched. "You don't know *how* to love nobody! How can you love me when you don't even love your damn self? Huh?"

She softly began to cry.

"Honey, please," I said apathetically, waving my hand in the air. "I don't know what you crying about. You can just keep your little crocodile tears to yourself."

Her shoulders shook, as the tears fell heavily with each of my words.

"How can I make this up to you?" she asked, looking up at me with her sorry little expression.

I took a deep breath, disgusted. I looked at her, sitting there in that teddy like a two-dollar hoe, and wanted to spit.

Enough was enough. I was *through* with her ass.

"You *can't* make it up to me. It's over. As far as I'm concerned, you and I are no longer friends."

Misty's face went through a million contortions.

"What do you mean, *we're no longer friends?!*" she asked with fear in her voice.

"Just what I said. From now on, you stay the *fuck* away from me. I'm moving out of your apartment, and I don't wanna have no parts of nuthin' to do with you!"

"You don't mean that," Misty said, jumping up from the bed. She made a move toward me.

I held out my palm, stopping her.

"If I were you," I warned, "I'd stay over *there*. I'm not feeling too cool right now, and I can't promise you that I won't whip your ass right here in your brand-new home."

Misty stared at me like I was a stranger.

She had her nerve. If anything, I didn't know who the hell *she* had turned into.

"Don't move out," she said. "The rent there is free. I'm sorry, Reesy. This was just an honest mistake."

"Well, it was the last straw," I replied. "I'm calling *game*. Friendship over. You forfeited. Stay your ass as far away from me as you can get."

I unlocked the door and snatched it open. Rick was standing there, his mouth wide.

"Get the hell out my way," I hissed, shoving him aside.

"Why are you treating your friend like this?" he asked. "You know Misty loves you!"

I turned around sharply and walked up to him, all in his face. I pressed my forefinger against his nose.

"You don't know *shit* about me and Misty," I growled. "So don't be telling me what's what. Actions speak louder than words."

I pushed his face with my finger, dismissing him, *and* his woman, from my life. I rushed toward the door.

Misty called out to me.

"Reesy," she begged. "Please. Don't trip like this."

I held onto the doorknob, listening to the pain in her voice.

It was nowhere near the pain I had felt tonight at the theater, when I realized, after an hour of waiting, that I was ass out and all alone.

I turned around and looked at her. She was standing in her bedroom doorway, looking every bit like the tramp she had become.

It occurred to me that I still had her robe in my hand.

I flung it at her.

"Put some clothes on!" I spat. "Your mama would die if she could see you right now!"

Misty gasped, throwing her hand over her mouth.

"And when this relationship turns raggedy, like you and I *know* it will," I chided, "make sure it's your mama that you run to, 'cause I don't wanna ever see your dumb ass again!"

I snatched the door open, and slammed it shut behind me.

I ran as fast as I could to the cab that was waiting. The motor, and the meter, were still running.

"Back to the train station," I panted, slipping into the back-seat.

My eyes were wet and my chest was hurting.

Inside my heart, there was a big ol' gaping, throbbing hole.

On the ride back on the train, I stared, zombie-like, out the window, my head feeling as though it were about to explode.

What was supposed to be one of the best days of my life had turned into shit.

Sure, the opening of the show had gone well. But the thing that mattered most to me, having my best friend there, who was, for all intents and purposes, my family, had been a total bust.

She had ditched me like a dirty diaper.

That hurt my heart like you wouldn't believe.

And I had allowed myself to get worked up into such a rage, that I had practically lost all control.

When pressed, I could be very physical, very emotional. I didn't handle anger well at all. At least I knew that much about myself. I'd gotten into many a scrap as a child. Whenever other girls tried to jump bad with Misty at school, I was always the one who had her back. No one ever dared to challenge me, 'cause they knew I'd whoop up on some ass in a hot second.

I don't think Misty realized how close she had come to that very thing happening to her today. It's good I got outta there before I let that side of me loose.

When the trained stopped again at 125th Street, I studied the black folks getting off a little more closely.

To my own surprise, just before the train was ready to take off again, I had jumped outta my seat and headed out the doors.

Into the great big ol' black world of Harlem.

I ambled across 125th Street.

I walked, noticing the people bustling all around me. There were bright lights everywhere, and black folks in all shapes, colors, and sizes.

There was enough fried chicken to feed all of Africa.

Kennedy Chicken, Kansas Chicken, Ya Mama's Chicken . . . *damn!*

African braid shops and clothing stores galore. Fried fish and shrimp joints.

It was late at night, and a lot of stuff was closed. But you couldn't really tell it from all the people that were out, that's for sure.

I looked up and saw that I was right in front of the Apollo Theater. I couldn't help but smile. I mean, *there I was,* right in front of it!

I considered all those times I'd watched the show on television. I thought of all those artistic giants from our culture that had gotten their starts there. I was overcome with pride.

As silly as it sounds, I wanted to feel the place. You know, just let some of that history pass right on to me.

I sidled up to the building, trying to play off what I was doing.

And as I walked alongside it, I just let my left palm kinda pass over the surface.

Touching it, I don't know, sort of made me feel better. Like I had been infused with the spirits of the masters. It may sound corny, but it's true. At that particular moment in my life, I was feeling mighty alone. I needed to make a connection with something. And running my hand along the Apollo Theater allowed me to do just that.

I kept walking, drinking in the sights.

There were sistahs with big hair, sculpted into all sorts of overgelled styles. There were braided heads, like mine. All kinds of braids—dookie braids, microbraids, blond braids, squiggly braids. A style for every reason and season. Dreads and locks were all over the place, and so were brothers, *and sistahs,* with zeroes.

I closed my eyes and breathed in the rich air. My heart began to heal a little around the edges, although the hole was still there and was noticeably tender.

"*'Zup, lady?*" said a fine chocolate specimen who was passing me by.

He smiled at me as he strutted his stuff down the street.

You know how brothers kinda lean to the side when they walk? Well, my boy had his lean goin' on and was rubbin' his chin, checkin' me out. He wasn't being obnoxious. Just friendly.

Harlem-style.

Didn't mean me no harm at all.

"Hiya doin'," I said and smiled in return.

"Lookin' good, girl!" he tossed back at me, never stopping to slow his roll.

I liked this place. I liked this place a hella-bunch.

I kept walking.

I turned corners here and there, feeling my way around, not in the *least* bit threatened.

People (read, *white folks*) always tried to make Harlem sound so battered. Made it seem dark and dangerous, like the jungle.

It felt like home to me. All the smells, sounds, and people filled the night air with a richness that reminded me of Carnival. It was like a party. And this probably wasn't even its busiest.

There were renovations going on all over the place. Harlem was being revitalized in a big way. It was getting its second wind. Or third, or fourth, for all I knew.

I found myself on Lenox Avenue between 126th and 127th. Right in front of Sylvia's. *Ummph, ummph!* A sistah could sure have gone for some of that good ol' soul food. But it was much too late for that. Sylvia's had closed hours before.

Oh well, I thought. At least now I knew where it was.

Sylvia's was historical. *Hell,* all of Harlem was. To think, this place had been right up underneath my nose the whole time I had been living in New York. And, even worse, it took having a blowout with Misty for me to take the time to discover it.

I needed my behind whipped for that.

This was a match that was obviously made in heaven. Harlem and Reesy went together like smoked neckbones and collards.

A million-and-one thoughts were racing through my head. My brain was on *fire*.

I had some decisions to make, and I wasn't going to waste any time about it.

To borrow the words of brother Julian . . .

Gotta make moves.

UPTOWN SATURDAY NIGHT

I moved out of the Milano with a dust behind me.

I took my stuff out piecemeal, so Len wouldn't notice, with his nosy behind. He would have been all up in my business, trying to assist.

I mailed the keys to *dem* and *dose*.

You know. *Dem* thangs up in Greenwich . . . *dose* fools that I no longer wanted to have anything to do with.

I did have to get a new phone number, but I explained that away by telling my parents that I was getting my own line inside the apartment.

I went to the post office, pronto, and filled out a change-of-address form. The last thing I needed was for my mail to be sitting around at the Milano, unanswered, and for me to have to go into it with Tyrone and Tyrene about why I wasn't living with Misty anymore.

I didn't tell Len I was moving. I just told him that I was going to be house-sitting a place for a friend for an indefinite period of time.

The fool believed it. Or, at least, he acted like he did.

"I don't see Miss Fine that much anymore," he commented. "She must come in at really odd hours."

"I guess," I shrugged. "I'm at work a lot."

He rubbed his chin, eyes scouring my body.

"Well, since the two of you are away so much, you want me to check on the place periodically, just to make sure everything's okay?"

"*Doowhatchalike,*" I said, stepping into a cab, instructing the driver on where to go, and watching Len and the Milano disappear out of my life for good.

My new place in Harlem was *all that*.

It was a newly renovated prewar apartment building, spacious and solid, around 138th Street, near the City College campus.

My building was very safe and well lit. The tenants were mostly buppies and youngbloods around my age or so. It was definitely a cool spot to be in.

My apartment was a two-bedroom, very roomy and comfortable. Why I got two bedrooms, I'll never know. I was so used to Misty's funky behind coming over and crashing at whatever crib I had. I guess I just got the extra space out of habit.

But it wasn't like she'd ever be crashing in my space again.

I loved the hardwood floors in my place. They reminded me of my Grandma Tyler's house . . . sweet, feisty thing that she was.

Tyrene and I got our attitudes honestly, that for sure. Grandma Tyler was *nots* to be messed with.

I thought about her as I walked around, looking at everything. She would definitely like it here. Even though I didn't get to see her very often, being the wandering spirit that I was, I still talked to her quite frequently. Maybe once or twice a week.

I loved Grandma Tyler. Sometimes talking to her was easier than talking to my own mother. Grandma Tyler took way more time to listen, and wasn't always sitting around trying to tell me what to do.

"Live your life, Tweety," she would say to me. "Ain't nuttin' to it but to do it. Wish I was younger. I'd be out there now, shaking my bony little ass right 'long witcha."

She knew about me dancing in *Black Barry's Pie*. She was the one person, other than Misty, who I wished could have been there opening night.

The day after my fight with Miss Divine, I called Grandma Tyler.

Admittedly, I wanted to hear her say *"Bump that hoe,"* but, of course, she didn't.

In fact, I would have truly been surprised if she had. But she did ask me all about how the show went.

She sat there on the phone, excited and intrigued, *oohing* and *aahing* as I described the music, costume changes, and crowd response.

It felt so good to be talking to her. I was able to share my moment with somebody who genuinely cared about me and never, ever judged me for what I did.

Matter of fact, Grandma Tyler was the only other person on the planet, other than Misty, who I ever confided in about my days as an exotic dancer.

She wasn't even shocked. She just laughed about it and said, "Tweety, baby, *do yo' thang*!!"

I never had to worry about her telling my business to Tyrene.

"Trust me, Tweety . . . yo' secret's safe wit' me. And you ain't got to always fret 'bout what folks gon' thank. That's just life, and either you got one, or you dead."

Hearing that always made me feel good.

"You know," she'd add, "I know some thangs 'bout yo' mama and daddy that would make your life look like teatime with the Queen. So don't you let them bother you. They done raised some hell in they day, and now they tryna ack all high and mighty. But them some rapscallions if there ever was any!"

Only Grandma Tyler could say *rapscallions* and make it sound worse than *muthafucka*. At least, you knew that's how she meant it.

And nobody else in the whole wide world called me Tweety but her. It was our little thang, and I loved her for it.

When I was a baby, she would pick me up and coo, "Look at my little piece of yella sunshine! Just as *tweet* as she can be!"

When I began to walk, she said I scampered around like a little bird, barely able to hold up my big yellow head. *Tweet* became *Tweety*. For obvious reasons.

And Grandma Tyler and me became spiritually connected for life.

Yeah, I thought, looking out the second-floor window at three little brown boys coming out of the bodega downstairs, *Grandma Tyler would definitely dig my new place.*

I leaned my palms on the sill and breathed in the balmy Harlem breezes. I liked to open the windows, let the fresh air in, and listen to the noise my people made as they passed up and down the street. I had put planters in the windows and filled them with pansies, fresh herbs, and plastic windmills. I hung a chime just above the planters.

It was paradise, people, I tell you. No lie.

All right, all right. So I'll bet you're wondering how I was able to do it all. Just up and move, *just like that.* Get a crib overnight. Check in, easy as you please, and set up shop all *lah-dee-dah* and so carefree.

Well, let me tell you . . .

I broke down and cashed in one of those stipends.

Money's money, and I needed it. End of subject. Put a *period* on that bad boy.

Forget about strength of conscience and taking the moral *I'ma-do-this-by-my-damn-self* high ground. All that shit flew out the window like a loosed pigeon when it got down to it.

Desperation is desperation. I needed to get away from Misty Fine. And, *uh,* wouldn't you know it, there happened to be some money sitting around, calling out my name, *begging* me to take it.

And I ain't deaf. My hearing is twenty-twenty like a mug.

I told myself that it wasn't like my folks were actually supporting me. I was going to put the money back, little by little, from my earnings in *Black Barry's Pie.*

The stipend was for ten thousand dollars.

Yeah, that's right.

Four times a year, my parents sent me a check for ten thousand dollars. Like I mentioned before, I always invested it, choosing to make and pay my own way in the world.

But a couple of days after that mess with Misty, one of those checks, the summer disbursement, happened to arrive.

Right on time.

It was like manna from the heavens.

I'd been trying to figure out how I was going to scrape up a way to get the hell out of that free space at the Milano. And as close as I was to Grandma Tyler, asking her for money was never even an option or a thought.

Tyrone and Tyrene took care of her, and my grandmother deserved every penny she got. She spent years baby-sitting white folks' kids and cleaning houses just so she could raise my mama and put her through school.

Nope. I definitely couldn't go to her for money.

So when the disbursement check arrived in the mail, I studied that bad boy long and hard.

Pay to the order of Teresa R. Snowden, it read. *Ten Thousand Dollars and No Cents.*

I stared at the check. If I didn't cash it and use it to get on with my life, *I'd* be the one who had no "sense."

So I took that check, deposited it into my checking account, and reveled in what it felt like to be a little bit liquid for a minute.

Wasn't a bad feeling, I have to admit.

I spent a lot of time knocking my parents for being such capitalists. But let me tell you, it felt damn good going out and being able to get what I wanted and needed. *When* I wanted and needed it.

I asked around of some of the dancers in the show about places for rent. I told them that I preferred something in Harlem.

Believe it or not, Donovan, with his fly, horny ass, was the one who hooked me up. He knew of a spot not too far from his own building that had just been reno'd.

It was right in the mix and hustle and bustle of Harlem. The rent wasn't even as high as I expected it to be.

At first, I wasn't sure if I wanted Donovan to know where I was living. But heck, available space is available space. It wasn't like he was going to be able to just come up in my place and *take* the punani.

You can't take what ain't up for grabs.

I got the place for nine hundred bucks a month. I paid the landlord five months' rent up front, plus all the requisite deposits.

When the dust settled, I still had a bunch of money left. I

went to Ikea and bought myself a couch, two chairs, a dining table and some of those cute little knickknacky things they sold to coordinate with your home.

I went to a few more places and picked up new towels, plates, utensils, and some colorful mugs and glasses. I stocked my home with food.

I was able to get all that stuff, and *still* I hadn't touched the money I was getting from my gig in *Black Barry's Pie.*

I was as happy as a tick on a toe. You couldn't tell me *nuthin'.* I was in my own crib. I was doin' my own thang, and I was makin' myself a little piece of change dancing on stage in an off-Broadway show.

My life was on the incline. Wasn't nothing but positive things ahead.

I was ready for the new. Out with all the old, including Misty Fine.

I had washed that triflin' heffah of an ex–best friend right outta my braids.

"You excited about the concert tomorrow?" Julian asked.

He stood there, sweaty, a towel draped around his neck. In his right hand, he held a towel for me.

"Am I?!" I breathed heavily, taking the towel from him. I was exhausted from that morning's workout. I'd just finished up an hour of high-speed walking on the treadmill.

Julian and I had begun working out together. In a very short period of time, he had gone from dissing me to praising me, to stopping to have idle chitchat with me during rehearsals and backstage, to having lunch. He had now officially become my friend.

Every weekday morning, at the crack of dawn, I met him around the corner from the theater, and we hopped it over to his gym. I liked the place, so I decided to join as well.

(Using some of that stipend money, of course.)

He had just finished the early morning aerobics class, and he stood there in his tights, with his ever-present bulge, the picture of physical fitness. He wasn't even breathing hard, and that morning class was an advanced level set that didn't take any prisoners.

Julian was looking at me kinda funny.

I made a grand gesture of lifting up my arms, sniffing at my pits.

"What are you doing?" he asked with a laugh. "You are *so* foolish!"

"Wondering why you're looking at me like that, checking to see if I'm stank!"

I stepped off the treadmill, and the two of us proceeded to head out. We walked down the street, sipping on Evian, duffel bags in hand.

"So why were you just looking at me like that?" I asked him again.

He appeared to be struggling with what he wanted to say.

"C'mon, negro," I pressed, "spit it out!!"

"I can't go to the concert with you tomorrow," he blurted.

"What do you mean, *you can't go*?!" I screeched. "They're *your* tickets!"

"We have a show tomorrow, remember? And it starts at eight . . . same time as the Maxwell concert. Gordon might trip a little if both of us book."

"*Oh God,* Julian! I had no idea the concert started so early! I figured I could go after the show."

"I know," he said. "I don't know what I was thinking when I bought those tickets. I didn't want to miss out. I should have known damn well there wasn't no way I could get off to go see Maxwell."

I walked along in silence. Freaking. Fuming. Flipping over the fact that I wasn't going to get to see my favorite singer in the whole wide world perform.

Julian must have read my mind. Or felt my fumes, one.

"That doesn't mean *you* can't go," he said in a serious tone. "You can always get one of the alternate dancers to stand in for your part."

I hadn't thought about that. That could work. I really wanted to see my man Maxwell at Radio City.

"You think so?" I asked. "I mean, it won't create any problems, will it?"

Julian shook his head.

"No. That's why they have understudies and alternates. Just

don't make it a habit of missing a lot of shows and mess around and get replaced."

I snickered.

"*Please.* You know seeing Maxwell is about the *only* thing that would make me skip out on *Black Barry's.*"

We dipped inside a diner on the corner. A tall, blond waitress led us to a booth. She looked dog-tired.

"Thanks," I said to her.

She very quickly walked away. I turned my attention back to Julian, who sat across from me.

"So how are you going to be able to handle not seeing Maxwell? You love him just as much as I do!"

Julian smiled, looking up past me. I followed the direction of his eyes. Our waitress had returned.

"What can I get you?" she droned in a sad-sack sort of a voice that made no pretense of trying to be friendly. Homegirl looked like she had just pulled a thirty-hour shift.

Julian deferred to me to order first.

"I'll have a large orange juice and a blueberry muffin," I said. "He'll have the same."

"*Oh,*" he said under his breath, "so you think you really know me now, huh?"

"Yep."

The waitress waited on him to confirm.

"I'll have what she's having," he said with a chuckle.

"Would either of you like coffee?" the waitress sighed.

She looked so pitiful, I felt like getting up and fetching our order for her.

"Could you bring two cups, with cream and sugar?" I asked pleasantly.

"How about if I just bring a pot?" she countered in an exhausted tone.

"That's cool," I replied.

She turned and walked away.

"*Damn!*" Julian laughed. "She's too tired to even pour the shit! She's just gon' bring us a pot and let us have at it on our own!"

"Leave her alone," I defended, thinking of how hard Grandma Tyler slaved, serving other folks all those years. "Some people work really hard for their money. We don't know *what* her circumstances are. Besides, there are already cups on the table. It ain't gon' kill us to pour it ourselves."

Julian was shaking his head.

"You never cease to amaze me, Miss Thang. Just when I expect you to go off about something, you suddenly turn into Mother Teresa."

The waitress came back with our muffins, juice, and a pot of coffee on a tray.

"Here's the cream," she groaned, plopping it down. "Sugar's on the table."

"Thanks a lot." I smiled, hoping to send some good feelings her way.

My good feelings missed her completely, and ricocheted off the wall somewhere back near the kitchen.

"Oh well," I mumbled. "So anyway, as I was asking you before, what are you gonna do about missing the concert? You love Maxwell just as much as I do."

"I'll manage. Besides, it's cool. Tonio really wanted us to see him together, so maybe he and I can see him some other time."

"I thought you said he was trippin'," I commented, pouring us both coffee.

"He's always trippin'," Julian replied.

I nodded, pouring in cream and opening a packet of sugar.

"What are you gonna do with the other ticket?" I asked.

"Have you made up with your girl yet? What's her name . . . Misty?"

I jerked my neck so fast, it almost snapped.

"*What*?! No, you *didn't* ask me that! Negro, *please*! That girl is *his-tor-ree*! You hear me?"

"I *hear* you," he mumbled, picking at his muffin, "but I don't *feel* you."

I glared at him.

"It's not a matter of whether you feel it or not. *I* do. She dogged me. She's toast. End of subject."

"*Mmmm-hmmm.*"

"*Mmmm-hmmm*, hell," I replied. "So stop talking 'bout her, ruining my good day. As a matter of fact, let's make it like

Pharaoh did in *The Ten Commandments*. 'Let the name Misty Fine be stricken from every mind, lip, and tongue . . .'"

"You are *sooo* ridiculous."

"While you bullshittin' . . . ," I mumbled.

He kept laughing as he bit down on his muffin.

"So what are you gonna do with the extra ticket?" I asked again.

"Actually . . ."

"Uh-oh. I don't like how that sounds."

"Well, Donovan had mentioned to me . . ."

"Donovan!!" I shrieked. "Oh, *hell* no! Ain't *no* way I'm going to no Maxwell concert with ol' stick-and-move Donovan!"

"He'll just be sitting beside you at the concert. What's the big deal?"

I laughed sharply.

"*The big deal* is that Donovan has been trying to make moves on me of late. What better place to come on to a sistah than at a Maxwell concert? I'll be feeling all good and shit . . . probably keyed up from watching my man workin' it on stage. Donovan will kick into overdrive on my ass."

He tossed the last bit of muffin into his mouth. For the muffin to be as big as it was, he wolfed it down pretty quickly.

"So how you know Donovan don't just wanna groove to Maxwell like you do?" he asked. "Brother's music moves everybody. Donovan couldn't get any tickets because the show was sold out."

"Trust me. I know Donovan."

"Well," Julian said under his breath, "he's already got the other ticket."

"*Damn*, Julian! Why didn't you tell me?"

"I'm telling you now."

"You could have asked me first."

"You would have said no."

I sighed, breaking a piece off my muffin.

"You're a pushover for a fine man, you know that? I don't know why you even give a shit about hooking Donovan up! You know *damn well* that he's as straight as a board."

"I know," he grinned. "But you can't fault me for looking and trying to help."

I cut my eyes at him.

"You ain't trying to help nobody but your damn self. You're feeling brother out to see if he's giving up the cheeks. I'm trying to tell you, it *ain't* gon' happen."

"You never know. I'm here to tell you, Miss Thang . . . you just *never* know."

"Well, I ain't trying to get with no Donovan. And you need to quit it, too, before I find your friend Tonio and tell him!"

He laughed and gave a wave of his hand.

I studied him closely as he sipped his coffee again.

"Julian."

"What?" he asked, looking up at me from his cup.

"If you had already given the ticket to Donovan, what made you ask me about Misty?"

His lips curled into a smile.

"Thought Pharaoh had stricken that name from our lips," he said with a grin.

"I was just curious," I said sharply. "Don't get flip."

"Well, if you really wanna know . . ."

"Never mind! You trying to get all sarcastic about it."

He held out his palms.

"Hey, I was just trying to follow your rules. You said don't mention her, and then you're the first one to bring her up."

"*Anyway* . . ."

"Anyway, nothing. When you asked about the extra ticket, I thought for a minute that maybe you had made up with . . . *you-know-who*. It just popped into my head to ask you about it."

"*Whatever,*" I replied dismissively. "Who cares anyway?"

"Obviously you do," he laughed. "You're the one that keeps bringing up her name."

Before I could come back at him hard-core, Julian reached into his duffel bag and pulled out a five-dollar bill and two ones. He placed them on the table.

"You get the tip this time," he said.

I reached into my duffel bag where I kept my cash. I had a small wad of green bundled up in a knot.

Julian eased out of the booth.

"Let's go," he said. "Gotta make moves."

"If I hear that *one* more time!" I laughed, sliding out right behind him.

"That's how it goes, baby," he smiled.

He walked toward the door. I glanced around for our bedraggled blond waitress.

I spotted her, over in the corner, barely able to walk as she carried a trayload of food over to some customers.

"Let's roll!" Julian called.

I dropped a ten spot on the table.

"It'll come back to me in the universe," I mumbled to myself.

"Ten . . . new messages . . . are in your mailbox. Main menu . . . to listen to your messages, press 1."

Good Lord, I thought. *This chick just won't quit.*

Misty had been bombarding me with phone messages, e-mail, postcards, flowers—*you name it*—since our big blowout.

I wasn't having any.

I wouldn't have even bothered to listen to the voice messages, except for the fact that I had to go through them all in order to delete them.

Actually, I didn't even have to listen to them all the way. As soon as the automated voice said, *"First message, 9:37 A.M. today,"* I realized that I could press 1 and the message would be gone. I didn't even have to bother to wade through them all.

The catch, though, was that I wasn't sure if all the calls were from her or not. Tyrene could be calling. Or Grandma Tyler. Or Julian. Or anybody.

Anybody other than her.

So I had to listen to at least the beginning of each message to determine whether or not it was her, in fact, harassing me.

Eight of them were from her. I deleted them all.

She tricked me on the ninth one.

"Reesy," a deep, manly voice said. "Y'all need to cut this shit out. I know you miss your girl. She's missing you like crazy. She got some Maxwell tickets for tonight because she knows you love him. Do you know she bought 'em as a surprise for you weeks ago? She didn't even want to take me. I think the two of you should go together and put all this mess aside. Maybe if you call around three—"

"Message erased. Tenth message, 3:54 P.M. today."

"Hey, sexy," a deep, manly voice droned again.

I was just about to press 1 and delete it, thinking it was Rick calling for Misty again, when I heard something different and familiar in the voice.

"You know we don't live five minutes from each other," Donovan's voice continued. "Why don't you give me a call around five, and we can arrange to hook up and do this thang together. I'll take you out to a nice quick dinner, and by eight, we can be over at Radio City. Zhane's opening up for him, you know. Those fine fillies can throw down!"

How did he get my number? I sat there wondering.

"555-3355," he said. "Call me, girl. We cah do dis."

I was about to press 1.

"I'm surprised you're listed," Donovan added. "You must have *wanted* me to find you."

"Message erased. You have no more new messages."

I hung up the phone.

Note to self: call the phone company and get my number unlisted.

I had thought that maybe Misty had called up my folks and tricked them into giving her the number, but I realized now that it was my own failure to request privacy when I set up the new phone.

Oh well. I let that one fall through the cracks. But at least she didn't know where I lived. All the postcards she had been sending were forwarded to me by the post office. The flowers she sent arrived at the theater.

The last thing I wanted to be doing was seeing her standing on my doorstep.

On second thought, the *last* thing I wanted to be doing was sitting across from fine-ass Donovan, having a quick dinner with him.

Seeing Misty on my doorstep rated maybe half a notch above doing that.

I eased into my spot at Radio City.

Julian had gotten excellent floor seats. I was up close. Only about four rows back from the stage.

I had on a new dress I had bought the day before. It was wine-colored, short, and sexy. It had at least a dozen straps crissing and crossing over my back.

I got some interesting stares in that thing. From men and women.

I knew I looked good. My body was tight, and I was feeling, as the Queen of Soul says, like a *natural* woman.

Zhane' was rocking the house with their smooth two-part harmony, and I was grooving to the sounds.

"Damn, girl! You look like a chicken thigh in that dress!" his honeyed voice dripped in my ear.

"Is that supposed to be a compliment?" I asked, not turning to even look at him.

"I *loooove* chicken thighs," he cooed. "Chicken and waffles. Ever been to Roscoe's?"

"Never."

I kept rocking to Zhane's rhythms.

"It's on the west coast. It's the joint." Donovan made smacking sounds with his lips. "You look like you need to be laying next to an order of hot waffles, with butter oozing down your sides. Chicken and waffles, baby. Chicken and waffles."

I rolled my eyes.

"Well's is the best," I said without looking at him. "I don't even have to go to Roscoe's to know that. I've had their chicken and waffles, and I can't imagine anything being better than *that*."

For some reason, I enjoyed being contrary whenever I talked to him.

Well's was a famous chicken and waffle restaurant I'd discovered over on 132nd and Seventh. The food was the *bomb*. I'd heard of Roscoe's, but, as far as I was concerned, Well's, which had been around far longer, ruled.

"Yeah," he agreed. "Well's is pretty tight. They got that good strawberry butter. I could just spread some of it all over you right now and lick you up!"

"Is that supposed to *excite* me?"

"It would if you knew how good I was at what I do."

I finally turned and looked at his sexy behind, standing next to me with all that hair.

"Where *the hell* are you from anyway, Donovan?" I asked, scanning him from head to toe.

He had really nice dreads, locks, *whatever* you wanna call them. They weren't too long or too thick, and they could be pulled back easily into a ponytail, showing off his well-sculpted face.

I wanted to grab one of those locks and just snatch his face down where it could be put to best use.

"L.A., baby!" he replied. "The Land of La-La. City of Angels. *Los Ang-geh-leez . . .*"

"All right! *Damn!* I get it, already!"

"Just proud of where I come from," he grinned. "I love La-La."

"If you love it so much, what the hell you doin' here?"

"Same thing you doin', baby," he cooed.

"And what's that?"

"Tryna to be a *star!*"

He flashed me those pearly whites. With his cute ass.

Looked like I was stuck with him for the rest of the show.

Well, I thought to myself with a sigh. *It could be worse. I could be with some ol' tired, broke-down nigga who took away from my flow.* At least Donovan made me look good.

"Don't forget," he whispered, a big grin on his face.

"Don't forget what?"

" 'Bout my brass *wawtah*bed, fool!" he laughed. "See dere? You done forgot already!"

I looked into those deep brown eyes of his, and couldn't help but laugh.

I got the feeling this was the beginning of a *very* long night.

Maxwell raised the roof on Radio City!!

It was truly one of the best concerts I'd ever seen.

And it was like a three-for-one, because, besides Maxwell and Zhane', two sistahs broke into full-fledged fisticuffs in the aisle while we were waiting for the 'Fro'd Wonder to take the stage. Had every neck in the house craning, trying to see.

Made me think about Misty. I quickly banished the thought.

A sistah couldn't ask for better entertainment. Getting to hear some of the best sounds of the century, and a ringside seat at the fights, to boot.

What a night!! It might as well have been my birthday.

When the concert was over, Donovan offered me a ride home.

"No thanks," I told him.

"Why you trippin'?" he frowned. "Ain't no thang. Didn't we have fun tonight?"

"It was *a'ight,*" I said, smiling reluctantly.

"See dere?" he grinned in return. "Now how was you gon' get home? Catch the train? Somebody'll be done raped your ass, lookin' all tasty like that in that dress."

"I took a cab here."

"Well," he persisted, cupping my elbow with his hand, "let me drive you home. We live right up the street from one 'nother. Don't be so mean, girl."

"I'm not mean."

I guess it couldn't hurt anything, him giving me a ride. We did live pretty close to each other. What could happen?

Donovan had, surprisingly, turned out to be halfway decent company.

We walked over to Fifty-first between Sixth and Fifth, where he had parked his truck.

Donovan opened the door for me and I slid into the passenger seat.

He smiled as he shut me in.

"What you grinnin' at?" I asked him when he got inside.

"You."

"Why you grinnin' at me so hard?"

"*'Cause,*" he mumbled. "You look good in my car."

I glanced over at him, observing the way he looked at me as he said it.

Damn, he was sexy!!

How long had it been since I last had some dick?

We cruised up Sixth Avenue, headed for Harlem.

Donovan had his lean going on in his black Jeep Cherokee,

looking all smooth and hard-core. The radio was tuned to HOT97. "One More Chance" by Biggie Smalls was playing.

I liked that song. It was one of my favorites.

Obviously, Donovan did, too. He sang along with the music, tearing the hell up out the song. And I don't mean that in a good way.

"So what's it gon' be, him or me?"

"You know what?" I said sweetly, cutting him off.

"What's that, baby?" he cheesed.

"Biggie's version was good enough for me."

His face froze for a second, trying to figure out the dis.

"Awwww dayum! Look at you! You *trippin'!* You tryna break on a brother, huh?"

"Just lettin' you know."

"Message received. You a mean little sum'n, you know that?"

"Tryna stay alive, my brother. Just tryna stay alive."

"You hungry?" he asked.

I shrugged.

"A little bit. I ate something before I left the house. I'm not really hungry, per se. Just a little bit lunchy, I suppose."

"Per se," he mimicked. "Your little smart ass. You got a piece of brain on you, don't you? I could tell when I first met you that you was one-a dem smart ones."

Good Lord, I thought, rolling my eyes on the sly. *Wait'll I tell Misty about . . .*

Oh snap. Forget it.

"I got some food at my house," he dropped casually.

"I'll just bet you do."

"Naw, see dere," he replied, trying to be serious. "I got some food there for real. I had a *bobbycue* earlier today. Some of my boys came over, and we hooked up some ribs."

"Mmmm. That sounds good."

"I can throw down on some food, girl," he said with a wink.

I glanced over at him again. What could happen if I decided to get a little something to eat over at his place? I was kinda hungry.

"All right," I said. "Show me."

"All right, then!" he laughed. "I'm about to hit you off."

I cut my eyes at him.

". . . with some good-ass food," he added hurriedly.

"All right, then. Hurry up. You got my appetite worked up now."

"Okay," he said, putting the pedal to the metal. "I got something else, though, that'll make the time go by."

He hit the stereo in the Jeep, changing from FM to CD player.

All of a sudden, the sweet sounds of Maxwell poured from every speaker. I was surrounded. The song "Ascension" filled the truck with heavenly rhythms from back to front.

I settled down peacefully in my seat, closing my eyes as I listened to that thoroughly perfect song.

My eyes were not destined to be closed for long.

Donovan began to sing along with the music, literally tearing the song apart limb from limb.

When he got to the chorus and sang, "Sugar pie, realize," I couldn't take it anymore.

I reached over and turned off the stereo.

"*Why'd you do that?!* Had enough of him for one night, huh?"

I looked over at him. He was as beautiful as sin, but the bulb, apparently, was only about ten watts total.

"I can *never* get enough of him," I replied in a firm, even voice. "*Ever. You,* on the other hand. *You're* another story, black."

"You're trippin', girl."

"No," I shot back, "*you're* trippin'. Just get me to those ribs."

"I'ma get you to 'em. Don't worry."

We rode along in silence for a few. But I just couldn't let it hang in the air like that.

"*And for the record,*" I said as we pulled up outside his building.

"Yeah?"

"For the record, it's '*Shouldn't I realize.*' Not '*Sugar pie, realize.*' You damn sure know how to fuck up a song. Where the hell did you get *that* from?"

"*Shouldn't I, Sugar pie. I-ran, I-raq.* Same difference."

"No . . . it's *not.*"

"Don't matter," he said, stepping out of the car. "I might not be able to get the words right, but I betcha I got something Maxwell can't never lay claim to."

"Oh really?" I asked, my eyebrows raising curiously. He opened my door. "And what is *that*, might I ask?"

"You at my crib, some bomb-ass *bobbycue* . . . and a brass *wawtah*bed."

I stepped out of the Jeep.

Donovan was looking mighty tasty.

Or perhaps a sistah was just a little too hungry for a piece of Adam's ribs.

If you know what I mean.

The next day, I made my way home, all fucked-out and funky.

(Don't act surprised that I spent that night with Donovan— you know how *that* goes.)

I tell you what, though. I see why sistahs be trippin' over his behind. Brother can handle his business. He worked me over like a brand-new job.

My first instinct was to want to call Misty and tell her all about it.

Couldn't do that, though.

Oh well. I'd tell Julian about it when I saw him on Sunday. He'd get a kick out of hearing about Donovan's indiglo condoms, the interesting uses he had for *bobbycue* sauce, and the fact that he did, *indeed,* have a brass *wawtah*bed.

Homeboy even had the nerve to play "If the Kid Can't Make You Come" by the Time as mood music.

Julian would really trip out over *that.*

We'd laugh about it long and hard, and shoot funny looks Donovan's way.

But it wasn't quite the same as telling Miss Divine.

I wondered if she was happy over there, all pushed up with her new man.

KNOCK, KNOCK, KNOCKIN' ON ~~HEFFAH'S~~ DOOR

Fourteen . . . new messages . . . are in your mailbox."

This mess was getting old.

And I'm sure she knew that she was tormenting me with this process. Like I said, I had to at least listen to parts of the messages before I could delete them. Which meant more tedious work for me.

Two months had gone by, and *still* I hadn't seen Misty Fine.

In my mind, I justified that I didn't need a friend like her.

I missed her something fierce, the way she always used to ask my advice for everything. But I guess that's the main reason why I was so angry. I knew she wasn't calling me because she needed me.

She hadn't needed me for anything since she'd starting hanging with Rick. She was more than likely just calling so that she could make amends for the dis.

Once that was resolved, it would be business as usual. Back to treating me like an unneeded, unwanted, second-class citizen.

No thanks. I think I'll pass on *that.*

Bad thing about it is that I can hold a grudge. I'm quick to forgive, but once I get my monkey on, I can hold out on you like nobody's business.

When I've decided that I've been wronged, I come to all sorts of conclusions and drastic decisions. Be they wrong or right, I come to them anyway. And I indulge the hell out of them.

So the conclusion I had come to was that Misty had not only dogged me, but she wasn't sorry that she had dogged me. She was just sorry that she no longer had me around to dog anymore.

Bump *that*. I don't let nobody go out on me like that. Not her. Not my folks. Not nobody.

Child please.

She could go somewhere and hide with *that* mess.

I was sitting backstage just before rehearsal, reading a card Miss Divine had sent. The card was accompanied by a beautiful bouquet of tulips in an assortment of colors.

She knew those were my favorites. She was going for the jugular now.

The card was just as touching. It read:

> *Reesy,*
> *I miss you. I came to the show last night. You were excellent!!*
> *I was so proud!!! I love you and am so sorry we aren't talking.*
> *Please forgive me and pick up the phone and call. No one else*
> *can ever replace you in my life. I know I can be stupid, but*
> *how can I get better unless you help?* :-)
>
> > *Your sistah-for-life,*
> > *Miss Divine*

I stared at the silly little smiley face she had drawn on the card. She was stupid. She always had been.

I couldn't help but smile at her note.

I sniffed the flowers. They were very pretty. Just what I needed to brighten up my little area.

I sat there admiring them, when I heard Julian come dashing over, calling out my name.

"Hey, hey, hey!"

"Hey!" I smiled, turning around toward him. "What you so giddy about?"

He came up to me and kneeled down alongside my chair.

"Guess what?" he grinned, his tone barely above a whisper.

He looked around to see if anyone was listening.

This piqued my interest, for sure.

"What?"

"Rowena's leaving the show!"

"What?!" I screeched, drawing the attention of one of the girls a few feet down from me. Her brow raised as she watched me and Julian huddled up together. After a second, she looked away.

"Sssssshhh," he whispered harshly. "I'm trying to keep this on the d-l. I came to you for a reason."

"Why is she leaving?" I asked, stunned. "And why do you seem so happy about it? I thought you liked her? What's Gordon going to do without her? Who's gonna play Mimosa? She's damn near the whole show!!"

"Calm down! *Damn!* I *do* like her. She's going to L.A. Rowena's been working on doing some things out there for a while now, and they've finally come through. She's got a part in a new Hughes Brothers film."

"For real?" I marveled. *"Wowwww."*

"Yep. She's wanted the big screen the whole time. Stage was just a little ol' playground for her."

"Man," I sighed, "do you think—"

He cut me off, smacking me on the leg impatiently.

"Stop asking so many doggone questions! Look, I think you should try out for the part of Mimosa."

I stared at him for a second. Like he was the man in the moon.

"Quit being *stupid*! How the *hell* am I supposed to try out for her part?!"

Julian frowned at me.

"Who's the one being stupid now?"

I clucked my tongue and turned away from him.

He stood and moved around in front of me, leaning on the counter where I kept my makeup. That big pelvic bulge of his was all in my face.

"Nice flowers."

"Thanks," I smiled, playing with the leaves on one of the tulips. I was glad we were changing the subject.

"No, Miss Thang," Julian said, reading my mind. "I'm not through with you."

"Julian! Quit it! This is nonsense!"

"It is *not*! I've worked with Rowena and Gordon for a long time. I know her talent. And in the little bit of time we've been working together, I've come to know yours. I think you should do it. I want you to audition for the part."

"But how can I . . . ?"

He shook his head.

"Uh-uh, Miss Thang! Don't sit there and lie to me and say you don't know the part. You've watched her rehearse more times than I have. You probably know her role better than she does."

I sat there, looking up at him.

"Get outta here," I said tiredly, pushing him off of my counter and out of my face.

"The audition is at eight in the morning," he replied in a whisper. "*Tomorrow.* And you'd *better* have your ass there! We can hook up tonight, if you want, and I'll go over the part with you, bit by bit."

"Uh-uh," I refused, shaking my braids wildly. "If I'ma do this, it's gon' be on my own. Fair and square. No legs up from you or anybody else."

He smiled down at me. Obviously proud.

"I can't believe you even suggested that," I mumbled. "When I first started, you were the main one accusing me of fucking somebody to get in the show. Remember, you clearly said to me, *You have to earn your breaks with me, Miss Thang.* 'Member that?"

Julian grinned at me, pleased as punch.

"I remember. I'm just glad *you* did. I was hoping you were going to refuse my help. I see I trained you well."

"*Who* you trained?!" I exclaimed, working my neck. "I *came* here prepared! Now, get outta here before you put somebody's eye out with that big ol' nasty bulge between your legs!"

He laughed, patting me on the shoulder.

"Now, *that's* how I like to hear you talk!"

He made moves to walk away.

"Five minutes till regular rehearsal," he reminded me.

"I'll be there, nigga," I answered, smiling slyly.

"I know you will, Miss Thang. I know you will."

He disappeared.

Damn!! Rowena was leaving the show. And *I* was going to be trying out for her part.

How the sam hell did all this just happen?

And how the *hell* was I going to pull it off?!!!

All that night, I sat up, wondering, worrying, trying like a mug to meditate on it all.

I had my incense and candles burning, listening to Erykah Badu. Her music was smooth enough to allow me to think and groove at the same time.

I sat in the middle of the living-room floor, folded up in the lotus position. I had rubbed some peppermint oil around my temples, in an effort to relax.

Lord. *What* was I thinking? How could I try out for Rowena's part? That woman had experience and presence for days. Whoever played Mimosa couldn't be half-steppin'. The crowds had come to expect too much.

To be able to step into that role, you had to come *correct.*

I didn't have any of the skills it took to be a lead.

On the floor in front of me was a business card.

M.C.D. Acting Lab. "Where the hidden talent is cultivated."

Well, that was me. My talents were about as hidden as they came.

I'd been given the card a while back by one of the other dancers, Marlisa.

She said the instructor, a young brother named Michael Cory Davis, was really good.

She said he was fine, too. A well-known up-and-coming film-maker and actor with business savvy to spare, this Michael guy was a sexy thang with a nicely carved body and a head full of locks.

I stared at the business card long and hard.

Naaaah.

The *last* thing I needed was to take acting lessons from a good-looking coach. It would be too easy to predict how *that* story was going to end. And, no doubt, it wouldn't be with me getting any real acting lessons. Not any that could be used on the stage, that is.

My phone rang.

I snatched the cord and dragged it over to me. My caller ID was in the bedroom, but I didn't care who it was at this point. Even if it was Misty, I wouldn't have been too against talking to her right now.

In fact, I needed to hear her voice more than anything, assuring me that I wasn't crazy for trying out for this part.

"Hello?"

"What you doing?" his smooth voice crooned.

"Trying to concentrate," I replied, annoyed.

"Having trouble relaxing?" Donovan asked. "I got something for that."

"I'll just *bet* you do. Maybe another time. Tonight's a full night for me, I'm afraid."

He made a moaning sound on the phone.

"But I really wanna see you, baby. I can be there in a coupla minutes and make everything okay."

I sighed into the phone. Real loud, so his ass could hear it and make no mistake.

"Not tonight, Donovan," I repeated. "What's up with you? Shouldn't you have dipped on me by now anyway? Ain't that your M.O.? Why you still hanging around, taking my abuse?"

I heard him chuckle on his end.

" 'Cuz, girl. You got me sprung. You my little chicken thigh. Light meat."

"*Hmmph!* Well, this little chicken thigh gotta go. And for the record, thigh meat is dark."

I hung up the phone on his ass without a goodbye, then waited a second to make sure he was off, and picked it up.

I activated call block to keep him from ringing me up again.

The last thing I needed was his behind harassing me the night before something as serious as this audition. I wondered if he knew about Rowena leaving the show.

I had been fooling around with Donovan ever since the Maxwell concert. And while he was damn good at what he did, he wasn't the smartest, most conversational *rapscallion* (and I mean that like my grandma says it) in the world.

It would have been nice to have a serious boyfriend. I hadn't had one in a while. And while none of the guys I'd dated in the recent past were jerks, none of them was anybody I would consider getting serious with.

In fact, what I really wanted more than I would ever admit was my own husband. A strong black man who let me be me, and who took pride in having a strong black woman by his side. Not someone who just gave a lot of lip service to the fact that that's what he wanted. And not some shell of a man who was all front and no substance, like the things I watched Misty date over the past few years.

I wanted someone like Tyrone was for Tyrene. Someone who could truly be my partner, and always have my back. I had high ideals, and I was more than willing to hold out for them.

A part of me, although I hate to say it, envied the fact that maybe that's what Misty had found in Rick. That's one of the reasons why I was angry with her, and why I kept secretly hoping her shit turned raggedy.

As callow as it sounds, I didn't want to be out here alone, with no one for me.

Well . . . for right now, Mr. Rent-a-Dick would do. And Donovan served the purpose of just that. He could slang it like a pro and give a girl just was she was itchin' for.

But sistah-girl wasn't itchin' for nunna that tonight.

I breathed deeply, in and out, and rubbed my temples again.

"Certainly" was now pouring from the speakers. I hummed along with the words.

"Who . . . gave you . . . permission to rearrange me? Certainly not me."

True dat, girlfriend. *True dat* like a mug.

I sat there, breathing and singing, trying to talk myself into doing this thang.

I mean, really, there wasn't any question about whether I would do it. Fear didn't drive me to the point of not making a move.

But I was terrified on the inside. Terrified of what it would mean if I didn't get it.

And what it would mean if I *did*.

My phone rang again.

I answered it quickly.

"How's my Tweety doing?" Grandma Tyler cooed.

"Hey, lady!" I exclaimed, genuinely pleased to hear her voice. It was right on time.

"How's that show going? You making waves? I know you are!"

I smiled to myself. I loved her so much. Like Misty, she felt me and usually knew when to call when I most needed her.

"You psychic, ain'tcha?" I kidded. "C'mon . . . tell me. 'Cause otherwise you wouldn't know to ask me that."

Grandma Tyler let loose with her raspy laugh.

"You was just on my mind, baby. I could feel you going through some changes 'bout something."

I paused for a quick second, then blurted it out.

"I'm trying out for the lead tomorrow, Granny."

"Oooooh, Tweety!!" she squealed. "See there, baby!! Already, they can see how talented you are!!!"

"I'm scared," I said in a small voice.

Grandma Tyler got bold on me. Her voice dropped down, all deep and scolding.

"What you talkin' 'bout, you *scared*?! I don't *never* wanna hear you say that! You know you good, Tweety! Always been able to dance from day one!"

"But, Granny, this is more than dancing," I whined. "I'll have to sing, and do some acting."

"Chile, you know you can sing! You was singin' long before you ever started walkin'. And don't talk to me 'bout no actin'! Baby . . . you's a natural at that if there ever was one!"

I smiled to myself, listening to her.

"Yeah, but Granny, it's one thing, having your grandma tell you that you can sing and act. It's another to be tryna do it in front of a bunch of folks who know what singing and acting is really all about."

"Umph," she muttered. She smacked her lips.

"What'd you say that for?" I asked.

"Tryna get the taste back in my mouth. If I'm not mistaken, you just slapped the shit outta me."

I laughed.

"What you trippin' 'bout, Granny? Ain't nobody slap you!"

"You may as well had. Tellin' me I don't know nothing 'bout no singin' and actin'!"

"I didn't mean it like that," I said, trying to recover.

"Well," Grandma Tyler rasped, "point is, you don't think I know what I'm talkin' 'bout."

I sighed heavily.

"Listen to me, Tweety," she began. "I'm seventy-five years old, and if there's one thing I done learned in life, it's this . . ."

"What's that?" I asked, feeling a lecture coming on.

"If you let me finish, *gotdammit,* I'll tell ya!" she said sharply, sucking her teeth.

"Okay," I giggled.

"Now listen to me: *good is good.* Don't matter who it is sittin' back saying so. If something is a winner, everybody can see it, and go outta they way to try to get next to it."

"True dat," I agreed.

"Hot-ta-mighty-no, chile!" Grandma Tyler exclaimed. "Hush for a minute and just listen!"

"I'm listening," I mumbled.

"All right, then. Just the same as good is good, shit stanks. And if it's shit, you don't see nobody running up tryna figure out what it is. They just move as far 'way that smell as they can git."

I chuckled, nodding my head. My grandma and her *Tylerisms,* as she called them. Words of wisdom.

To me, they were as precious as gold.

"You hear me?" she asked.

"I hear you," I replied softly.

"Now I'm seventy-five years old."

"You said that already," I muttered.

"I *know* I did!! You the one take gingko biloba, not me. My mem'ry's fine!!"

I hollered with laughter. Wasn't no one like my Granny.

"You ain't got no sense, Granny! You know that?!"

"Well, I got sense enough to know shit from Shinola. And you ain't neither."

"Hmmph," I chuckled.

"You *tugar,* baby," she cooed. *"Taste toe tweet."*

"Thanks, Granny. I needed to hear that."

"I know you did, Tweety. That's why I called."

"I gotta go," I said, blowing her a kiss into the phone. "Love you, ol' lady."

"Love you, too, Tweet-tweet," she rasped. "And don't you worry your braided-up head. You gon' get this part. Mark my words."

"We'll see, Granny. We'll see."

"Mark my words," Grandma Tyler repeated. "Bye, baby."

"Bye," I said, and hung up the phone.

I sat there for a minute in that lotus position, listening to Erykah singing about how she couldn't believe that we're still living. "Drama." My cut.

I let the song wash over me, lulled by the music, her words, and my grandma's confidence.

Finally, I shook my shoulders, untucked my legs from underneath me, and stretched like a cat.

I let out a long feline squeal while I was stretching.

"I'ma do this," I declared out loud. *"For me, my grandma . . ."*

I thought for a minute, wondering if I dared to say it. I did.

I got up from the floor and walked into the kitchen, singing with the music along the way.

Thank goodness for Erykah's music. It helped me chill and put everything in perspective.

I was there, bright and early the next morning, ready to do this thang.

"Good to see you," Julian whispered, giving me a kiss on the cheek.

"How many people are trying out?" I asked, trying not to appear nervous.

"Just two," he replied, giving me a serious look. "This part really only boils down to two people who could take it on. You and Tamara."

"Tamara?!!" I asked, not ever once having considered that the competition would be only one person, or someone that held such a grudge against me.

Tamara H. was this chick in the show that Donovan used to mess around with. No one knew, or perhaps cared, what the *H* stood for—it was her attempt to give herself some sort of

pompous air, like Madonna or Cher, I suppose. She was the last
person Donovan had been seeing, before he and I started hittin'
it on the regular.

She also happened to be the very same girl who elbowed me
and got the other part when we first auditioned.

In true *stupid-female-with-misdirected-anger* fashion, ever
since she found out about me and Donovan, she had been taking verbal stabs at me on a daily basis.

Shooting me nasty looks. Standing around with some of the
other girls, whispering as I passed their way.

I couldn't care less whether she liked me or not. But I certainly didn't care for being turned into the bad guy.

Tamara still continued to flirt with Donovan, as if he wasn't
the one who did her wrong. The more he igged her, the meaner
she was to me.

And now she and I were going to be in a face-off for the lead
part. One of those *and may the better woman win* things.

If that wasn't a metaphor for something else, then I don't
know what a metaphor is.

The deal was, the two of us would do the audition at exactly
the same time.

We would sing the parts, in tandem, dance the dances, and
pretty much act out the role as though there was only one of us
on stage.

However, really, the both of us would be there. Putting an
unbelievable amount of pressure on each other and ourselves.

I mean, how can you really concentrate when you've got
someone else beside you, doing the same damn thing, but
putting her own spin on it?

You'd have to try your damnedest not to focus on that person's act, and try your best to lose yourself in your own.

Gordon, Julian, Dreyfus, Rowena, and an older brother I had
never seen before were going to be checking us out and making
the decision.

Turns out, the older guy was Gordon's partner. He only
showed up for serious stuff. Otherwise, he was invisible.

I watched the five of them, sitting out there in the audience, staring up at the two of us on stage. We were about to get this show on the road.

Tamara shot me a nasty look. I didn't give it much consideration.

In my head, I said a quick little prayer. (Not for Tamara to break her ankle, or anything like that.) I just prayed that God would grant me the ability to be the best that I could be, and that He let me, no matter how this thing turned out, become a stronger person as a result of the experience.

I thought about my grandma and her encouraging words from the night before.

Also, for some odd reason, thoughts of Misty shot into my mind. Why did I suddenly feel her presence, of all people, as I stood there waiting?

Weird thing about it was, the thought of her was comforting. I didn't try to push it out of my head. Something told me that if she could see me doing this right now, she would be very proud.

"Okay, Tamara and Reesy," Julian shouted from the shadows, "we're going to take this thing from the top. Just do it the way you know it. If you don't know it all, then act like you do!"

We both nodded.

"All right, ladies!" he said, clapping his hands together. *"Let's make moves!"*

I breathed in and out deeply, three times. Tamara stood there beside me, checking me out like I was crazy.

The music began, and my body begin to move.

This was my moment. I wasn't going to even think about it.

I was just going to let loose and do my thang.

And, like I always say . . .

Let the chips fall where they may.

Thirty minutes into things, I was singing my heart out, kicking my legs around, cabaret-style.

"Black Barry's Pie has a wonderful taste! Come on inside and just check out the place! You'll dig the sights and the people you meet! Just take a bite, ooh, this berry's so sweet!"

It's funny, but from the very opening of the show, I'd never really paid attention to the lyrics as Rowena sang them. I had been so excited about being a part of the whole theater experience, that I hadn't taken the time to dig into the minutiae.

I mean, I knew the songs by heart because I'd watched her rehearse so much, but I'd never really noted (as in, *examined*) the actual words.

For some ridiculous reason, in the thick of this grueling audition, I examined them now.

"Black Barry's Pie, get your slice à la mode! We'll heat it up, take this show on the road! This dish is hot, baby let's shake it loose! Why don't you try some of this tasty juice?"

If *those* weren't some of the *cheesiest* lyrics I'd ever heard!

What's strange is that when you're watching the show, or when you're performing, the energy is enough to sweep you up and draw you in.

That song was a freaking lyrical *atrocity*!

I wondered who the songwriter was. I'd be willing to bet that he was somewhere tropical right now, laughing his ass off, marveling over the fact that he had gotten paid for that shit.

And that it was going over big, to boot.

The critics seemed to love it. Since it opened, the show had gotten nothing but rave reviews. *Black Barry's Pie* was pulling in mad loot.

There was even a buzz in the air that a couple German investors would be coming around to give the show a look-see.

They had apparently financed quite a few successful Broadway productions. Word was, if they liked what they saw, these super-rich muckety-mucks might even be considering taking it to the Great White Way.

All that hype made me realize that it wasn't so much the songs as it was the person singing them. That made all the difference in the world. When Rowena performed, you didn't want to take your eyes off of her. She was electricity incarnate.

All the more reason that the role of Mimosa be cast just right. Whoever got it had to really be able to set it out for the people.

Tamara and I sang in unison, although, admittedly, she did flub a couple of words.

But she more than made up for that, because girlfriend could *move*!! She was all over that stage, matching me lick for lick and kick for kick. I tried not to focus on her too much, because the thought of how good she was truly made me nervous.

We shimmied across the stage and around each other, singing and dancing like a couple of savages. I could hear my voice resonating around the theater. It was almost like having an out-of-body experience.

I sounded damn good. For a minute, I had to wonder whose voice it really was coming out of me.

Tamara didn't have the best singing voice. I mean, she could hold a tune okay, but she wasn't necessarily all that captivating.

But Tamara could dance her ass off! As I did my thang, I secretly wondered why Julian didn't shower all the attention upon her that he gave to me.

Tamara's footwork was lightning fast, and she was so limber, she was almost liquid. As much as I was trying not to be distracted, I couldn't help it. She was *fantastic*.

My voice cracked a few times, from paying too much attention to her. And then, I messed up a couple of the words.

I saw her shoot a look at me, her eyes narrowed mockingly.

In the audience, I could see Julian stirring uncomfortably.

I kept dancing, trying to recover.

Sweat began to run down my back. My coochie was itching, but wasn't no damn way I could scratch it.

Tamara looked dry as a bone, maintaining her damn cool.

As I tried to dance and check her out at the same time, my shit began to get a little raggedy. Okay, a *lot* raggedy. At one point, I tripped over my own ankle kinda funny, and almost fell.

Tamara danced right around me, like I wasn't even a blip on her radar.

After a few more moves where I was miserably trying to recover my grace, Julian yelled up at us from the audience.

"Okay, ladies!" he shouted. *"Very good! Let's take five! And I mean only five!"*

We stopped, and I leaned forward, hands on my knees, panting.

Tamara walked real close to me, so only I could hear her, and hissed, *"You need to go somewhere and sit your tired ass down!"*

I looked up at her, and she glowered at me, as if she dared me to say something back.

She even had the nerve to have one of her fists clenched, like she was getting ready to wax dat ass.

Before I could respond, Tamara walked away.

Within seconds, Julian was up on the stage. Ostensibly, I suppose, it was just to give the both of us a little praise and encouragement.

But I know he came up there expressly to see me.

He walked over to Tamara and gave her a pat on the back.

"Nice going so far," he said with a smile.

She grinned at him like the cat that ate the canary.

Julian sauntered over casually to me.

"Good job," he said, loud enough for her to hear.

Then he leaned a little closer to me and whispered sharply, *"Stop trippin' on her and pay attention to what you're doing!! You know this part like the back of your hand!!!"*

"Okay," I mumbled. "But she's good, ain't she?"

"You're *better*, dammit!" he said. "Don't embarrass me now and let that heffah beat you! I recommended you for this, after all!"

He patted me on the back again and casually walked away.

Tamara shot me another one of those *I'll-coldcock-you* looks.

It finally dawned on my dumb ass.

She was trying to scare me out of the competition. All those mean looks and comments were meant to make me nervous and just plain screw up what I was doing.

And I was falling for her little ghetto tactics, hook, line, and sinker.

Not this go 'round, I thought to myself. *She wants to see an ass-whoopin'? I'm about to show her one, right here on this stage!!*

Julian disappeared back into the shadows of the audience.

"Five minutes up!" he called, once he settled into his seat.

I walked back over to center stage.

I could feel Tamara staring at me once more, ready to dish out one of those intimidating looks, with a side order of balled-up fist.

Not this time. *This time,* it was all about me and getting this role.

I stood there, panting, wringing wet, in the middle of the stage.

I was exhausted, but energized.

Tamara stood a few feet away, still trying to get me to look at her. She was breathing just as hard as I was. I was pleased at that.

The fact that I had tuned her ass out for the rest of the audition made that heffah have to work harder than a pack mule.

I sang every note, hit every high, shook every shimmy, and busted every move right on time.

I didn't know how I looked compared to her, but I didn't give a shit. All I knew was that I gave a thousand percent of myself out there on that stage, and that's all that mattered to me.

I could walk away feeling good about my performance.

They couldn't get anything better because there wasn't anything extra inside me to give.

A few times, while I was up there doing my thang, I thought I saw Julian's teeth. Looked like he was grinning like it was going out of style. Rowena even had an impressed smile upon her face.

Now, I'm not saying they were smiling at me. But what I *do* know is that I was up there, working that role like my life depended on it.

I didn't know what the hell Tamara was doing, nor how good she was at doing it.

My mind had totally, completely, blanked her out.

"Great work, you two," Julian said, coming up to us.

"Bravo!" the other four yelled, clapping from the audience.

"Take a chill pill." Julian smiled, putting his arms around both of us. "Go home, relax, and shake this off. You two were fantastic today."

"When should I be hearing something?" Tamara asked, batting her eyes at him, like that shit was going to work.

That let me know right then just how clueless she was.

Every damn person involved with the show knew that Julian was gay. He was quite up front about it. He had no interest, *whatsoever,* in what was between a woman's legs.

Julian stared at her blankly. I could tell he was amused that she was attempting to flirt her way into his good graces.

Tamara rubbed her sweaty palm across her breasts, leaving a streak that made her nipples more pronounced.

Julian was not moved. His ubiquitous bulge did not get bigger. As if it could anyway.

"You should hear something by late this afternoon," he replied. "Before tonight's show."

"When is Rowena officially leaving?" I asked, hoping I could see, in his expression, some hint of whether my performance had redeemed itself.

"In a couple weeks. She'll work with whichever one of you gets the part up until her last day."

His face was poker. For once, since we'd become friends, I couldn't tell what the hell was going on in his head.

Tamara smirked, knowing, I guess, how unnerved Julian's distance made me. It was common knowledge to everyone in the show that he and I had become pretty tight.

I was, admittedly, nervous. Julian didn't raise his eyebrow, twitch his lip, wiggle his nose, nothing, to let me know if I had done all right. If I had really been as good as I felt like I was during the last part, he would have winked or grinned, or something.

"See you two ladies later," he said distantly, dismissing us both.

"Okay," Tamara replied, cutting her eyes at me to see what my next move would be.

I watched Julian closely, wondering if he would give me some signal to hang around.

He didn't.

In fact, he just turned and walked away from us both, leaving the two of us standing there on the stage, looking a tad bit silly.

"Kee-kee-kee-kee-kee," Tamara cackled evilly under her breath.

Her eyes were locked onto mine.

I gave her my friendliest smile, and said, "*Well* . . . gotta go meet Donovan!"

Her face drew up like a sphincter.

That oughta fix her ass.

I turned and walked away, heading for the exit that emptied out into the alley. I hated alleys. It was a new phobia I'd earned since my arrival in New York. From when I danced at that spot in Times Square and had such a bad experience there.

As I walked toward the train station, I was seriously worried about the look, or lack thereof, on Julian's face. This was beginning to feel like when I first tried out for the show, only worse. I didn't know what to think. No expression from Julian could be a good thing, or something terribly bad.

Instinctively, my heart sank as I deposited my token, passed through the turnstile, and waited for the train.

As soon as I got home, I went straight to the bed and lay down.

I didn't even take a shower. I just kicked off my Nikes and crawled in.

I was so depressed, all I wanted to do was hide under the covers and shut my eyes. I wanted to lose myself in the world of sleep and act like none of this had just happened.

I had more to lose this time than when I first auditioned for *Black Barry's Pie*. This time, not just the role, but my ego, was at stake.

You see, if Tamara got the part, not only would I have to live with seeing her play the lead. I could deal with *that*. That's one of those *I-just-wasn't-meant-to-have-it* kind of things.

But it wouldn't end there with Tamara. She was a straight-up bitch. She would go around and tell everybody how she whooped my ass and made me look stupid on stage.

Tamara would brag at my expense. Every time I turned around, I'd be running into her, and she'd be giving me those looks. And she'd stay huddled up with the other chicks in the show, talking about me in front of my face.

My stomach was hurting.

I curled up in a fetal position, feeling miserable and sorry for myself.

I should have never even tried out for that stupid role. I was nuts for letting Julian make me think I was good enough to get it.

To make matters worse, I had let him down. Julian was barely able to look at me when I left. If I had done well, he would have called by now, telling me that I had bagged the part, no problem.

But he didn't even call me to tell me that I sucked.

I kept picturing his expression. Julian had looked at me as if I was an absolute stranger.

I picked up the phone and dialed Grandma Tyler. I needed someone close to me to hold my hand.

The phone rang and rang and rang. It had rung about ten times before I even noticed that it was still ringing.

I let it ring some more.

Grandma Tyler wasn't home. And she didn't have an answering service, or even an answering machine to pick up her calls. Either you got her, or you didn't.

And that's just how Grandma Tyler liked it.

I lay there, balled up in the bed, moaning. My stomach felt like it was tor' up. My bowels made rumbling sounds like I was about to have the shits.

I got up and went to the bathroom, but all I managed to pass was a puff of nervous gas.

I sat there, trying to give up the goods.

No dice. All that happened was that my bowels bunched up tighter.

I fired a flurry of rancid poots, but that was it.

I needed someone to talk to. I needed a friend.

(*I needed some air freshener.*)

The one friend I had become accustomed to talking to of late, Julian, was off-limits. I couldn't call him until he called me.

Of course, there was one more option.

I was trapped. I had no recourse. And right now, I needed her more than I'd ever needed anyone in my life.

I raised my raggedy ass up off that toilet full of rotten airballs and walked back into the bedroom.

I sat down on the side of the bed, contemplating.

Then, I *did* it.

I picked up the phone and called Miss Divine.

"Misty Fine's office," Mare answered.

What was Rick's secretary, Mary, doing working for Misty?

Damn. I didn't want her to recognize my voice.

Mare (her nickname) and I had gotten a little tight, right before I left. But our friendship was limited to our time together at Burch, and when I split from the company, I left my connection with her right along with it.

"Is Misty available?" I asked, trying to deepen my tone.

Mare seemed suspicious. I heard hesitation in her voice.

"May I . . . ask . . . who's . . . calling?" she replied cautiously.

"Is she available?" I repeated.

"Who *is* this?" she probed.

"It's me, Mare," I sighed, giving in.

Her voice went up a notch.

"*Me* who?" she asked excitedly. "Is this *Reesy*? This most certainly is *not* Teresa Snowden?!"

"Yeah," I said, my voice monotone. "It is."

"*Heeyyyyyyyyy, girl!*" she squealed. "How's it *goin'*?! Whatcha been doin' these days?!"

I really didn't have time for this. I was not in the mood for her and her white-girl antics. That *tell-me-all-your-business-and-I'll-tell-you-all-of-mine* shit.

Besides, white women always confided *way* too much information. Told you personal shit that you had no business knowing about. Sometimes, only five minutes after meeting you. Like how they just went to the doctor for their herpes medication. Or that they finally bought a bigger, better vibrator.

Shit that sistahs just didn't talk about or do.

I wasn't up for that. Not right now. Actually, not ever.

"Sorry to cut you off, girl," I replied anxiously, "but this is a bit of an emergency. Is she there? I *reeeeaaalllly* need to speak with her."

Mary sighed.

"Well," she said, drawing the conversation out, "she's not here this afternoon."

Her voice dropped into a whisper.

"Neither is Rick. He's got a surprise for her."

"Oh really," I responded dryly.

I couldn't care less about whatever it was.

"Yeah," Mary replied, still speaking in hushed, conspiratorial tones. "You know they're dating, right?"

So much for Misty thinking she was keeping that situation under wraps.

Mare giggled.

"Of *course,* you know they're dating! Silly me! You're her *best* friend!"

This was getting stupid. I had to cut this fool off at the pass. *Quick.*

"So you work for her now?" I asked.

Despite everything, I was mildly curious as to why she was answering Misty's phone. Mare was working as Rick's assistant when I was with the company.

"Yeah," she whispered, "I do. I work for her and Rick now."

"Hmmph," I managed to snicker.

"I know." She giggled again. "It's funny, isn't it?"

Mare mistakenly thought that I was laughing with her. But I wasn't. I was merely thinking how cute that whole setup must look.

The only two black faces in the house happen to have the same assistant, and also happen to be dating. The fact that Misty was the boss only made matters worse.

And Mare was doling out Misty's business to anyone who didn't ask like it was Halloween candy.

This was a Human Resources disaster waiting to happen. I didn't even want to dwell on it anymore.

"I gotta go, Mare."

She stopped giggling and jumped back into girlfriend mode.

"Okay. Let's do lunch sometime. I really miss hanging out with you."

"Sure," I lied.

Homegirl still didn't get it.

We ain't friends, I said in my head.

"I'll leave Misty a message that you called," Mare chirped. "She'll be checking in at some point, I guess. But then, I don't know . . . she might not."

She said the last two sentences in a kind of cryptic, singsongy way, as if she was dangling some secretive information over me that she wanted me to jump at.

"You think she's at home?" I asked.

"Ummmmm, probably," Mare dragged.

"Okaybye," I said quickly, without ceremony, and hung up the phone.

I didn't want to waste any more of my time.

I stuck my feet back into my Nikes, not bothering to untie and retie the laces.

I went into the living room, grabbed my purse and keys, and jetted for the train station.

I didn't know what I was going to say when I got there. I didn't know what I was going to do.

All I knew was that I needed to see her.

To maybe calm my nerves, and help make this rumbling in my bowels just up and go away.

She was the one who opened the door when I rang the bell.

She stood there in a pair of faded blue jeans and a pink tank top. Her hair was all fluffed out and curly. I'd never been so happy to see someone as I was to see her right then.

How could I be mad at her, the way her face broke out into that wide-mouthed grin when she saw me?

"Girl!!!" she exclaimed, flinging her arms around my neck. *"I'm so glad to see you!!!"*

Misty studied me from head to toe, that broad smile of hers not diminishing in the slightest.

"I missed you, boo," she said. "I'm sorry."

"Sorry 'bout *what?*" I replied nonchalantly. "I don't know what you talkin' 'bout."

Misty chuckled.

"I see my girl's still the same," she prattled, shepherding me into the house. "I'm glad you're back. You must have felt me calling out to you. I needed to talk to you today like you wouldn't believe!"

Her mouth was going a mile a minute. My heart skipped a beat when she said I must have felt her calling out to me.

Made me think about that old commercial where a mother gets burned by a pot in Iowa and, at that exact same moment, thousands of miles away in Indonesia, her son gets a boil on his ass.

Something like that.

"Hey," Misty exclaimed, pausing for a moment. "How'd you get here?"

"I took the train. There's a cab waiting for me outside. I wasn't sure you were going to be here."

"Thought so," she replied. She yelled in the direction of the hallway. "*Rick!* Go outside, honey please, and send that cab away!"

She leaned close to me, whispering.

"Have you paid him yet?"

I shook my head no.

"Honey!" Misty called out again, giving me a quick grin and a wink, "pay the man, too, please! Thanks!"

Rick wandered out of the back in a pair of khaki shorts and an army-green T-shirt. He was a pretty darn good-looking guy.

When he spotted the two of us, Misty's arm around me tightly, he broke out grinning, too.

"Boy, am I glad to see *this!*"

He walked over and gave me a kiss on the cheek.

Caught me clean off guard.

"You have no idea how miserable this lady has been without you!" Rick smiled, pointing at Misty.

I glanced at Misty. She nodded in agreement.

"Life around here has been pure hell. *I want my Reesy,*" he mimicked. "That's all a brother heard!"

"Stop it, Rick," Misty giggled, blushing. "I just missed my sis-tah."

"I missed you, too," I replied softly, looking at the floor in embarrassment.

Misty knew all this mushy stuff was making me nervous. That girl knew me like a book. I could tell she was getting ready to change the subject.

But the funny thing was, Rick seemed to have the same intu-ition. He changed the subject on his own.

"Cab's outside, right?" he asked.

"Yeah," I said.

"Let me go pay him and send him off," he said, rushing out the front door.

Misty led me over to the couch.

"Men can come in pretty handy," she said with a smile.

"I see."

She reached out for my hands, holding them both in her own.

I noticed the finger next to her pinky on her left hand. Perched on that finger was, *easily,* a five-carat rock.

I let out a gasp.

Her eyes followed mine.

I looked up at her.

"He just gave it to me this afternoon," Misty said, smiling. Her eyes were moist. "Isn't it beautiful?"

"Yeah," I said softly. "It is."

"Scared me to death when he whipped it out. I can't believe he wants to marry me, the way I've been acting around here these days."

For her sake, I forced a smile onto my face.

"I've been wanting to see you all day," Misty prattled. "I wanted to share this with you before I told anyone else. What am I going to do? I don't know the first thing about being married!"

I did my best to suppress a sigh.

"This is what you always wanted, isn't it?" I replied, struggling to keep my voice from sounding sarcastic. "Girl, you've been preparing for this moment your whole life!"

She laughed.

"Yeah, I guess. But I never thought it would actually come!"

Misty moved her hand around and around, admiring her ring.

"You gon' be my maid of honor, right?" she asked.

"Sure. If that's what you'd like."

"Of *course*, fool!" she quipped happily. "You're my one and only choice, girlfriend! I want you to help me with *everything*!"

A fresh ball of gas waged war in my bowels.

Rick came back inside.

When he walked in, the two of us glanced at him guiltily, like a couple of trapped rats.

He chuckled, shaking his head.

"Go back to whatever it is y'all are in the huddle about. Don't mind me. I'm going to disappear in the back and make a few phone calls."

"Bye, baby," Misty whispered to him as he passed.

"Bye, *wife-to-be*," Rick replied with a grin.

Good Lord, I thought, invisibly rolling my eyes.

"Y'all are cute," I said obligatorily.

"Ya think?" Misty asked with genuine interest.

I nodded, not really wanting to get into it any deeper.

"So!" she finally asked, tapping me on the hand. "What's up with you? You bumpin' anybody? How's it kickin' with the show?"

"What's up with you? Bumpin'?!" I repeated. "What's with all this ghetto talk of yours? You used to be so prim and proper, now you're all laid back and hip-hoppy. I don't know if I can take this from you."

She chuckled.

"Girl, it's the company I keep."

"Uh-uh." I frowned, refusing to fall for that as answer. "You hung around me for damn near all my life, and you spent all that time chiding me for the way I talk."

She shrugged.

"But I sleep with Rick. He's around me all the time."

Yeah right, I thought.

There was still another litmus test.

"What radio station do you listen to? Is it still KISS-FM?"

Misty cut her eyes at me sheepishly.

"HOT97."

Damn!! Now *that* was a major switch. While KISS and HOT were sister stations owned by the same company, KISS played the kind of music Misty loved. Easygoing old-school flava from when we were growing up.

HOT97, on the other hand, was *Puff Daddy Central.*

I listened to HOT on the regular, but I was a flat-out hip-hop mama. No shame in my game. HOT97's slogan was "Where Hip-Hop Rules the World."

97.1 on the dial was the *last* place I expected to find Miss Divine hanging out.

"Ed Lover and Dr. Dre are *off the chain!*" Misty said in her own defense. "Girl, you ever hear them play that game True Dat in the morning? And do your hear how Red Alert be rippin' it up with that old school lunchtime mix! I listen to them in the office all the time!"

"True Dat?" I asked.

"Yes, girl," she exclaimed, "true dat! They are bomb-diggity!"

She thought I was bigging up what she was saying. Naw. I was too busy being stunned by the fact that she was listening to Ed, Lisa, and Dre, HOT97's morning crew, and that she knew they had this crazy-ass call-in contest, True Dat.

"Hmmph!" I mumbled. "What a difference a dick makes."

Misty smacked me on the hand.

"Girl, that's *nasty!*" she giggled. "It ain't got *nuthin'* to do with no dick!"

"It has *everything* to do with dick, and you know it!" I replied.

"Anyway . . . ," she went on, "how are things with you and the show?"

I was really disturbed about how much she was changing, starting with the obvious aberrations in her speech. But I really needed to talk, too. I needed her to hold my hand, literally and figuratively.

I let go with that heavy sigh I had been holding back.

"What's the matter?" Misty asked with concern, immediately sensing that something was wrong.

I leaned back against the couch, running my hand over my forehead.

"What's wrong, Reesy?" she repeated. "You've really got me worried. You didn't quit the show, did you?"

I frowned.

"*No,* I didn't quit the show, Misty."

She put her hand on my arm.

"I'm sorry. I didn't mean that in a negative way against you. I was just wondering if something happened that upset you and made you quit."

"Oh," I said with a sigh of relief. "Sorry. I'm just sensitive right now, I guess."

"So what's up?"

I paused a second, trying to get a grip on my emotions. They were going in a bunch of different directions at this point, especially with the little announcement she'd just made.

"I tried out for the lead today," I replied finally.

Misty's eyebrow shot up.

"Are you serious? Did they ask you to? What happened to Rowena?"

My head snapped toward her.

"How do you know about Rowena?" I asked sharply.

"I've been to the show. Rick and I have checked you out. You're really good. So is she."

"Oh yeah," I said, remembering the tulips she sent me and the note that said she'd been in the audience. "I forgot about that."

"Did you like the flowers?" Misty asked with a hopeful smile.

"I loved them. You know I love tulips."

"I was hoping that would crack the door a little so you'd let me back into your heart."

"Why'd you send all those other types of flowers before, then?" I asked out of curiosity.

"Honestly?"

"Honestly."

"'Cause I *forgot* about the tulips!" she laughed. "Girl, I didn't remember how much you liked them till I passed by one of those corner flower stands and the merchant was putting out fresh ones in different colors. Then it hit me."

I giggled at that.

"Had I sent them earlier, we probably would have made up a long time ago," she said.

"Probably," I replied. "I don't know, though. I was pretty mad."

"I know," Misty said, laughing softly. Her hand was still on my arm.

"So what's up with Rowena?" she asked again.

"She's going to L.A."

"Hmmmmmm."

I nodded along with her.

"There were only two people trying out," I added. "Me and this other bitch, Tamara. She was pretty good, though. I don't know if I'll get it."

"Who told you to try out?"

"Julian."

"Oh *please*! Girl, why are you even worried?! If he asked you to try out, he must be confident in your talent."

I rubbed my forehead again, balling and unballing my lips.

"But you're not, are you?" Misty asked.

"Uh-uh," I mumbled, shaking my head.

"Aww, baby," she cooed, putting her arm around me. "Are you scared?"

"Uh-huh," I whined. "My stomach's been tor' up all afternoon."

She rubbed my back.

"When was the audition?"

"Today," I replied.

"Did you come here straight from there?"

I shook my head.

"I went home first and tried to lay down. I can't rest. I feel sick."

Misty folded me up in a hug. I hugged her back. It felt so good to be with my friend.

"You still feel sick?" she asked.

"Uh-huh."

Misty got up from the couch and went into the kitchen. I heard her open the refrigerator door and pop the top on something. She opened the cabinet, reached for a glass, and poured something that made a fizzing sound.

She walked out of the kitchen with a glass of what looked like water.

"Here. Drink this."

"What is it?"

"Sprite. It should settle your stomach a little."

I sat up and took the glass from her. I began to sip. The cool liquid felt good coursing down my throat.

"Drink it all," Misty insisted.

I did. I was beginning to feel better already, just because she was there.

"When are you supposed to find out the results?" she asked.

"Late this afternoon," I said, letting out a little belch.

"Reesy," she chided, "it *is* late this afternoon."

"I know," I said with a weak smile. "I had to get outta there. The waiting was killing me."

She rubbed my back again, taking the glass from my hand.

"Feel better?"

"A little."

"Good," she said with a sweet motherly smile.

I exhaled deeply, leaning back against the sofa again. I closed my eyes for a minute.

"So how you gonna find out if you got the part if you're over here?" Misty asked.

"I don't know if I wanna know," I groaned.

"*Of course,* you wanna know, girl!" she insisted. "Stop being so pessimistic! This isn't like you."

I opened my eyes again and began to chew on my bottom lip.

"I guess it's because I want it so bad," I said in a small voice.

"*Hmmm,*" she responded, nodding her head.

I closed my eyes again.

"I haven't said that aloud to anybody," I muttered. "Not even myself."

"Sometimes it helps just to speak it out loud, girl."

Misty leaned back against the couch along with me.

"So how are you supposed to find out?" she asked. "When you go back to the theater?"

I shook my head.

"No. Julian's supposed to call both of us and let us know."

"Oh. Suppose he calls and you're not there? He might have already called."

I sat there, thinking. I sorta figured that's how it would happen. Julian would call my house and leave me a message. That's one of the reasons I got out of there, I think. I wanted him to leave me a message. I couldn't bear hearing the fatal news from him firsthand.

"Yeah," I said. "He probably has."

"You wanna call and check your messages?"

"*No!!*"

"Yes, you do. It's killing you. Not knowing is killing you way more than knowing ever could."

I looked over at her.

"Ya think?"

"You forget," she grinned. "I *know* your azz."

We both giggled.

Misty reached over for the portable phone on the end table beside her.

"You gon' dial, or you want me to do it?" she asked, holding the phone out to me.

I stared at it for a minute, like it was a lethal weapon. In a way, it was. That little white portable phone held the power to make me or break me at that point. One way or another.

I stared at the phone a minute too long for Miss Divine.

"What's the number to your voice-mail service?" she demanded.

I told her the number.

She dialed.

My heart was in a knot, and something in my stomach did a swan dive that would have earned a perfect 10 on the Olympic scale.

"It's ringing," Misty said.

She listened to all the appropriate prompts, then pressed star and entered in my phone number.

"I've dialed that bad boy so many times, I know it by heart," she said with a sheepish grin.

Misty paused a second.

"It's asking for your code," she said, handing the phone to me.

"*No!!*" I screamed, refusing to touch it. I sat there, chewing my lip. "*You* punch it in. It's 461971."

Misty was the only person on the planet I felt secure enough to give any of my access codes to.

She punched it in.

"Why so many numbers?" she asked. "How the heck can you remember a code like that? What's it stand for?"

"The date we first met on the playground," I muttered.

"*Wow.* That's pretty deep."

She was silent for a second, looking at me with a saccharine expression. I quickly looked away.

"You have five new messages," she said.

I looked up at her again.

"Four of them are from me," she added quickly.

I giggled nervously, unexpectedly. I found a spot on the floor to fix my attention to, and kept it there.

"You want me to retrieve them?" she asked.

I kept my eyes fixed on the floor, and nodded my head swiftly.

She pressed 1.

After a second, she said, "That one's me."

I sat there, my insides quivering like fresh Jell-O. Blood was rushing and roaring in my head like a full-fledged hurricane. I thought I was gonna pop a vein, I was freaking so bad.

Misty, feeling me, slipped her hand into mine and squeezed.

She pressed 1 again and paused.

"Me," she said, and pressed 1.

"Me."

Pause. Press.

"Me."

Pause. Press.

She was quiet, listening intently.

I looked up from the floor at her, trying to read her expression. It was stone.

My stomach lurched and made an ugly, churning sound. My sphincter felt dysfunctional. I thought I was going to shit, right there on that couch.

Misty pressed a button on the phone several times, in rapid succession.

"Here!!" she said quickly, handing the phone to me.

I recoiled, sick to my stomach.

She pressed the button several times more, and thrust the phone at me again.

"Take it, fool!!" she exclaimed.

I reached for it, my hand shaking violently. I put the phone up to my ear.

I heard the deep drone of Julian's voice. It was curt and brief.

"You got it, bitch" was all he said.

The message was so brief, it took me a second or two for it to really sink in.

I pressed the number 4, the code to rewind, three times in a row, to take the message back to the beginning.

"You got it, bitch."

I pressed 4 again three times.

"You got it, bitch."

Press press press.

"You got it, bitch."

Press press press.

"You got it, bitch."

Misty snatched the phone from me, squealing as she did so.

"You got it, *biiiiiiiiiiiiiiitch*!!" she screamed at the top of her lungs.

I sat there, shaking, grinning, sick to my stomach, about to blow a lobe. And my lower intestine.

"I got it," I repeated nervously. "I *got* it. He said I *got* it."

Misty was up on her feet at this point, hopping around the room.

I would have gotten off the couch and jumped up and down with her, but I was afraid that the imaginary cork in my behind that was holding everything together would come undone, and shit would be all over the place. I needed to keep my ass still, and let all this sink in.

Rick rushed out from the back.

"What's going on out here?"

Misty continued to hop up and down. She bounced her way over to him like an oversized brown Energizer bunny.

"Reesy just got the lead in *Black Barry's Pie*!!!" she sang happily.

When she reached him, she flung her arms around his neck.

"*Getdafugout!*" Rick cried. "*Gon', girl!* Congratulations! Couldn't have happened to a nicer girl."

"Thanks," I replied, still catatonic over the whole thing.

Misty grabbed his hands and danced with him around the room, singing the same phrase over and over.

"*Reesy just got the lead in* Black Barry's Pi-ie!"

I smiled at the two of them, every now and then catching the glimmer from her ring as she bounced my way.

"This was a banner day for both of us, huh, girl?" Misty panted, still dancing.

"Looks like it," I said with a smile.

"Don't count me out," Rick said, giving Misty a kiss on the lips. "Don't forget, I just got engaged. It's my lucky day, too!"

"Yeah, baby!" she cooed. "I know what! Let's break out the 'pipple!"

"*'Pipple?*" I asked, confused.

"*Cham*pipple," Rick explained. "Champagne. Time to celebrate. We always keep some chillin' in the fridge. I'll go get it."

He freed himself from her clutches and rushed off to the kitchen.

"I *luh* dat man." Misty grinned. "I sho'nuf do!"

I pressed my lips into a smile, silently wondering why they always kept champagne chillin'. Were they doing that much celebrating these days? I thought she had been missing me so.

Misty scampered over to me, throwing her arms around my neck.

"And I luz you, too, baby! I'm so glad we're back together again!"

"Me, too."

Rick came back in with three glasses and the bottle of 'pipple. It was that Veuve stuff she had ordered at the Soul Cafe. I recognized the yellow label. He handed us each a glass and began to pour.

"To friends," he toasted.

"To friends," Misty repeated.

"Ditto," I mumbled, a semi-fake smile plastered on my face.

"And to family," Rick added, looking at Misty with special meaning.

"To family," she repeated in a soft voice.

They leaned in toward each other and kissed.

I suddenly felt like a voyeur.

As I watched them, a part of me was filled with a bittersweet feeling. Misty had found her man and was about to move on to the next level.

But another part of me, this very strange, weird, funky jealous side of Reesy Snowden, was very much annoyed.

Miss Divine was acting just a little too giddy for my tastes. Over a man, albeit an ostensibly nice one. Just because he had asked her to marry him, she suddenly seemed to think that everything was right with the world.

I felt somewhat guilty and ashamed, knowing that a side of me wasn't exactly reveling in her joy. Inasmuch as she was there for me at that moment, genuinely reveling in mine.

I wanted to bust her bubble a little bit. Sprinkle a little rain on her parade.

(Like I said, I'm not proud that I felt that way.)

But I wanted to put a halt to some of that *happy happy joy joy* she was suddenly flinging around at the universe.

I wanted to see it stopped.

'Pipple and all, if you know what I mean.

RETURN OF THE MACK

Gordon and Julian threw a big bash at Nell's to celebrate Rowena's moving on to bigger things in L.A. and me taking over the role of Mimosa.

Everyone in the cast was on hand to get their boogie on. We had that place jam-packed, upstairs and downstairs.

I was there doing it up with Donovan, much to Tamara's dismay.

I now posed a double threat to her. I had *two* things she had desperately wanted and lost.

I didn't rub it in, though. All I had to do to put myself in check was remember how I felt, sitting there on Misty's couch, terrified within an inch of soiling myself at the prospect that I hadn't gotten the part.

Tamara was handling all this far better than I probably would have. Her mouth was stuck out a lot, but she was still around.

If *I* hadn't gotten the role, I can't say for certain that I would have been able to show my face in that theater again.

I expected Misty and Rick to show up sometime around ten.

In the meantime, I was whooping it up with Julian, Donovan, and the gang.

"You ready to take on your first show as the star, Miss Thang?!" Julian yelled over the loud, bumpin' sounds of Janet Jackson's "Got 'Til It's Gone."

Julian, Donovan, Gordon, Rowena, Rowena's man Jeff, and I were all sitting around on couches downstairs, chillin'.

"I'm 'bout as ready as I'm gon' get," I squealed, a drink in my hand.

I had my buzz on, and I was feeling *reeeeaaaaallll* good. My body swayed to the music as I spoke.

"You'd *better* be ready, girlfriend!" Rowena snapped with a twisted grin. "My ass is history as of tomorrow morning! I'll be *leeeeeeeevin'*, on a jet plane!"

She stretched her arms out like wings and pretended she was flying.

Ol' girl was flying for real. She had downed her fair share of drinks along with me. We had been tossing 'em back since around six that evening.

"It's all good," I replied, still rocking my body to the music. "Don't even sweat it."

"All right, now!" Gordon chuckled, in that thick pea-soupy laugh of his. "First time I see a slipup, I'm trading you in for Tamara!"

He was drinking Courvoisier, and had one of those smooth grown-folks' highs going on. Not the *get-loose, let's-fuck, all-loud-and-wrong* delirious state of drunkenness my generation and under tended to fall into.

We all burst out laughing at his comment.

"Let's dance," Donovan whispered in my ear, smelling like gin.

"All About the Benjamins" was playing. As much as I liked the song now, I wondered if I'd even remember it existed in a year or two. Or a month or two.

Another Puff Daddy hit soon to be come and gone.

I let Donovan lead me out on the floor, and immediately began to shake my body down. I waved my hands around in the air and worked my hips with abandon. I was feelin' *too* good.

I had my braids pinned up in a ball, but I reached up and, one by one, pulled the hairpins out. I let them drop on the dance floor where they may.

My braids now free, I slung my head around like a wild

woman, doin' my thang and rubbing up on Donovan for no reason other than just to make his dick hard.

Mr. Brass *Wawtah*bed responded accordingly.

"If you're good," he crooned, coming close to my ear from behind, *"I'll let you work the stick in my ride!"*

"Get some new lines, nigga," I mumbled over my shoulder.
"That ol' tired-ass Morris Day shit is long played out."

I kept dancing, bending my back and working my butt deep
into his crotch.

I hadn't been with Donovan sexually in a long while. I had
closed that chapter, having rapidly become bored and unenthused by his recycled banter. But he still made for entertaining
company sometimes. Gave me somebody to laugh at.

He *was*, however (as he himself professed), *sprung*. And he refused to give up, putting all his other women down in the hopes
of bedding me again.

I wasn't in the least bit interested.

Someone came up to me on the dance floor and handed me
a drink. A glass of champagne.

I took it, without question, and tossed it back. It was delicious.

"Bednot do that, girl," Donovan warned, like he was my
daddy. "Somebody'll be done slipped your ass a mickey."

I spun around, dancing all up underneath his nose, slanging
my braids.

"How do *you* know 'bout slippin' folks mickeys, is what *I*
wanna know!" I replied, and spun back around, once again giving him my rootie-patootie to dance with.

And kiss.

Another glass of champagne came my way.

I took it and was about to chugalug.

Donovan stopped my hand as I brought the glass up to my
lips.

"Stop taking drinks from people you don't know!" he said
harshly.

I turned back around and glared at him like he was crazy.

"Who you think you talkin' to?" I snarled. "You better step
off!"

I was about to shove him out of my way, when I noticed who
it was that had given me the drink.

It was Misty, standing just a few feet away. She was all smiles.

I began cheesing instinctively, delighted to see my girl up in the house.

"Miss Divine, Miss Divine!" I sang, dancing over to her and throwing my arms around her neck.

"Hey, baby!" she grinned. "Enjoying the 'pipple?"

"The 'pipple's got it goin' on, girl!"

We walked away, leaving ol' tired behind Donovan standing right there in the middle of the dance floor like the fool that he was.

"How long you been here?" I asked, sipping on my drink.

" 'Bout ten minutes," she said. "We were upstairs for a few, then came down here 'cause I had a feeling you'd be out there shaking your azzz."

"You know me so well," I slurred, beginning to feel some serious effects from my alcohol binge.

The deejay dropped the first few beats of DMX's "Get At Me Dogs." I grabbed Miss Divine by the arm and doubled back out onto the floor.

"Girl!" I squealed. "C'mon! That's my jam!"

"Okay!" she said excitedly. "Just let me find Rick."

As she spoke, I scanned the dance floor, looking for Donovan. I saw Tamara walk up to him, grab him by the waist, and pull him toward her. He glanced my way, looking seriously uncomfortable.

Like I was gon' be mad. Like I actually *cared*. Tamara was welcome to him and his entire collection of Morris Day memorabilia.

One less Stacy Adams–wearin' monkey on my back.

I turned my attention back to Misty, who was intently scanning the room for her man.

I moved my body to the music, still sipping on 'pipple. A perfectly good song was being wasted away.

"Ooh!" she shrieked. "There he is, over there in the corner!"

She pointed, waving her hand high, trying to catch his attention.

I glanced in that direction and spotted him, standing over there, looking all hip and cool.

Then I noticed what was standing to the right of him, and my eyes nearly popped.

Beside Rick was this *fiiiiiiiiiiiiiiine* mofo. Lookin' *hella-good*, in some black jeans, a black jacket, and a black T-shirt.

Any other time, I would have been easing my way over there, tryna get wit' a brother like that.

But *this* particular brother posed a serious problem.

As I stood there, staring at him, my body did a slow burn.

Rage was steeping in me with a deep, dark simmer.

I *knew* this guy. We'd only met once, but it had been enough to wreck shit up for me.

It was Rick's best friend, Dandre Hilliard.

The one who blew my cover at Burch by announcing that I used to be an exotic dancer. He was the reason I lost my job there. Or, at least, was the catalyst that set things in motion.

I had personally, privately sworn to myself that I'd get even with him for what he did to me if I ever saw him again.

And now, here he was at *my* party, all up in Nell's, looking like a hot fudge sundae, smiling at me like what happened at Burch Financial had just been a figment of my decruited (the *new* term for firing) imagination.

From across the room, I saw him give me a sexy look and a wink.

I was so mad, I could have spit fire.

"Okay girl, now. Don't freak out . . ."

"What the *hell* is he doing here?" I asked Misty through gritted teeth.

She moved closer to me, trying to explain.

"You know, Reesy," she began, "I've really gotten to know Dandre much better over the past few months."

"Oh yeah?" I mumbled, still moving my body to DMX. "*And?* Now you can confirm that he's a bona fide ass?"

"No, Reesy!" Misty exclaimed, putting her hand on my arm. "As a matter of fact, he's a really nice guy! He's the type of guy that will do anything for you, and he'll give you his last. He and Rick grew up together, just like you and I did. Now that I know him, I realize he didn't do what he did to you on purpose."

"Oh really?" I remarked dryly, draining the last of the champagne from my glass. "Then why'd he do it?"

"He just didn't know any better," she replied. "He had no idea of all the trouble he stirred up at the office that day. Dandre would have *never* done that on purpose. He felt awful when he found out that you lost your job!"

I fell out laughing. I laughed so hard, Misty started laughing, too.

"I didn't *lose* my job," I stated flatly. "I quit, remember?"

"Yeah, girl. I know you quit. But he still felt bad about you having to go."

"You realize how ridiculous you sound, right?" I shouted over the music. "That's a grown-ass man over there."

I pointed Dandre's way.

"How you gon' tell me that grown man ain't got sense enough to know that you don't just come up in a corporate office and drop people's personal business like it's a dime on the street?"

I was laughing, but it was more of a drunken laugh. Inside, I was quite perturbed.

Misty laughed on.

"Really, Reesy," she giggled. "Dandre just doesn't know any different. He's never worked in a structured environment, so he doesn't really know the rules that apply."

"I'm laughing, Misty," I smirked, "but this shit *ain't* funny. That was my fucking life he was playing with that day."

Ol' girl sobered up quick. Her laughter stopped on a dime. A hot minute of silence hung between us before she ventured to speak again.

"I know," she sighed at last, her hand resting on my arm. "Seriously though, Dandre's not used to the working world. He makes his own rules, so he's kind of oblivious to the fact that the rest of us don't have that luxury."

"What do you mean?" I snapped. "Does he work out of his home or something? Besides, what's structure and rules have to do with anything? We're talking plain ol' common sense!!"

"Well, actually," Misty countered, "common sense is relative. Dandre, in a way, has kind of lived in a bubble his whole life."

"What do you mean?" I asked again.

Misty hesitated a second, then replied, "He's never worked at all."

I stared at her with disbelief.

She stared back at me, her eyes wide with confirmation.

"Get *outta* here, girl!!" I said finally, waving my hand dismissively. "Everybody's worked at one time or another. Even drug dealers are considered employed."

"Not Dandre," Misty countered. "He's a classic rich kid. I used to think *you* were, but you and he are nothing alike in that regard."

I noticed Rick and Dandre advancing our way. Misty followed my gaze and glanced in their direction. She shot Rick a quick look and made a funny waving gesture with her hand that she thought I didn't catch.

I did.

Rick and Dandre hung back for a minute.

"Dandre's dad's a gynecologist," Misty said. "He teaches at Howard Medical School and supposedly has this very lucrative practice."

"The son of a gyne, huh?" I snickered. "Figures. Explains why he used to be all up in my coochie at the Magic City."

"Yeah," she said with a nod, totally missing my sarcasm. "Dandre's mom died when he was a baby, so his dad just spoiled him, and pays for everything. Dandre went to college just for the fun of it. He never had any intentions of pursuing any real career."

The guys were almost near us.

"How old is he? He's kinda big to be a daddy's boy."

"Thirty-three," she whispered. "Be nice. Please. This is your night. Don't make a scene."

I held up my hands innocently.

"You'll get no scenes from this sistah. It's a party, remember?"

Misty grabbed my hand and squeezed it.

"Promise?"

"I don't make promises," I replied.

"You *used* to."

"Wrong girl," I answered. "You must be talking about another Reesy. This one don't make promises and shit that she can't keep."

"Stop cursing."

"Fuck you. Why you defending this Dandre character so?"

Misty let go of my hand.

"Because," she replied, her brows knitted with frustration, "you're being an ass! Let all this stupid mess about Dandre go!

Do you know how much convincing I had to do to get him to come here tonight?"

My eyes narrowed. I felt steam fizzing in my ears.

"*You* invited him here to my party?"

My words were sharp and deliberate.

"Yes, I did," she emphatically replied. "You and Dandre need to move past this, and you need to do it now. He wasn't going to come tonight, but I told him you were a very forgiving person, despite how tough-as-nails you may appear. Rick confirmed it. You know you're just a big ol' marshmallow on the inside, Reesy. I don't know why you try to act so hard!"

I chewed on my bottom lip, listening to her words. She was trying to kill me with kindness. Trying to shame me into getting over my grudge.

I glanced undereyed over in Rick and Dandre's direction.

Rick was patiently waiting for the go sign. Dandre smiled pleasantly, his expression sweet and helpless.

I let out a heavy sigh.

"*Fuck it!*" I said, waving my hand. "Just tell them to come on! They look like a couple of street dogs over there, waiting for a biscuit to be thrown their way!"

The sentence was barely out of my mouth before Misty made her move. She began gesturing wildly, signaling to Rick that the coast was clear.

Rick was just as anxious, parting the crowd like Moses did the Red Sea. At his side, moving with equal ease, but obvious uneasiness, was Dandre.

"*Dang,*" I mumbled. "Give me a chance to speak the words."

Misty kissed me on the cheek.

"Thank you, baby! You're gonna like him, just wait and see!!"

"*Whatever,*" I grunted.

She clasped my hands tightly in hers.

"Be nice," she chided sweetly. "And please, don't curse. You look very pretty tonight."

"*Ummmm-hmmm.*"

I refused to be wooed by her words and her saccharine behavior.

Rick arrived in front of us, beaming happily. He bussed Misty on the lips.

"Hey, baby," he said.

"Hey, *boo*," she cooed.

Just as I thought. *Everyone* was her *boo* these days.

Rick leaned over and gave me a kiss on the cheek.

"Happy party to you!" he sang, doing a little goofy dance.

Dandre stood there beside him, trying not to be conspicuous, but standing out like a very sexy sore thumb.

I studied him, feeling even more intense rage than I'd suspected. Now that he was close to me and I was able to examine his face, the vivid memory of that humiliating incident at Burch returned.

Millicent, that old evil wench of an assistant who hated my guts, had been looking for something to hang me with. Anything to try to get me and Misty fired.

Dandre had walked up that fateful day, after returning from lunch with Rick, and opened his mouth right in front of Millicent about seeing me do my thang at the Magic City in Atlanta. He bragged that I was one of the best he'd ever seen, insanely thinking that I was taking his comments as some form of a compliment.

Millicent ran wild with this revelation, and I slapped the taste out of her mouth. The result of it all was that three people—me, Millicent, and her boss Bob—ended up phased out of the company.

For a minute, there was even worry that Misty might lose her job, but she came out of it okay.

That had been months ago. Still, how could I forgive Dandre for that? As attractive and friendly as he was, standing there looking at me now, what he'd pulled was some low-life mess.

And as for Misty's comment about him not knowing any better?

Well, honey . . . I wasn't buying it for one bit.

But I decided to keep my cool, as I stood there beside him, studying him out of the corner of my eye.

The brisk sensation of giddiness rushed through my body as a bit of a plan began to brew up in my tightly braided head.

The deejay, that evil waxmaster, put on Maxwell's "Luxury: Cococure."

Rick immediately grabbed Misty and pulled her out onto the floor, leaving Dandre and me standing there, just kinda staring at each other.

"Wanna dance?" I asked after a minute.

From what I could see from his behavior, Rick must have thoroughly warned him to tread carefully with me.

"I'd love that," he smiled.

Damn shame. Brother was just too fine for his own doggone good.

I wanted to hurt him so bad I could taste it.

Be still, my vengeful heart.

We slipped out onto the dance floor, and the two of us began to move.

A few people in the house called out his name. The deejay gave him a big up from the booth.

"You're mighty popular," I commented.

"You're mighty pretty," he returned.

"Hmmmph." I smirked, and turned away from him, giving him my back to dance with.

Dandre placed his hands gingerly on my hips, mirroring the movements of my body with his own. It felt good, but, at the same time, I felt like turning around and spitting in his eye.

"Do you forgive me for what happened?" he whispered close to my ear.

"I don't know what you're talking about."

"Are you serious?"

"Sssssssh!!" I answered. "Maxwell's singing. Just let it be."

He did. And we continued to move synchronously to the music.

I felt it best that I not go there with him regarding the Burch Financial issue. Then I'd really get hot, and end up messing up what I was beginning to formulate in my head of how I could get back at him for what he did to me.

In the words of rapmaster Rakim, I was *"thinkin' of a master-plan."*

Dandre swayed against me, moving so close to my back that we were now snuggled like spoons. It wasn't so oppressive that it invaded my space. But it was close enough to let me know he was interested in getting personal.

Maxwell sang on.

"*I found a cure for this . . .*"

I closed my eyes, letting the music take me away.

"You are *sooo* beautiful," Dandre whispered.

I said nothing, caught up in the rhythm.

"I can't even believe I'm dancing with you."

"*Sssssssssssssh!*" I hissed. "Don't fuck around with Maxwell! Could you just let the damn song play?!"

When I heard him breathe in, as if he was about to say something else, I turned around and placed my palm across his mouth.

This move definitely caught him by surprise.

Dandre looked me in the eye, a smile forming on his lips underneath my hand.

I gave him back the same stare, allowing the corner of my lip to curl upward in acknowledgment.

He put his hands around my waist and pulled me close to him.

I let him, finally taking my hand from across his mouth and resting it upon his hip.

Over his shoulder, I could see Julian, Gordon, and the whole crew grinning at me.

They raised their glasses.

Donovan was with them. Glaring.

Standing behind the sofa where they were sitting was Tamara. She was glaring at me, too.

I closed my eyes, tuning them all out, letting my body meld into Dandre's. Regardless of what he'd done, he felt damn good pressed up against me.

But that was just physical. It had *nothing* to do with what I felt in my mind. And I knew how to separate the two, damn near better than anybody.

It's a good thing.

I was going to need to rely upon the physical quite heavily to help me achieve what it was I had planned for ol' boy.

Dandre and I stayed on the floor.

The next song the deejay played was that seductive slow groove by Joe where he talked about doing all the things your man won't do.

Dandre pulled me close and we rocked to the music. By this time, he had learned to let me lead the conversation. He seemed to be happy just holding on to me.

I glanced over at Rick and Misty. She kept checking out the sparkling diamond perched on her hand, which was perched on his shoulder, as she held on to him tightly.

I did my best to keep my eyes from rolling. Those two were *another* story altogether.

"Can I get you a drink when we finish dancing?" Dandre asked, still holding me close.

"Why? You tired or something?"

"Uh-uh," he muttered. "I could stay like this with you all night."

He pulled me toward him a little bit tighter.

I felt his bulge securely in place, as hard as a rock.

"Ummmph," I groaned inadvertently.

He chuckled softly in my ear.

"*You* did that, you know."

"I know my handiwork when I see it," I replied.

Dandre held me tighter.

Damn, damn, damn.

Donovan's eyes were burning like lasers through me. But he knew better than to come up and try to make a scene. He knew he couldn't play me like that. Not for *one* minute.

I snuggled my face inside the curve of Dandre's neck, letting my warm breath settle there.

"You're killing me, girl," he moaned.

I softly sang along with the music.

"Nothing can be sweeter than the sound of making love . . ."

He moaned again.

I felt the insides of my thighs getting warm. I pressed against him a little harder.

"I don't want to leave you tonight," he whispered, gently nibbling at my ear.

My body melted at the feel of the heat from his mouth.

"You don't have to," I murmured.

In the distance, I saw Donovan's ears prick up, like some sort of six-million-dollar Doberman with supersonic hearing. He eased up off the sofa and headed toward the dance floor.

Tamara was right behind him.

He brushed past me, whispering in my ear,

"Meet me at the bar in thirty-two measures . . . cool?"

I burst out laughing, totally breaking the mood Dandre and I had set.

Donovan was a *mess*. Those Morris Day lines absolutely, *positively*, had to go.

Dandre quietly observed the exchange, maintaining his composure.

"Everything straight?" he asked.

"As a board," I replied.

He pulled me back toward him.

"Let's get outta here," I whispered in his ear.

He leaned away from me, enough so that he could see my face.

"Are you sure?" he asked. "I mean, only if it's what you want. No pressure from me, okay?"

"You talk too much," I said.

"I'm officially shutting up," he laughed. "For now."

He took me by the hand and led me off the dance floor.

"You wanna say goodbye to Misty and Rick?" he asked.

I glanced over at them, still out there grooving. They were locked together tighter than a nun's legs.

"No," I said. "Let's just go. Trust me, we won't be missed."

As I passed by the crew on the couches, Julian shot me an interesting look.

"Later for you," I mouthed. *"Gotta make moves."*

Before Dandre and I disappeared through the doorway to head upstairs, I caught a glimpse of Donovan and Tamara dancing together.

He was staring at me.

She was staring at him staring at me.

The both of them looked as miserable as a couple of death-row inmates on Fry Day.

"Did you drive here?" Dandre asked, as we headed out the door of the club.

"No," I said. "Did you?"

"Yeah. My car's right over here."

He pointed to a white 300z parked up the street.

"That's a hot-looking little ride," I declared flirtatiously.

"It gets the job done," Dandre replied, suddenly sounding somewhat shy.

He held my hand as we walked up the street. I breathed in the night air, my body hot and bothered, my mind hoppin' mad. I was about to go get it on with this man, no question. This fine man, whose hand I was holding, who was electrifying my body with the slightest of touches, was about to take me home and get rocked.

I *knew* it was going to be good. I could tell *that* already. What was flitting through my mind at that moment wasn't necessarily the *what,* but the *why.*

I knew what I had to do. I had to get even. No doubt about it. But *why* did I have to get even? That's what I wanted to know.

Of late, I was beginning to discover a range of dark emotions within me that were starting to surface. I had no explanation for them. Had they always been there? Or was this something new?

Maybe I was going through some sort of a life change. Maybe my vindictive attitude toward Dandre was all a part of that. Like my jealousy over Misty's relationship with Rick, it was a feeling that I wasn't too proud of. But I couldn't deny that it was there, alive and well.

And since it was there, I had no choice.

I *had* to indulge it.

Despite the repercussions.

Dandre and I wrestled in my bed like a couple of savage animals.

I don't know if I was still intoxicated from the liquor, or if I was intoxicated with him. All I know is that I was craving this man. I couldn't get enough of him.

I wanted him *on* me, *in* me, *over* me—everywhere he could fit.

I kept reminding myself that this was all for a reason, but every time his tongue caressed me, I almost forgot.

He whispered sweet, wicked words in my ear, asking me to tell him how he could please me.

I did.

Sometimes with words, sometimes with just a nudge here and there. He responded to them all.

Dandre was daring and willing, ready to take on whatever I was dishing out.

When he finally mounted me, I held on to him desperately, flailing my body against his in a nervous state of excitement.

I watched his face as he moved above me. His eyes were locked onto mine. His expression was intense.

"Lady," he moaned, "what are you doing to me?"

I slowed down, setting the pace. He closed his eyes and moaned again. When he tried to speed things up, I sent him a signal, with a firm squeeze from inside.

"*Ahhh . . . Reesy!*" he called out.

"This is my show," I whispered. "Let me run it like it's mine."

I traced my nails down the small of his back, stopping just below his butt.

Dandre moaned again.

I clung to his body, encouraging his movements with my own.

I began to move faster, faster, faster against him, until he was thrashing and pounding above me.

Right when I felt that he was just about to pop, I squeezed again.

"*Aaaaaaaaaaaaaaaaaahhhhhhhhhhhh!*" he cried, and held on to me tightly.

He shook for a few minutes, his body tense and rigid.

I lay beneath him, quivering as well.

When Dandre stopped, he rested his head upon my shoulder, his breathing fast and heavy.

His mouth was pressed against my ear.

"When can I see you again?" he gasped.

I lay there beneath him, my eyes closed.

"I *have* to see you again," he repeated. "When can I see you?"

"*Sssssh,*" I whispered, kissing his cheek. "I told you, you talk too much. Let's just get through tonight."

He wrapped his arms around me, holding me close.

Thirty minutes later, after a very quick nap, the two of us were kung-fu fighting again.

I woke up early the next morning, watching Dandre as he lay sleeping in my bed.

My thoughts were troubling me.

As I stared at him, the memory of that scene at Burch Financial was intensely vivid.

I wanted to loathe him, and I did.

At the same time, my body had total recall of how he had made it feel just a few hours before. He had been so gentle, so kind, so fierce, and so passionate. Nothing like what I had expected.

But none of that mattered.

Dandre had to pay.

As I studied him now, I thought about how good I would feel when I finally got him back for what he did to me.

Hopefully, the feeling would far outweigh the pleasure he had given my body, and make this whole thing worthwhile.

Dandre stirred under my gaze. I stayed still, trying to keep from waking him.

He was a *very* striking man. He could have easily been a model or an actor. His face was beautifully chiseled, and his smooth café-au-lait skin cried out to be stroked.

I didn't move, resisting the urge to touch him.

His eyes batted open anyway.

"Morning, beautiful," he said groggily, a smile on his face.

I smiled innocently. "Good morning."

"Hey," he yawned, "you know what?"

"What?" I asked, raising my eyebrow in question.

He flung the covers back, revealing a massive morning missile. He leaned up, pointing at it.

"*You* did that," he said.

My smile took a turn for the naughty, and I slid down alongside him.

"I know my handiwork when I see it."

LET THE SIDESHOW BEGIN

There it was. As big as day.

As my cab pulled up to the Nexus, all I was able to focus on was the marquee.

Just beneath the huge lettering of *Black Barry's Pie* were the words *Starring Reesy Snowden* in slightly smaller letters.

My name in lights!! It was every performer's dream.

Rowena had rehearsed my butt off for the two weeks leading up to her departure. I'd gotten the songs and the moves down to a science, impressing not only Julian and Gordon, but her as well.

"You act like you've been waiting on something to happen to take me out of the show!" Rowena kidded me a couple of weeks before, during one of the last rehearsals we had together.

"I think I just knew my time was coming," I said with a smile. "Like they say, *When opportunity knocks, you'd better be dressed and ready to go.*"

"*Who* says that?" Rowena scoffed. "I ain't never heard that phrase in my life!"

"Somebody," I mumbled. "I heard it somewhere once."

I knew where it came from. It was one of Grandma's *Tylerisms*. She had a million of 'em, I swear. Her twisted *isms,* in one way or another, had populated my life for years.

I pulled open the stage door and rushed to dressing room.

Tyrone and Tyrene were going to be in the audience. I had finally called them and revealed everything—all in one fell swoop.

They were loaded down with so much information at once, they couldn't process it all quick enough to grill me thoroughly over the phone. But the grilling was inevitable. It would happen at dinner that night, after the show, for sure.

Grandma Tyler was out there, too. She hated flying with a passion, but she got on a plane, just for her Tweety, and was going to be there in the crowd, with Tyrone and Tyrene, to show me love and moral support.

Rick and Misty, too.

And Dandre. Dandre was going to be front and center, waiting for his baby's entrance. I was his *baby* now. The object of his untiring adoration. He professed it endlessly, hopelessly, every possible moment of the day.

Brother was pussywhipped lovely. For him to be such a major mack, I was amazed at how quickly he'd submitted.

The rich perfume of roses filled the room. An enormous floral arrangement sat on my dressing table, in front of me now. A gift from my indefatigable swain.

Dandre wanted to be the first to give me flowers.

He was.

And, as was his flair, his bouquet was, by far, the largest and the most exquisite.

I stroked the petals of a pink rose as I sat at the table, checking myself out in the mirror. I sat there like that for a minute, letting it sink in that this little kingdom was now officially mine.

I had inherited it all from Rowena. And while no one except Julian, and maybe Gordon, would have figured me to be her heir apparent, I'm sure all of them were out there now, wondering if, indeed, that's what I was really destined to be.

Even *I* wondered. I had no idea, one way or another, how I was going to pull this thing off.

It's amazing . . . Sometimes you think you know the stuff you're made of. You think you know all that you possess inside. Then there are moments like this, when you're standing on the verge of *whatever*, and you wonder just what the hell it is you've got within.

I knew that, for me, the question wasn't whether I could do it or not. I *definitely* had the skills. Everybody knew that by now, without a doubt.

No . . . the real question was *Does Reesy Snowden have star power?* Was I big and bad enough to be leading a well-known off-Broadway production?

Hmmph!! I guess I'd know the answer to *that* by the end of the night.

Hell, by the end of the night, I'd probably know the answer to a whole lotta things.

I sat there, trying to redirect my jitters. I played with my nails. They were painted a rich royal purple. The color was stunning against the tone of my skin.

Purple was Mimosa's signature color. No matter what she wore, purple was always present on her in some way or another.

Ironically, though, none of that really mattered. All the pretty colors in the world wouldn't make a difference if the audience didn't get fired up from my performance tonight.

I stared ahead, studying myself in the mirror. My face was painted to perfection, and the clingy, royal purple evening gown with its spaghetti straps and thigh-high slit hugged my body like a glove.

My skin was silky smooth, a beautiful golden hue that was radiant under the light.

I looked fantastic, and that was the straight-up truth. Even *I* had to give myself props on that.

My braids were pulled back in a tight, severe bun. I didn't even have any tendrils hanging. It was all face, all me. No hair to act as a buffer. No tendrils to distract.

The goal was to make these people look at *REESY.* To have them get a load of *THE NEXT BIG THING.*

At least, that's how *I* saw it.

Let's just hope that I was right.

• • •

"Two minutes, everybody! Places!"

I could hear Dreyfus walking around backstage, announcing the curtains.

When the band/orchestra began to play, I stayed planted in my chair, in my dressing room, still doing my breathing exercises and trying to focus my thoughts.

Mimosa didn't make her entrance until the dancers finished their opening number. I had about six minutes to wait.

My left leg was moving like a jackhammer.

I let it do its thing. It was a way to let nervous energy escape.

There was a quick knock at my door.

"Come in."

The door opened partway, and Julian stuck his head in.

"How you doin'?" he asked.

"I'm okay," I answered with a smile, trying to appear confident.

He nodded, appraising me.

"You look terrific."

My smile widened into a genuine grin.

"Thank you, Julian," I replied, grateful for his encouraging words. "To tell you the truth, my heart's going a mile a minute."

"Scared?" he asked.

I shook my head.

"No. I don't think so."

"Nervous?"

"A little. Nervous *good,* though. I'm realizing that my whole life may be about to change within the next few hours."

Julian pressed his lips together, thoughtfully, nodding his head in agreement.

"Yes, Miss Thang. You're absolutely right about that."

I sighed heavily.

"But don't let that scare you," he added quickly. "Just concentrate on the show, and don't think about anything else. Become Mimosa. Let her spirit take you over when you hit that stage."

"I *am* Mimosa," I breathed. "Right now, she and I are one and the same."

"Good!" Julian exclaimed. "That's the way I like to hear you talk! Come on, let's get out of here."

He opened the door wider and held out his hand to me.

I carefully pushed up from my chair. Heat raced over the surface of my skin as I grew flush from the thought of finally going on stage.

It was happening. My God, it was happening. I was about to go out there, front and center, with no surrounding dancers for me to blend into and get lost. This time, it was all eyes on me.

My heart was going *thunkety-thunkety-thunkety-thunk.* I gave myself a quick check in the mirror.

"You're beautiful, lady," Julian assured me. "Perfection can't get any better than that."

I walked over to him, grabbing hold of his still-outstretched hand. I leaned over and kissed him on the cheek.

"If this goes well, I have you to thank, ya know."

"Then start thanking me now, heffah!" Julian laughed. "Your undying gratitude has been long overdue!"

I smiled broadly at him as he pulled my dressing room door closed. Still holding hands, we walked toward the stage.

Actors were rushing about, changing into and out of costumes and putting on makeup. A few people stopped and watched as Julian and I walked by.

"Lookin' good, girlfriend!" one of the stagehands, a sistah named Trina, whispered loud enough for me to hear.

"Thanks!"

The dancers on stage were wrapping up their opening number.

Dreyfus was beckoning frantically to me.

"C'mon, Reesy! You're about to go on!"

I glanced quickly at Julian. He smiled and gave my hand a firm squeeze.

"Knock 'em dead, Miss Thang!" he uttered softly, his mouth close to my ear. "Show 'em some of what you whipped on us, way back when you first tried out for the show!"

I nodded, hurrying over to Dreyfus. He caught me by the waist, positioning me close to the stage, just inside the curtain.

I raised my arms, readying my pose. I entered singing "Pie in the Sky," an upbeat tune, full of gusto and bravado, that established Mimosa as a woman of fire and vigor.

"We're all behind you now, Reesy," Dreyfus whispered. "Go out there and bring down the house!"

I nodded again, blood rushing hot hot hot through my veins. I was burning up from the inside out. So hot that I felt I could have fainted.

I heard my cue from the band.

I opened my mouth and began singing from offstage, surprised to hear my voice soaring, so loud and crystal clear.

Arms outstretched, I strutted confidently, my hips swaying with mad exaggeration, out onto center stage. The other dancers whirled away, disappearing into the shadows. The theater grew dark and a spotlight focused on only me.

I looked up and out, right into its brilliance. Every hair on my body, except for my braids, was standing on end.

As I danced across the stage, the light followed me. It dipped and dived, mirroring my every action.

The more I moved, the more I became caught up in the heat of the song. The feeling I had from being out there was electric.

As I pranced around on that stage, singing my song, I was becoming quite hot and hellafied horny.

I stared out into what I knew was the audience. But I couldn't really see any of them. Julian, Rowena, and Gordon had assured me that the lights would be so bright, the last thing I had to concern myself with was the look on folks' faces.

They were absolutely right.

For once, though, I kinda wished they weren't. I would have loved to lock onto the individual faces of the people in the audience. I was good at that. It was an art I had perfected as an exotic dancer. If I were able to look into the eyes of my prey, I knew with certainty that I could captivate them with my singing and movements until I felt them sucked in by my spell.

I'd have to wing it the best way I could. My imagination would have to get me through.

In my mind's eye, I drew imaginary faces. Complete with Grandma Tyler, Rick and Misty, and Tyrone and Tyrene.

Most of all, I pictured Dandre's face. The sexy image of him turning to putty as he watched me strut my stuff in front of God and everybody.

Something was happening to me. I was consumed with the lust of being the absolute center of attention.

I knew the faces were fixed upon me intently. All of them. I could feel the vibes they were sending out as they ricocheted all around the theater.

As I neared the end of the song, I moved closer to the edge of the stage. I got down on all fours, and crawled toward the audience.

The person crawling toward the edge of the stage had a mind of her own. Inside, I watched, horny and horrorstruck, as she lowered her voice with every gesture she made.

The band director quickly adjusted, directing the band/orchestra to play softer, so as not to drown out the singing.

This person, the one who was now crooning to the audience so provocatively, leaned up on one arm, her finger crooked. Her body slithered liquidly as she sang the very last lines of the song.

She ended with barely a whisper, on her belly, both elbows on the stage, her face in her hands. The orchestra had faded to silence.

The audience broke into a roar. A deafening cheer.

The woman at the edge of the stage smiled seductively.

I watched it all with disbelief.

That woman wasn't *me*!! At least, not the me that *I* knew myself to be.

I knew I had a lot of nerve, but I was pretty sure that I didn't have enough nerve to go out and try to rework the show's already successful formula.

I stared at the woman long and hard. Finally, I realized who it was.

It was Mimosa Jones.

On stage, beneath that riveting light, I had become Mimosa Jones.

And ol' girl wasn't about to take the conservative route this time around.

No way.

This new incarnation of Mimosa was ready for her close-up.

And she wasn't about to wait on Mr. DeMille to give it to her, either.

● ● ●

The rest of the show was just as dramatic, with Mimosa re-working each version of the songs she sang.

Everyone in the show, although thoroughly surprised, happily followed suit.

For a little while, through the first couple of songs at least, I was puzzled about why this had happened with me.

Then, suddenly, it all made sense.

You see, it was one thing for me to learn the part from Rowena. Instruction is instruction, and that was what she gave me.

But my natural rhythm was so innate and my personality so defined, there was no way I could have just done the part and not put my own physical spin on it.

If I'd really thought about it, I would have realized that long before. But I just got so caught up in rehearsing with Rowena, I never even considered what might happen once I had taken from her all that I needed and was ready to fly on my own.

When I dashed backstage to change costumes for the first time, Julian rushed into my dressing room, nearly catching me unclothed.

He closed the door behind him.

I was so horny and excited from the high of my performance, that I would have considered fucking him. I didn't have time, though.

Besides that, it would have been a lost cause.

Right in front of Julian, I stripped off the purple gown and snatched the red sequined number from the rack. I knew my lack of modesty was of no concern to him.

"What did you just do out there?!"

I glanced up at him as I squeezed into the dress.

"I sang the song. Why? Did I not do okay?"

"You were un*fucking*believable!!"

I plopped down in the chair, touching up my makeup.

"So, is that a *good* thing?"

I dusted my face with a fresh coat of powder.

"Do you even have to ask?"

"Quit bullshittin', Julian," I said. "Just give it to me straight."

He came over and stood behind me. I could see his face in the mirror as I continued to apply my makeup.

"Reesy, you were *incredible*!! You must have been practicing that for weeks without anybody knowing!! I'm the damn choreographer!! You ain't told me shit!!!"

I shook my head as I smoothed my eyebrows.

"Tonight was the first time."

"No way!!!" he snorted. "That shit was too tight to be spontaneous! You can't just pull a move like that out your ass!"

"Calm down, nigga, calm down," I said quietly, looking into his face through the reflection of the mirror. "You forget, I know this show inside out."

I pushed back from the counter and rose from the chair. Julian backed up, getting out of my way.

I smoothed down my dress and walked across the room to the shoe rack.

"It's such a risk, Reesy," he replied. "Suppose someone else is thrown off by what you're doing?"

I slipped my feet into a pair of red satin pumps.

"Has that happened yet?" I asked, looking up at him.

"No."

I ran my fingers casually across the top of my hair.

"So I looked good out there, huh?"

"I told you, girl—you were *da bomb*!"

"Good!" I said with finality. "Then I'm not gonna stop. I'm just gonna let Mimosa do her thang."

I walked over to him and squeezed his chin between my fingers.

"Don't worry . . . I won't screw anybody up. I know exactly where I'm supposed to be."

I let go of his chin and peered into his face.

"Damn, I'm horny!" I added, for no reason other than the fact that it was true.

Julian just stood there, shaking his head.

"You are something else, Miss Thang. It's like I don't even know you. I thought I did, but it looks as though I haven't even scratched the surface."

I rushed past him, about to exit the room.

"Then that makes two of us," I commented, as I headed back toward the stage.

He stepped out of my dressing room, into the bullpen area.

"*What* are you talking about?!" Julian asked with surprise. "You know practically every damn thing about me!"

I still had about a minute before it was time to go on. I stopped in my tracks and waited for him to catch up.

"That's not what I said," I replied when he was finally beside me.

"Then what did you mean when you said *that makes two of us*?"

I stood there, staring into his eyes, contemplating just what it was I *had* meant by the statement.

"Well?" Julian persisted.

I glanced over toward the stage. Dreyfus was beckoning to me.

"I meant that I'm just as in the dark as you are, Julian," I replied hurriedly, racing over toward the stage. "I haven't figured me out yet, either!"

Suddenly, Dreyfus caught me by the arm and pushed me out onto the stage.

I disappeared among the lights and let Mimosa Jones handle her business.

The crowd was on their feet, screaming, as I came back for my second bow. Five different men walked up front and handed me bundles of roses. My arms were filled.

I bowed again, and disappeared backstage with the roses.

I tossed them into a nearby chair and rushed back over to the curtains, sneaking a peek into the audience.

The stage lights were down and the house lights were up. I could see everybody and everything as the crowd got up and made their way out of the theater.

There was Dandre, standing next to Misty and Rick. He was beaming at them like a happy little schoolkid.

Misty and Rick were all teeth and grins. Rick was pumping his fist in the air. Misty was hanging on to his arm like a piece of Velcro.

I scanned the room in search of the obvious.

Straight ahead, there they were. My family. Tyrone and Tyrene. Smiling conservatively, which was a major display of emotion for them. They stood there, all prim and proper, and seemed to be quite impressed by the fact that their daughter had brought the entire house to its feet.

Tyrene wore a royal blue velvet turban around her head and was garbed in royal blue velvet, loose-fitting, African-styled attire. My mother looked quite the regal picture. My father wore a tux, with a kente cloth bow tie. Unmistakably her kingly counterpart.

Yup. By the look on their faces, they were definitely impressed. But there would be questions, without a doubt.

Question number one, I could already guess. It would come from Tyrene.

Reesy, why did you have to play such a sexual role?

It would never dawn on my mother that perhaps *I'd* made the role sexual. That I was the one who put that kind of a spin on it.

As much as she was my mother, Tyrene really didn't know me. It would never occur to her that maybe I'm just that way.

Sitting beside them was the woman who wouldn't have to ask me anything. She already knew the answer to the question of me.

Grandma Tyler stood beside my parents, all petite and radiant, with her hands clasped together. She wore a red suit, and her face was touched with a delicate hint of makeup. Her hair was wound into a beautiful gray french roll.

It had been almost two years since I'd last seen her. As I peeked at her from behind the curtain, I turned into mush and my eyes, at last, filled with tears.

My relationship with Misty was the tightest bond I had with anyone. But my grandma laid claim to a special place in my heart that no one else could ever reach.

I secretly waved to all of them and blew them a kiss.

Then I turned, snatched my flowers up from the chair, clutched them tightly to my breast, and disappeared backstage.

My dressing room was so packed with people, I could barely breathe.

Julian was all over me, smothering me with hugs and kisses.

"Oh my God, girl!! You were awesome!!"

I grinned, squirming uncomfortably under all the attention.

Still, this was the most exciting moment I had ever experienced. I was so keyed up, I just wanted to run up and down the streets, screaming.

While we were talking, Donovan stopped by, peeking inside the room as though he were terrified to enter.

I beckoned to him.

"Come in! Why are you just standing over there?!"

Julian chuckled under his breath.

Donovan walked over to me like he was scared.

"C-c-congratulations," he stammered. His eyes were wide with wonderment. "Reesy, you flipped that shit lovely tonight! You were . . . Man, I can't even *describe* it!"

His voice was barely above a whisper, he was so nervous. I was impressed. I expected him to drop another Morris Day line.

"Thanks, Donovan."

He stood there, fidgeting nervously, tugging absently at one of his dreads. People continued to spill in and out of the room. He awkwardly glanced around.

"You got a full house in here," he mumbled.

"Yeah," I replied. "Everybody's being so gracious. 'Cept your girl. I don't think she'll be stopping by."

"*What* girl?!" he snapped quickly. "I ain't *got* no girl!" He hesitated a moment. "I been waitin' for you."

Hmmph!! Like I didn't know this.

In fact, I knew what he wanted, standing in front of me like that. He wanted to get with me tonight. But he knew things had changed. So much so, that he was now afraid to even step to me the way he had always done so confidently before.

My energies were running high. I felt like fucking with him.

"Still got that brass *wawtah*bed?"

Beside me, Julian snickered.

"Huh?" Donovan asked, surprised and confused.

"You heard me," I whispered, batting my eyes at him seductively.

A cautious smile began to form on his lips. Brother actually thought he stood a chance.

Thankfully, at that moment, Gordon burst into the room, his block head casting a shadow across my dressing table.

"You were magnificent, young lady!" he bellowed.

Donovan, not nearly as familiar with Gordon as I, faded away discreetly, eventually disappearing from the room and taking his tiny piece of false hope with him.

"A star was born out there tonight!" Gordon announced. "You know that, don't you?"

I blushed, looking down at the floor.

Gordon lifted my chin.

"Don't you play that role with me, Teresa Snowden! I knew you were a fireball from day one, cussin' me out on the phone like that!"

"Oh!" I laughed. "So you had to go *there*, did you?!"

"Of course, I did," he chuckled thickly. "Who knew that hiding behind all that fire and contention was the kind of talent you showed us out there tonight?"

"I knew it!" Julian beamed, his arms thrown around my neck. "I knew she was special from the very first!"

"Yeah, right!" I countered. "That's why your azz treated me like *shit* during all those weeks of rehearsal!"

I pushed him away, laughing as I did so.

"Get off me!" I exclaimed. "Don't be tryna jock me now!"

More people were crowding into the room, offering their congratulations and hugs.

Gordon picked up my hand, kissing it respectfully.

"I gotta go, my queen. There's some folks outside I need to see. There were a lot of press people out there tonight. Did you realize that?"

"Really?!" I asked, surprised. "Did you know they were coming?"

"Of course! The show's pretty popular. Any time a popular show has a major cast change, they always show up to see how it's going to affect things. That's to be expected."

"It's a good thing I didn't know about that," I replied. "That probably would have really made me nervous."

Gordon put his hand on my shoulder.

"You? Nervous?" He gave that soupy laugh again. "I don't think there's a soul alive out there that could do that to you!"

I smiled.

"Gotta go!"

He patted me on the hand and walked away. As he was walking out, someone knocked on my open door.

I turned around in my chair, trying to peer around the people standing in the room to see who it was.

It was Misty and Rick.

"Come on in, y'all!" I yelled.

Misty pushed her way through, maneuvering around everyone, until she made her way over to me. I stood up from my chair and gave her a big hug.

"Girl . . . you were *phenomenal* out there!" she exclaimed. I grinned proudly.

"Phenomenal woman, that's me!"

"I'm so happy for you!" she said. "This is obviously the place you're supposed to be. Reesy, girl, you were meant for the stage! No question about it!"

"For real?" I asked desperately, clasping her hands in mine. "Did I really seem like I belonged out there?"

"Yes! You were so natural! And you did the show totally different! Did you and Julian change it up this way?"

Julian, hearing her speak his name, chimed in.

"Hell naw!" he shrieked. "Miss Thang ain't even tell me she was planning on trying something new! Shocked the shit out us all!"

"I didn't expect to, Julian," I muttered. "I told you, it just happened when I hit the stage. I just got caught up in the role!"

"You damn sure did!" Rick said, finally coming over to where we were standing. He gave me his usual kiss on the cheek, this time followed by a hug.

"Girlfriend, you were bomb-diggity out there!"

"Thanks a lot," I replied graciously. "I appreciate all the props!"

"Props, hell! You were the shit! You should see my boy! You got my man flippin'!"

Dandre. I glanced around the room to see if he was there.

"Where is he anyway?" I asked Rick.

"He ran out real quick to get something. He'll be here in a few, though."

"Cool," I said as Tyrone, Tyrene, and Grandma Tyler stuffed themselves into the room.

Grandma Tyler was the first to greet me. She swallowed me up in a great big ol' hug.

"Granny's Tweety!" she rasped. "Baby, I'm so proud of you!"

Her wizened yellow face was just a-glowing.

I hugged her tightly, kissing her on the cheek.

"It's so good to see you, Grandma! I've missed you so much!"

We stood like that for a few seconds, just holding each other.

"What about us?" Tyrene asked sharply. "What are we, yesterday's trash?"

My mother. *Gotta love her.*

"Hey, you two!" I said, letting go of Grandma Tyler and giving them both quick hugs and kisses.

"You were good, baby girl," Tyrone announced. "I never figured you for doing this with your life, but if it's what you want, you seem to have a knack for it. Of course, you know, your mother and I would rather you do something different. Something with a little more prestige and dignity. But, *sela.*"

"*Sela* is right!" Grandma Tyler piped in, cutting her eyes at Tyrone.

Sela was Tyrone's way of putting an end to a discussion. It was kind of like amen or so be it. To me, it was more like *c'est la vie.*

As in, *that's life* . . . and ain't jack shit you can do about it.

As such, him saying *sela* to me right now was about as appropriate as you could get.

"I'll take what you just said as a compliment, Tyrone," I chuckled.

"Well, take it how you want. I'm just speaking my mind."

"As you always do," I muttered.

Tyrene stood there, beside him, studying me intently. Her eyes grazed my body from head to toe, checking for any new cracks or crevices that might have arrived since she'd done her last inspection.

"You look good, daughter," she finally admitted, sucking her breath in dramatically as she spoke.

"Thank you, Tyrene," I replied, with just as much drama. "You look good, too."

She nodded, concurring with my comment.

"So this is what you do these days, yes?" she asked, giving me a penetrating stare.

I gave her back the same stare, locking my eyes onto hers.

"Yes, Tyrene. This is what I do."

She nodded her head again, and began to walk around the dressing room, picking up things here and there, studying them.

She moseyed over to the clothes rack, checking out the various costumes. Her lips were pressed tightly together. That was always a giveaway. Tyrene was in research mode. Gathering data for her assault.

"Slinky, yes?" she asked rhetorically, holding up a very short, very sheer white cocktail dress.

In the scene where I wore it, I was required to do a lot of kicking and bending, showing much ass and plenty thigh. My variation on that theme tonight added even more ass and thigh than usual.

"Mmmmm" was all I said in reply.

"How you doin', baby?" Grandma Tyler said to Misty, giving her a hug. "I ain't seent you in years! You shole is pretty!"

Misty beamed.

"Thank you, Grandma Tyler! You look beautiful, too!"

"So, people!" Julian's voice rang out. "What's the plans for tonight, everybody?! We need to celebrate Miss Thang's triumphant debut!"

"Miss Thang?" Tyrene sneered. She turned toward me. "Since when did you become *Miss Thang?*"

"It's just a figure of speech, Mrs. Snowden," Julian interjected quickly. "That's my nickname for her. She's got so much talent, spunk, and attitude, Thang is about the only word I can come up with that's sufficient enough to describe her."

"Well, we didn't raise any *Thangs,* young man!" Tyrone huffed. "I'd kindly appreciate it if you would show our daughter more respect!"

Julian was stunned.

"Tweety, baby, you know where I been wantin' to go?" Grandma Tyler chimed happily in her raspy voice, coming toward me as swiftly as her time-weathered legs would allow.

"Where, Granny?" I replied, humoring her, trying not to sound as frustrated as I actually was.

"This my first time in New York. I always wanted to go to Tavern on the Green. You heard of that place? I read about it in a magazine once."

"I have two words to say to you, Granny," I replied.

"What's that, baby?"

"Gingko biloba."

Grandma Tyler burst into laughter.

"You little *heffah!*" she rasped. "Ain't *shit* wrong with my mem'ry!"

Tyrene rolled her eyes at her mother's words. I couldn't help but giggle.

"Granny, you know I've heard of Tavern on the Green. You talk about it every time you mention New York. I already made us reservations. That is, if anybody still feels like celebrating."

Misty spoke up quickly.

"We'd love to go, right, honey?" She looked at Rick.

Rick took a second to answer. I glanced over his way. He was watching the door.

When I looked in the direction of his gaze, I noticed Miss Tamara switching by in a skintight outfit.

Hmph! Looks like somebody still had a bit of a roving eye.

"Rick," Misty repeated. "You wanna go to Tavern on the Green?"

"Sure, baby," he finally answered. "And don't forget, Dandre's coming with us, too."

"Wherever he is," I mumbled.

"He said he was coming back," Rick insisted. "Trust me. He's a man of his word. He will."

Niggas and flies, I thought to myself.

Grandma Tyler had told me that phrase once. I thought it was hilarious, and so very apropos. I didn't consider it a put-down to the race. It wasn't meant that way.

She only used it in reference to tired-ass people that you couldn't depend on. It was actually part of a longer saying. The phrase went *Niggas and flies I do despise. The more I know niggas, the more I love flies.*

Right now, 'bout the only people in the room I had any semblance of love for were Grandma Tyler and Julian. The rest of them, I would have gladly traded.

For a swarm of nasty flies.

"Who's Dandre?" Tyrene asked nosily.

"Bzzzzzzzz," I hissed at her, and happily walked away.

Julian chuckled as I went by.

"Good for you," he mumbled. "They're a mess!"

"You *never* lied," I mumbled back, sitting down at my dressing table.

"You guys need to get going and get us a table," I said. "Our reservations are for eleven o'clock. It's almost ten-thirty now."

"When are you coming?" Tyrene demanded.

"Go ahead. I'll be right along, as soon as I can get out of this makeup and these clothes. Just take a cab over. Tyrone, you know where it is."

I glanced over at Misty, beckoning to her with a subtle jerk of my head.

She eased over.

"Why don't you and Rick hang around for a minute," I whispered.

"Sure thing."

Tyrone, Tyrene, and Grandma Tyler began to spill out of the dressing room.

"You'll be there by eleven?" Tyrone confirmed as he was walking out of the door.

"On the dot."

Within moments, they were gone, and it was just the four of us. Me, Julian, Misty, and Rick.

I was able to collect my thoughts for a minute.

The silence was short-lived. As I was sitting there, reveling in the afterglow of success, Gordon stuck his head back in the room.

"Reesy!" he boomed.

I turned around. He had his finger crooked.

"Yeah?"

"Could you come here for a minute?"

I stepped outside.

"What's up?" I asked.

Gordon was smiling brightly.

"Got a couple of people I want you to meet."

Two distinguished-looking white men were standing a few

feet away. One of them was very tall and thin, with sparse blond hair and a ruddy complexion. His keen blue eyes were small and curious. His lashes were so pale, they were practically nonexistent. The other man was also tall, though not as awkwardly so as the other. His physique was tight. This I could tell by the way his immaculate gray suit conformed to the shape of his body. His dark brown hair fell in a heavy lock that stopped just above his left eye.

He looked like a cross between one of the guys from Devo, that techno group from the late seventies, and the lead singer of Depeche Mode.

Out of nowhere, a tune played in my head.

"Trans . . . Europe . . . Express."

Both men stood there, solemn expressions on their faces.

Gordon led me over to him.

"Teresa Snowden," he began, "meet Gustav Schwartz and Helmut Wagner."

"It is an honor," the tall, gangly one said with a slight bow of his head. His words were delivered with a slow, deliberate enunciation. His accent was faint and elegant.

"The pleasure is all mine," I responded automatically, my tone empty and flat.

What a trite thing to say, I thought. *I don't even know these jerks.*

Whatever. My brain was fried. I was in no mood to be thinking up clever things to say. Who the hell were they anyway?

"You were brilliant," the dark-haired one remarked. He had a serious German brogue.

"Why have you chosen not to grace Broadway with your presence before?" he asked.

"What?!"

"Helmut, *Black Barry's Pie* is Teresa's first foray into theater," Gordon explained. "And tonight was her debut in the role of Mimosa."

"Surely you jest!" Helmut exclaimed. "Is that true?"

"I kid you not."

I was getting hungry. I was already bored. My eyes wandered, checking how empty things had become backstage.

"Well, Gordon," the tall one, Gustav, began, "tonight convinced us. We want to do the show."

Now, that caught my attention.

"We'll make the show grander, bigger," Helmut was saying. "We're going to need more dancers, so that she'll truly stand out as the centerpiece that she is."

Gordon was nodding emphatically.

"We'll want to make the move as soon as possible," Gustav stated. "How long will it take to train new dancers?"

"No more than a month, I'd guess," Gordon replied.

"*Fantastic!*" Helmut exclaimed. "We'll let the show run here for the next three months. That'll give the audiences time to really get to know her and fall in love. It will also give us time to put things together. New sets, new dancers, the works. Then we'll shut down, and reopen a few weeks later."

"*Yes!*" Gustav agreed. "We want people salivating by the time we reopen. It'll be a major stage production. The biggest thing since *Dreamgirls*!"

"Who *are* you guys?" I demanded. "And Gordon, what the hell is going on?!"

Gordon was cheesing so hard, I could see practically every tooth in his mouth.

"Gustav and Helmut are investors, Reesy. They came here tonight to check us out. After seeing you, they've decided that they *definitely* want to take the show to Broadway."

"With you as the lead, of course," Helmut interjected.

My heart stopped for exactly one second.

I know, because I felt my blood shift when it started back again. *"Broadway?"*

"Yes, Teresa!" Gustav beamed. "Broadway! We're going to make you a star!"

"A *star*? You're going to make me a star?"

"The brightest one in the heavens!" Helmut said with a smile.

I shook my head slowly, in utter disbelief. Something good was actually happening.

Something really exciting and wonderful and good was actually happening for me.

My hands were shaking violently. I clasped them together, but that didn't work.

"I gotta go," I announced. "People are waiting on me."

"Sure, honey," Gordon said, rubbing me on the back. He studied me with his head slightly cocked. "You're okay, aren't you?"

I swallowed a big gulp of something—air, spit, I don't know—and nodded.

"Yeah," I answered softly. "I'm all right. I can't believe this. I just gotta let it sink in."

"We'll talk," Helmut vowed. "All of us. Very, very soon."

Gordon nodded. So did Gustav.

"Well," I struggled, trying to control the quavering in my voice, "it was really nice meeting you two."

"And you, Teresa," Helmut smiled. "Or do you prefer Reesy?"

"Reesy," I stammered. "I'm much more comfortable with that."

"But is that befitting a star?" Gustav asked the two men, bringing his hands to his lips contemplatively. "It doesn't quite roll off the tongue as well. Teresa Snowden sounds much more dignified."

"We can always change it," Gordon said.

Helmut searched my face.

"Would you have a problem with that?" he asked. "If, for the show's sake, we publicly referred to you by your formal name?"

Please, I thought. *They can call me Kizzy if they want!*

"I don't have a problem with Teresa."

Helmut grinned, his dark eyes dancing.

"*Good!* If you like, we'll still call you Reesy backstage."

I was about to burst with glee.

"Gotta go, guys!"

I stuck out my hand, offering it in a handshake to both men. Gustav's grip was firm and swift, strictly business.

Helmut's was warm and lingering.

I leaned over and kissed Gordon on the cheek.

"Thanks for everything!" I whispered.

"We'll talk," he gurgled in response, the best he could do with a voice as deep as his.

I dashed away, back toward my dressing room.

Misty was standing in the doorway, watching.

"What was *that* all about?" she asked as I rushed inside.

"Girl, c'mere!" I squealed, grabbing her by the hand. "You won't *believe* what just happened!"

Julian was beside me. Rick was sitting in one of the chairs.

"Now, how you gonna tell her a secret and not tell me and Rick?! You may as well tell everybody."

The three of them stared at me expectantly.

I held on to Misty's hand. She squeezed my palm tightly as a gesture of support.

I took a deep breath.

"Okay," I finally said. "Guess what just happened?"

"What?!" Julian asked.

I clutched Misty's hand tighter. I needed my sistah now, more than ever, for this.

"Gordon just introduced me to these two guys. Germans. They wanna take the show to Broadway, with *me* as the lead!"

"Oh my God, Reesy!" Misty exclaimed, wrapping me up in a tight hug. She hugged me so tightly, her shoulder was smothering my mouth.

Julian was jumping up and down, shouting and clapping his hands.

"So it happened!" he screamed. "It *really* happened!"

"What do you mean?" I asked, surprised by his outburst. "Were you expecting this?"

"You remember," he panted, pacing around excitedly. His hands were going a mile a minute. "A few weeks ago, there was a bunch of talk about some investors coming by to check out the show. These guys had a string of Broadway hits that they'd been involved in. Major Big Willies with some serious cash flow."

I stood there, thinking, trying to recall.

"Hmmm . . . I kinda remember something about that. But that was way before Rowena left. Before I even auditioned for her part."

"Yeah," Julian said, his breath coming quick. "Gordon had no idea when they were going to show up. He'd gotten word they were curious a long time ago, after we started getting all that good press.

"We were just praying that, if they did come, they were really in the market to take on the show. After a while, we didn't hear much about it anymore. We just figured that they weren't interested."

"Reesy, girl," Rick said grinning, "you lead a very charmed life."

I blushed uncontrollably.

"I've had my moments," I said with a sigh.

He kept grinning. Although I was feeling pretty high, I hadn't forgotten the fact that he had been checking Tamara out a little while ago, right in front of me, Misty, and everybody else in the room.

Misty hugged me again.

"I love you, girl!" she said.

"I love you, too," I returned, feeling really sentimental.

"Well," Misty smiled, "we'd better get going. We've got to meet your folks over at the restaurant. You mind if I tell them about the Broadway thing?"

"Not at all! In fact, please *do*! Less explaining for me to have to do."

"All right. You're gonna wait for Dandre, right?"

"Girl," I smirked, waving my hand, "that boy ain't coming. I don't know *why* you keep on bringing him up. But I'll be right behind y'all, don't worry."

"He's coming, Reesy," Rick insisted again. "Listen . . . is there a bathroom around here somewhere?"

"Yeah, sure," Julian replied. "Come here with me for a sec."

He led Rick to the dressing room, pointing.

"Just around the corner, bruh. It's the first door on your right."

"Thanks, man," Rick said. "I 'preciate it."

He turned to Misty.

"Babe, I'll meet you guys outside in front the theater. I gotta hit the head."

"Okay, baby," Misty purred sweetly, walking over to Rick and kissing him on the lips. "Don't keep me waiting out there too long."

"I won't," he said as he rushed out of the room.

I watched them through the mirror.

Misty and I *definitely* needed to have a talk. I was beginning to have some serious concerns about ol' Ricky-poo.

A true friend would say something, right? That was to be expected. Hell, I would want to know if my man, my fiancé, was making eyes at other women.

Julian walked over to me and gave me a peck on the top of my head.

"You coming to dinner with us?" I asked.

He watched me as I removed the shadow from my eyelids with a moist cottonball.

"Hell *naw*, Miss Thang!" he piped. "I was gonna go, but after the way your folks just busted my chops, I done had enough of your family for one night!"

Misty and I burst out laughing.

"Boy!!" I squealed. "I told you how they were!"

"Uh-uh, girlfriend!" he countered, shaking his head. "You left out some *major* details! Your parents are *sick*!"

"All right, now!" I laughed. "Watch it! They *are* my peeps, after all!"

He rubbed his hands against his thighs. There was a trail of moisture from the area that his palms had touched.

"Why are your hands sweatin' like that?" I asked.

He shrugged.

"I'm too excited, I guess. I'm about to go home and tell Tonio the news."

I snickered.

"Don't hurt him, Hammer."

Julian headed toward the door.

"Oh, I'ma hurt him, all right," he said, grabbing his crotch. "And more than likely, I will be using my hammer to do it."

I screamed with laughter.

"Get outta here, you nasty dog!"

Julian had his hand up, waving, as he exited the room. Misty was right behind him.

"Bye, girl!" she added. "See ya in a few. I'm going up front to wait for Rick."

It had been about five minutes since everybody left.

I had taken off all my heavy makeup and was heading to the bathroom to wash my face.

I heard voices around the corner. I thought everyone was gone.

I slowed up, not wanting anybody to see me with my face all greasy and streaked.

I hung back, listening, trying to figure who it was.

"Well," the man's voice said, "I gotta run. I got people waiting on me. Call me. I really would like for us to hook up."

"I'll call you," a woman's voice replied. "When's a good time?"

"During the day. Call me at the office. That's the best time to catch me, anyway."

"Okay."

"You look good, girl! Had me flippin' out when I saw you walk past that dressing room!"

I couldn't *believe* him!! And he was talking loud, not even making an attempt to be discreet.

She giggled.

"Well, I'm sure you ain't never got kicked outta bed for eatin' crackers, neither, you know."

"You tryna tell me I'm cute?" he chuckled.

"You don't hear me, tho'!"

He laughed again.

"Bye, sexy! I gotta bounce!"

"I'll call you," she yelled after him. "Remember, *don't tell nobody*!"

"*Word is bond!*" he called back.

I quickly dashed back to my room, trying to avoid getting caught.

I plopped down in my chair.

I sat there, staring at myself in the mirror. I leaned forward, examining my face. My brows were knitted tightly and my lips were pressed together.

Damn!!

Tamara and Rick.

I wasn't *even* surprised. As I suspected, his ass was counterfeit, just like all the rest.

What got me was that he had the nerve to be trying to hook up with somebody in the same show I was in! How *low-life* could you get?!

I mean, he could have at least had the decency to pick somebody we'd never ever know about. Not some chick that was right up underneath my nose.

Tamara walked by my dressing room, cutting her eyes at me as she passed.

That *bitch*. What was she doing still hanging around anyway?

I guess she couldn't get to me, so now she was going after my best friend's man.

Still, I couldn't blame it all on her. After all, it takes two to tango and three to clean it up.

I had to tell Misty. It was the only thing to do.

I sat back, sighing heavily.

It was for the best. She didn't need to be marrying a jerk like him anyway.

I'd tell her later, maybe tomorrow or Monday, during lunch, my treat. That would put an end to all this nonsense.

Better she get out now than be stuck with him legally.

As my eyes skimmed over the outline of my face in the mirror, they were suddenly drawn to my lips.

I noticed that they weren't pressed together anymore.

Funny, the corners had curled up nicely into the shape of a smile.

(OME ON AND TAKE A FREE RIDE

I changed into a lavender mini-suit and applied a light coat of makeup. I slipped into a lightweight rose-colored swing coat to keep out the night air.

I was just about to shut my door and head for the restaurant. I was running more than thirty minutes behind, but that scene with Tamara and Rick had thrown me off a little.

I had my hand on the doorknob, peeking around inside to make sure I had turned everything off.

A gentle shove from behind placed me back inside the room. *"What the . . . !!!"*

It was Dandre.

"What the *hell* are you doing here so late!!" I demanded.

He had the nerve to come rolling into my dressing room now, damn near an hour after the show had ended.

Dandre pulled me close to him, kissing me full on the lips. His tongue tried to press its way into my mouth.

"What *the fuck* do you think you're doing?!" I snarled.

"What's wrong, baby?" he asked. "Why are you so upset with me?"

"Let me tell you something," I began, waving my finger in his face. "I don't like being dissed. Especially by no *niggas*! You might be used to playin' that with your other hoes, but you can just turn around and raise the hell up outta here with that shit!"

Dandre chuckled.

"Oh. So you're a *hoe* now?"

"What the *hell* did you just say?!"

"You just said *my other hoes,* like you were including yourself in that category. Personally, I don't think of you that way."

He stood there, all sexy and calm, just a-smilin'.

"You see me laughin'?!"

After what his boy Rick had just pulled, the last thing I was in the mood for was another triflin'-ass nigga. Birds of a feather, flocking all over the place. They were probably just alike. They'd known each other way too long not to be.

"And listen, baby," he said, moving close to me again, "there *are* no other women. You're the only one for me."

"Negro, *puhleeeeze*!!" I scoffed. "You *obviously* don't know who you're dealing with. Those stupid little lines don't mean a thing to me, okay? Now let me by. I gots to go!"

I tried to push him aside. He stayed fixed.

"I'm sorry I'm late," he explained softly. "I had some business I needed to take care of."

"I'm sure you did," I replied. "Let me by."

"Don't trip like that, now," he pleaded. "It had to do with you."

"Of course it did," I said, ducking around him.

I turned when I got to the doorway.

"Maybe we can get together one of these days, and you can tell me all about it. In the meantime, *step off*!!"

I turned and rushed out of the dressing room, toward the exit that emptied out into the alley.

As I sped toward the door, a sense of dread began to build within me.

I didn't want to have to go into that dark alley by myself.

(Like I said . . . I had a thing about dark alleys. After all, I'd almost been raped in one when I first moved to the city. When I took a job as an exotic dancer at that sleazy joint in Times Square, the One Trick Pony, the owner had practically watched as this cheesy bastard tackled me and tried to do his thing, all in an alley behind the club. That shit scarred me for life. And ain't too many things can claim they done scarred me.)

Anyway, though, since I'd already made a move toward the alley, I just couldn't turn around. Dandre would probably be standing there, waiting on me to do just that.

I was only a few steps away from the door. There was going to be no way around it.

I felt myself shaking as I got closer to the exit. The sound of blood was rushing in my ears.

Just as I put my hand on the pushbar, someone gripped me by the arm.

"Where do you think you're going?" he asked quietly.

I stood there, shaking, my heart thumping away. He had no idea how close I had just come to fainting.

"Let me go," I whimpered.

"You're trembling," Dandre whispered. "Are you *that* mad at me? God, Reesy, you don't cut a brother *any* slack!!"

I said nothing. I just stood there, my eyes fixed on the floor, allowing myself time to calm down.

Dandre wasn't playing anymore. Now he was as grave as I was.

"Listen to me, lady," he said, pulling my face around so that I could look into his.

I tried to avert my eyes. He persisted until our gazes finally met.

"Listen," he repeated. "I don't know what you *think* I did, or what you expect of me. Whatever it is, you're wrong. Dead wrong."

I was still trembling, trying my best to calm down. Too much had happened to me that night. My emotions had been on a damn roller-coaster ride.

"I know you think you know all about me," he kept on. "Ever since that thing at Burch, which I know was fucked up, you've just reached this conclusion about me that can't be changed. No matter what I say or do, you handle me like you're expecting me to turn into some sort of callous dog at any moment."

I listened to him talk, surprised to hear him bring up the Burch incident. Since I'd been seeing him, we hadn't mentioned it at all. Except for that one brief moment on the dance floor at Nell's.

Not that it wasn't always fresh at the top of my mind. It was. It stayed there.

"If I've been handling you so wrong, then why the hell do you keep coming around?" I asked.

He hesitated.

"Well?" I persisted.

He sighed.

"*Because,*" he finally said.

Dandre quickly looked away. This time, *I* was the one to search out his gaze.

"*Because?!* Because *what?!* What kind of kindergarten answer is *that?!*"

He sighed again. This time, it was a heavy sigh. Like he was letting out a breath that he had been holding his entire life.

"*Because,* Reesy," he murmured with exasperation. "Just *because.*"

My expression told him that his answer was a crock of shit, as far as I was concerned.

Out of frustration, he began to babble.

"*I* don't know!!" he rambled. "I mean, *yeah,* of course I know! I just don't know if I wanna *say.*"

"I don't have time for this," I snapped, turning around and starting to walk away.

In the other direction. Away from the alley door.

"*Wait,* woman!!" he exclaimed, pulling me back.

"I don't play games with people, Dandre," I said through gritted teeth.

An obvious lie, but it sounded good as it came out.

"So either let my arm go, or 'fess up. Either way, I gots to hurry up and leave."

"Where're you going?" he asked.

"Away from you," I replied, staring point blank into his face.

He sighed again and shook his head.

"Maybe it's just better if I show you," he mumbled. "For some reason, my words aren't coming out right tonight."

"Show me *what?*" I frowned.

"Just come with me," he said, and pulled me by the hand.

He pushed open the door to the alley.

My heart skipped a couple of beats, but I wasn't as scared as I ordinarily might be. Dandre was a strapping brother. He led me by the hand, through the alley and out onto Twentieth Street.

"Where are you taking me? I'm seriously late. My folks are waiting for me at a restaurant. And, unlike yourself, I respect people's time. I don't intend to have them waiting all night for me."

"Calm down," he said. "Just bear with me for one more minute."

I had to admit, it was nice walking with him like that, his palm entangled with mine. The night air was a tad bit brisk, and his body was close enough to keep the wind from getting the best of me.

We rounded the corner onto Fifth Avenue. The street was pretty empty. Most of the people were gone, except for a police cruiser quietly double-parked.

Dandre quit walking.

"Why'd you stop?" I asked suspiciously.

"Because," he replied, staring at the street. "We're here."

My mouth formed into the shape of a question that never came to be.

Dandre led me over toward the police car.

"Hey, bruh!" he called out.

The police officer, a short, dark brown fellow with a thick set of muscles, broke into a grin once we got close.

Dandre held out his hand. The brother gave him some dap.

"Good looking out, G!" Dandre said. "I owe you for this, man."

"It's cool," the officer replied. "You're good for it. I know you'll hit me back."

"No doubt. Just holler when you need me."

I stood there awkwardly, holding on to Dandre's hand.

"This her, man?" the officer asked.

Dandre grinned, pulling me closer.

"Yeah, bruh, my bad! Reesy, this is Vandel."

"*Vandel?*" I repeated, trying not to sound sarcastic.

That was a pretty monked-up name for a cop to have.

"Yeah," he replied, holding out his hand.

I shook it.

I watched him give me the obvious once-over.

"Makes sense now, man," he said to Dandre.

"Told you it would." Dandre smiled.

I didn't dig this little exchange at all.

"Dandre, I gotta go. Now."

"Okay, baby," he submitted, reaching into his pocket and pulling out a set of keys. He placed them in my hand.

"What's this?!" I asked. "I don't wanna drive your car!"

"Those aren't my keys," he returned.

"Then why are you giving them to *me*?!" I shouted, thoroughly pissed.

I'd been messing around with him too long already.

It was now eleven-fifteen. Grandma Tyler wouldn't understand why I wasn't there. She'd worry and think that something had happened to me.

"Yo, man," Vandel chuckled. "I'm audi. Handle your bizzzzness."

"I got it, bruh," Dandre declared confidently, giving Vandel some dap for the road.

Vandel the cop got into his car, started it up, and, with a wave goodbye, pulled away. In search of some real vandals, I suppose.

I stood there with Dandre for only a second.

"I'm going to catch me a cab," I announced, flinging the keys back at him and walking toward the corner.

"Reesy, why would you wanna walk when you already got a car?"

"I told you, I'm not riding with you!" I said, and kept walking.

I stuck my finger up in the air.

Not the middle one. My forefinger. The universal sign for hailing a cab.

"I didn't say you had to ride with me!" he yelled. "It's your car! You can drive by yourself, if you want!"

I stopped dead in my tracks.

What car was he talking about? I didn't *have* no damn car. I hadn't brought my black Montero up to New York when I made the move. I sold it. I didn't think I'd need a vehicle because of all the public transportation.

I was partially right. But every now and then, it would have been nice to have a car to take an occasional road trip. Or just to go for a weekend drive.

"I don't have a car, Dandre," I said without looking back.

"Yes you do," he answered back. "It's right over here!"

I turned around, my lips pressed together, and walked back toward him.

He was still standing there, the keys dangling from his fingers.

I walked up to him deliberately, stopping only a few inches away.

"*Now.* What car are you talking about? You know I don't have a car here. Is this another one of your silly little games?"

Dandre turned his face to the right, staring. I followed his gaze.

There, parked close to the curb, was a brand-new black Porsche Boxster. With a big ol' red ribbon wrapped around the top.

"This is . . . for me?"

I cleared my throat as I stared at the car.

Dandre nodded, a broad grin on his face.

"Yup, baby! It's all yours!"

"Are you out of your *mind*?!" I whispered. "You can't just *give* me a car!"

"I just did," he countered, grinning happily.

He dangled the keys in front of my face.

I allowed my eyes to focus on them. I couldn't believe it. This was the craziest day I had ever experienced. I was floored.

"I can't accept this from you," I replied, shaking my head. "I'm not comfortable with it. You hardly even know me. How can you just give me a car?"

"It's just a car," he insisted. "I wanted to do something nice to celebrate your debut tonight."

Dandre's expression was now as serious as serious could be.

I realized something. He didn't even know about the show moving to Broadway. He wasn't around when I shared the news with everyone else. Goodness knows what he might do if he found out about *that.*

"Dandre," I sighed, "you don't give someone you barely know a car! You could have just taken me out to dinner or something. That would have had the same effect."

"No, it wouldn't," he protested. "And I wanted you to have it. The first time I saw it, it reminded me of you."

The car was a beaut. And I could easily see myself in it. Top down. Braids flying back in the wind.

Inside, I was salivating. I was just itching to claim that ride. It would suit me perfectly, now that I was about to become a Broadway star.

But I couldn't do it. It would be too complicated. He'd try to lay claim to me and think he had the right to boss me around. All because I accepted a high-priced gift from him.

I wasn't having any of that. I wasn't about to let a man try to rule me with his wallet.

"Nope!" I said. "I'm not gon' be able to do it. I appreciate the gesture, Dandre, but I can't let you just flat-out give me car."

"Then borrow it," he insisted. "Consider it a loaner until you get one of your own."

Hmmm. Now *that* was doable. No strings. No commitment. No ties that bind.

Dandre continued to dangle the keys in front of me, noticing the hesitation in my face.

"I'll keep it cleaned up for you and make sure all the maintenance is done. Just drive it around until you get tired. Then, if you want, you can just give it back."

I paused for a moment, thinking.

"Now, that's a thought," I finally replied. "It just might work."

I ran my fingers over the top of my head, seriously considering the idea.

I cut my eyes at him.

"As long as you understand that I'm not taking this from you as a gift."

"Understood," he agreed, proffering the keys again. "Here. Take 'em. Let's go for a spin."

"No time for a spin. I gotta get to Tavern on the Green. That is, if everybody's still there. They're probably pretty pissed at me by now."

"This'll get you there in no time flat." He smiled.

The keys kept dangling.

I reached out and gingerly took them from his hand. I stood there, studying them, running my finger over the Porsche crest on the keychain.

"Go on!" he exclaimed. "Get outta here!"

I rushed over to the car and opened the door. It was absolutely beautiful. The interior was a deep, rich tan. There was a phat azz stereo system and a very sexy dash.

I slid into the driver's seat. It hugged my booty like a glove.

I stuck the key in the ignition. The engine revved up strong, then began to purr like a kitten.

I pressed the Power button on the stereo system. Immediately, the sounds of Maxwell's "Whenever Wherever Whatever," the Spanish version, came pouring out.

That song was an *instant* panty soaker.

"You *dog*," I muttered under my breath. "You know you're wrong. You're not playing fair."

Dandre stood there in the middle of the street, watching me.

I began to soften, and reconsider.

"So what are you doing over there?" I called out. "Are you getting in or not?"

I saw his eyebrows raise.

"I thought you had somewhere to go?" he answered, surprised.

"*Oh!* So you're not coming with me? You're not my man anymore?!"

Dandre's eyes narrowed. He crossed his arms. Brother was looking quite delicious in his dark chocolate jacket and black slacks.

"Don't bullshit me, woman. Don't mess around with my heart."

"Then get in the car."

He sauntered his fine behind over to the passenger side. I leaned across the seat and opened the door.

"Thank you," he grinned.

I smiled back. "My pleasure."

I revved the engine again, listening to the power of all those ponies. Maxwell's heavenly voice washed over us like a fog.

"Why are you guys eating dinner so late?" Dandre asked, watching me.

"Because," I replied, looking straight ahead, my hands gripped tightly on the wheel. "When I talked to my parents this afternoon, they insisted on waiting and eating dinner with me after the show. They expected it to be just family so they could interrogate me. I guess I fixed them."

I sat there for a few seconds, listening to the music. My foot was still playing with the accelerator. I was becoming seriously aroused.

I glanced over at Dandre seductively, crooking my finger.

"What?" he laughed.

"C'mere," I whispered.

Dandre leaned over toward me. I pulled his face toward mine, closed my eyes, and kissed him deeply.

His tongue outlined the shape of my lips, and probed the inside of my mouth.

We kissed like that for no more than a few seconds.

It felt like an eternity. Pure bliss.

"You are *sooo* beautiful," he whispered, kissing my face all over. He clasped my chin in his hand, stroking it with his fingers.

Maxwell's words wove themselves between his.

"*. . . por siempre más un día, baby . . .*"

"I wanted to do something to make you happy. That's why I bought you the car. I was so proud of you."

I opened my eyes, studying him.

I'd never seen him so serious. He gazed at me with an intention that I didn't quite comprehend.

My body was feverish.

The music played on.

"*. . . amor bay-beeeeeeeee . . .*"

I lowered my lids, afraid of falling into the deep wells of Dandre's dark brown eyes.

He caressed my neck with his tongue.

Dandre was killing me. The man was a doggone sexual wizard.

My hand wandered purposefully to the center of his being. He was rock solid and hot to the touch.

"*Oooh, baby,*" I moaned. "Are *you* gonna get it! Just wait until after dinner when I get you home!"

"*Mmmm,*" he groaned, writhing beneath my touch. "I don't wanna wait."

"We have to," I whispered, pulling away from him. "We can't waste any more time."

Dandre sighed heavily, leaning back against the seat. He closed his eyes, his right arm resting across his forehead.

I shifted into first gear and pulled away from the curb.

He reached over, slipping his hand under my skirt.

"*What* are you doing?" I breathed.

He kept probing, pulling my panties to the side.

I tried to keep my focus and drive as I turned west onto Nineteenth Street. The album version of "Whenever Wherever Whatever" began to play.

"*Stop it, Dandre!!*" I pleaded. "*You're gonna make me have an acciden . . .*"

My voice trailed off.

"*Lead me on, girl, if you must . . . ,*" came the honeyed voice crooning through the speakers.

I continued to drive, turning onto Sixth Avenue.

We stopped at a traffic light. A cab pulled up alongside us. There was an older brother, he looked to be my father's age, sitting in the backseat.

He winked at me.

I fidgeted nervously.

Dandre never saw it.

The guy in the cab never saw Dandre either.

That's because Dandre was busy taking care of business.

His hand, and, *somehow*, part of his head, were burrowing deep beneath my skirt.

On my face was plastered a nervous, intoxicated grin. I glanced about, all around me, trying to see if I was giving myself away.

The light changed, and I sped off.

I began to sing along with the music.

It was all I could do to keep from crying out Dandre's name.

We pulled into the parking lot for Tavern on the Green.

I grabbed Dandre by the hand and raced inside the restaurant, ready to face the barrage of lip Tyrone and Tyrene would be firing because I was showing up so late.

"How do you feel?" Dandre whispered.

"You *know* how I feel, you dog!! I can barely walk, my legs are so weak."

"There's more where that came from when I get you home tonight."

"*Ssshhhh,*" I chided, as we made our way over to the table where everyone was sitting.

We were barely seated before the questions began.

"So what took you so long?" Tyrene demanded. "We deliberately didn't order, sitting here waiting on you!"

"You could have ordered." I smiled, refusing to be riled. "I didn't ask y'all to wait."

"Oh, don't mind them. We did order, Tweety," Grandma Tyler piped. "In fact, I done et already. I'm just waiting on some dessert."

I cut my eyes at Tyrene. She was busy studying Dandre.

"Congratulations, baby!!" Grandma Tyler added. "Misty told us about the show going to Broadway! With you as the lead! Remember what I told you before? You see? I was right all along!"

"Yes, Granny." I beamed. "You told me, but I didn't wanna hear it."

"Let's order some champagne, so that we can make a toast to Reesy's success!"

This comment came from Rick.

He signaled the waiter.

I didn't want to toast my success with him. After what I'd heard between him and Tamara, I was barely able to look at him, sitting across the table from me.

It especially annoyed me to see the way that Misty was pushed up against him, all loyal and lovey-dovey.

"We don't need no champagne," I protested. "We can do that some other time."

"Oh, yes we do, baby!" Dandre insisted.

I saw Tyrone and Tyrene zero in on him simultaneously.

"And just *who* are you, young man?" Tyrone bellowed.

"He's a friend, Tyrone," I quickly replied.

Tyrene leaned back in her chair.

"Well, daughter," she said, sucking in her breath, "it seems all your friends disrespect you. This one calls you *baby,* and the other one, Julian, calls you *thang.*"

"He calls her *Miss* Thang, Tyrene," Grandma Tyler snapped. "You heard him. And we all call her *baby,* so why can't this young man? Tweety *is* a baby. Everybody who meets her just falls in love."

"Tweety?" Dandre smiled.

"Don't ask," I muttered.

"I'll tell you what it means one day," Grandma Tyler said, patting Dandre on the hand. "Once she tells me it's okay to let you know."

I laughed at her remark.

Tyrone and Tyrene sat at the table, sharpening up their verbal swords.

"Teresa, you didn't tell us that Misty and Rick were engaged," Tyrone commented.

"It wasn't my news to tell."

"So when are *you* going to get married and stop blowing in the wind?" Tyrene interjected.

My nerves were still keyed up from the high of the performance on stage and in my new car. I was feeling quite feline and sexual with the heat of it all.

When Tyrene made her comment, I felt a good chunk of that heat turn into something molten. A kind of liquid rage, if you will.

Misty, being a true sistah, tried to intervene on my behalf.

"Reesy's been so caught up in working in the show, Mrs. Snowden. Looks like she's found her niche. Wasn't she wonderful out there tonight?"

It was a pitiful attempt at creating a diversion. But my mother was having none of Misty Fine's red herrings tonight.

"Hmm?" Tyrene repeated, staring into my eyes. She didn't even acknowledge the fact that Misty had so much as breathed. "Is this young man your beau? Are you two serious? Because it's time for you to settle down, you know, like Misty here. You're much too old to be gallivanting around as you do. *Christ,* you'll be *forty* in a few short years!"

"Tyrene," I said evenly, trying to keep my cool. "I'm thirty-two. Forty is still quite a ways off, don't you think?"

"It is closer than you realize," she replied.

"Yes, Teresa," Tyrone concurred. "It's not that far away. That's retirement age, for people who invest well. Look at you. You're just getting started on what you're calling a career. God knows, in eight years, which is *nothing,* you will have barely made any progress at all."

I was fuming. Hot like fire. It's a wonder smoke wasn't coming out of my ears. This was supposed to be a celebratory night for me.

"You didn't retire at forty," I replied. "So why would you suggest it for someone else?"

Tyrone stroked his full, neatly trimmed salt-and-pepper beard casually as he responded.

"I can if I want to, though. That's the difference between you and your mother and me."

Dandre rubbed my leg beneath the table. That helped calm my nerves a little.

"Tweety, I like this place!" Grandma Tyler said. "It's just like I thought it would be!"

"I'm glad, Granny. Did you have a good time at the show?"

"I had a *wonderful* time, baby! I agree with Misty. You've definitely found your niche!"

Misty smiled at me. I smiled back at her across the table, silently wondering how I was going to drop that dime on her about her man.

"Now, Teresa," my father began. "How many years do you plan on doing this theater thing? Keep in mind that you're starting your career late. You can't really build a future on this."

Everyone else at the table, with the exception of my mother, seemed to feel a little awkward. Under the table, Dandre gave my hand a supportive squeeze.

"So everyone here has eaten?" I asked.

"Uh-huh," Misty nodded.

"Good. Then I don't feel so bad."

I stood up, holding Dandre's hand, and thereby pulling him up with me.

"*Well, folks!* It's been a *long* day! I'm too tired to eat, too tired to fight, too tired to do anything but take my butt to bed!"

I leaned over and kissed Grandma Tyler on the cheek.

"Love you, Granny. I'll call you when you get back home."

"You'd better give me a hug, Tweety!"

I did. A nice, long, warm and fuzzy embrace that made us both tear up a little.

"Love you, lady," I whispered again.

"Love you more," she rasped right back.

I walked around to Tyrone and Tyrene, and bent down and kissed them both on the cheek.

"Thanks for coming up here to see me. It meant a lot to me to know you're so supportive. I love you guys."

I beamed at them. It knocked any iota of wind remaining right out of their gusty sails.

Misty turned around and reached for me. I gave her a great big hug.

"We'll talk tomorrow," she said.

"Yeah. Perhaps we can do lunch."

"Cool."

Rick gave me a quick peck on the cheek.

"Later, lucky lady."

"Yeah, Rick," I said, managing to pull off a pseudo-politeness. "Much later for you, too."

I clasped Dandre's hand tighter and pulled him away from the table.

"Goodnight, everybody," he said.

"Yeah. Goodnight, y'all," I said with a grin.

The last thing I saw as he and I happily walked away was the *o*-shaped mouths of Tyrone and Tyrene.

Their lips were so tight, they looked like they were about to whistle.

O, WHAT A TANGLED WEB

I was sitting across from Misty in Dolce on Forty-ninth, wolfing down the calamari salad with the lime vinaigrette.

I was in heaven. That salad was *da bomb*.

Unfortunately, the salad was probably going to be the only thing good to come out of that lunch. What went down today, I knew for sure, wasn't going to be nuthin' nice.

See, I had asked Misty to lunch for a reason.

She thought it was for us to do more planning for the wedding, which was only a month away.

They were getting married quick. I guess she didn't want to give him a chance to back out.

She'd brought samples of bridesmaids' dresses that she had torn out from magazines, and a picture of the wedding dress she'd finally decided on.

I had no interest in any of that stuff whatsoever.

This was probably the most exciting time in her life—the planning of her wedding—and I had been barely involved at all. She had called me quite a few times here and there, asking my advice about things.

My comments were usually agreeable. I very rarely indulged

her topics. It was hard, because I really didn't endorse the marriage to begin with.

And here she sat now, wanting to chatter on about what to wear and who to have wear it.

Like I said, *I couldn't care less.*

I wanted to talk to her about what I had seen between Rick and Tamara the night before.

And, knowing Misty the way I do, I could pretty much guess that she wouldn't like hearing it. She'd be miserable and hurt. Ol' girl had been down this road one time too many before.

"I still can't believe that he bought you a *car!*" Misty was saying now, as she daintily cut away at her blackened salmon.

I nodded, swallowing a mouthful of food. The salad was huge, but I was giving it my best shot.

"Actually," I said haltingly, still trying to force down a corner of calamari, "he's just letting me borrow it."

Misty's twisted her mouth up tightly and clucked her tongue.

"Child, *please!* How can you even sit over there and tell me that lie?! You know he bought that car for you! Dandre is totally *sprung!*"

She dragged a piece of salmon through a rich yellow cream sauce on the side of her plate.

"How do you know that?" I replied. "Just because he's dropping dollars for an expensive gift, that doesn't mean he's sprung. You yourself told me he was a rich kid who did nothing but spend his daddy's money. No skin off his teeth. I'm sure I'm not the first woman he's done something like this for. It's just his dick talking."

Misty shook her head as she forked another morsel.

"I wouldn't be so certain about that. You're not giving yourself enough credit. And you're not giving him credit for being real with you. Rick said this is the first time he's ever seen Dandre act like this. He said Dandre's not even seeing anybody else."

"*Rick said,*" I mimicked sarcastically. "And, *of course,* he's the epitome of ironclad truth."

A bite-sized, coral-colored, fleshy piece of salmon was on its way into Misty's open mouth.

At my words, her fork froze in midair.

"What do you mean by *that* statement? You were much too nasty in the way you said it."

I chewed my food slowly, mouth closed, eyes fixed on her.

She sighed with frustration.

"What's up with you? Why can't you just give a brother a break? *Damn!!* Everybody ain't out to screw you over, like you think!"

"Trust me," I said with a smack, "I ain't *eeeemuch* worried about *that* happening. I demand my respect, and I don't take no mess. From *no*body."

"Wait . . . So are you trying to say that . . . that *I* take mess?"

Misty had put her fork down by now. Her arms were resting on the table.

"Are we having a fight?" she asked with concern. "Are you mad at me about something? 'Cause if so, then why don't you just spit it out, instead of directing it at Rick and attacking him."

"Look at you. Always defending the man. I hope he's out there defending you the same way. If he's not too distracted."

"*All right, Reesy!!* That's *enough!!* He *is* my fiancé. I'm not gonna just sit here and let you run him down like this. Why the sudden turn on Rick? He's done nothing but be respectful to you!"

"But is he respecting *you?*"

"I've gotten too old for your games," she mumbled dismissively, looking off into the crowded restaurant. "This dumb shit you pull doesn't even faze me anymore."

She thought I was playing with her, as though I had time for that.

"Listen, Miss Divine," I began, my tone firm and direct. "If I were you, I would *check* my man. While you're sitting around tearing pictures outta magazines and trying on dresses, brother's still out there hoe-hoppin' and chasing skirts!"

"I'm not gonna even dignify that with a remark," she replied.

I threw my hands up in frustration.

"What motive would I have for wrecking up your shit?" I demanded. "It's not like my plate ain't full of more important things these days."

"I don't know, Reesy. Just what motive *would* you have? You haven't been all that enthusiastic about Rick and me from day one. I see how you roll your eyes at us sometimes when we're cuddling or kissing."

I sat there, a smirk on my face. She didn't even get it.

"Can't you be happy for me? Look at how supportive I am of all the wonderful things that are happening in your life!"

I was surprised to learn that she'd been so aware of my growing negativity. I had no idea she'd even been paying me that much attention.

"This is not about me *not* being happy for you," I protested. "This is about the fact that your fiancé is a *dog*!!"

"That's it!!" Misty announced, removing her napkin from her lap and tossing it atop her plate. "I'm outta here. I don't have time for this bullshit of yours!"

She pushed back from the table.

"I saw him coming on to another woman Saturday night," I blurted. "That bitch Tamara. The one I told you about."

She reached into her bag, pulled out her wallet, and threw two twenties on the table.

"I got lunch," I said, holding up my hand.

"No!!" Misty snapped. *"I'll pay for my own shit!!"*

She turned away and stormed out of the restaurant.

I let out a deep sigh. This whole thing had gone all wrong. I mean, I knew that she was going to be upset. That was a given. But *never once* did it occur to me that she just flat-out wouldn't believe me.

Rick obviously had her wrapped around his finger. He was playing her ass like a trump-tight hand of spades.

I picked up her money and dropped it inside my purse. I had no intentions of spending it. I was going to turn around and give it right back to her.

I pulled out my own money and placed it on the table.

I got up, determined to follow her and talk. It was not my intent to alienate her again. She just needed a reality check. Dude was dogging her and she didn't even care.

I saw her a few feet ahead, her heels clicking angrily down the sidewalk.

"Misty!!" I yelled. *"Misty!!"*

"You just stay the *hell* away from me!!" she shouted, her hand up in the air. "I've had *enough* of you! I don't want to hear it anymore!!"

She didn't even bother to turn around.

A few people passing by gave me curious stares.

Great. To make matters worse, this was now beginning to look like a lesbian lovers' quarrel.

I stopped walking after her, realizing it was useless.

"Whatever," I said to myself, as I walked back down the street and around the corner, to where I'd parked the car.

Well, I'd done my part. I tried to tell her what was going on. She didn't hear me, though.

I opened the driver's side of the Boxster and slid into the seat. I sat there like that for a minute, my head resting against the steering wheel.

I was tired of this. Misty and I were fighting way more than usual. I couldn't figure out why.

Both of us were so sensitive these days. We'd been trippin' harder in the past few months than we'd ever done before.

Maybe it was me. I'd been having a lot of negative feelings about her and Rick, but it wasn't like I'd done anything deliberate to cockblock their relationship. I'd kept my thoughts to myself.

What I told her today was totally different. It had nothing to do with anything else. Today was all about Rick's behavior, not mine.

It wasn't like I didn't have a history of telling Misty things I noticed about her men. She'd always listened before.

Well, maybe not *all* the time.

But she'd never turned on me before, or called me a flat-out liar. What I said always had, at the very least, carried a little bit of weight.

I suddenly thought of the words to that old Carole King song from the seventies, "It's Too Late."

"One of us is changing, or maybe we both stopped trying."

I raised my head and put the key in the ignition.

I began to worry, thinking about the rest of that song. I hoped it wasn't too late. I didn't want to lose Miss Divine.

But I wasn't going to sit there quietly, either, and watch her get hurt.

"So sue me for caring," I mumbled as I cranked up the Boxster and pulled away.

I stopped by the Nexus to see if Julian was around. The first thing I noticed before I even went inside was that the marquee was different.

It no longer said *Reesy.* It had been changed to *Teresa.*

The Germans weren't wasting any time.

I made my way through the dark and empty theater, back to where Gordon's offices, and, consequently, Gordon and the fellas, could usually be found.

It didn't take me long to locate Julian.

He, Gordon, and Dreyfus were, as I suspected, in Gordon's office backstage, chattering loudly.

I stuck my head in the door.

"What's up, y'all? What are you three in here cooking up?"

"Hey, nigra!" Julian said. "You get my message?"

I walked in and sat down beside him on the couch.

"What message?" I asked, letting out a big sigh.

"About the *Village Voice* and the *New York Times*," he replied.

He raised up off the couch and reached for a stack of newspapers that were sitting on Gordon's desk. He handed me the one on top. It was the *Village Voice.*

"There was a really nice write-up in there," Gordon said.

"Where?" I asked, riffling through the pages. "Show it to me."

Julian took the paper from me and leafed through it.

"Here it is," he said, pointing.

I took it back from him, my eyes rapidly scanning the article.

My heart practically stopped when I read the line "Reesy Snowden is the newest, brightest star in the Nubian sky."

"Did you see this?" I babbled stupidly, pointing at the words.

"Of *course* we did, fool!" Julian laughed. "We're the ones showing it to you!"

I couldn't *believe* it. The press was actually embracing me specifically. In all the great things that had been said about Rowena, no one had ever said anything as glowing as this.

"Woooooo-hooooooooo!!!!"

I kicked my feet up in the air.

"I didn't even know there *was* a Nubian sky," I squealed excitedly, my eyes still glued to the paper, "and now I'm a star in it!!"

"Hey," Julian laughed. "At least we got one."

He was right about that. Thanks to productions by the Fats Wallers, Duke Ellingtons, and the contemporary August Wilsons, Savion Glovers, and Gordon Stocks of the world, among others, more and more stars would get a chance to be added.

"Show her the other one," Dreyfus said.

"Oh yeah," Julian remembered, going through the pile of papers in his lap.

He flipped through a few pages and found the one he was looking for. It was earmarked.

"Look at this," he said, tapping the page with his finger. "This was in the *Times*."

I took the paper from him, searching for my name.

I found it in a tiny, unassuming blurb in the lower right-hand corner of the page.

Black Barry's Pie, *a popular new off-Broadway musical, opened Saturday night's show wearing a different face as the lead. Newcomer Reesy Snowden replaces mega-talent Rowena Shaw (now Hollywood-bound) as the irrepressible Mimosa Jones, to the surprise and delight of the audience and this reviewer. Snowden is pure vamp and energy, giving an already-tight show a clever, seductive spin. Featuring an all-black cast,* Black Barry's Pie *is a must-see. Reesy Snowden, despite her name, has the makings of a stellar career.*

"Despite her name?" I said, looking around at the guys.

"She bypasses all the positive stuff," Julian mumbled, throwing up his hands, "and singles out that one line."

"But Helmut and Gustav were right," Gordon said. "Teresa does have a much better ring."

I leaned back on the couch, still clutching the paper.

"Which explains why the marquee has been changed," I replied, nodding.

"Yep," Julian concurred. "Did it first thing this morning. Hope you don't mind."

"I ain't mad at cha," I laughed.

I raised up off the couch.

"Can I take these?" I asked, holding up the two newspapers.

"Y-y-yeah," Julian answered hesitantly. "I suppose. We can always go get more."

I headed for the door.

"Where you going?" Gordon asked. "You just got here."

"I gotta go see somebody," I replied. "And take care of some business."

Julian's eyes narrowed suspiciously.

I looked away, avoiding his gaze.

"See y'all later," I said with a wave and took off out the door.

I rang the doorbell three times.

Nobody answered.

I banged on the door.

I looked up, trying to see if I saw any movement through the windows upstairs. His car was parked out front and the engine was cold.

How do I know this?

Because. I felt the hood. A trick reserved for suspicious heffahs such as myself.

"*Hey!!*" I called. "Open up if you're in there!!"

One or two people passed by on the sidewalk, going about their business. I stood there, looking around, trying to figure out where in the heck he could be.

I'd never dropped in on Dandre before, even though I had a key.

Yes, girl. Home slice had given me a key. He bust out with it one night when we were laying up in his bed and he was feeding me strawberries. He had just finished eating a slice of cake off my thigh.

Freaky, yes.

But I ain't gon' tell you no lie—*that* shiznit blew me the hell away!

So, *of course,* I had to return the favor and eat some cake off of him, too.

And you can guess the strategic spot I decided to dine from. I ate it *all,* leaving nary a speck. (Tyrone and Tyrene taught me always to eat all my food.)

Moments later, he was proffering me a key.

How long he'd been planning this move, I'll never know. Perhaps he'd had the key all the time, and was waiting for the proper moment to drop it on me.

The gesture seemed totally unplanned when he did it.

Perhaps it was his very own key, and that cake trick I pulled on him inspired him to give it up like a kidney to a transplantee. I saw him take the key off his keychain. So either he had a spare, or he knew where he could get another.

Any way you look at it, brotherman gave me total access to the cribbo.

See there? Just goes to show you that you *never* know what can happen when you decide to eat out!!

But, like I said, Dandre always knew when I was coming.

(*To the crib,* you nasties. To the *crib.* I always called ahead to let him know.)

His brownstone was on the Upper West Side. It was phat and comfy, and I'd spent plenty of nights there since he and I hooked up, getting my freak on and laying out my plan.

This trip to his house was a test. To see if Miss Divine was right. I wanted to know if brother was, indeed, *sprung.*

Or if I was just another random piece of punani for him to conquer and discard.

Where could he be this time of day? He didn't have a job. His two hangout partners, me and Rick, had jobs that kept us occupied during the day, for the most part. For me, it was usually rehearsal.

Most of the time, whenever I called, Dandre was home.

Suppose he was in there, hoeing it up someone else?

The thought made me burn a little.

What the hell was I burning for? It wasn't like I was falling for him or anything. This was all just a part of the game.

As I stood there, I felt the key singeing my hand as it hung off my keychain. Calling my name.

Use me, use me, use me, it cried.

I tried to ignore it, but the key would not be ignored.

Girl, put me in the lock! What the hell do you think he gave me to you for?!

I heard the key, and I knew it was right. Why else would he give it to me if he didn't want me to use it?

I knew that was true. But a part of me was a little uneasy. Just in case he was in there with somebody else.

How would I handle *that*?

Reesy, please!! I knew my ass. I would go slam *off*!!

But why? Why should I even give a shit if Dandre got his freak on with some other heffah? It wasn't like I cared one way or the other.

But there were butterflies in my stomach, and those bad boys were kung-fu fighting at the thought of me just opening that door unannounced.

I took a deep breath.

Bump the butterflies. I'd had them before. Dandre was a free man. He could mess around all he wanted. He was just a toy for me play with for a minute, get even with, and then move on.

I just wanted to test him for the principle of it. To see if he was as true as he claimed.

I put the burning key in the door, quietly turning the lock. I heard it click. I quickly opened the door and shut it back.

I rushed over to the alarm system, punched in the code he'd taught me, and disarmed the system. Then I armed it again.

The foyer, a beautiful splash of lemon yellow walls and mahogany wood, was quiet and unlit. Being careful not to make a sound, I crept stealthily into the living room.

I stood there for a moment, just drinking everything in. I did this every time I came to his home.

Dandre's crib was laid. If you saw it, your freaking jaw would drop.

My feet sank deeply into the plush bone carpeting and admired the view from where I was standing.

I walked around the living room, casually checking out Dandre's things.

His big, comfortable cream-colored couch was sitting in the middle of the room.

If cushions could talk. We'd done some nasty things on that sofa, I tell ya.

In front of the couch was a coffee table made out of pure ivory. On top of it was Dandre's pride and joy: a mahogany chess set that he'd bought on a trip to West Africa.

The chess pieces were half a foot high and were carved into the shapes of the people found in an African village. There were griots and tribesmen, chieftains and a shaman.

We had played chess often in the little bit of time we'd spent together. Dandre played well. I would have never figured him to even be interested in the game.

The walls of his house were covered with just as much black art as mine. He had an impressive collection. We both favored the works of Varnette Honeywood, Charles Bibbs, and Leroy Campbell.

I headed toward the bedroom upstairs, running my hand along the massive cherrywood armoire that was the focal point of the living room. That's where the TV was housed, along with all the other audiovisual equipment.

"Dandre?" I called softly, walking gingerly up the staircase. "Dandre?"

I listened carefully for any noises. My ears were particularly pricked to pick up any sexual sounds that might be jumping off somewhere in the house.

When I got to the landing, I looked in the direction of his bedroom.

The door was closed.

Aha!!

He was probably in there, getting it on. Why the heck would his door be shut, unless he was in there up to no good?

The butterflies in my stomach were doing demolition work. I could feel the lining of my belly being stripped from the inside out.

I tipped over to the door, and put my ear against it. I heard heavy breathing.

The thought that he might be in there getting his boogie on actually enraged me.

Without hesitation, I flung the door open, determined to catch him in the act.

I did.

The act of being balled up, sleeping like a baby.

He lay there in the middle of the bed, the covers partway off.

He was naked. I could tell, because the comforter was bunched up around his legs, exposing vital parts of his body.

I felt kinda silly.

I also felt kinda horny.

Dandre had passed my test, *dammit,* and turned me on in the process.

I unzipped my jeans and stepped out of them. I pulled my cotton T-shirt over the top of my head.

A few seconds later, sans panties and bra, I crawled up onto the bed, quietly hovering over the top of his body.

I wanted to take him in his sleep. That's when he'd be most vulnerable. *If* he'd be most vulnerable. If he was still seeing other women, now would be when he'd most likely call out the wrong name.

I kissed him gently around his neck and shoulders.

He stirred a little in his sleep.

"*Mmmmmmm . . . ,*" he groaned "Baby, what do you think you're you doing?"

I didn't respond. Not verbally, anyway.

His hands reached out for me, pulling me closer to his body. I craftily dodged my head out of the way, not wanting him to feel my braids and thereby know.

"*Mmmmm,*" he kept moaning, his eyes still closed.

I burrowed my head deeper. Dandre writhed beneath my touch.

When I heard him cry "*Reesy!!*" I smiled.

He flipped me over and stared into my face. He was groggy, but wide awake.

"Get a condom," I whispered.

Dandre leaned over and reached for one inside the nightstand. I kept a straight face as I watched him put it on.

Inside, I was pleased, amazed at his compliance.

Just a little bit ' ger, I thought, *and my work here is done.*

"I'm crazy   you, you know."

I lay there in bed staring up at the ceiling. Dandre was holding me in his arms, stroking my braids one by one.

I had other things on my mind.

Like those reviews in the paper. And the move to Broadway. My spirits were on cloud nine.

"How come you didn't call me and tell me you were coming?" he asked.

I wondered if the move meant Mimosa would get a wider selection of costumes. That would be awesome if she did. I wanted to be involved in picking them out. I'd talk to Gordon about it.

Or maybe I'd have to talk to the Germans. It seemed like they were in charge of things already, considering that marquee change.

I felt a tug on my braids. I looked up.

"*Hey!!*" Dandre whispered. "I've been talking to you for five minutes, and you haven't answered me yet."

"Sorry," I replied, rubbing his leg. "I got a lotta things on my mind."

"The show?"

"Yeah. I'm pretty excited about it. Especially after what they said in the papers."

"They mentioned the show in the paper? Which one, the *Times?*"

I nodded.

"And in the *Village Voice.*"

"Well, what'd they say?" he asked.

I repositioned myself in his arms. My right buttcheek was falling asleep.

"The *Times* said I had the makings of a stellar career. The *Village Voice* said I was the 'newest, brightest star in the Nubian sky.'"

"*Baby!!*" he exclaimed, hugging me tightly and kissing the top of my head. "That's fantastic!! Have you told Misty and Rick yet?"

"Uh-uh," I grunted.

I'd almost forgotten about my little squabble with Misty. Dandre reached for the phone on the nightstand.

"What are you doing?" I frantically asked.

"Giving them a call at Burch. We have to share your good news! Let's have dinner with them and celebrate before you do the show tonight!"

I stayed his hand.

"Just chill. Give me a chance to digest all of this."

I kissed his neck, trying to create a distraction. He groaned softly.

"I didn't call you because I wanted to see if you would pass my test," I mumbled, sucking the area just below his ear.

"What test?" he asked, his tone suspicious.

"Just a test."

"Hmph," he grunted, nodding. "And did a brother manage to pass this hidden test?"

I kissed his left shoulder, running my tongue along the muscles there. His eyes were closed.

"I'm still here, aren't I?"

"That doesn't mean anything," Dandre muttered. "You could have just been horny."

My fingers were playing with the hairs on his chest. It was a jungle of thick, black curls that were soft to the touch.

I snatched one out, as punishment for his flip remark.

"Owwwwwwwww!!!" he yelped, grabbing hold of my hand. "Cut that *shit* out!!!!"

His brows were knitted tightly in instinctive anger. I ran my tongue across his lips, following the shape of his cupid's bow. The creases in his brow very quickly fell away.

"If you wanna know how I feel about you, Reesy, you don't have to be sneakin' up on me to find out. I can tell you right now that you're not gonna find me holed up in my crib with another woman."

I kept playing with his lip lines.

"Because I know that's what your little test was, wasn't it?"

I said nothing, just kick licking my way around his mouth.

"Huh?" he repeated.

I began to chew on his chin, ever so sweetly.

Dandre groaned, throwing his head back just a little.

"I wouldn't have given you a key if I wasn't serious about you," he mumbled.

I tasted the stubble that was beginning to grow in.

We stayed like that for a few minutes, me silently nibbling and tasting his face, as he savored the flava of me savoring him.

"What happened to your moms?" I asked, feeling unusually close to him for some reason.

Dandre remained quiet.

"Never mind," I added quickly. "You don't have to tell me."

"Naw, babe," he said, hugging me tightly. "I can talk about her. I just *don't* ever really talk about her. 'Na mean?"

"I guess," I said.

But I really didn't.

Dandre let out a big sigh.

"My moms died in childbirth," he said. "Having me. What's jacked up about it, though, is that my pops was the doctor."

I leaned above him, surprised, but maintaining a reserved look on my face. This was a mode I'd never really seen him in.

"Dang . . . Really?"

"Yeah," he mumbled, playing absently with my hair. His expression was deep, reflective, and serious. "But it wasn't his fault. Moms had a bunch of complications, starting with the fact that she wasn't supposed to be able to carry me full-term to begin with. But you couldn't tell her otherwise. She carried me around until damn near the end of the ninth month."

"Wow," I whispered.

"Yeah. Then, on top of that, the cord was wrapped around my throat when I came out. I was strangling bad, and lost a lot of oxygen. Everybody expected both of us to die. Soon as I was born, Moms started hemorrhaging real, real bad."

I listened, watching him closely. His face bore a look of abstract pain . . . something I couldn't quite put my finger on. Like he was telling a story that had really impacted his life in a big way . . . but it was still a story to him, nonetheless. A fable that had been taught to him in order to explain an absence.

"Pops took it real hard. Other doctors were called in during the delivery, and they explained to him that there was nothing anybody could do."

He chewed on his top lip pensively.

"But you couldn't tell my pops that. I think he always believed that he could have saved her, ya know? Like, if he was such a good doctor, he should have been able to at least save his own wife. He's been trying to save the world ever since."

"But he delivered *you*. He saved *your* life. Doesn't he feel like that counts for something?"

"He does. He really does. And he's tried to make up for her loss by doting on me."

"With money?" I asked.

"Yeah. And with love. Pops always shows me a lotta love. Say what you want about the money thang, can't nuthin' take the place of that."

I laid my head down on his chest. Suddenly, at that moment, he wasn't Dandre-the-would-be-villain to me. He was a fragile thing that walked and talked like a man, but had something altogether different going on underneath.

"My pops was mad crazy about my moms," he said softly. "I can't imagine loving someone that much, and then watching them die right before my very eyes. I think that I'd die right along with them. Ya know? My soul would just raise up and go."

I heard something crack in his voice.

My eyes stung a little. I blinked a couple of times to fight back the invasion.

"Do you feel like you missed out on a lot because she wasn't there?"

"Oh yeah. I know I did. Pops never let me forget her. Everyone in my family kept her memory alive. She's like this legend, ya know? This superwoman that I've been using as a standard for most of my life."

"Wow. Do you have a picture of her?"

"Uh-huh. Raise up a sec."

I sat up. He reached over and opened the top drawer in his nightstand. He pulled out a cigar box. Like one of those kinds you keep crayons in when you're a kid.

"I've had this box forever," he said, sitting up as well.

"What is it?"

"Pictures. Of my moms. Of my moms and my pops."

He flipped open the box and began handing me photos, one by one. Each one was dominated by a tall woman with delicate bones and a beautiful brown face. Her hair was a short tangle of curls, and her cheeks were deep with dimples.

"She's gorgeous."

He nodded.

"Yep. That she was. That she was."

I looked up at his face, realizing something. She was, apparently, never really dead to him. Perhaps because she'd never really been alive.

I put the pictures back in the box, then leaned over and hugged him.

"What's that for?" he asked.

"For being deeper than I deserve," I mumbled.

"What does *that* mean?"

"Sssshhhhh," I whispered. "Just hold me. I want to be like this with you for a quiet minute, okay?"

We did, gently rocking to some inaudible rhythm. A million emotions were racing through me, the strongest of which I didn't even want to address.

I felt like crying and holding him close like that forever.

"I wanna take you somewhere," Dandre sighed at last, stroking my braids. "I wanna go away with you for the weekend. I've got a place on Martha's Vineyard. You'd love it there."

"Ummm-mmm," I mumbled. "Can't do it. Not for a while. I'm too busy with the show."

He sighed again, this time in frustration. I felt our beautiful moment beginning to dissolve.

"Besides," I added, "I've heard about that place."

"What have you heard?"

"Lots. That you call it your *pussy pad*. That's where you take your women and do your thang. I heard Rick experienced some kind of personal tragedy out there. All kinds of stuff."

"Damn!!" Dandre chuckled. *"Pillow talk is a muthafucka!!"*

"So all of that is true? I thought it was a bunch of bullshit that Rick had been feeding Misty."

He laughed again. We were still embracing each other.

"Why would he feed her bullshit? It *is* all true."

I let go of him, leaned back, and looked at his face.

"So that's your pussy pad for real?"

"Yeah. It was for years. I took lots of women there."

"And now you wanna take *me*?" I snapped. "Talk about a damn *pattern*!! And you're not even trying to lie about it!!"

"Would you prefer I deny that I used the place for that?"

I turned my head away and stared out of the window . . . fuming.

Son of a bitch. So I really *was* just another hoe.

Dandre gently rubbed my arms.

"That's not why I want to take you," he said. "I mean, on one level, it is. I want to make love to you everywhere. But on another, it's for something totally different."

I threw my legs over the side of the bed.

"I gotta go."

"Reesy. I haven't taken anyone there in a year. That lifestyle gets kinda old after a while, you know?"

I searched for my panties and bra. I put them on. I didn't have *jack* to say to him.

"I go to Martha's Vineyard sometimes by myself, and I sit out by the water and meditate on my life. I do it a lot. Have been ever since I got the place."

I pulled on my jeans. Dandre kept babbling. *Where the heck was my T-shirt?*

"That's something I've never done with anybody," he prattled. "Not a woman, not Rick, not a soul."

I found my T-shirt and slipped it over my head.

"That's why I wanted to take you," he said. "I wanted the two of us to go out by the water. Just to sit. Maybe hold hands. Contemplate the sea."

I stopped what I was doing. I turned around and looked at him.

"Okay," he grinned. "And maybe sex a little."

I smirked.

"All right," he laughed. "A *lot.*"

"You are *so* stupid. Why do I even bother with you?"

He was sitting up with the covers around his waist. His golden brown body was tight and ripped.

"Could it be that you're falling for me?"

"Don't be so cocky."

"I thought you just said I was deep?"

"I lied."

A few seconds of silence hung in the air.

"Are you really leaving now?" he asked.

I sat down on the edge of the bed.

"Yup. Got things to do."

"Will I see you tonight?"

He rubbed my back with his big toe.

"Maybe."

I *did* have things to do. I needed to give Misty a call.

"After the show?" he persisted.

"Perhaps."

His big toe drew designs on my back, sending unexpected chills of passion through my body.

"Be in my dressing room by the time the show's over."

"Sure," Dandre agreed. "I'll wait for you backstage."

"No. I want you in my dressing room when I get there."

"All right."

"And I want you ready. You never know what kind of mood I might be in."

"I'm *always* ready when it comes to you, baby."

I raised up off the bed.

"Just make sure you are tonight. But for now, I gotta bounce."

"All right. I'll see you this evening. I'll bring condoms. And honey."

"What's the honey for?"

"The better to trap you with, my fly," he said with a leer.

As I walked down the stairs, I smiled to myself.

He was *clearly* mistaken about who was the spider, and who was the fly.

He'd know soon enough.

But by then, it'd be much too late for him to pry himself loose.

LIKE WHITE ON RICE

I couldn't get Misty to return my calls for the next two weeks.

But that was cool. I could understand her being upset and not wanting to deal with the situation.

Dandre mentioned that Rick was also acting kinda moody.

From what I could guess, that meant things were not so great at home.

Good. Misty needed to ditch that loser. It was two weeks away from the wedding. There was still plenty of time for her to get out.

Better late than never. Who knew how many times he and Tamara had kicked it by now.

Things were going really well for me with the show. We had a full house, night after night. Standing ovations became the norm. I began to look for them, and welcome the adoration.

Word got out about the show being Broadway-bound, and the crowds just kept on coming.

I officially had an underwear drawer and an area in the closet for my shoes over at Dandre's house. He was growing more and more serious by the day.

I did my best to keep things arm's length. I wasn't trying to get serious with him.

But, *goodness knows,* the sex we were having was slamming.

I was sitting in my dressing room, killing time.

Taped to my mirror were the rave reviews I had clipped from the papers. Every now and then, I ran my fingers across them, just to confirm that they, and my success, were, in fact, real.

It was just shy of noon, and I was leafing through a copy of *Vibe* magazine. I had my feet kicked up on the table.

"May I come in?"

I looked up. It was Helmut, standing in my doorway.

"Sure." I smiled, closing the magazine, and subtly slid my feet off the counter.

He stepped inside, looking around.

"This room . . . it's very small."

I glanced around. It seemed fine to me.

"Small is relative," I commented. "This is the biggest dressing room I've ever had."

"Really?" he asked, his eyes growing wide with disbelief at first, then returning to normal. "Oh yes, I remember. Gordon did say this was your first show. That's still hard to believe. You're such a professional."

He moved over to an empty chair.

"May I?" he asked again, pointing to the seat.

"Sure. Sit down, please."

Helmut settled himself graciously into the seat, and studied me for a few quiet seconds.

"You deserve a much bigger dressing room than this. We'll make sure your new one is sprawling. You're doing a wonderful job in the show. The critics are madly in love with you."

I folded my arms on the table in front of me, resting my chin on them.

"Really?" I grinned. "Are you hearing good things?"

"Teresa . . . *Reesy* . . . don't be *insane*!" he exclaimed. "They're practically bursting with excitement over you!"

I felt giddy. Helmut was in a position to hear far more than I would, so if he said it, it must have been true.

Still, you never knew with white folks. I wondered if he was blowing smoke.

"All I saw was a couple of articles. Have there been more than that?"

Helmut nodded, flicking that heavy lock of hair that hung over his eye out of the way.

"I've got stacks," he said. "I'll bring them in and show them to you."

"That would be cool," I replied with a smile.

Helmut smiled as well, his gaze deep and penetrating. He was looking at me as if I was transparent. It didn't make me uneasy. But it did give me pause.

"Are you excited about what's happening?" he asked.

"Very. Having this role is a dream come true."

He abruptly got up from the chair and began to walk around. He riffled through the dresses on the costume rack, and examined all the different pairs of shoes.

"Nice," he said, glancing over at me. "But we'll get you better. We'll get you the best."

He worked his way over to where I was sitting.

I raised my head, watching him with suspicion.

Helmut began to pick up things from my dressing table. The first thing he grabbed was the copy of *Vibe*.

"I subscribe to this," he said, flipping through the pages. "Quincy Jones, right?"

"Yeah," I replied, impressed.

Helmut studied a picture of Biggie Smalls.

"Quincy is a very powerful man. I've worked with him before."

"Oh really?"

"Yes. I've worked with a number of stars over the years."

I wondered how old Helmut was. He looked to be in his late thirties. Maybe he'd gotten into the business at a very young age.

He was standing a little too close. Closer than I'd ever allowed a white guy to get.

He glanced down at me.

"So, would you like to have lunch?" he asked in his usual, out-of-nowhere manner. As though the question had been posed already.

"*Uh* . . . cool," I responded, somewhat startled. "Yeah. That would be fine."

He held out his hand to me.

I stared blankly at him, not quite understanding the gesture.

"Let me help you up," he offered, after he realized that sistah-girl just wasn't getting it.

I gave him my hand.

"Thanks," I mumbled.

"You're more than welcome," Helmut said with a smile. "Have you been to the Rainbow Room before?"

I chuckled.

"Why are you laughing?" he asked, his brow furrowed.

"Because, I've been trying to go there since I moved to New York. I haven't made it yet."

Helmut led me to the door.

"Good," he smiled again. "Allow me the pleasure of introducing you to the finer side of the city that never sleeps."

We sat in a darkened corner and chatted all afternoon.

If anybody had told me that I'd be conversing with a white man from Germany for four hours with nobody around but us, I would have laughed in their face.

Helmut was very intriguing. He knew something about everything that had to do with the theater. He was particularly knowledgeable about a number of black productions.

"I've always found the darker culture much more alluring," he admitted. "There's so much depth, an intensity that's just not present in other races."

"That's an odd thing for a white guy to admit, don't you think?" I boldly commented.

Helmut held up his hands as if conceding a point.

"What's true is true," he replied.

I sat across from him, listening to him talk. I wondered if he was always this open, or if it was just because he was with me.

"How did you and Gustav hook up?" I asked.

Helmut took in a deep breath and rolled his eyes to the side, considering.

"We were children together in Berlin. Then his family left Germany and moved away to Vienna. We lost contact for many years.

I ran into him again here, when we were both twenty-one. I was fresh out of Juilliard. Gustav was putting together his first production for the stage. A larger-than-life version of *Faust*. It failed miserably."

I sat there, drinking in his words. He was so deliberate with the language, that I could picture everything as he was saying it.

"We decided to put our wits, and our monies, together and see what we could do. It was an uphill climb, but, soon enough, we learned to make it work."

"And now you put on major theatrical events," I said.

"Yes. That's what Gustav and I do best. We know how to create a showstopper. And, if we're not the creators, we certainly have a knack for spotting a winner."

I smiled and took a sip of water.

"No misses?" I asked.

"Not in the last eighteen years," Helmut declared.

Wow. The translation was that *Black Barry's Pie* was a shoo-in. With Helmut and Gustav behind it, it was destined to be a runaway hit.

And I had the starring role.

Luck didn't get any better than this.

Helmut's limo drove us back to the Nexus.

"What are you doing after the show tonight?" he asked.

I sat in the car, pondering what I had lined up. Other than Dandre, which was not so much plans as it was an always-open invitation, I didn't have anything.

"Not much," I replied. "Why?"

"Would you have cocktails with me? I'd like to take you somewhere special."

The hairs on my arm stood on end.

Helmut put his hand on my arm.

"Will you have a drink with me tonight?" he asked again. "After the show?"

Oh Lord. This man was asking me out on a date.

I couldn't go out on a date with him.

He was white.

I didn't *do* white.

End of subject.

Besides that, Tyrone and Tyrene, whose favorite refrain was *Don't trust whitey,* would bust two guts.

I mean, don't get me wrong. It wasn't like I found white folks unattractive as a whole.

There were lots of good-looking white guys. Brad Pitt. Tom Cruise. Richard Gere. They were easy on the eyes, no doubt. But they weren't people I fantasized about. Whenever I dreamed, it was always in Technicolor. My men didn't have to be colorized. They already came that way.

I sat there, having a major dilemma. How was I going to tell Helmut no and, at the same time, try not to alienate him?

After all, he was backing the show. I couldn't afford to have him at odds with me. The success of my career practically rested in the palm of his hand.

Speaking of hands, Helmut's was still on my arm. He continued to press me for an answer.

"I won't keep you out long," he assured me. "I know you have to get your rest."

I looked into his eyes, trying to find a flicker of intent.

I saw nothing but pleasantry. Perhaps I was reading him wrong.

I thought about it.

It couldn't hurt me to have a drink with him. I'd allow myself an hour to chitchat, then I'd insist that I had to go home.

"All right," I consented. "I'll have cocktails with you."

Helmut was beaming.

"*Fantastic!* I know just the place to take you! Trust me, you're going to *love* it!"

I laughed nervously, trying to feign enthusiasm.

Inside, I was hoping that there wouldn't be any black folks there.

Especially not any brothers. I wouldn't be able to deal with the looks I knew they'd give me once I rolled up in the house with Helmut. It would be like dying a slow death.

Way too much drama for me to wanna deal with.

Helmut picked me up at exactly 10:30 P.M. at the Nexus.

The show had ended at ten, giving me just enough time to change clothes and relax my mind for a minute.

The limo whisked us away, off into the night.

"Where are we going?"

Helmut offered me a glass of champagne. I took it, tossing it back with lightning speed.

I wanted to dull my senses so I wouldn't have to really deal with what was happening.

He poured me another. I tossed it back with equal alacrity.

"You're going to get dizzy," he warned, smiling. "Those bubbles will go straight to your head, and then what will we do?"

Then you'll take my ass home, that's what, I thought.

I was reminded of Donovan on the night of my party at Nell's. He kept telling me what and how I should drink. I ignored his advice then, just as I was ignoring Helmut's now.

The car pulled up in front of the Four Seasons Hotel.

"Why are we stopping here?"

Helmut smiled.

"This is where I'm taking you, Reesy."

The limo driver stepped out of the car and walked around to open my door.

"You're bringing me here?!"

"Yes. I'm taking you to 5757."

My heart began beating fast and loud. He had to be kidding. No way did he pick me up to bring me straight to a hotel.

"Is that your suite number?" I asked.

The limo driver was standing there, holding my door open.

"*Nooooooo!*" Helmut cried. "I don't live in hotels. I have a huge apartment on Central Park West. 5757 is the name of the bar."

My shoulders went limp. I was never so relieved in all my life.

"Madam, may I help you out?" the driver asked, offering his hand.

"Oh. Yeah. Sorry about that."

Helmut exited on the other side of the car and walked around. He extended his arm, waiting for me to attach myself to it.

Shit. That meant I was going to look like I was with him. I mean with him with him. People would naturally assume that we were a couple.

Lord! What was I going to do? I couldn't get out of it. I had to take his arm.

I did.

The doorman smiled at us pleasantly as we passed into the lobby.

I prayed to God that I didn't see any colored people.

See, it was one thing to go to lunch with Helmut. That was safe. It could always be construed as business.

But to go *out* with him? *At night?* In a *limo?* With him holding me by the arm? That would be interpreted one way, and one way only.

I knew this. I had come to that conclusion about many a sistah I assumed had defected, just because I saw her with a white man at night.

Lord Jesus.

I knew I hadn't been the most religious person of late. I hadn't been as in touch with the Almighty as I should be. But, *just this once,* I hoped that God would hear my prayer. I needed Him to cut me a little bit of slack.

Just this *one* time.

We followed the stairs and rounded the corner. I could hear a lively buzz as we approached.

The place was with thick with people.

Instantly, God's message to me was revealed.

He had given me the finger.

Right off, I spotted five brothers, and I'm talking goodlooking black men, standing by the bar. They were all in suits, and were obviously of impressive *ilk,* as Tyrone would say.

A smattering of other black folks were speckled around the room.

The host, a dark-haired man with a grim face, responded familiarly when we walked up.

"Good evening, Mr. Wagner," he greeted in a gravelly monotone voice. "So good to see you again tonight. Will this be all in your party this evening?"

"Yes, just us two," Helmut confirmed. "And Orin, we'd like something against the mirrored wall. Preferably in the corner, if you please."

"No problem, sir," he replied.

Orin led the way across the room, and Helmut followed behind him, leading me along.

I was afraid to look at the brothers at the bar. At the same time, I was afraid *not* to acknowledge them, either.

I glanced their way.

All of them, *every single one,* was watching as Helmut and I crossed the room.

A couple of them were shaking their heads. One of them locked eyes with me, then turned away in disgust.

I don't know what the other two did. My head was spinning by that point. All I wanted to do was find a table and sit down.

Preferably, somewhere in the dark.

It was like I was moving in slow motion. We were just walking and walking, but it didn't seem like we were getting anywhere. I was suffocating. My lungs felt like they were smaller than raisins.

Orin finally got us to our table.

Actually, the side against the mirror was a cushioned seat that stretched the length of the entire mirrored wall. Small square tables were placed in intervals, in front of the cushioned seat. The tables were about a half a foot apart. A chair was placed on the other side of each table.

So, basically, there really was no seclusion. At least, not any to speak of. Sure, we were in the corner. But there were other people beside us, barely an elbow jab away.

I slid into the side that was cushioned. I did it so quickly, I actually got a little dizzy.

The champagne from the limo was obviously having an effect.

I was afraid to sit with my back to the brothers. I knew that that would have really pissed them off.

I expected Helmut to sit across from me, on the other side of the table. Instead, he slid in next to me on the cushioned seat.

I thought I was going to faint.

The brothers stared at me like I was out with David Duke.

"Can we order a drink?" I whispered.

I whispered *not* because I was trying to be discreet. *Oh no.* You see, I was almost hyperventilating. A whisper was all I was able to muster.

"As you wish," Helmut replied, signaling a waiter.

The waiter, a towheaded kid who looked fresh out of college, arrived at our table. He also greeted Helmut by name.

"Good evening, Mr. Wagner. What can I get for you and your guest?"

Helmut looked over at me.

"What would you like, darling?"

I winced at the word, glancing around to see who could hear. No one nearby seemed to care.

However, the brothers at the bar were still giving me the evil eye.

"I'd like a gin and tonic, minus the tonic," I breathed, refusing to make eye contact with Helmut.

"Would you like a twist with that?"

"Twist all you want," I gasped. *"Just hurry up and get it here. Please. Thank you."*

(Tyrone and Tyrene taught me to always say *please* and *thank you*.)

"Yes, ma'am," the waiter replied. "And what will you be having, Mr. Wagner? Your usual?"

"Yes, Billy," Helmut answered, reaching into a pocket inside his jacket and pulling out a wallet. He handed the waiter a credit card. *Platinum.*

"Open a tab. And bring two glasses, if you will."

"Yes, sir. Most certainly."

Billy Boy dashed away. I watched him disappear.

Out of the corner of my eye, I could see the brothers standing there, watching us. I was afraid to look.

Billy returned, posthaste, with my gin and a bottle of port.

He poured a little into a champagne flute and offered it to Helmut.

Helmut swirled the glass slightly and inhaled the wine's delicate perfume. He tilted it by the stem and tasted a sample, thoughtfully working the liquid around in his mouth.

Helmut nodded at Billy, who then proceeded to fill both glasses.

Meanwhile, I quaffed my gin.

While Helmut was bullshittin' around with his examination of the grape, homegirl was gettin' ready for drink number two.

"One more, please," I said to Billy.

Helmut and Billy both looked at me like I was crazy.

"Are you sure?" Helmut whispered, placing his hand on mine. I could feel the brothers as they watched our every move.

"Yeah. I need another, Billy. The sooner the better, if you don't mind."

Billy hurried off.

"Is this mine?" I asked, reaching for the extra glass of port.

"Yes, it is. But Reesy, *please! Calm down!* What on earth is the matter?!"

His hand was still on mine.

I grabbed the drink and tossed it back. I rested against the cushion, allowing myself to catch my breath.

Now it was safe to look at him.

I peered into Helmut's face. I studied the shock of brown hair hanging heavily over his eye.

His dark eyes were penetrating. He began to gently stroke the top of my hand.

What am I doing here with him? I wondered. As I stared at Helmut, he seemed like the whitest man in America.

"Can I have some more wine?" I asked.

Before he could answer, Billy arrived with my drink.

"Never mind," I said to Helmut.

I held the glass of gin in my hand for a few seconds, preparing myself for the shock of its kick.

As I went to toss it back, Helmut stayed my hand.

"All right, young lady. Talk to me. Something is obviously seriously wrong here."

I looked around, undereyed, at the people in the room. The brothers were still leaning against the bar, checking us out.

"I'm just a little uncomfortable," I admitted with a sigh. "You might find it stupid, but it's the absolute truth."

"I figured as much," he replied. "Now. Tell me, what exactly is it you're uncomfortable about?"

I sat the untasted glass of gin down on the table and leaned back against the cushion.

Might as well tell him. And besides, I could always blame my frankness on the liquor.

"I'm uncomfortable being here with you."

Helmut's left eyebrow raised.

"Why is that? Are you afraid of someone from the show seeing us?"

"No," I answered, shaking my head.

"Good, because it's a silly concern. If you're afraid people are going to think you're trying to win me over, you're wrong.

How can *I* improve your status in the show? You've already got the lead."

"I could give two fucks about that."

"Then why are you so uncomfortable? I don't understand."

"Because you're white."

Helmut instantly laughed.

I looked over at him.

"Is *that* the reason? Are you *serious?*"

I picked up the glass of gin and tossed it back.

"Yep," I choked.

I bit my lip. My head was swimming.

'Round and 'round and 'round.

Out of nowhere, Wesley Snipes walked into the room. He nodded at the brothers at the bar, then sat down a couple of tables away from us.

A brown-skinned sistah with short hair was already sitting there. They were obviously friends.

I tried not to stare at him, but I couldn't help it.

He was a rich, beautiful black that was so dark, it was intoxicating. Like Hershey's bittersweet chocolate. I'd always found him sexy, but seeing him now made me realize that the big screen didn't do him half the justice he deserved.

I was so drunk, it wasn't funny. My jaw was slack. I was two steps shy of drooling.

Helmut was now sitting so close to me, I could feel his hot breath against my neck.

I gazed into his face. After having the image of Wesley's heavenly mocha emblazoned on my eyeballs, Helmut literally paled in comparison.

It was as though he read my mind.

"I'll never be Wesley Snipes," he muttered. "But don't judge a book by its cover. Not just yet, Reesy."

He smiled seductively.

"I'll bet that I can give you just as much excitement, if not more, than Wesley Snipes ever could."

An image of Wesley working his stuff on that balcony scene in *Mo' Better Blues* flashed through my head. The one where Cynda Williams hollered *"Oh Shadow!!!"*

Helmut had to be outta his mind.

Just as I had to be for sitting there with him.

"I'm ready to go," I announced.

He sighed, studying my mouth.

"As you like."

Helmut held up his finger, barely gesturing. Billy quickly made his way over to us.

"Another drink, sir?"

"No, Billy," Helmut said. "I'd like for you to close out the tab and bring me the check."

"Yes, sir!" Billy replied, rushing off again.

I sat there, staring off into space.

I was too drunk. My breath could melt steel.

I did my best not to look at Wesley. How I managed it, I'll never know.

His luscious blackness was like a flame, and I was a kamikaze moth who was desperately trying not to burn.

I didn't look at Helmut either. He sat there beside me, still clutching his wolf tickets, writing checks with his mouth that he knew damn well his ass couldn't cash.

Outfuck Wesley Snipes indeed!!

I wasn't about to have him try to prove it to me. Not in this lifetime. Or the next.

I stared into the open area of the room, watching the people move around and mill about. My eyeballs began to feel funny, like they were covered with trash.

I rubbed them with both forefingers, in an attempt to clear them up.

I blinked a few times, trying to focus.

A battalion of Billys returned with an army of checks.

I blinked again, trying to consolidate them.

They refused to merge.

As I stared ahead, the whole room became a kaleidoscope. It was like looking through a fly's eyes. All hundred of them. A whole bunch of everything was moving every whichaway at once.

I had a thought.

I glanced over at Wesley.

Sure enough, there were literally stacks of him pushed up together.

Mocha delight.

I grinned.

"Let's go, Reesy," Helmut whispered. "You're looking a little green."

I glanced at him.

A host of Helmuts caught me by the arm and guided me gently from my seat.

"How da *fuck* Umma look green?" I slurred, wobbling. "Nigga, I'm *black*!"

"No, you're not," he countered politely. "At best, you're *yellow*."

I pushed away at all the Helmuts, trying to pry myself free.

They kept a firm hold on my arm as they led me away from the table, toward the door.

We made our way past the Wesleys.

"*Heyyyyyyy, Wesley!*" I called out foolishly. "*Gotdam*, nigga! You look *good*!"

The Wesleys chuckled heartily.

"She all right, man?" he asked Helmut.

"I'm *fine*!" I interjected. "Umma *star*!! You needa come see my show!! *Black Cherry's Thigh*!"

"She'll be okay," Helmut answered, moving me along.

We strolled past the brothers at the bar. They glowered at me. Legions of them.

I grinned at them, waving my hand.

"*Hey, y'all!*" I squealed. "You know what? Y'all some *mean* muthafuckas!"

"*Trick*," I heard one of them mumble.

"That's not necessary, man," another one said. "She's drunk. Be chill."

"*That's right!*" I yelled over my shoulder. "Be *chill* with that shit!"

The Helmuts got me out of the bar, through the lobby, and into the car in no time.

I collapsed back on the seat.

I closed my eyes, completely out of control.

Within seconds, I was fast asleep.

It was morning when I finally woke.

I stirred under the covers, relieved to be in Dandre's bed. I pulled the satin sheets close, languishing in the feel.

As usual, I was barely conscious, but horny as hell.

I snuggled up to Dandre, who was lying on his side with his back to me. I reached my hand around the front of him in search of my favorite missile.

It was on standby.

He moaned at my touch.

"C'mere with that," I whispered.

He did.

I rolled over onto my back. He rolled over on top of me.

"Get a condom," I added.

Dandre reached across me and pulled one out of the drawer.

I lay there with my eyes closed while he slipped it on. I was expecting him to be mad at me for getting in so late, but, obviously, he wasn't.

It wouldn't have done him any good to be mad at me anyway. Not with the rock-hard boner he was packing.

I was still very tired. But I had to get my sex on. I silently hoped Dandre didn't want to talk when we finished. As soon as we were done, I planned on going right back to sleep.

He climbed on top of me and slipped it in. I wrapped my arms and my legs around him and began to move.

"*Mmmmm, baby,*" I moaned, my eyes still closed.

Dandre kissed my neck, sucking it fiercely. I found it immensely exciting.

"*Babyyyyyyyyyy . . . ,*" I cooed. "That feels *sooooo* good."

I held on to him tighter.

He leaned above me and pinned my shoulders down. With force and intensity, he began to pound my body.

The feeling was incredible. It was almost like we were fighting, it was so rough.

I gripped him harder, clamping him down with my legs.

Dandre pounded on.

Perhaps he is mad at me, I thought, writhing with pleasure. *I should get him mad more often. He's trying to bang my living brains out!*

I was much too excited. Usually, I was in control of our lovemaking. This time around, Dandre was completely in charge.

I cried out, screaming crazy words that didn't make sense to me or anybody I would have wanted to know. I began to feel myself about to burst. I tried to pull back and gain control.

I couldn't.

"*Oh, God, baby!!*" I screamed wildly, thrashing about.

I felt the starburst at my center begin to radiate throughout my body.

I clutched at him desperately, grabbing him by the hair.

By the *hair*???!!!!

Since when did Dandre's hair become long enough for me to grab? And why did it feel so soft and straight?

My eyes popped open in horror.

Above me, Helmut kept on pounding, staring directly into my face.

He was smiling.

My mind was running wild with panic, only serving to excite me more.

Caught in the frenzy of the impossible, shocked clean out of my natural wits, I came again.

Hard.

So did Helmut.

"*Reesy!!!!!*" he cried, rearing his head back toward the ceiling.

I shuddered beneath him, still grappling with my own release.

He collapsed upon my shoulder, his breath heavy against my ear.

I lay there, staring up at the ceiling, still quivering, allowing myself to focus. I glanced around the room. There were huge, fanciful paintings of nude women covering the walls.

Black women.

There were also an assortment of photos of Helmut with what appeared to be important people.

Most of them were black as well.

Heavy gold drapes hung from the windows. There was a fireplace with embers still glowing.

This was *definitely* not Dandre's crib.

Helmut kissed my neck.

"Now, tell me you didn't enjoy that," he whispered.

I said nothing. I just lay there, catatonic, once again staring at the ceiling.

Out of the corner of my eye, I could see Helmut's pallid body lying on top of me. I felt bile rise in my throat.

I didn't want to deal with this right now. I *couldn't* deal with it right now. Especially with what it meant. The repercussions were too far-reaching and catastrophic.

The scary thing about it was that Helmut had felt so wickedly delicious. And his, *um*, thing seemed to function quite well.

This wasn't supposed to be. After all, he was a *white* guy. No *way* was I supposed to like it.

I blinked hard, trying to shake the thought.

I know what, I mused desperately to myself. *I'll just do like Miss Scarlett.*

Gone with the Wind had been one of my favorite books as a teenager. It had been one of Misty's favorites, too. Misty liked it because it was a powerful love story.

I liked it for other reasons. Mainly, for Scarlett O'Hara. I admired the way she handled her business.

She did what she had to do. If somebody did her wrong, she got her revenge. If she wanted something bad enough, she had no shame in going after it. She was looked down upon by people who thought they were better, but did she give a shit?

Homegirl just went out and claimed what was (and oftentimes, *wasn't*) rightfully hers.

She was a woman after my own heart.

When things got so bad for her that should couldn't deal, she just chucked it in a corner, and went about her business. *I'll think about it tomorrow* was her motto. *Tomorrow is another day.*

I closed my eyes and tried to block out the whole incident. I breathed in slowly and deeply.

After a while, I felt myself beginning to drift off to sleep.

Yeah. I'll pull a Scarlett O'Hara and think about it all tomorrow.

Tomorrow's still another day.

STANDING ON THE VERGE OF GETTIN' IT ON

*W*here were you last night?!*"* Dandre demanded.

The show had just ended. We were in my dressing room. We competed for space with what had to be a couple hundred red roses. I didn't even *want* to know who they were from.

"I got in late," I mumbled, my head down on my dressing table.

Dandre was hovering behind me. I didn't have to look at his face to tell he was pissed.

I didn't need it right now. I had too much other shit I was trying *not* to deal with.

"Why didn't you return my calls? I left you a ton of messages today."

"Dandre, baby," I whispered, reaching back for him with my hand. I still didn't bother to lift up my head.

"Don't *Dandre baby* me, Reesy!!" he snapped, shaking my hand away. "*Damn!!* What do you think, that you can just play me like I'm some sort of knucklehead off the street?"

I could hear him pacing around behind me.

"And where the hell did all these flowers come from?" he asked in an annoyed tone.

He was jealous. How cute.

"I'on know," I grunted. "Fans, I guess."

Someone knocked on the door.

"Go away!!" he yelled.

I finally looked up. That shit wasn't cute anymore.

"*What* do you think you're doing?" I asked sharply, gazing at him through the reflection of the mirror. "This is *my* room. You don't dictate who comes in and who doesn't."

Dandre was standing there in a black jacket and a tight navy blue turtleneck that hugged the contours of his chest. He had on a pair of navy blue wool pants.

He made a good bully. It was a total surprise. He'd never jumped bad with me before.

"We were having a discussion," he replied flatly, his face all balled up.

"So that means you get the right to disrespect me in my space? I don't *think* so!" I glared at him through the mirror.

"Disrepect *you*?" he cried. "I've done nothing but do right by you! You're the one disrespecting *me*!"

"Nobody disrespected you," I mumbled, grabbing a handful of cotton balls and the bottle of baby oil on my table.

Dandre was now the one glaring.

"If I had done what you did, you would have screamed bloody murder! The least you could have done is give me a call. It's not like you didn't check your messages."

I began stripping away my makeup.

"How do you know I checked my messages?"

Dandre was standing behind me again.

"Because. You always check your messages. Why should today be any different?"

"Well, I didn't check my messages today."

He sighed loudly and sat down in a chair just behind me. I could still see his face quite clearly in the mirror.

"Don't lie to me, Reesy," he said in an even voice. "I haven't given you cause to, so don't lie just to be lying."

My hand froze in place, still gripping the cotton ball. I looked at his reflection.

"So now you're calling me a *liar*?"

He stared back.

"I'm not calling you anything. I'm just asking that you don't try to play me. I think you're confusing the fact that I'm openly expressive to you with weak behavior. I'm far from weak, baby. A *long* fucking ways away."

"Nobody called you weak."

"Well, I'm just setting the record straight," he replied. "If you're not gonna respect me enough to give me a courtesy call for damn near twenty-four hours, then don't bother to call me at all!"

Dandre got up and walked toward the door. When he got to it, he didn't even look back. He just pulled it open.

Damn. He was going to leave. Just like that. He wasn't playing around at all.

This was a surprise. I figured he'd indulge me. At least a little bit.

"Hey!!" I called out.

"What," he answered flatly, not even turning around.

I sat there a moment, thinking. I chewed my bottom lip.

He began to pull the door closed.

"I'm sorry!!"

The door opened back.

"What was that?"

Dandre still had his back to me.

"I said I fucked up."

Dandre walked back into the room, leaving the door open. He came back over to the chair and sat down again.

"You happy?" I smirked, this time looking into his actual face.

His expression was still the same. He shook his head.

"It's not about getting you to say you're sorry, Reesy. It's about showing each other respect."

"So I slipped. It's not like it happens all the time. You don't have to turn it into a federal crime. *Jeez.*"

"You slipped for twenty-four hours."

"So I'm sorry. Damn. Let it go."

I got up from my chair and went over to his lap. I stared into those deep brown eyes of his.

I kissed him gently, lingering against his lips.

"Kisses can't fix everything," he muttered.

"Depends on where you get 'em," I replied with a grin.

I picked up his arms and put them around me. He half-held me at first, then his embrace grew tighter.

"Don't do that to me again," he chided in a soft voice. "You had me worried for hours."

"Sorry, baby," I whispered, relieved to have gotten myself out of a potential mess.

As we sat there like that, someone passed slowly by the door, trying to look in.

I was nervous, hoping desperately that it wasn't who I expected.

It was Tamara.

She saw us embracing. She saw me see her. Dandre, noticing a diversion in my attention, looked over at her, too.

Tamara rushed away.

"Hey!!" Dandre called out.

"What's up with you?" I asked in surprise.

He patted me on the booty, trying to get me to move.

"Hold up for a minute," he insisted.

I did, and he dashed out of the room, running after her.

Well I'll be damned, I thought. *Ain't this some shit?! Right in front of my damn face!*

I stood there like that, fuming for a moment, at a loss for what to do.

It didn't take me long to react.

I stormed out of the dressing room, in search of him. He and Tamara were standing in the hallway, talking. He had his arm around her. Both of them were grinning.

I walked up to the two of them, my face riddled with anger.

"What's going on here?" I demanded.

"Reesy, you didn't tell me Tamara was in the show!" Dandre exclaimed.

"I didn't know I needed to make an announcement," I answered sharply. "Besides, you come here damn near every night. You've seen her before!"

"Baby," he grinned, "you know I can't see past you. You get all my attention."

Tamara clucked her tongue.

I glared at her, daring her to do it again.

"Do you *know* her?" I asked.

"Hell *yeah,* I know Tamara! I've known her since she was crawling around in dirty draws!"

Tamara cheesed at him all cute and friendly.

"Then that would be last week," I replied.

"Damn, baby!!" Dandre laughed, unaware my animosity. "That's *fucked* up!!"

Tamara ignored me.

"I was bigger than that when we first met," she declared.

"Girl, you weighed a pound wet when I first saw you! What were you, about eight? Remember? It was at that family reunion?"

"Oh yeah!" she said, laughing. "I forgot that's when I first met you. It's been so long."

I was beginning to feel like an outsider, and I wasn't having it.

"*What* family reunion?"

Dandre turned to me.

"Rick's," he replied, as though I should know this already. "Tamara is Rick's first cousin."

Whoooooooaaaaa.

I thought about it. Tamara *H.* Rick *Hodges.*

Oh snap!!

I'd never even made the connection. Hell, why would I?

An assortment of thoughts started rushing through my head. My words to Misty during our lunch at Dolce were the first to come to mind.

Good Lord. How was I going to tell her I was wrong?

"I'll be in my dressing room," I announced, turning away.

"Hold up, baby," Dandre said, grabbing my hand. "I'll walk back with you."

He turned back to Tamara.

"Does Rick know you're in the show?"

She nodded.

"Yeah," she said. "I talked to him a couple weeks ago when he was here. I hadn't seen him in a while, but since then I've called him at the office a few times."

"I wonder why he didn't tell me that he saw you," Dandre mused.

I watched Tamara now with a whole new fascination. I could

actually even see some resemblance between her and Misty's man.

"I told him not to tell anybody," she remarked. "You know my folks. They'll be calling me asking for money if they find out I got a part in a show. It ain't like I'm making a whole lot. I ain't got none to spare."

I cleared my throat. Dandre caught the hint.

"I'll check you later, Tamara. It's really good seeing you, girl!"

"Yeah, I'll see ya around," she replied, scouring his body with her eyes. *"Wit' yo' fine self."*

That last part was uttered under her breath. It was meant for only him and her.

Dandre knew I caught it.

"I appreciate the compliment," he said, putting his arm around me. "A brother's just tryna stay in shape for his lady."

I couldn't resist a smile.

We turned and walked away, leaving Tamara standing there with her tongue practically hanging out.

When we got back inside my dressing room, I shut the door.

Dandre wrapped me up in a hug. I hugged him back, choosing my words carefully.

"Baby?" I cooed.

"Yeah, sweetie?"

"Does Misty know that Tamara is Rick's cousin?"

He squeezed me tightly, kissing my cheek.

"Don't know the answer to that one, baby."

"Hmmph," I muttered absently.

Dandre led me over to the chair he had been sitting in before. He sat down in it first, and then pulled me down onto his lap, facing him.

He wrapped my arms around his waist and held me close.

"I don't think she knows," I mumbled, looking past his shoulder at the wall.

"Who, baby?" he asked, obviously not listening.

"Misty," I replied with annoyance. "She's never mentioned knowing anything about Tamara before, other than what I've told her. I don't think she knows."

"Then tell her," he insisted. "Introduce her to the girl."

Not hardly, I thought.

I sighed heavily.

I had to do something. For once, I had really put my foot in it. I had gone off on ol' Rick without due cause.

As Dandre rubbed my back and played with my braids, I tried to figure out just how I would tell her. I had to find a way to make amends.

I was wrong, and the least I could do was own up to it.

I didn't go home with Dandre. I was too tired to hang, and I didn't want to even put myself in the position to try.

After a good deal of explaining and reassurance, I begged off and took my butt home.

I just wanted to go to bed. I was whooped from that morning, which I was still not emotionally prepared to deal with, and my blood felt quite toxic from all the drinking the night before.

I took a long hot shower, called Dandre up and told him good night, crawled under the sheets, pulled the covers over my head, and fell out.

I was awakened a few hours later by a frantic knocking at my door.

I glanced over at the clock. It was 3:52 A.M.

Who the hell could it be at this hour? How'd they get in the building?

I dragged myself up from my warm, cozy bed, grabbed my thick pink chenille robe from the floor, and trudged into the living room.

"Who is it?" I mumbled, peering through the peephole. I never opened my door for people I didn't buzz in after they rang me first from downstairs.

"Me," I heard a muffled voice cry.

"Me, *who?* Stand back so I can see you!"

"Open the door, Reesy!!" the voice cried again. *"It's me!! Let me in!!"*

I unbolted the top lock, clicked off the bottom one, and opened the door.

She was standing there, looking like a wreck. Her face was tear-streaked and her hair was a mess of tangled curls.

"*Girl, come in!!*" I exclaimed, snatching her by the arm. "*What the hell happened?!*"

Once Misty stepped inside my apartment and I shut the door, she burst into hysterical tears.

"Oh, *honey!*" I whispered, pulling her close to me in a hug. "What's the matter?!"

She just stayed there, limp in my arms, her body wracked with uncontrollable sobs.

"*Misty!!*" I demanded. "Tell me what's wrong! Did Rick hit you?!"

"*Noooooooo!!!*" she whimpered.

I held her at arm's length.

"Then tell me what happened," I said softly. "What's wrong?"

Misty wiped her streaked face with both hands and wandered away from me, over to the couch.

I followed her, sitting across from her in a chair. I waited for her to speak.

It took her a few minutes. She sniffled erratically, catching her breath in gasps, like a little kid.

"We h-h-had . . . ," she sniffled and gasped, ". . . a . . . big . . . fight."

I sat back in my chair.

"What about?" I asked.

"Things . . . have . . . been . . ." She gasped and sniffled again, unable to get her words out all the way.

I got up and got her a glass of water from the kitchen. I handed it to her and sat back down.

Misty took a sip, still trying to catch her breath.

"Take your time," I said comfortingly.

She nodded and took another sip.

"Things have been . . . *strained* . . . ever since that day I talked to you."

"Um-hmmm," I mumbled, feeling a bit unnerved.

"I started accusing him of, of stuff every time he was l-l-late, or had to make a private phone call."

I kept listening. I didn't say anything.

"I stopped having sex with him."

Uh-oh. I knew that heralded problems. Misty, like me, was

definitely one to get her sex on, especially if she had a constant man nearby.

"How was he dealing with *that*?" I asked, my voice as understated as I could make it.

"He . . . he . . . he . . . ," she sobbed gasping.

She took another drink of water.

"H-h-he was very upset. He kept saying that he wasn't doing anything wrong."

"Did you believe him?"

"I didn't know wh-what to believe!" Misty cried.

I rubbed my chin, a ton of guilt sitting on my shoulders.

"So what happened tonight?"

Misty's eyes filled anew with tears.

"I told him I knew all about T-T-Tamara and what happened that night!"

Oh Lord.

"And he stood right there and told me a blatant lie!"

"What'd he say?" I whispered, almost afraid to hear the answer.

Misty was angry now.

"He said she was his *cousin*!!!" she hissed. "Like that's not the oldest lie in the freaking book!!"

"Did you tell him I told you?" I had the nerve to ask, trying to make sure I'd been kept out of the mix.

"*No!!*" she cried. "He was too busy denying it for me to get a word in at all! That's when I left!"

Although I didn't deserve it, inside, I heaved a sigh of relief.

My phone started ringing.

"Don't answer it!!" Misty shrieked hysterically. *"It's him!! He probably knows I came here!!"*

"Of course he knows you came here," I replied. "Where else would you go?"

The phone continued to ring. It was like a death knell.

She sat there on the couch, her hands shaking out of control.

It was confession time. I was scared. This bomb of a doozy would probably tear us up for real.

I let out a deep breath.

"Misty, I think that we should answer the phone."

She shook her head violently.

"*Nooo!!* I don't wanna talk to him!"

"But you owe him that much," I implored. "He's your fiancé, after all."

Misty's face was twisted with confusion.

"I don't get it! *You're* the one that told me he was a dog! Now you want me to talk to him?!"

I sat there, staring at the floor.

The phone was still ringing.

"I'm not answering it," she declared. "I don't care what you say."

I had to say something. I couldn't just keep it to myself.

"Misty," I began, looking up at her, "you need to pick up the phone." I hesitated, then, just let it out. "Tamara *is* Rick's cousin."

She stared at me, her mouth growing very small.

"But you told me you heard him—"

"I did hear him," I said, cutting her off. "It sounded like he was trying to pick her up. But I didn't know she was his cousin. Now that I know, their conversation makes sense."

Ring, ring, ring went the telephone.

I kept my eyes fixed on hers, ready to take my lumps. Her expression was a mixture of betrayal and relief.

"How do you know she's his cousin?" Misty whined. "Why didn't you call me up and tell me?"

I exhaled deeply.

"I just found out tonight. I was going to tell you. Dandre was talking to her outside my dressing room."

I saw a dark look flit across her face.

"In front of me," I stated. "He's known her since she was little. She's Rick's first cousin."

"How do you know Dandre's not just covering for Rick?" she asked, now suspicious beyond the call of duty.

"He didn't know there was anything to be covering up," I protested. "I never told him about what I heard. I only told you."

The phone hollered.

Misty still seemed in doubt.

"Think about it," I explained, "Tamara's name is listed in the playbill as Tamara H. Nobody knew what the *H* stood for, but now it makes sense."

The phone was raising holy hell.

"So you were wrong?" she asked at last.

"Yes, Misty," I replied, not trying to dress it up. "I was absolutely, *one hundred percent* wrong about your man."

Her glistening eyes narrowed at me.

"You admit this freely?"

I nodded.

"Uh-huh. In trying to look out for your best interests, seems like I almost fucked them up."

The ringing phone was on a mission.

She twisted her lips together.

"Will you admit that you *wanted* things to get fucked up between us?"

Wow. That was a tall order.

She didn't bat an eye.

I smiled weakly.

"Maybe," I mumbled.

She clucked her tongue.

"Yeah, I guess," I added quickly. "A little. I didn't want to be out here alone, by myself."

Misty shook her head, still clucking her tongue. She looked up at the ceiling, tears spilling out anew and running down her cheeks.

"You are *soooo* stupid!" she exclaimed.

"I know."

Ring!! Ring!! Ring!! Ring!!!

"When are you gonna realize that I'm not trying to leave you?"

"I'on know," I mumbled. My eyes were now wet, too. "I got a little jealous, okay? I admit it. You seemed so happy, I almost *wanted* it to go wrong."

She pressed her lips together. We both sat there like that for a few moments, with nothing but the sound of the ringing phone dominating the room.

"Don't let this happen again," she said with finality.

I moved my head rapidly, agreeing. Then I had a thought.

"But what about if I see something for real?" I asked with a certain amount of seriousness. "Do you want me to tell you, or should I just keep it to myself?"

"You'd better do your homework first," Misty replied.

Her tightly pressed lips began to form a soft smile.

"Then, if you don't tell me, I'll personally come and *kick* your ass!"

I chuckled.

"Okay. I will. I promise."

"And do you promise to start helping me with my wedding plans?" she added. "Things are getting down to the wire."

"I promise," I answered sincerely.

There was a knock at the door.

"Now, who the *hell* could that be?!" I asked, springing from my chair.

The phone had never stopped ringing.

I looked through the peephole. Again, it was dark.

I *definitely* needed to get another peephole.

"Who is it?" I demanded.

"It's Rick!!!" he bellowed. "I know Misty's there. Let me in!!"

Misty jumped up from the couch, rushing toward the door.

"Here," I said as she approached. "You let him in. I'm gonna answer the phone."

She undid the locks while I raced for the receiver.

"Hello?" I answered, slightly winded.

"Hey!! What took you so long to answer the phone?"

It was Dandre.

"I was handling some business."

"Handling some business? What *kind* of business?"

I started to say something flip, then remembered our conversation from earlier in that evening.

"Misty's over here," I said with a sigh.

"That's why I was calling. Is Rick there yet?"

I glanced over at the door. The two of them were standing there, locked in an embrace.

"Yeah, he's here."

"Good. They need to work that shit out. I can't understand why two people would start trippin', right before they're getting ready to get married."

I stood there, holding the phone, feeling like the devil in a pink robe.

"Come get me," I said.

"What?" Dandre responded.

"You heard me," I snapped. "Come get me. I'm gon' let them stay here tonight. It's too late for them to be driving back to Greenwich."

"That's a good idea," he agreed. "Okay, let me throw on some clothes. I'll be there in a minute."

I hung up the phone.

Rick and Misty were still standing in the doorway. Misty was crying, talking, and grinning, all at the same time. Rick was holding her hands like she was the last woman on earth.

Suddenly, I remembered something. I walked into the bedroom, found my purse on the dresser, opened my wallet, and pulled out some money.

I went back into the living room.

"You guys come over here and sit down," I said.

They glanced at me, all starry-eyed and euphoric. Rick led Misty by the hand, over to the couch. When she sat down, I held out two twenty-dollar bills toward her.

"What's this for?" she asked, puzzled.

"Dolce," I answered. "I told you I was paying that day. But you wouldn't take my money."

"Reesy, please," Misty sighed, pushing the money away.

"Take it," I insisted. "Consider it hush money," I added with a smile.

Rick looked at her.

"Hush money for what?" he probed.

Misty's mouth twisted into a crooked smile as she cut her eyes at me.

"Nothing really," she mumbled. "It's more like a penalty fee for an honest mistake."

"Oh," he replied, rubbing the back of her hand.

I was quite weary.

"I'll be in the back for a minute," I yawned, "then Dandre's coming to pick me up. You two take my place tonight—it's much too late for you to head all the way back to Connecticut."

"Okay," they answered in unison.

I went into the bedroom and shut the door. I sat down on the edge of the bed, my head in my hands.

Boy!! What a disaster *that* almost was!! Thank God I was able to salvage it.

I really did love Misty and definitely didn't want to do anything to hurt her.

Breaking up with him, especially under false pretenses, would have really been devastating for her.

In my mind, I could still see the way Rick was clutching her hands. Misty was so lucky to have him.

I'd do anything to have somebody love me like that.

Instead, I was dealing with a man who gave great dick and fantastic toys, but was, for all intents and purposes, my mortal enemy. I had been setting him up for weeks to get him back for humiliating me. What kind of a love affair was that?

And then there was that *other* thing. But I still wasn't ready to deal with *that* just yet.

Tomorrow, I reminded myself.

And, as long as it was dark outside, tomorrow was still a day away.

Well, tomorrow came upon me, whether I was ready for it or not.

And, like Scarlett O'Hara, ready or not, I had to belly up and deal.

Helmut was waiting for me in my dressing room when I came in that evening for the show.

When I opened the door and flicked on the lights, he was sitting there, like the Ghost of Christmas Past.

"You didn't acknowledge my flowers," he said with a smile.

At the sound of his voice, I felt an unmistakable tingly throb between my legs.

Oh, hell no!! Please, Reesy, girl, *say it ain't so!!!* No *way* could my cat be aching for this . . . this *WHITE* man!!

It had to be a slip. I was just horny. My poor cat was merely responding to the fact I was feeling a little bit in heat.

He was at my dressing table, in my chair. In his hands, there was a little box wrapped in silver paper, with a little silver ribbon.

Aw, damn. What was I going to do? I couldn't leave. I had a show to go on with.

"Yesterday was hectic," I replied casually, tossing my duffel back on the floor and walking over toward him.

Helmut rose from the seat, waving his hand graciously. My cat was growing warmer by the second.

This was starting to become a very serious concern.

"Your throne, my queen," he said nobly.

"Hmmphh."

I sat down and immediately began pulling out my makeup and applying it to my face. I squirmed a little in the seat, trying my best to squash the little feline flames flickering below.

It only made matters worse.

"You can't stay in here," I announced, not bothering to look at him. "I have to get dressed."

Helmut stood there, smug and content.

"What's the big deal?" he murmured seductively. "I've already seen you naked."

Behind me, he gingerly ran his forefinger across the nape of my neck.

"And what a lovely sight it was," he added.

By now, my cat was a raging conflagration. I mean, flames were practically shooting out from under my chair.

"That was an accident," I countered in pitiful protest.

"Then it was a helluva crash," Helmut returned, bending down toward me. He kissed my neck.

"I want us to do it again, as soon as possible," he whispered.

I stopped applying my foundation, weakly shrugging him off me. I fixed my eyes on the surface of the dressing table.

On the inside, I was freaking in a big way. This was *definitely* a problem. A real problem for sure. I could *not* be attracted to this white man.

That mess just *couldn't, wouldn't,* and *didn't* fly.

"Helmut, what happened was an accident. I was drunk. Very drunk. It's *never* going to happen again."

His breath was hot against my skin. From below, I swear, I heard my kitty give a squeal.

"Sounds like someone doesn't believe you," he murmured.

My eyes grew wide. Ol' boy had obviously heard my kitty squeal, too.

"Never say *never*, Reesy," he warned tauntingly. "That's a powerful word that many a person has ended up eating."

"I *never* eat my words," I stated, ignoring the fact that I had almost just ruined Misty's relationship because of that very thing. "When I say *never*, that's exactly what I mean."

Helmut chuckled. Both he and I knew that I was obviously turning into putty about this whole ordeal.

"Good," he replied. "That means I'll enjoy watching you eat crow, among other things, all the more."

He sat the silver box on my dressing table.

"A little gift for you, my dear."

"No gifts, Helmut," I refused, pushing the box away. "I think we need to keep our relationship purely professional."

"Then take it as a professional gift," he insisted, gently pushing it back.

"*No!!*" I replied sharply, helplessly. "Now, if you would, please leave so I can get dressed."

"As you like."

He left the gift on my dressing table and walked away.

"You're forgetting something," I said.

"Of course I am."

"I'm not taking your gifts, Helmut! So stop messing around!" I turned toward him.

He was nowhere to be seen. And the door had been discreetly closed behind him.

I huffed and turned back around, staring at the silver box sitting on my table.

I squirmed again in my seat.

My eyes were still fixed on the box.

I don't know *who* I was trying to fool. *Shit*, I love myself some gifts. Always have. The mere fact that I got mail with my name on it was enough to excite me.

And since I had begun spending those stipends, giving myself gifts and allowing myself to get them had become a somewhat regular, almost orgasmic, indulgence of mine.

Hell, when Dandre gave me the car, it's a wonder I didn't nut up right there on the street.

(Hmmph . . . Considering what we did in the car that night, I guess, in a way, you could say I did.)

I allowed my fingers to run over the surface of the silver wrapping.

Just because I'm taking this gift doesn't mean *I'm gon' get with him,* I thought to myself. *I didn't ask him to give me this.*

I played with the ribbon on the box. I was excited by the mystery of its contents.

I can keep it, I justified. *Helmut owes me this for that stealth fuck he slipped on my ass.*

I loosened the ribbon and tore into the gift.

It was from Tiffany's. At least, that's what it said on the box.

I lifted the lid, and gasped.

It was a dazzling diamond tennis bracelet. That bad boy had to be at least six or seven carats total weight.

"Wowwwwww!!!" I whispered.

I lifted the bracelet from the box and draped it across my left wrist. I gingerly held it in place as I fastened it.

I held up my arm to the light, blinded by the glimmer.

"I've got a problem," I mumbled to myself. "I've got a *biiiiiiig* problem."

That was a freaking understatement. I had some serious shit going on. I needed to talk to somebody about it.

I needed to talk to Misty.

Now that things were back straight with us again, I needed to bounce this nonsense off her. I knew she'd help me make heads or tails of it.

'Cause, right now, I damn sure couldn't.

What with my fiery cat and the dazzling ice dangling off my arm, I was at a loss about who I was turning into.

I'd always considered myself to be in charge of my life.

But right now, I felt like an out-of-control, materialistic, no-scruples-having hoe.

I called Misty up as soon as the show was over, and asked if she had time to see me.

"Are you all right?" she asked with concern. "It's kinda late for you to be coming out here to Greenwich."

"I'm straight," I lied. "I just need to talk."

She paused, listening for something else in my voice.

"It's nothing we can talk about on the phone?" she asked.

"I didn't say that when your ass rolled up at my crib last night!" I blurted. "Can you see me or not? I need to dump this shit *now*!"

"Then come on," Misty said. "You know I'm here for you, girl."

"All right. I'll be there in a few."

"Be careful, Reesy!" she warned. "Don't drive too fast trying to get up here. Whatever it is, just be cool and take your time."

"Yeah, right," I mumbled, and hung up the phone.

I didn't even bother to go through my usual *presto-change-o*. I didn't have time. I just grabbed my duffel bag and bit my lip as I rushed out of the side door and braved my way through that frightful alley, still in my outrageous Mimosa getup.

I just wanted to get outta there before Dandre or Helmut had a chance to find me. I could always change my clothes later at Misty and Rick's.

"So what's the matter?" Misty asked over a hot cup of coffee.

We were sitting on the bed in their room. She was in the middle of the mattress, facing me. Rick was in the den checking out the Giants game.

I was leaning back against the pillows, my feet tucked up under me. I had changed out of my costume, and was in some jeans and an oversized gray sweatshirt. I had stripped my face of any trace of makeup.

I cradled a cup of coffee damn near bigger than my whole head. Misty's was straight java. Mine had enough cognac in it to choke a cheetah.

"Girl," I said evenly, staring her straight in the eye, "I think I'm a hoe."

Misty burst out laughing, almost wasting her coffee.

"Reesy, quit playing!" she sputtered. "You almost made me scald myself!"

I kept staring at her, my gaze unwavering.

Misty wiped a touch of coffee from her leg, looking up at me, surprised that I hadn't joined in her laughter.

Her expression froze when she saw that I didn't find it funny.

"*Oh my God, girl!* You're *serious,* aren't you?"

"Yes, I am. I've never been more serious in my life."

She took a sip of coffee, her eyes peering curiously at me over the rim.

"Okay," she said, after taking a swallow, "talk to me."

I sighed and took a swig of my industrial-strength drink.

"Just what I said," I replied finally. "I think I'm a hoe. I seriously think there's something wrong my libido and, maybe, my state of mind."

"I don't understand what you're talking about, Reesy. This is the most stable I've ever seen you. I mean, you're in a serious relationship with Dandre."

"Am I?"

"What do you mean? Things aren't going well between you guys or something? I thought you two were a perfect pair."

I exhaled a gust of wind that burned my tongue as it blew out.

"*Whatever,*" I replied dismissively. "And what do you mean by *this is the most stable* you've seen me? You act like I've been acting like a hoe all along."

Misty reached over and touched my hand.

"No, baby, that's not what I mean." She had a funny little semi-smile on her face. "But you know how you always used to make me so nervous, the way you'd just go out there and pick up a hardhead in a heartbeat. Look at that guy Donovan. And remember that guy you brought back to our place that time? The one with the black booty and the Joe Boxer drawers?"

I sat there, quiet, thinking about it. She was referring to the night I got upset about all the trouble at Burch, and went out and picked up this roughneck and brought him home.

But it wasn't like he had been a total stranger. I mean, I had seen him around a time or two when Misty and I first moved to the city. We had even conversed on the casual a few times. So when the urge finally needed some closure, I just went out and tracked him down. Homeboy had long given me the digits to access him.

"Well, his booty wasn't the only thing that was black."

"*Oooh, child!*" she laughed.

Misty kept on talking as I took another sip of my *coffgnac.*

"Think about it," she said. "Since you've been here, you've

been with that guy you brought home that night, and then Donovan, and now Dandre. At least, those are the only ones I *know* about."

"That's all there've been," I countered.

"Okay," Misty replied. "And while that's not a whole heap of men, it's way more than I've been with, total, in the past five years. You've always been unihibited. I'm much too scared to be out there swinging it like that."

"Scared of what?" I mumbled, letting the *swinging it* remark go by without comment.

"AIDS," Misty exclaimed. "It's a different day and age, girl!! We've had this conversation too many times! You just don't mess around like that."

"You know I practice safe sex, and I get tested every six months."

"I know this," she agreed. "I'm not judging you. We've just always been different in that regard. You've always explored the limits of your sexuality. I've always been the conservative, uptight, *what-exactly-does-it-mean-to-be-in-the-buck* person in this friendship."

I giggled and sipped some more of my drink.

"Remember when you told me what that meant? I had no idea! I had been misusing the phrase for years. Had started plenty of conversations with *Whenever I'm in the buck . . .*"

"Misty, shut *up!*" I laughed. "Don't remind me. Besides, this ain't funny."

"*That's* what I'm saying! The fact that you like sex and know a lot about it doesn't make you a hoe. So don't even sweat it. And don't worry about Dandre. Things are gonna work out. He really loves you."

I shook my head.

"You don't even feel me," I murmured.

Misty knitted her brow.

"Obviously, I don't. Run your mouth. Tell me what's up."

I took one more swig, bracing myself for the confession.

"Dandre's not the only one I'm seeing," I admitted.

Misty was quiet. I saw a hint of disapproval in her eye.

"*I know, I know . . .*" I protested before she could speak. "You really like him. I like him, too. Sometimes I'm confused about how much I like him. I'm not *supposed* to like him."

"Why aren't you supposed to like him? That's a crazy thing to say!"

"Because of that shit he pulled at Burch."

Misty clucked her tongue.

"Damn, Reesy. I thought we were adults. I truly thought that you'd let that whole thing go."

My eyes flashed at her.

"Have you let go of what Roman did to you that time? Marrying someone else without even a *bye bitch*?"

"Yes, Reesy. I've let that go."

"Liar."

"I've moved on with my life," she insisted.

"*Whatever,*" I replied.

"So who's this other guy?"

I didn't say anything. I just dipped back into my coffee.

"*Come on!! Tell me!!*"

I lowered the cup.

"Helmut," I barely whispered.

Misty sucked in a breath of wind so deep, it's a wonder she didn't pop her stitches. Her eyes were bugged clean outta her head.

"There's something wrong with me, ain't it?" I asked.

Misty was turning blue, she was holding her breath so tight.

"Girl, *answer* me!!" I cried, shoving her on the arm. "You're making me feel worse than I already do, looking at me like that!!"

She exhaled and stared at me like I was crazy.

"*Girl!!*" she whispered. "The show's backer?! The *white* guy?! Oh no, ma'am, not *you*!!! Not Miss *Welcome-to-the-Revolution*!! I can't freaking believe this!!"

"Stop it, Misty," I pleaded.

"Are you sure this is *you*?" She felt my forehead, then rapped it with her knuckles. "Are you sure you're not Reesy's doppelganger?"

"What the fuck is *that*?!" I exclaimed.

"An evil twin."

"Hmmph!" I grunted. "Shit. The way I've been acting these days, I'm beginning to wonder about that my damn self!"

Misty sat her cup of coffee on the nightstand beside her. I took another big gulp of mine. Bump that fact that I had, by this point, singed off nearly all my taste buds in the process. I handed her my empty cup and she placed it alongside hers.

"Look at this," I said.

I pulled up the sleeve on my left arm and showed her the bracelet. I'd had the sweatshirt pulled down over it, hiding it from plain view.

"Don't tell me he gave you that, girl!" she exclaimed, grabbing my wrist and ogling the ice.

She spun the bracelet around.

"Girl, this aint' no *joke*! How could you take this from him?"

I shrugged indifferently.

Misty pressed her lips together.

"Now, you *know* that nuthin' is for free," she warned.

"I didn't ask him to give it to me," I replied.

"But still," she countered, "you took it. And possession is nine-tenths of the law, baby."

I sucked my teeth and clucked my tongue dismissively.

"Does Dandre know?" she asked.

I shook my head, reaching behind me for one of the pillows. I wrapped my arms around it, suddenly feeling alone and insecure.

"Reesy," she said quietly. "Don't hurt him, please. He's a really nice guy. He's in love with you."

"He hasn't told me that. And I'm not planning on hurting him."

How I managed *that* one with a straight face, I'll never know.

She leaned back against the remaining pillows beside me.

"So what you gonna do? Mildew or barbecue?"

Another obvious *Rickism* slipping into her conversation. I shrugged.

"I'm thinking about maybe going to see a shrink. I think that maybe I've got sex issues or something. You know. Some kinda power or control thing. Maybe nymphomania."

"You'd go to a psychiatrist?"

"I'on know. I don't want to. Maybe. *Yeah,* I guess. I never really believed in that shit. And black people ain't really ones to go running to no head doctors to be talkin' shit out, ya know? We're problem-solvers, not whiners."

"That's good in theory, Reesy," Misty said, "but the truth of the matter is, sometimes you *do* need someone with medical expertise to help you work your way through stuff. Ain't nuthin' wrong with that."

"You say that like you've been to one," I said.

Misty nodded.

"I have."

Now, *that* shut me straight up. Ol' girl had actually been holding back something from me.

"Let's work through this together," Misty said, holding my hand. "Just keep the lines open and talk to me. I'll help you. It would kill you to go to a shrink. You're *definitely* not the type."

"You're right."

"And Reesy . . ."

"What?" I asked, feeling silly for even being in such a fucked-up situation.

"You're . . . not . . . a . . . hoe," Misty said dramatically.

"You just play one on TV!" she threw in with a laugh.

"Bitch!" I shrieked, and smacked her with the pillow.

We fought and threw pillows until we ended up in a giggling heap, relieved to have each other to dump our burdens on.

I spent the night at Misty and Rick's, borrowed some of her clothes, and the next morning she and I went out shopping for wedding stuff.

I had to give it to her. She had everything in order. The hall was lined up. The dresses were all made. Her wedding dress was bought, and the cake had been ordered.

It was going to be a pink and gray wedding. Misty had seven bridesmaids, our line sistahs from when we pledged back in college.

Misty was the type who kept up with everybody.

I, personally, had no idea where a number of folks had gone after graduation. I stayed in touch regularly with three of my line sistahs, but had long lost track of the other four.

Shoot, half the time, I barely knew where I was my damn self.

Misty joined the graduate chapters in each city she lived in. I, however, was always too scattered to join anything more than a candid conversation.

But when we were in school, my sorority had played a major role in my maturation. I learned so many things from my sisters. They were my family away from home.

Me and my sorority sisters forged a tightness and love that, even though I'd lost touch with some, was there for the long haul despite the passage of time. If I saw them tomorrow, I knew we could pick things up right where we had left off.

We stopped by the caterer's.

Misty and Rick were getting married in Mount Vernon, where he was born and raised. His family still lived there. He and Misty were getting hitched in the neighborhood church.

"What denomination is Rick?" I asked, flipping through a pricing book of all the different catering plans a person could get for a reception. There was the fifty-dollar-per-head deal. The sixty-dollar-per-head deal. The seventy-dollar-per-head deal.

"He's a Baptist," Misty answered absently as she wrote out a check. "But he said they never really went to church when he was growing up. His folks just started going to this church a few years ago."

I flipped through some more pages. *Whoa.* The *eighty-dollar-per-head* deal. That meal included fried chicken, ham, and shrimp for the guests.

What a combo. It was a recipe for gastronomic disaster.

And besides, wasn't no fried chicken, ham, and shrimp dinner worth eighty dollars a head!!

Shit. For that price, you oughta get to take home the freaking plates, and at least a couple of pies!!

The name of the catering company was Soulful Savorings. I kept looking for things on the menu that could justify the prices they were charging.

I remember shopping with Grandma for some of the things they listed. Like greens. Greens were dirt cheap. A dollar, dollar-fifty a bundle, at most. And fried chicken didn't cost *anything* to make.

But Soulful Savorings had themselves a little racket going. For fifty bucks a head, you got the base meal: fried chicken (dark meat only), a side of mustards (the funkiest, least-liked greens of all), yellow rice, and cornbread. No dessert was included. And the tea was unsweetened.

They knew *doggone well* nobody wasn't going to want to serve their guests no dark meat chicken and mustard greens. Most people just naturally gravitated to the next level up. The sixty-bucker.

It had candied yams instead of yellow rice, which was better, but no cigar. And, of course, those stankin'-azz mustards were still hanging around on the plate.

For seventy bucks a pop, you got fried chicken (mixed), collards (the best), macaroni and cheese (which every negro on the damn planet wanted), candied yams, and a selection of cornbread, rolls, and biscuits. The tea came sweetened or unsweetened, and each guest got a slice of sweet potato pie and a piece of peach cobbler.

Soulful Savorings should have been ashamed of themselves. With the prices they were commanding, they were flat-out *janking* people.

Misty tore the check from her checkbook and handed it to a sistah behind the counter. I continued to peruse the catalog, now totally intrigued at the endless variations on a theme it offered.

"How many people are coming to the reception?" I asked, still riffling through pages.

"A hundred and sixty have RSVP'd," she answered, putting her checkbook back in her purse.

"A hundred and sixty?!" I exclaimed, looking up at her. "Which package are you getting?"

"The one for seventy dollars a head," Misty replied.

"That's eleven thousand two hundred bucks!!" I exclaimed.

"I know how much it is, Rain Man, thank you," Misty said with a gritted-tooth smile. She cut her eyes in embarrassment at the sistah behind the counter.

Sistah was a petite li'l brown thang with short curly hair. She was immaculately groomed, down to every last detail. Her makeup had a lacquer finish, and her lipstick was a fiery red shellac that, if you stood in just the right spot, you could see your own reflection in. Face was so glossy, it looked like it had been dipped in Wesson. Somebody needed to teach sistah-girl the meaning of the word *matte*. She had on a velour pantsuit in that deep purple color you saw so much of in the winter. It was sharp. 'Cept it was a *wee* bit too early for her to be busting out with just yet.

But, despite the season, girlfriend was fly. You could tell she had doled out some paper for her getup and her look.

No wonder she's so decked out, I thought. *She's making a fortune picking folks' pockets in broad daylight.*

Misty smiled at the sistah.

And the damn customers were aiding and abetting the crime.

I shook my head and closed the book.

"You ready?" I asked.

"Let's go," Misty said to me graciously. "I'll be talking to you, Imani."

"*Hotep,* my sistahs," Imani chimed.

We were barely out the door before I was running my mouth.

"*Hotep,* my *azz!!*" I snapped. "How the hell she gon' give you that Afrocentric send-off after she just *raped* you the way she did!!!"

Misty slipped her arm through mine and rushed me toward the car.

"Girl, stop tripping! How did she *rape* me? She's just charging what any caterer would charge. And I wanted to give the business to my people."

"Yeah, Misty," I protested, "but seventy bucks a head for some damn fried chicken?! Do you know how many buckets you can buy from the Colonel for that?"

Misty burst out laughing. We were standing beside the Boxster.

"Get in the car, fool!" she giggled. "You ain't got the sense God gave Goober."

"Whoever the fuck *he* is," I mumbled, unlocking the car. "I bet Goober ain't stupid enough to buy eleven thousand dollars' worth of fried chicken, I know *that* much."

We both got in and I cranked up the car.

"All caterers charge you too much for too little," she said. "And chicken is what they specialize in."

"Then you should have gotten your mama to fry it, and saved yourself some money."

I pulled away from the curb.

"You remember my mama's chicken, right?" Misty asked, giving me a twisted little smile.

I thought about it. Then it hit me.

Mrs. Fine couldn't cook worth *nothing*. That's why Misty was always coming over to my house for Sunday dinners when we were growing up.

Her mama cooked everything on high. I mean *everything*. Bacon, chicken, rice. Actually, nothing was ever cooked, per se. It was always just kinda seared. Charred on the outside, but mostly raw on the inside.

I mean, Mrs. Fine was a nice lady. She really was. But ol' girl just didn't have time to be lingering over no meals. She had better things to do.

She'd throw some food on the stove, turn the eye up as high as it could get, and then proceed to go about her business. She actually burned up the kitchen wall that way once.

It's a wonder Misty and her dad had ever made it out alive, living in that house with her.

Misty sat there, still smirking, waiting for my answer.

"Naw, girl," I laughed. "I wanna make it outta your reception without a case of ptomaine!"

"That's what I thought," she replied. "So drive, heffah. We got other thangs to do!"

We had one more trip to make.

She had taken the day off to get stuff done. And since she was the boss, she could do whatever the heck she wanted.

Saks Fifth Avenue was the last stop on the schedule. It was an easy drive into the city from Mount Vernon.

I put the Boxster in one of those overpriced parking garages that cost damn near seventy-five dollars a day.

We sifted our way through the third floor, looking through all the designer clothes, for suitable evening wear. We made our way through each boutique.

Misty and Rick were going on a Mediterranean cruise for

their honeymoon, and she was looking for something breezy and seductive.

They were going away for a month. Some honeymoon, huh?

"So what are you going to do about Helmut?" she asked, picking through a rack of strappy dresses by Calvin Klein.

"Don't know," I mumbled, looking through the rack along with her. "Here, this one's nice."

I handed her an electric blue number with straps all across the back. It would have accentuated her figure quite nicely.

"Not my color," Misty said, dismissing the dress. "That thing has Reesy Snowden written all over it. Shop for me, not for you."

I stuck the dress back on the rack.

"So what are you going to do about Helmut?" she repeated.

Damn. Now, why was she bringing this up? I was not in the mood to talk about any of that mess, you know what I mean?

"Told you before. I don't know."

I found a ruby-colored velour dress with thin spaghetti straps.

"This is pretty. It looks like you."

Misty took it from my hand and held it a ways from her, studying it.

"Now . . . that could work. That could *definitely* work."

"It should definitely set things off if you wear it that night after you leave from the wedding."

"Ya think?" Misty asked, smiling wickedly.

"Oh yeah, honey," I laughed. "I know. That dress is *da bomb!*"

She threw it over her arm.

"Okay," she said, convinced. "I'm going to go try it on."

"Cool," I replied, lingering at the rack of dresses.

Misty walked toward the dressing rooms.

"You're not coming?" she called. "I need you to tell me how this thing looks on me."

Dang! I thought I was gon' have a minute of peace.

I knew her. Once she got in that room and got to changing, she'd begin her grilling all over again.

A razor-thin salesgirl who looked like she could use a few sandwiches let Misty into the dressing room. The girl was really pretty, with dark black hair and deep-set blue eyes. She was very tall. I guess, to some people (more than likely, the ones who hired her at Saks), she looked like a runway model.

But, child, let me tell you . . . that waif look was doing her *too* wrong. Her legs were so spindly and weak, if she happened to mess around and stumble or twist her ankle, she probably would have just crumbled up into a bundle of bones.

It's a shame how white girls go for that starvation thang. A quick bite of chicken wouldn't have done her no harm.

I found myself a seat while Misty tried on the dress. Maybe she would just slip into it and not go into her usual mode.

She was quiet for a few. Cool.

I closed my eyes, letting my body sink into the cushy chair outside the all-beige velvet dressing room.

What was I going to do? I hadn't seen Dandre all day, and I had dipped on him last night before he could even get a chance to see me backstage after the show.

Damn. I couldn't just avoid him forever.

"So what you gon' do about Dandre?" her psychic behind hollered. "You can't just string him along, you know."

I sighed. I wasn't really ready to be trying to solve my problems out loud. Especially not in no department store.

"Ixnay, IstyMay," I hissed. "Why you tryna air my business all up in this big-ass store?"

"My bad, girl," Misty said in a softer tone. "But I'm worried about you. This is a bit of a mess you got yourself in."

Her voice was muffled momentarily as she pulled her top over her head. But that didn't stop her from trying to talk.

"I still can't believe you did it with him!" she whispered.

It was such a loud whisper, she may as well have just said it straight out.

"I can't believe I did it either," I replied, keeping my eyes closed. I rubbed my temples with my forefingers.

I could hear Misty in there, sliding into the dress. She was still running her mouth.

"So? Was he good?" she asked.

"What?!"

"Girl . . . you hear me! Was he, you know, good? How big was his . . . um . . . thang . . . ?"

"Just hush, okay? We'll talk about it some other time. I'm not feelin' up to it right now."

I heard her squirming around.

"All right. But I thought I was supposed to be your shrink. How you gon' let this out if you won't let me in?"

"Quit trippin'," I replied. "I'ma let you in. I just don't think it's appropriate in a department store. And what's taking you so damn long?"

"Wait a second. There's a hook on here on something. I'm trying to fasten it. Give me . . . one second."

I blew air out of my mouth and leaned my head against the back of the chair.

"Honey!!!" a woman's voice called loudly. "Honey!!! It fits me real good!!! Come over here and see!!!"

I opened my eyes, annoyed at the interuption. It was coming from the dressing room next to Misty's.

A fair-skinned sistah walked out, wearing a sequined black mini-dress.

Now see there!!! Misty had been right next door, blabbing all my business, calling out names and everything!! For all I knew, homegirl could have been a friend of Dandre's!!!

"Is that you, Reesy?" Misty whispered.

"No. Hurrup."

"Honey!!!" the woman called again. "Honey, where you at?!"

Now this sistah looked familiar to me. Where did I know her from?

"Honey!!! Roman!!! Where you at?!"

"Chill out, baby," I heard a deep voice answer. "I'm right outside checking out these dresses."

He held one in his hand. The exact same one Misty was trying on.

"This would look good on you," he said, grinning, walking over toward her and stopping beside me.

He looked down and pleasantly nodded my way.

He was a tall man with a rich chocolate complexion. Was nice and buff.

Suddenly, it all became clear.

"Roman!!" the woman exclaimed. "That color's too red for me!! Red against red don't look right!!"

"Baby, you know damn well you'd look good in this! That's how I like my women. Ain't nuthin' but redbones for me!"

He glanced down at me and winked. I guess that was supposed to make me feel good, since I was considered a redbone, too.

The woman cut her eyes at me. I knew she didn't recognize me. But I damn shole recognized her. I wondered how long it would take for the rest to occur.

"Roman, quit playing!! Ain't no *other* women!! You are *locked down and married*." She glanced over at me again. "So don't you even be tryin' to front!!"

In my head, I silently counted backward from ten. If it didn't happen by then, well, *dammit,* I was going to take over.

Nine . . . eight . . . seven . . . six . . . CLICK!!!

The dressing room door opened and Misty walked out. She had the dress on. It hugged her every curve. Ol' girl was stunning.

Roman's jaw damn near separated from his head when he saw her.

"Roman!!" Misty sang cheerfully. *"How you doin'?!"*

She sauntered over to him and gave him a hug. She kissed him on the mouth.

What?! No crying?! No screaming?! Something was *definitely* wrong with this picture!

This was the man who had used Miss Divine for a year, then up and left and married a woman he had been engaged to the whole time.

I expected her to at least gouge his eyes out. Hit him with her shoe. Kick him in the nuts. Bite him on the cheek. Joog him with an ink pen. *Something.* Her behavior was *much* too dignified for my tastes.

Stacy, Roman's unsuspecting wife, rushed up beside him, openly indignant about watching her man get bussed on the lips right in her face. She looked Misty up and down, apparently freaked out by the fact that she had on the same dress Roman held in his hand.

"Roman, *who* is this?!"

Misty stood beside him, throwing her arm across his shoulder.

"Me and Roman go *waaaay* back," she said with a grin. "You must be Stacy."

Misty extended her hand.

Stacy seemed a little relieved.

Roman, on the other hand, was catatonic. Brother couldn't say *shit*. I mean, he didn't run, he didn't talk, he didn't do nuthin'.

He just stood there, looking like a fucking fool.

"What's your name?" Stacy asked Misty. "Honey, how does she know you?"

Roman didn't say anything. His top lip was beading up like the morning dew.

Misty kept grinning.

"I'm Misty, Stacy. What, are you guys out here on vacation?"

"No. We're just in town to see a show," Stacy said. "How do you know my man?" She gave Roman a heavy shove. "Baby, what's wrong with you?!"

His top lip was soaking wet.

"Stacy, let's go," he finally mustered up the nerve to say. He touched her on the arm.

Stacy instantly sensed that something was wrong. She violently shook his arm away.

"*No*, Roman!! Who *is* this?!"

Stacy's was the kind of mad that let you know she had gotten mad like that before. Like it happened on a regular basis.

I just leaned back in my chair and watched the fireworks fly.

I was majorly impressed with Misty. She had flipped the script on me. Caught me, *and* Roaming Roman, totally off guard.

"Tell her how you know me, baby," Misty beamed into Roman's face.

"*Get off me!!*" he declared, shrugging her arm from around his shoulder.

"*Awwwww,* now look at you!" Misty cooed. "That's not what you were saying all those nights you came to my house and fucked me silly." She looked over at Stacy. "This man's got stamina! He still setting out those all-night fuckfests? Girl, I know your cat is *too* raw!!"

Misty threw her head back and laughed.

I burst out laughing along with her.

Stacy was in a rage. She was scooching forward kinda funny, like she was getting ready to pounce on Roman. Doing a sort of semi-squat with her arms raised, like that thing Ralph Macchio did in *The Karate Kid*.

Our superthin saleswoman began to look nervous.

I couldn't blame her. Two sistahs were standing there, all g'd out in some of the best rags Saks had to offer, about to throw down.

This was some Jerry Springer shit.

This was going to be a sight to see.

"Let's go, Stacy," Roman announced in a more commanding voice.

Stacy clenched and unclenched her fists together, about to make her move.

Misty kissed Roman sloppily on the cheek and went back into the dressing room. He angrily wiped the kiss away.

Damn!! It was over before it began. I was hungry for more fire, more brimstone. I wanted to see some doggone gnashing of teeth!!

Roman and Stacy stood there, still in a face-off.

I could see Misty's feet under the door as she began slipping out of the dress. She was talking.

"Yo, Stacy!!" she called. "How was Roman's dick when y'all got married? Did it still have that big white bump on it?"

Woo-hoo!! The party was on again!

"How she know 'bout your bump?" Stacy hissed.

"Girl," Misty giggled, "he had this rising on his dick, right up underneath the head. We couldn't do much 'cause it was too sensitive, so those last few times we were together, a few days before he married you, nigga ate my cat like it was going outta style! It's a wonder y'all were able to even fuck on your wedding night."

Stacy's mouth was balled up tighter than two sphincters. I think Misty had struck a chord.

"If we don't go now," Roman threatened, "I'm leaving you right here. I don't know this fuckin' bitch!"

Misty was still in there talking.

"He's got a red spot on his left ball. Right inside a little tangle of hair. Never could understand how somebody so brown could have such a bright red mark. I know you've seen it, girl. It's right at eye level when you're . . . well, *you know*."

I burst out laughing so hard, my stomach hurt. I bent down in my chair, breathing heavily and clutching my belly.

Stacy reached over and slapped the living shit out of Roman.

"I'm tired of this muthafuckin' shit!" she cried. *"Gotdammit, Roman, I'm tired of your ass!!"*

The undernourished supermodel saleschick drew nearer.

"I'm sorry, ma'am. You're going to have to leave the store," she whispered diplomatically.

Stacy glared at her as if she wanted to rip out her lungs. I prayed she didn't hit ol' girl. The supermodel would not survive the blow.

Misty came out of the dressing room.

"You ret, girl?" she beamed.

"Yeah," I said, still laughing. "Girl, you're a mess!"

"Lying-ass hoe!" Roman spat angrily.

"You're the master of lies," Misty sneered. "I just wanna see your ass get outta *this* one!"

She covered his face with her palm and shoved his head.

It snapped back and then forward like a Rock'em Sock'em Robot.

"Punk muthafucka!" she laughed, and walked away.

I followed on the heels of my girlfriend, giddy with laughter and a new sense of regard.

I looked over my shoulder. The Sickly Supermodel was blocking Stacy, apparently trying to talk her into changing out of the dress. Stacy's fists were still clenched.

Roman stared after us, his eyes popping like a fire in a furnace.

If looks could kill, me and Misty would have been reduced to volcanic ash.

"So you're not gonna get the dress?" I asked.

Misty shook her head. Her face was radiant.

"Nah. Think I got all the wear out of it I'm gonna need!"

We walked out of the store.

"I can't believe we saw him today," I said. "Must have talked him up when we mentioned him last night."

"True dat," Misty snickered.

I put my arm around her shoulder.

"Thought you said you had gotten over what he did."

We wandered down the sidewalk, our steps peppy and brisk.

"I *am* over it, girl," she said with a grin. "As of this very second, I have freed myself from his karma. I finally got my chance to give it back to him, just the way his ass dished it out to me."

"So you think you're bad now?" I asked with a smirk.

"Naw, girl," Misty said. "I don't think that."

We turned the corner, headed a few blocks over to where I had parked the car. I caught the tone in her voice.

"Oh," I laughed, finally getting it. "But you *know* it, right?"

Misty stared straight ahead, her expression firm and confident.

"Damn skippy, I do!" she quipped.

My girl. I was mighty proud of her.

Sistah had *definitely* come a long way.

FOR WHOM THE BELLS TOLL

I was sitting at home, watching *VIBE* with the sound on mute.

I was eating a big hunk of caramel cake.

I'd gotten it earlier that evening, before I did the show, from Make My Cake over on 110th and Lenox.

Make My Cake was a bakery run by the Baylor brothers and their sister, and the desserts were mind-blowing, homemade delights, with *real* frosting, like your mama made.

(Well, *somebody's* mama. Not mine.)

I went by there at least three times a week. They had *everything*. Sweet potato cupcakes, banana pudding, chocolate chip cookies, coconut cake.

Every time I went, Dedan Baylor tempted with me a new confection. The last time I was there, he did me in with a bag full of hot, fresh cherry rugalah.

The glow of the big-screen TV glimmered off the pale beige walls of my apartment. Shadows danced on the Honeywoods, Campbells, and Bibbs that hung from the walls.

I was loungin' on my gold couch. It was deep, cushiony, and plush. I had my arms wrapped around one of the pillows and my feet were dangling over the side.

I had on an oversized Urban Hang Suite T-shirt, and had it

pulled down over my knees and tucked up under my booty. All I had on underneath was a red satin thong.

I had once again managed to dip out from the theater right after the show, pretty much unnoticed and undeterred.

Dandre had been nowhere in sight.

I knew he was mad at me. I hadn't called him the night before to tell him I was staying at Misty's. He had left me a concerned message around eleven that evening, but I hadn't answered it just yet.

He didn't bother to bombard me with phone calls. I guess he'd had his fill of that approach.

And I remembered how angry he was the last time I went a whole night without a word.

Dandre had made it very clear that if I wasn't going to respect him enough to give him a courtesy call for twenty-four hours, to not to bother to call him at all.

Well, *I didn't.*

(Although, admittedly, I knew it was a dangerous move. I was really hammering a nail into the coffin this time. I knew I had better be pretty damn sure that I was ready for him to be gone from my life.)

I knew he was frustrated with me. I also knew I was wrong.

But something in me seemed to live for the thrill of rebellion. It was an issue that I really needed to deal with, but old habits are hard to change. I was too deep in it.

Besides, a sick part of me got off on that *fuck-you-I-control-my-own-damn-destiny* kick.

(For further clarification, see my jacked-up relationship with Tyrone and Tyrene.)

Misty had called a little while before and said that Rick had talked to Dandre, and that he was really upset. He thought I was trying to play him.

Misty asked me if I was.

I, of course, *denied, denied, denied.*

(And she, of course, could see right through my twisted little lies.)

As I sat there watching Sinbad's bright, perky face fill the screen, I actually found myself missing Dandre. As much as I had to do what I had to do, he was still my nigga.

I stayed like that, transfixed, daydreaming . . . mentally trans-
posing Dandre's face over that of Sinbad's. I focused hard. I
found that if I squinched my eyes tight enough, that mess actually worked.

I laughed to myself. A sistah had issues.

No. *Ishas.*

My shit was *waaaaay* beyond just being a plain ol' problem.

Well, no matter how much squenching I sat there doing,
Dandre had to go. As much as I had grown to like him, wasn't
no changing my mind about it.

I still had to get him back for what he'd done to me at Burch.

In the face of Misty's absolution with Roman, Dandre's retri-
bution seemed even more pressing. I wanted him to feel as small
as he'd made me feel. When he did that shit to me in front of all
those people, especially Millicent, I felt like I'd been raped.

"It'll be for the best," I said to myself, playing with the buttons
on the remote. "I'on need to be too attached to him, anyway."

The phone rang.

The caller ID box was in the bedroom, but I wasn't about to
go run in there and look. I was too comfy to move. If it was
Dandre, I'd find a way to keep the conversation curt and short.

"Speak," I mumbled.

"Reesy?"

I sighed. It wasn't him.

"What's up, Helmut?"

I didn't even bother to ask how he got my phone number. He
could get it from anybody, easily. Julian, Gordon, Dreyfus.
None of them knew about what had happened between us, so
why wouldn't they give up the digits if he asked?

"How's the rest of your night been?" Helmut asked in that
suave-ass accent of his.

My eyes were fixed on the TV screen. Sinbad was bouncing
around the screen, up to his usual antics.

D'Angelo, with his wicked, talented ass, was jamming with the
band. I took the TV off mute so I could peep out his sounds.

"It's straight," I replied in an even, indifferent tone. "I'm just
chillin', watching a little TV."

"You left right after the show tonight and last night. Is everything all right with you?"

I thought I heard a roaring sound in the background. I lowered the volume on the TV.

"All is right with the world," I answered, checking out the dreads of one of the guys in the band.

I wanted dreads. I had been thinking about growing them for quite some time. But now that I had the role of Mimosa, I wondered how it would go over.

"Would you mind if I came upstairs?" Helmut asked.

Now, *that* got my attention.

"Come upstairs where?"

"Where you are. I'm in my limo outside."

I got up and rushed over to my window. I looked out.

Sure enough, there was his big-ass black stretch pulled up alongside the curb. The headlights were off.

"Why did you come over here?" I asked in a panic.

I didn't know why I was freakin' so. I think it was mostly because I was confused.

Part of me was annoyed that he had just popped up on me like that. Another part was excited by the fact that he had the balls to locate me and just arrive, unannounced, at my crib.

"To see you," Helmut said. "I have to see you. I must see you. I won't take no for an answer."

I was silent, still peering out of the window.

"I can see you from here," he remarked with quiet confidence. "I'm coming up, but I want to hear you say you want me to come first."

I scrunched my face up in response to his audacious statement.

"What makes you think that I want you to come up?" I demanded. "I didn't even ask you to come by!"

"You willed me here," he answered. "You're running from me, but you want me to follow."

Damn. That was a trip thing for him to say.

It was a trip because, as jacked up as it sounded, I think it was true.

"So go on," Helmut whispered. "Say it. Do you want me to come upstairs?"

I stood there at the window, silent, nervously shifting my weight from foot to foot.

"Reesy, do you want me to come up? Speak now, or Jarrod and I are pulling away."

I didn't say anything.

I saw the headlights flash on brightly, lighting up the street ahead.

"All right," he whispered. "I'm leaving. Go ahead, Jarrod."

The car began to pull away from the curb.

"No!!" I blurted in a quick, small voice.

"Don't leave? You want me to stay?"

I was quiet.

"Helloooo?" he teased in that quirky brogue.

"Yes," I murmured. I hesitated again, studying the shimmering diamond bracelet on my arm. "I want you to come back."

I clicked the phone off before he could say anything more.

Before I could change my mind.

I saw the car back up to the curb and the lights flick off.

The door opened and Helmut stepped out. From where I was, I could see that he held a bottle in his right hand.

He looked up toward the window. I backed away, my heart racing at what I was about to do.

I thought about Dandre with his sweet, caring brown face, and something inside me went soft.

Just as abruptly, I pushed the thought away.

I bent my head down, then slung my braids back, smoothed down my big T-shirt, and walked to the front door.

I clicked the lock and waited with the door cracked so I could listen out for the elevator and hustle him inside as quickly as I could.

I peeked out into the hallway, looking for my neighbors.

The *last* thing I needed was for them to see me let a white man into my place in the middle of the night.

I was lying in bed, my body entangled limply around Helmut's.

We had polished off a massive bottle of Dom, and bounced around that apartment and bedroom like a couple of wild hyenas.

For me, it was the excitement of something taboo and forbidden.

Verboten, as Helmut called it.

(He'd actually used the word in reference to how whites usu-

ally considered blacks as sexual partners. He had been talking
about why that very mystique had piqued his curiosity about the
darker-skinned versions of the opposite sex.

Never once did it occur to Helmut that *verboten* was exactly
what I considered him.)

I was fucked out and limp, knee-deep in a dream about me
and Dandre sitting on a beach, the foamy water lapping playfully
over our feet.

His arm was around my waist, and I was happily telling him
about what I'd just done with Helmut.

In my dream, Dandre was laughing.

Laughing like he was my best girlfriend. Laughing like I could
tell him anything, good or bad, and he'd still be right there, by
the water's edge, sitting peacefully with his arm around my waist.

The roar of the ocean was our soundtrack, and it played on in
a melody that was, at once, savage and soothing.

I felt Helmut shift around in the bed, but I was too deep into
my slumber to be consciously aware. I rolled away from him,
over to the other side. I balled up tighter and pulled the covers
over my head.

I could heard Dandre speaking in my dream so clearly.

"So you actually *fucked* him?" he asked with a grin.

"Yeah!!" I exclaimed, seeing myself with crystal clarity as well.
"Can you *believe* it? I don't know what possessed me to do it! I
think it was that *final frontier* thing. Something that I never
thought I'd ever do in my life, so it became the most obvious
thing for me to do in my life. Does that make any sense?"

We both laughed at that. The salty water lapped across our toes.

"I feel ya, baby," Dandre chuckled, "witcha silly azz. I still
love you, though."

I glanced over at his brown face, shining under the summer sun.

"Do you love me?" I questioned.

"I love you like no other. Remember, you're up in my spot. I
ain't never brought nobody here."

Happy, I leaned my head against his shoulder and we stared
out into the sea.

The roar of the ocean played on in my head, as he and I stared
at the horizon and watched the ships and seagulls pass us by.

The roar of the ocean grew stronger, and, after a while, it

began to drown out even the *caw-caw-cawing* of the seagulls overhead. We couldn't hear the murmur of the boat engines for the roaring of that sea.

We sat there like that, close together, trying to revel in the stillness. However, we were both rapidly growing annoyed at the rising frenzy of the ocean roar.

In my dream, I closed my eyes, trying to focus on just being. In the dream, I chanted a mantra.

Nam myoho renge kyo . . . nam myoho renge kyo . . . nam myoho renge . . .

. . . DAMN!!!

All right, now. That roaring ocean was getting quite outta hand. A sistah couldn't even meditate for the distraction it became.

The sound filled my ears with such chaos, growing higher and more erratic, that it forced my eyes open. I rolled over in the bed, groggy, barely functioning, and felt around for Helmut.

His spot was cold.

I could hear the noise in the living room, muted, but still roaring. The bedroom door was closed. My eyes were as weak as a newborn's. I managed to struggle up and sit on the side of the bed.

I felt like I had been asleep for a thousand years. My eyes were so cruddy, they were practically stuck together.

In fact, for all intents and purposes, I *was* still asleep. I had been sleeping so hard, it would take me at least twenty or thirty minutes, and a couple of cups of black, black coffee, to wake the hell up.

I pushed up from the bed and made my way awkwardly to the bedroom door. My eyes were so sensitive, they were barely open at all.

I groped for the doorknob and pulled the bedroom door open.

The blinding light made me squench up my eyes even tighter, and, in a stupor, I stumbled into the living room.

"Helmut?" I whispered, groping around for something concrete, like the back of the couch or a chair. *"Helmut!!"*

Whatever it was that had been roaring came to absolute silence when I walked naked into the room.

"Brrrrrrrr!" I shuddered. "It's *cold* in here! Is the door open?"

My teeth were chattering. I wrapped my arms around my torso.

"*Yes, it is,*" an angry voice declared. "Maybe if you kept your ass covered, you no-good *trick,* you wouldn't have a problem, now *would* you?!"

My heart stopped on a dime.

I'd know that voice anywhere in the world.

It was roaring all right, but it definitely wasn't the ocean.

That voice belonged to Dandre. *Oh snap!!!* How'd he get into the building?! That buzzer system, apparently, wasn't good for *shit.*

"What did you just call her?" Helmut asked.

"If I was you," Dandre snapped, "I'd shut the fuck up, white boy. Just watch your mouth. You're a breath away from a beatdown as it is."

Not surprisingly, Helmut was quiet.

I really couldn't make out either of them, because my eyes were much too weak from the champagne, the deep sleep, and the torturously bright light in the living room.

And there I was, as naked as Cooter Brown, standing right in front of Dandre. I couldn't go away. That would be an admission of shame and that I had done something wrong.

No. I had to take this like a woman.

I had to play this one out the way that it was going. Just stand there like I was in my own house, which I *was,* and act like I could be there naked with another man if I wanted to.

Which I could.

It was nobody's business but mine.

Dandre didn't have no damn papers on me.

Well . . . this was the moment I'd been waiting for. I had finally humiliated Dandre the way that he'd humiliated me.

In front of somebody white, just like he'd done to me.

Made him look like a fool.

Just like he'd done to me.

I could hear him over there breathing like a loosed bull, hurt and livid.

"I *hate* you for this, Reesy," he hissed in a deep, bitter voice. "This shit was uncalled for. You coulda just been a woman and told me to back the fuck off!"

I stood there, my arms folded tightly across my chest.

Inside, I felt a twinge of success.

So why didn't any of it feel so good?

What I was most surprised about was that he was being so calm and dignified about it. I expected him to just bust out and start whipping azz. If not mine, at least Helmut's. And I definitely expected him to give me a reason to go off.

So far, he hadn't.

"So you were trying to play me the whole time, huh?" he asked through gritted teeth. "All this time, all through everything, you were just playing me for a chump, right?"

"Apparently so," Helmut remarked sarcastically.

"What the *fuck* did you just say?!" I heard Dandre shriek.

"Do you have a hearing deficiency?" Helmut asked. "If Teresa wanted to be with you, you'd be the one in bed with her tonight, don't you think? Instead of standing here screaming like an idiot!"

I don't know if Helmut was finished talking or not.

Point is, he *was* finished talking, whether he wanted to be or not.

A bone-crushing blow landed somewhere on his jaw. I couldn't tell where, because I couldn't see it. All I could make out from where I stood was that the blow was delivered from the *black-hand* side.

And I heard an ugly popping noise that I can only guess must have been the place in Helmut's face where bone met cartilage somewhere along the jaw.

I heard Helmut stagger back a bit, slump to the floor, and quickly recover. He leaned on the back of one of the chairs and raised himself up.

"Reesy!" he demanded. "Let's call the police, *right now*! If this brute won't leave, we'll get him thrown out!"

My eyes were clearing a little.

I noticed that Helmut was totally naked.

Goodness! He looked like a big block of Philly cream cheese standing next to Dandre's brownness like that.

"She ain't got to throw me out," Dandre snapped, his voice thick with hurt. "I'm leaving. And don't worry about seeing me again, Miss Magic City. I thought you were different. Special. But I see I was wrong. Once a hoe, *always* a hoe."

Now, *that* hurt.

Dandre knew damn well it did, too, because I'd confided to him once in bed that the only thing I hated about exotic dancing was the fact that people sometimes mistakenly thought I was a prostitute.

He had assured me that he'd never believed such a thing about me. Told me that I had class.

The *lying* muthafucka. I guess it took something like this to find out how he really felt.

Fine. At least now I knew up front where I stood in his mind.

"Get the fuck out my house!!" I snarled.

I walked over to a bowl where I kept my keys. I opened my eyes as wide as I could and tried to make out the ones that went to the Boxster and his brownstone. I pried them off my keyring and threw them at him.

Dandre stepped slickly out of their way.

"Keep the car," he said coldly. "You *earned* that shit. The sex was worth it, if nothing else. And I'm changing the locks at my crib and reconfiguring the alarm system, so I don't need the house key, either."

He reached for the doorknob. I thought the door had been open, but it was only a little cracked. That was how the draft had gotten in.

"I'm audi, y'all," he said evenly. "But tell me this, white boy. What'd you give her for the sex? Clothes? Money? Jewelry? 'Cause if I was you, I wouldn't get too attached to her. She's a trick-ass bitch if there ever was one."

He snatched the door open and, without ceremony, politely walked away.

Helmut just stood there, looking a whole lot like I felt.

Stupid.

Dandre had flipped this whole thing around on me. While I was biding my time, to make him flail around in humiliation, he had walked away dignified.

I, however, was standing there naked, cold, and embarrassed once again.

Wondering *why the hell* I was smarting so much about the fact that Dandre had reduced me to a whore.

Helmut was standing there, rubbing his jaw.

"I think it might be broken," he murmured. "Who was that man to you?"

My eyes were blurry with tears. I felt like Dandre had just wiped his ass with my face.

I wanted to be by myself. The sound and thought of Helmut in the room made me want to vomit with disgust.

"I need for you to go," I announced.

"*What?!* You don't mean that, darling. You're just upset."

"Get out, Helmut," I repeated calmly, tears beginning to splash down my cheek. "Just get the fuck out *now*, before I call somebody to make you go."

"That wouldn't be a good idea, Teresa," he said just as quietly. "You forget who I am and what I can do."

"I don't give a *damn* who you are!!" I hissed. "Just get your shit and go!!!"

I ran into the bedroom and grabbed up his clothes in my arms. They were in a heap beside the bed. He had stepped out of them so fast earlier, they'd practically come off in one continuous motion, like the skin off a snake.

I flung them at him.

"Now get out!!!" I screamed.

"You're going to regret this, Teresa," Helmut warned. "You forget, I'm a starmaker *and* a starbreaker. You either do it my way, or there is *no* way, do you understand?"

I walked toward the phone. Tears were now streaking down my face, and my heart felt like it was being crushed to smithereens.

I put my hand on the receiver.

"Go now," I threatened, "or I call the police."

"What are you going to tell them?" he laughed. "That we just had a great night of wild, passionate sex, and now you want me to get out?"

"I'll make up something if you don't go," I said in the most serious tone I could muster. "I am not afraid to lie."

Helmut began to step into his clothes quickly, realizing, I think, that I was not about to play. He didn't bother to tuck the shirt inside his pants, and he casually threw his jacket over his shoulder.

"This is the dumbest thing you've ever done," he remarked.

I stood there, my hand still on the phone.

"I've done a whole lot dumber than this," I commented. "So ain't nuthin' you can say to scare me. All you can do is just raise the hell up out of my home. *Now.*"

Helmut walked out of the door, pulling it tightly closed behind him.

I expected him, too, to leave with more sound and fury than he did. Instead, his quiet, quick departure made me feel all the more stupid standing there naked and alone in the middle of my living room.

I walked over to the couch and flopped down. I had a pink and green afghan that Grandma Tyler had made for me years ago. I wrapped it around me tightly, and let the tears flow freely down my cheeks.

I sat there like that, hurting, heavy, hollow on the inside, wondering how all my shit had suddenly backfired on me, all in one abrupt night.

The telephone rang.

I jumped at it. Maybe it was Dandre.

Because, even though he had called me a hoe, a bitch, *and* a trick (and, truth be known, I couldn't really be mad at him for doing so), I still wanted to hear from him. His dismissing me that way had hurt more than anything.

I didn't want to believe that he really thought I was just some cheap hoe. He'd actually had me believing for a while that perhaps, *just perhaps,* he was really beginning to fall in love with me.

"Hello?!" I answered in a frantic tone.

"Reesy," Helmut began, "if I were you, I'd think about this. You have until tomorrow at 9 A.M. to let me know. Otherwise, you're not going to be a very popular person with your fellow castmates."

"Let you know *what*?!" I demanded. "What does what happened here tonight have to do with the show?"

"It has *everything* to do with the show," he replied in that now-diabolical accent of his. "If you and I stop seeing each other, and if I can no longer have access to you for sex, there is no more *Black Barry's Pie.* Not for Broadway, anyway. Gordon and his partner will just have to find another backer to take them there."

I sat there on the phone, seething, listening to him talk.

"So many hopes would be dashed. Gordon's. Yours. Your good friend Julian. He was most excited, I believe."

"You can't make me sleep with you," I snapped. "That's blackmail."

"Is it?" he asked derisively. "You know, perhaps it is. But I wonder how far your career would get if anyone at the *Times* or the *Village Voice* ever found out about that lovely past of yours. What's the name of that place? The Magic City, I think it was?"

My skin was beginning to flush.

"And, good Lord, the One Trick Pony in Times Square sounds like a particularly sordid place! I'd hate to have *that* leak into the paper and be the reason Gustav and I have to back out of supporting the production. After all, we have our reputations to protect."

I could barely breathe.

"How do you know about those clubs?" I whispered.

"Because I have investigators who work for me, Teresa," Helmut chuckled. "Never underestimate a man who knows what he wants. He covers all his bases, and makes sure all the exits are sealed."

I couldn't even speak anymore. I just sat there, clutching the phone, feeling everything falling down all around me.

"Nine A.M.," he repeated. "As of 9:01 A.M., the faxes will go out to the newspapers. Doesn't matter to me that this won't be big news. All I need is for it to show up in the paper at all. Just a little blurb. Something tiny. Anything that's enough to give us grounds to pull out."

I was shaking violently.

"Good night, Reesy," Helmut purred.

Before he hung up the phone, he made a loud kissing sound.

I couldn't take it. The stress of the night had become too much for me to handle.

I burst out crying. Hysterically. Uncontrollably.

How did I let things come to *this*?

I lay down on the sofa in a fetal position, pulling the afghan over my head. In the darkness, I could still see the glimmer of the tennis bracelet.

I frantically clawed at it, unfastened it, and flung it off my arm.

I flung it as far across the room as I could.

I pulled the covers back over my head and allowed myself to cry out loud underneath their shelter.

Tonight was a milestone, as milestones would go.

For the first time in nearly two decades, I had done something that I'd sworn to myself I would *never* allow to happen again.

For the first time in nearly two decades, I had totally lost control.

And cried because of a man.

I deliberately slept in the next day.

You see, I wasn't about to break down and farm myself out to Helmut like I was some kind of common tramp.

That was *not* going to be happening, no matter *how* scared I was.

I'd rather die than do some mess like that.

No. Instead, I just forced myself to sleep on through the morning, until it was practically noon. That way, what was past was past. If he was going to do it, then he had done it by now.

But if he had done it, at least he knew that I was not about to bow down to him. Reesy Snowden was not afraid of being down. Or out.

I had *been there* before, and had long mastered the art of the *done that.*

What was the hardest part of it all wasn't what would go on with the show.

As much as I loved that show and everybody in it (with the exception of one Miss Tamara H.), I knew everybody would be able to land on their feet somehow. The show might even survive.

Helmut could have very well just been bluffing.

For me, what was the hardest was staying asleep until noon.

I was taunted and tormented by a parade of dreams, all of which featured various manifestations and incarnations of Dandre Hilliard, starring as the wronged strong lover who had been trying desperately to do right by his tawdry hoe.

(Needless to say, I played the role of the tawdry hoe with an Academy Award–winning tour de force.)

When I finally allowed myself to rise, I was wringing wet with sweat. Without bothering to look at a clock, I got up and went straight to the shower, hoping desperately along the way that my phone would ring and that Dandre would be on the other end of it.

It didn't, and he wasn't.

I must have stood in that shower letting hot water course all over my frazzled nerves for more than thirty minutes. I was actually surprised the water stayed hot that long, considering how it tended to fluctuate from hot to cold at a moment's notice.

My ears were strained for the phone the entire time that I was in there.

Never once did it ring. No calls from Dandre, Helmut, or anybody.

When I finally got out of the shower, I figured it was best to just get my behind dressed and head on down to the Nexus. May as well be in the slaughterhouse when the ax wielder came to lower the boom.

Things were business-at-usual at the theater.

Julian was the first face to greet me as I walked through the doors.

"Your behind don't even work out with me no more in the mornings!" he admonished with a grin. "So what, you think you too good for me now that you the main reason this thang is going to Broadway?"

I laughed a fake, nervous laugh. My eyes avoided his.

"Oh, you too good to talk to me now, too?" Julian persisted.

He walked briskly alongside me as I beat it to my dressing room.

"Everything's cool, Julian," I answered quietly. "I've got a real bad headache, though. Plus I got some things on my mind."

"I see," he replied. "You want some Aleve? Or you gon' try to meditate it away?"

Julian was being his usual jovial self. It wasn't his fault, but a sistah was not in the mood for any of it right now.

"I just need a few minutes of peace in my dressing room, if that's all right with you," I replied.

We had stopped and were standing next to my door. Julian was searching my face for a hint of something. I was looking all around him—at the walls, the floor, anything *but* him. He had gotten to know me *much* too well. If I made eye contact with him, he would read me with a quickness.

"All right, Miss Thang," Julian said in a calmer tone. "So when's that wedding jumpin' off?"

"What wedding?" I asked, caught off guard.

Julian's brow furrowed.

"Your girlfriend, Misty's."

"Oh," I replied with relief. "Next weekend."

"Don't sound so excited," he joked, putting his hand on my arm. "Contain yourself, please! *Whose* wedding did you *think* I was talking about?"

"Misty's," I lied.

Julian cut his eyes at me.

"*Bullshit!* You're trippin' on something. You may not want to tell me what it is, but don't be trying to lie to me. This is Julian. I know there's something wrong."

"I just need some time to chill, okay? Maybe I'll talk to you about it later."

If you don't talk to me about it first, I thought.

"Cool," he said with a shrug. "Whatever. You know where I am when you need me."

I leaned over and kissed him on the cheek.

"Thanks, Julian. I love you for that."

Julian gave me a genuine smile, then narrowed his eyes suspiciously at me.

"Something's definitely up with you," he remarked, waving his finger. "I'm like a bloodhound. I'm gon' sniff that shit out. Watch me!"

"I don't doubt that you will," I mumbled, as I walked into my dressing room.

Probably much sooner than you think.

Well, that night, *Black Barry's Pie* went on as scheduled. Without a hitch.

No negative words from Gordon, no comments from Drey-fus, and definitely nothing from Julian. If anybody knew any-thing, Julian would be the first to know.

Perhaps ol' Helmut had been as full of shit as I suspected.

After the show that night, I hung around in the dressing room, hoping that Dandre would perhaps show up and have some words for me, good or bad.

By eleven, he still hadn't shown. Neither had Helmut.

(Helmut's absence was definitely a *good* thing.)

I went home and crawled up on the couch with my afghan again, chatting on the phone with Misty.

"Has Rick said anything to you?" I asked.

"Naw, girl," she said. "I'm sorry, but, sad to say, that's not our biggest priority around here right now. We got all these peo-ple coming into town for this wedding. Mama and Daddy are gonna be here tomorrow."

"Are they flying or driving?" I asked.

"Girl, you know my ol' crazy daddy won't fly. They are driv-ing all the way up here from Mississippi. They left two days ago and are making a bunch of stops along the way."

"Umph," I muttered, my attention not fully committed to what she was saying.

I was too busy wondering what must have been going on out there somewhere in Dandre's head.

"Rick's brother and his wife are coming out Wednesday from Seattle," Misty rambled.

"He's got a brother?" I asked absently. "Is he cute?"

I didn't even care as I asked the question. It just popped out of my mouth out of instinct. I didn't give a damn about no cute men.

All I wanted was my Dandre.

"Uh-huh, from the pictures I've seen. His name is Trane."

I pulled the blanket up tighter around me.

"What kind of name is that?" I sighed, just asking dumb ques-tions out of obligation.

"It's short for Coltrane. Michael Coltrane Hodges."

"Oh," I mumbled. "So what do you need me to do this week?"

"Can you help me in the mornings with some of this last-minute rushing I got to do?"

"Yeah," I said. "I don't really have to be down at the Nexus until the afternoon, anyway."

"Okay," she said, then paused for a moment. "You're scared, ain't you?"

She got my attention back with that.

"Scared about what?"

" 'Bout Dandre, and Helmut, and the fact that he might mess things up for you with the show."

"I'll be *a'ight*," I answered abruptly.

"*Reesy*. Don't try to front with me. This is scaring you to death. You can admit it. It's not like I'm gonna think any less of you for admitting that there are things in life that make you afraid."

I was quiet.

She was quiet, too, waiting for me to confess.

"*All right, then,*" she finally conceded. "You know where I am if you need my shoulder. No matter how crazy this week is, I can always squeeze in time for you."

"Thanks, girl," I sighed. "I appreciate it."

"No problem. Look, I gotta go. I got too much stuff to do here before I go to bed."

"Okay," I responded reluctantly.

I wasn't quite ready to get off the phone. I needed an encouraging voice to hear me out. If not Misty, there was no one else that I could call.

Other than Grandma Tyler. But I knew she was probably sleeping by now, and it would scare her if I called her up and woke her at this hour.

"Bye, Reesy," Misty said. "Love you girl!"

"Love you, too," I mumbled. "Hey, Misty?"

"Yeah?"

"I *am* scared."

My voice was so small, it was a dot in the wind.

"I know, girlfriend," she said. "I know."

"Okaybye," I said abruptly.

"Bye, baby."

I hung up the phone and stared at the blank TV screen.

Miserable, lonely, sad, and blue, I traipsed my pitiful behind into the bedroom.

I climbed in under the covers, pulled them over my head, and prayed to God that my sleep would be a dreamless one.

Four days passed, and *still,* all was well with *Black Barry's Pie.*

Nobody said a thing to me about Helmut pulling out, and I damn sure didn't bring up nothing about it on my own.

Dandre had erased me from his mind like a reformatted disk. He didn't call, come by, send messages through anybody, or anything.

I, of course, couldn't call him. After all, he had called me a hoe and a trick. *And* a bitch.

If I called him, that would mean I didn't respect myself, and Reesy Snowden *definitely* respected herself.

And while I would have shouted for joy if he would have just called me, I wasn't about to lose my dignity and pick up the phone for him.

The wedding rehearsal and the rehearsal dinner were scheduled for this evening, but I wasn't going to be able to go to either because I had to do the show.

Misty and I were going to practice on our own, though, earlier in the day.

All that night, during my performance on stage, my thoughts kept wandering to the fact that at that very moment, Dandre was there at the rehearsal with them, gracing the group with his handsome face.

I thought about some of my line sistahs. A number of them were in town for the wedding. They were some pretty girls. The sorors of Alpha Kappa Alpha were some beautiful, together women.

They'd be at the rehearsal party, because some were bridesmaids.

Any one of them would be a decent match for Dandre.

As I thought about this, Reesy-as-Mimosa began to sing some of the songs with a little too much pomp, venom, and circumstance. I saw a few brows go up among my cast members alongside me.

Bump *that.* They were lucky I even managed to stick it out.

I was so upset at the thought of Dandre with someone else, it took practically all I had not to storm off that stage and out the door. I was itchin' to make an appearance over at the rehearsal dinner.

Afterward, Dandre was throwing Rick a bachelor party. Misty said that Dandre was inviting a lot of girls. Women that he knew long before he ever started dating me.

I was jealous of this, too. But what could I do about it? I was the one who had played him like a bad hand, and had told myself I didn't want him to begin with.

He was pretty much lost to me forever. Brother was fair game to anyone who wanted to have a shot.

As much as I tried to block that thought out, I couldn't. I knew that he'd be sleeping with one of those chicks tonight, whether it was some li'l hottie from the bachelor party or one of my line sistahs from back in the day.

Actually, though, a soror wouldn't do that. Not my line sistah. I'm sure Misty would put a buzz in their ears about the situation with me and Dandre, without revealing too much.

While I boogied away on stage, singing up a bevy of Mimosa's greatest hits, in my head I chanted a frantic mantra in hopes of some centered peace.

Nam myoho renge kyo. Nam myoho renge kyo. Nam myoho renge kyo.

Nothing. The more I chanted it, the more rampant my imagination became.

Meditation wasn't helping me at all.

I needed relief.

A sistah was missing her man something fierce.

And, in the words of Diana Ross and the Supremes, *"there ain't nuthin' I can do about it!"*

THE WEDDING BELL BLUES

I watched her as she gracefully slipped on her *full marital jacket,* ready to slide into it with an ease that she obviously had been prepping for her whole life.

I couldn't help but envy her.

She was absolutely radiant in her dress.

The bodice was satin, a pouf-sleeved, apricot-and-cream-colored delight with a plunging backline. On the poufs were tiny apricot roses done in satin. Where the plunging back formed a V, there was a beautful bouquet of cream and apricot flowers. The dress hugged her figure closely and accentuated all of her best features.

Misty was like a butterfly who had spent way too much time trapped in her cocoon, and was now ready to bust that joint and fly away to wider, more varied skies.

It's funny. I expected this, her wedding day, to be a day when she and I would be our closest. I would be there to see her realize something that I knew was a lifelong goal.

Instead, it was turning into one of the most separated times we'd ever spent together.

I spent most of the morning gathering up the bridesmaids.

It was good to see so many familiar faces again. The dresses were soft pink tea-length numbers that clung to the waist, then flared out into a classic, clean A-line.

"Wow, Peggy, you look fantastic!" I exclaimed.

Peggy had been number three on our pledge line. She was slender and graceful, with an angular yellow face that was very pretty and regal. Her hair was a short little tuft of curls. She came from a lot of money, and she looked every bit of it.

Dandre would like her, I thought.

"What about me?" Shawnee asked. "Is my dress on right? The back feels kinda funny."

I helped her adjust her dress. Shawnee had been a cheerleader in college. Some eleven years later, she still looked like one.

I'll bet he'd probably like her, too.

Once I finally made sure everyone's dress fit just right, I stuffed the girls into the white limos that Misty had rented. I wanted to make sure they were at the church with plenty of time to spare.

The groomsmen were already there. They'd been there for at least a solid hour. Guys were nowhere near as troublesome as women about getting dressed.

They just slipped into their tuxes, brushed their teeth, and they were done.

Already, I was exhausted.

If I didn't know it then, I damn sure knew it now. The term *maid of honor* wasn't necessarily some lofty privilege. The word *maid* should have been the giveaway. What it basically translated into was *honorary grunt.*

It seemed like a compliment of the highest order to be bestowed with, but when it got right down to it, you were your homegirl's pack mule. Someone to shoulder all the burdens so the bride could make it through the whole experience with as little stress as possible.

After I got the bridesmaids in order, I was sent off to check on getting more ice (I'd thought that was the two-million-dollar-a-plate caterer's job), chase down a blow dryer, and look for some cement glue for one of the bridesmaids' heels that fell off.

It was some of the most frustrating work I'd ever done.

The wedding was slated for noon.

By 11:45, I was almost as nervous as the bride herself.

"Reesy," Misty smiled, holding my hand, "you look great. I couldn't have picked a better, more appropriate dress."

I studied myself in the full-length mirror. I did look good.

The pale pink, floor-length gown was cut asymetrically, with one shoulder bare. The satin material made a rustling sound when I moved.

"We've got to get you outta here and over to the church," I said. "It's almost 11:50 A.M., and that's at least a five-minute ride. We don't want you to pull up at the church too early or too late."

"I'm a little nervous, girl," Misty whispered, clutching my hands.

"That's normal. If you weren't nervous, then I'd have cause to be concerned."

"Thanks, Reesy. For being so strong and supportive of me."

I gave her a warm hug and a squeeze.

"Now, get out there and get in that limo!! You're starting to make me nervous for real!!"

I wasn't aware that I would be walking down the aisle with Dandre as a part of the bridal procession.

We were required to walk arm and arm with each other.

For me, just being near him again was enough to make my heart soar.

Dandre held on to my arm like it could have been attached to anybody. Like it *wasn't* attached to anybody.

I marched alongside him, step by step, listening for the beat of his heart, a grunting noise, *something* to indicate that he cared.

I got no signs from him.

Once we made it up to the altar, he broke away from me and moved to the side, planting himself to the far right of Rick, who cut his eyes at me real quick, then just as quickly looked away.

I knew that Rick had already come to a conclusion about me. As much as Misty insisted that he was staying out of whatever it was that was going on between me and Dandre, I knew he wasn't.

How could he?

Dandre had been his boy for almost as long as Misty had been my girl. When you have a friendship that spans that amount of time, at some point it transcends the ordinary and turns into a love that is amost identical to that of family concern.

I knew Dandre had talked about me to Rick, and that Rick had offered him advice.

But it would be *crazy* of me to think that advice included him telling Dandre to give me another chance.

I mean, what brother would encourage his best friend to get back together with a woman he'd caught naked with a white man?

Shoot, with *any* man, for that matter!!

Brothers didn't play when it came to that mess, and I can't say as I blame them on that one either. I had zero tolerance when it came to infidelity.

So why wasn't I able to apply my standards to myself?

If I'd walked in on Dandre butt-nekked with a white girl, I'm sure Misty would have encouraged me to get away from him as fast as I could.

Not that I would have needed her advice, if I'd caught Dandre in some mess like that.

He woulda been missing a testicle. I woulda bagged one-a dem bad boys as a souvenir, that's for sure. I woulda fucked up his shit sumthin' lovely.

Then I would have treated him like the kryptonite that he was, and stayed as far away from him as a negress could get.

No *ifs,* no *ands,* no *buts* about it.

So I knew that Rick had advised him to do just as much when it came to me. And I knew that it had nuthin' to do with whether Rick liked me or not.

It was just a matter-of-fact thing that needed to be done. No question about it.

In the words of Brand Nubian . . .

"*. . . a hoe is just a hoe, and that's without no controversy . . .*"

How could I contest it? I couldn't say a damn thang in support of myself.

We stood there awkwardly, as the rest of the bridesmaids and groomsmen made their way up the aisle.

I could hear my blood rushing through my veins as I did my

damnedest to not acknowledge Dandre's presence so very near mine.

It was like trying to ignore the sun.

During high noon.

Vixen, a soror of mine that I hadn't seen in more than eight years, sang a beautiful version of Maxwell's "Whenever, Wherever, Whatever."

(That was *my* influence at work there.)

When she finished, the pianist played the first few bars of "Here Comes the Bride."

Everyone in the church rose and turned in Misty and her father's direction.

Mr. Fine was decked in a dark gray suit with a pink cummerbund. It went quite well with his dark brown skin.

Misty was so lovely, the way she floated up that aisle, her dark eyes gleaming brightly through her veil.

Rick was beaming like he was the happiest man alive. His eyes were glistening as he watched his woman waft so heavenly his way.

I'd never seen a man look that way at another woman before. I guess brother was feeling a bomb-ass kinda love. Something I might have, up to this minute, refused to believe a brother could truly feel for anybody but himself.

Once again, I was finding myself wrong about a person. Misty told me Rick was a good man. I'd been so insistent upon shooting him full of holes, that I never once looked for any of the good in him.

I cut my eyes at the ground, embarrassed at how mean-spirited my thoughts had been over the past few months. I'd misjudged so many things, and not recognized so much of the beauty that I'd been blessed to be surrounded with.

When I looked up again, Dandre's eyes and mine met briefly.

My heart danced a momentary jig. I knew he couldn't help but see the hopeful look that flitted briefly across my face.

I, in turn, saw nothing but death and indifference in his. As if I were the last person he'd ever want to be near or know. In that nanosecond of time, I was able to capture a message so odious, so loud and clear, that it would ring in my head for the rest of the day.

I looked away, over toward Misty's mom.

Mrs. Fine, a pleasantly plump little yellow woman, was there in a beautiful soft pink dress made out of chiffon. She was sitting up front in the first pew on the left, all smiles.

She was thrilled that her daughter was finally getting hitched.

Tyrone and Tyrene and Grandma Tyler had come back into town for this. They were sitting a few rows behind Mrs. Fine.

Of course, Tyrone and Tyrene's expressions were their usual stoic fare.

Grandma Tyler, however, was beaming happily.

Dandre and I were seated next to each other at the reception.

He didn't say anything to me the whole time.

I didn't attempt to make conversation. For once, I didn't know what to say.

The two of us sat there and watched Misty and Rick take their very first dance.

They danced to "Forever in My Life" by The Artist. It was an extremely popular song for weddings, but Rick was a Prince/The Artist fan from way back, and insisted that this be the song they cut their first connubial rug to.

He held Misty's waist gently and twirled her around the room, singing loudly and shamelessly to her in front of the crowd.

Misty was all teeth as she grinned at her new husband.

When the song was over, they glided back over to their seats.

"The next song is for the maid of honor and the best man," Darryl, the deejay, announced.

He played the record. The crowd let out an *oooooooooh*.

It was ". . .'Til the Cops Come Knockin'" by Maxwell.

I expected Dandre to protest, but he didn't.

He stood, pulled out my chair, took my hand, and led me out onto the dance floor.

The music flooded the room like a tidal wave.

"Didn't you dig the way I rubbed your back, girl? Wasn't it cool when first I kissed your lips?"

What kind of cruel shit was this?

Dandre held me tightly around the waist, and had his right palm pressed firmly to mine. I could feel every nerve in my body as I moved with him across the floor.

I wondered what he was thinking. His mouth was so close to my ear, I could feel his breath warming the surface of my skin.

I pressed my body closer to his, hoping to touch his soul, as well as his heart. My own heart was beating wildly beneath my flesh. I wanted Dandre to feel the effect he had on me. I wanted him to know how much I cared.

When I moved closer to him, he instinctively pulled away. He made some kind of resistant grunt and cut his eyes darkly at me.

I don't remember much more about that dance, other than the fact that I found it embarrassing.

However, I could never forget that barren look in his eye as he moved away from me with such haste.

Like there was nothing there, and nothing ever would be.

Like I had dropped a nuclear bomb on whatever it was that had once been vibrant and alive in him, and now all that remained was devastation and waste.

It made my heart grow tight.

And left me teary-eyed for what would be the rest of the day.

I must have run to the bathroom a hundred times or more during that reception.

My nerves were shot and my stomach was tor' up.

My heart was absolutely crushed at the fact that Dandre didn't want to have anything, period, to do with me anymore.

Misty and Rick sat at the head table, smiling, happy, kissing every time the guests tapped their glasses with their utensils.

They were so beautiful and natural together, that it made me feel like a fool for ever wanting to try to tear them apart.

People were on the floor, dancing up a storm. The deejay was playing a nice mixture of hip-hop, seventies old school, and new school/retro R&B.

I eased my way through the crowd and disappeared into the bathroom again.

When I finished emptying my already-exhausted innards, I went to the sink and washed my hands first, then turned off the hot water, and let the cool remain on and course over my hands.

I leaned down close to the sink and splashed some soothing water on my face. I glanced up at my reflection.

I looked so tired, so unhappy. My skin had a pallid, almost leathery hue that made me appear, as Shakespeare said, "sicklied o'er with the pale cast of thought."

So many things were changing for me. I didn't have anybody to love. I might not even have a job anymore, for all I knew, even though Helmut's threat had proved empty to date. My best friend had just moved on to another level in her life, so I had no idea how that was going to affect my relationship with her.

For Misty, she was standing on the threshold of a whole new limitless frontier.

For me, I was standing at the brink of hell, and its jaws were yawning wide, beckoning me to drop my little yellow ass on in and feel the fire.

I walked out of the bathroom, smack dab into the sound of a couple of voices that I knew quite well.

"I'm 'bout to break, dog. A nigga done had his fill."

"Why you goin' so soon? You ain't gon' stay and see us off? You done made it this far, won't you just come on and hang?"

"Naw, man. It's killing me to even sit next to her like that, you know? Sistah's straight trash. I hate her so much, I just wanna fuckin' spit in her eye."

My heart plummeted. Did a straight vertical drop. All the way down to the very bottom of my little corn-covered, barely-had-a-nail-on-it-big-enough-to-paint left pinky toe.

"You don't hate her, man," Rick said sympathetically. "You're just feeling a lotta anger right now. That's all."

I had to respect Rick for that. I really appreciated him being logical and fair. It would have been much too easy for him to dis me just to please his boy, but he didn't choose to go that route.

"I *do* hate her, man," Dandre insisted. "I showed that sistah nuthin' but love, told her all my personal shit, and gave her access to damn near everything that was me. And look at what she did. She ain't human, bruh. Wouldn't no human do some shit like that."

I heard Dandre pause.

"Naw, man. Wouldn't no human being do some shit like that. I don't know what she is, but *whatever* she turns out to be, and I *personally* think it's Satan, I don't want her sittin' next to me for one minute longer."

"I hear ya, bruh," Rick sighed. "Well, I ain't mad at cha. If you gotta go, you gotta go. I'll tell Misty. I'm sure she'll understand. You stuck here with me through the hard part, so you know you straight with me for doin' that."

"Yeah, man. You know you my nigga. I ain't gon' just be leavin' you in the lurch. *Muthafuck* a hoe."

I heard the two men embrace and pat each other on the back.

"A'ight, man," Rick said. "I'll be checkin' in with you. Maybe I'll holler at you from the ship."

"Naw, nigga. You know how much those damn ship-to-shore phone calls cost? Sometimes they're almost twenty dollars a minute! Be wit' your lady, man. You can hit me when you're back on dry land."

"But that's a month from now. You sure you gon' be a'ight? You'on need nuthin'?"

"I'm straight, dog," Dandre said. "Handle your business. You're a married man now."

"True dat," Rick chuckled. "She's beautiful, ain't she?"

"Yeah, man. Ol' Misty was a vision coming down that aisle. Treat her right. You got one-a the good ones."

"Don't I know it."

I stood there like a mute as their voices drifted away. It was as if someone had just poured a bottle of Liquid Drano down my throat and cleaned me out of everything I had inside.

From the rooter to the tooter.

Damn. He loathed me so much, he didn't even want to sit next to me.

That was some powerful hate. I knew I'd done some damage, but I had no *idea* that it had cut that deep and to that degree.

I waited a few minutes before I walked back into the room.

I saw Dandre standing next to Misty, apparently deciding to say his goodbyes to her directly.

She spotted me as I lingered around the fringes of the crowd. She gestured to the deejay to give her the mike.

It passed through a few hands until it landed her way.

"Could you turn that down for a quick minute, Darryl?" Misty asked the deejay. "I'd like to make a toast to someone in my life who's very special to me."

Darryl the deejay paused the music for a minute.

"Speech, speech!" the crowd called out.

"Riiiiiiiiiiiiiiiiiiiiiiiickkk!" some loud-ass fool somewhere in the back shouted.

"No," Misty chuckled. "This toast ain't for my baby."

The rest of the room laughed. There were a smattering of *uh-ohs*, *damn dogs*, and *so-soons* that went around the room.

"*No, no, no!*" Misty laughed. "Don't y'all be trying to start nuthin' already! I plan to spend the rest of my life toastin' this man . . ."

The men barked and pumped their fists in the air.

"Dawgggggggg!" someone yelled.

". . . as long as he spends the rest of his life toastin' *me!*" she added.

The women cheered, and a few *you go, girl*s flew around the room.

"But seriously, y'all," Misty continued. "This toast is for someone very special in my life. Someone who's been there for me through thick and thin, good and bad. And even though we fight, I still love her like a play cousin."

Everybody burst out laughing.

A smile began to creep across my face.

"No, y'all," she said. "On the real, though. This is to my girl. My sistah. My *nizigga* for life."

I couldn't *believe* she said *nizigga* with all them white people in the room. That was straight-up Rick's influence. Misty had a lot of white friends, and she was usually careful about not mixing her professional and personal diction. There were even people there from Burch.

But, now that I think about it, they probably didn't get what she meant.

"This lady's got so much love in her, if they broke her up in chunks and sprinkled her around the world, no one would ever feel lonely or unloved again. She's had my back for years."

My eyes began to fill up.

"She's fierce, loyal, and strong on every count. They just don't make 'em like Reesy Snowden anymore."

Misty smiled at me from across the room.

"So raise 'em up, y'all," she beamed. "Put 'em up high for my girl. Here's to Teresa Snowden. Ain't no love like a sistah's love, baby!!!"

Everyone had turned toward me and raised their glasses. A waiter came by and handed me one.

I raised it.

"To you, girl!!" Misty declared.

I nodded back in her direction and took a sip.

As everyone took sips of champagne, I noticed Dandre doing his best to ease out of the reception hall.

He was very quiet about it. He didn't even look back to acknowledge Misty's words. Other than me, I think the only other person who noticed him making moves to leave was Rick.

Rick glanced over my way, his expression a little sad. I guess he kinda felt for me. More than anything, though, he commiserated with his friend.

And, obviously, the *last* thing his friend wanted to be doing was toasting my skanky ass.

I needed to do something to keep from falling apart.

"May I make a toast as well?" I called out.

Misty smiled.

"Could you pass her the mike, please?" she whispered to a man standing in front of her table.

The man took the mike from her and it passed from hand to hand, until it made its way to me.

I took it and sucked in a deep breath at the same time.

I glanced around the room quickly for Dandre, but didn't see him anywhere. There was a tall, skinny brown-skinned brother now standing in the place where he had been.

I guess he was officially gone, and I was now officially unattached.

So now my man was gone. On top of that, my girl was about to bounce.

There I was, surrounded by a crowd of people, in a room thick with family and friends, and feeling lonelier than I'd ever been in my life.

My voice was small when I spoke.

"I want to make a toast to Rick and Misty. They have a love that is strong . . . a lot stronger than the naked eye could ever see, and I'm happy my girl finally found someone who can love her the way she deserves to be loved."

Misty beamed and looked over at Rick. Rick's face was a mixture of surprise and appreciation.

"Misty has been here for me through a good chunk of my life. We grew up together, went to college together, pledged together . . ."

Random *skee-wees*, my sorority's signature call, erupted around the room.

"We've had each other's back for so long," I continued, "that it's automatic. I don't know how to do anything else. She's never really realized it . . . probably because I've never really told her before, but she's truly my role model. I look up to her as a standard of excellence. I learn more and more from her with each day that passes."

Misty's hand was clasped over her mouth in surprise. I could tell from that gesture that she was about to cry.

"I-I know this is a mighty long toast . . . ," I stammered, my throat now thick with emotion, ". . . and I know I'm starting to ramble a little, but I w-w-wanted to let her know how much I love her and appreciate her for being such a strong force in my life."

I stopped to catch my breath, trying desperately not to cry.

"Miss Divine has meant more to me than she can *ever* realize. She's kept me from falling apart many a time, simply because she believed in me."

Misty was now rushing across the room. Her eyes were streaming with tears.

She threw her arms around my neck in a tight embrace.

"Girl!!" she choked. "You know I love you, right?"

"I know," I said, tears falling heavily upon my cheeks. *"I know, I know, I know . . ."*

We stood like that in the middle of the floor, my body racked with sobs, her patting my back and us rocking from side to side like we were about to be separated for life.

I was crying for a lot of reasons. For her and her happiness, for me and my pathetic state, for the loss of Dandre.

Misty knew that, and she stood there, comforting me for them all, on this—*her* wedding day.

Even on her wedding day, she was willing to deal with my drama. *Damn.*

The sorors gathered in a circle around us, preparing to sing the sorority hymn to Misty. This was a long-standing tradition that Misty had been looking forward to for years.

She was virtually oblivious to it now, so caught up was she in the emotion of our moment.

For me, it was a welcoming sight to see them surround us.

My heart was so heavy it hurt.

The sorors stood around us, holding hands and swaying.

Misty was still clutching me close. I glanced over her shoulder. I could see Dandre staring at me from across the room.

I thought he was gone. Apparently he wasn't.

The look on his face was not one of sympathy or compassion for me and what I was feeling.

It was one of flat-out disbelief. Like he thought I was the biggest actress in the world.

He turned abruptly and walked out of the reception hall.

The sorors were singing the hymn loud and strong.

"Oh, Alpha Kappa Alpha! Dear Alpha Kappa Alpha!"

Misty was now singing along with them as she held me close.

I didn't feel like joining in.

As I watched Dandre's back move further and further away, all I wanted to do was just lay down and moan.

ONE MONKEY DON'T STOP NO SHOW

Two days after Misty and Rick's wedding, the shit hit the fan.

The *Times* carried a small comment in the Arts & Leisure section. The *Village Voice* had a nasty little dishonorable mention. And the *Post* actually had the nerve to dedicate a quarter-page article to my nasty little deeds. The *Daily News* ran a photo of me as Mimosa next to their item.

It must have been a piss-poor news week in New York City, I tell ya.

As if anybody cared or gave a damn about whoever the hell Reesy Snowden was.

I sat at home in bed that morning with a stack of the papers strewn alongside me. I had been waiting, checking for days, to see if Helmut would carry out his threat. I had gotten up early this particular day and gone down to the corner newsstand to check again.

Julian was the first one to call.

I stared at the caller ID box, deciding whether to pick up the phone or not.

I may as well. I'd have to face him sooner or later.

"Hey," I said.

"Hey," he replied curtly.

"What's up?" I asked with nonchalance.

"You read the papers?"

"I seen 'em."

Julian was quiet for a minute. So was I.

"So you weren't gonna call nobody?" he said finally. "How'd all these papers find out about this?"

"Sources, I suppose."

No way could I admit that I'd been fucking Helmut. It was moot to tell anybody at this point anyway.

"Is it true?" he asked.

"S'pose it is?" I returned.

Julian sighed.

"I suspected as much. But I ain't mad at cha. Ain't none of us here no saints."

Wow. That was an unexpected comment, but it was a relief to hear.

"I got a call from Gordon a few minutes ago," he said. "Helmut and Gustav wanna back out. They don't want the association."

Hmmph! Obviously, ol' Helmut was a man of his word.

I didn't say anything in response.

"There goes our chance at Broadway anytime soon," Julian lamented. "Which is kinda fucked up, because we'd gotten all that press and hype about the show being moved to the Great White Way."

"Yeah, well. Sorry I fucked it up for y'all."

My eyes were once again filling up with tears. This was jacked up. I was way too weepy lately. I must be really wearing thin.

"So what happens now?" I sighed.

Julian's voice was so deflated and unenthused that it was painful for me to even hear him speak.

"I guess the show just goes on. Same venue, same deal."

"I see."

"There is something good that will come out of this, though," he added. "At least, I *think* it will."

"What's that?"

"The house will be packed. People who didn't know about the show will be flocking to see you after all that press."

I rubbed my forehead unconsciously.

"I don't know if I wanna meet the kind of people that are gonna be showing up just because of those articles."

"Well, Miss Thang," he replied, "money's money. We can't knock what's our bread and butter. And since we won't be moving to Broadway, we're gonna need all the press and hype that we can get."

"Yeah," I said, my voice small and pitiful. "I guess so."

"Yeah. Well, look, I gotta bounce. Me and Tonio are having lunch together."

"Okay."

There was a time when I would have asked him about how things were going with him and Tonio. There was a time when he would have told me on his own. We would have joked about Tonio and how Julian was going to leave him, but knew full well he wasn't going nowhere.

But not now. Not today.

I knew Julian wasn't mad at me. Not really. But this had stymied his career, too, not just my own. This was going to be his first time being choreographer of a Broadway show.

Now his dream was being temporarily derailed before he even had a chance to grab ahold of it.

We said our goodbyes and hung up the phone.

I decided that I wasn't going to answer any more calls.

I'd just deal with it when I got to the Nexus.

When I flipped the light on in my dressing room, Helmut was sitting there at my table.

"You still have time to change your mind," he said with a smile. "They're just stupid articles. They don't really have to change things."

"Get out," I hissed. "Just get the *fuck* outta my room before I scream and call somebody."

"That wouldn't be very smart, now would it?" he asked. "Wouldn't want to have to tell everybody the truth."

I threw my duffel bag on the floor.

"What? That I slept with you twice? One time when I was drunk? The other time when I was crazy? The people here know that I ain't down with being with nobody like you."

"That's not the truth," Helmut smirked. "The truth is, you

seduced me, and have been trying to blackmail me to keep you as the lead for weeks. But I had a replacement lined up and that pissed you off. You didn't like the fact that I didn't think you were a big enough draw for Broadway. So you've been threatening to tell my wife that we're sleeping together."

"Your *wife*?!" I shrieked.

"Yes. Everyone here's met her before. So you can't say you don't know I'm married."

"*I've* never met your wife before! You never said you had a wife, you low-life bastard! You took me to your house!!! You fucked me in your wife's bed!!!"

"Well, the people that matter have met her. So they'll know that you're lying." He chuckled to himself. "And do you really think that was my primary home I took you to? That's my love nest. It could have been your home, if you wanted."

He got up from my chair and came toward me by the door.

"But," he sighed, "I couldn't take any more of the blackmail, Reesy. And when those articles came out, that was the last straw. Gustav and I had to pull out."

Helmut was right up close to my face.

"It's a shame, because so many people associated with the show were finally going to get their big break. You've ruined it for everyone now. Well, almost. You can still change your mind."

He traced along my neck with his finger.

I spat in his face.

"Fuck you!!! Get outta here now!!!"

"So be it," he said flatly, walking away. "But you're not gonna emerge a hero out of this. You'll be the most hated woman in show biz. I'll make sure of that."

"I'd rather be hated than your whore any day!"

"Guess what?" he said with a wink. "You're already *both*."

He stepped out of my dressing room and into the hall.

I was so upset, I was shaking violently, my body almost out of control.

I stood there in the doorway, my eyes burning a hole through his back.

"Bitch," a voice behind me sneered. "You fucked up the whole show for everybody. I oughta *kick* your ass for this."

It was Tamara. She was *not* the person I needed to be seeing just then.

"C'mon, then, you so bad!!" I yelled. "I been *sick* of your tired shit for a long time!!!"

I pushed up against her, point blank in her face.

Tamara's eyes grew wide and she backed away from me.

I couldn't believe it. All those times she'd been frowning up at me, clenching and unclenching her fists, like she was ready to whoop up on some ass. All that time she'd been selling straight-up wolf tickets.

I should have kicked her ass right then for frontin' all those months.

"Get your *tired* ass out my face," I hissed, " 'fore I wear you out right here in this hall!!"

Tamara scooted out of the way, retreating around the corner in a brown blur of dust.

I stepped back inside my dressing room, closed the door, and went over to my chair to sit down.

I put my head down on the table and quietly began to cry.

My life was so damn raggedy, I couldn't even bear to face the crowd that I knew would be coming in that night.

I couldn't do it. My best bet would be to quit the show.

But that would really screw Gordon and Julian. They wouldn't have a lead, so they'd probably end up sticking Tamara up front, and shit would spiral down until there wasn't much of nothing left of *Black Barry's Pie*.

I know it was arrogant of me to think that nobody could play Mimosa like I could. But I believed quite the contrary—I was *sure* somebody out there could do it, and do it well.

I just didn't know if Gordon could financially afford that person.

And everybody knew for a fact that Tamara damn shole couldn't fill my shoes.

I began to cry harder. I couldn't see a way out. I couldn't go on stage. But I couldn't leave the show and fuck Gordon over like that, after he'd been so good to me and given me my first break to begin with.

I finally knew how Misty had felt all those times she just wanted to raise up and run away from her problems. When she moved to Atlanta that time, she was running away from a man. When we moved to New York, she was running away from the bad memory of another.

I was always so judgmental of her. But, right now, with my world tumbling down all around me, I wanted to run as far away from New York City as I could get. As much as I loved this town, there was a whole lot of shame and failure surrounding me and reminding me of my obvious shortcomings.

I closed my wet eyes tightly, keeping them pressed against my arm.

I knew I hadn't called on the Lord in a long time, but I needed Him now. More than ever.

I couldn't do this by myself. Maybe if I asked God to hold my hand, he'd feel a little sympathy for me and show me some compassion.

"Our Father, Who art in heaven . . . ," I whispered, sniffling heavily. "Hallowed be Thy name. Thy kingdom come. Thy will be done . . ."

There was a knock at my door, and then I heard it crack open.

I stopped praying and kept my head on the table. I couldn't let anyone know I was crying.

I'd just pretend like I was asleep.

"*Hey,*" a deep, familiar voice called out. "Hey!! Are you awake?"

I raised my head up and turned around.

It was Dandre.

I wanted to get up and run over to him, but I was afraid. I couldn't really make out his face, so I didn't know why he was here. Perhaps he'd come to rub it all in.

"I'm not sleeping," I answered softly. "What are you doing here?"

Dandre walked over toward me and sat down on one of the chairs behind mine.

He looked right into my face, sighing heavily.

"I saw the newspapers. That was some pretty fucked-up shit."

I blinked a few times, trying to clear the tears from my eyes so that I could read him better.

"Are you all right?" he asked, reaching over and wiping tears away from my face.

"I'm okay," I replied, shocked and suspicious. "I thought you hated me."

Dandre blew out a gust of wind that made his cheeks puff up and his chest go flat.

"I do," he answered. "I hate you more than words can say. But I don't want to see anything bad happen to you. You don't deserve this."

The tears fell fresh down my cheeks.

"Stop crying on me," he chuckled. "You know that I can't deal with this from you."

I couldn't stop. My shoulders shook uncontrollably, and I held my face in my hands.

"You're not supposed to be here," I whined. "I was really nasty to you. I tried to hurt you for what you did to me at Burch. Why are you here being nice to me now?"

"Because. I finally figured out that that's what you were probably doing," he replied. "Trying to get me back for wrongs long past. But karma's ugly like that. When you do something bad to somebody, it always comes home to roost. I never should have done what I did to you. I should have known better. I guess when I saw you with ol' boy, I got just what I deserved."

"You didn't deserve to be treated like that," I whimpered.

I kept holding my face in my hands. He reached over and took my face and lifted it up until I was looking into his eyes.

"Stop crying. Everything's going to be fine."

"No it's not. Helmut was blackmailing me. I slept with him twice, and he wanted me to keep sleeping with him, or he was going to pull out of backing the show. He's the one that leaked those stories to the papers."

I saw Dandre visibly flinch when I mentioned sleeping with Helmut.

"You know that killed me, right?" he remarked.

I nodded.

"It was like somebody just reached in and snatched my heart out. You just don't do that to a brother. Not when he's got feelings for you deep like I do. My pride and ego took a permanent hike."

"You just said *feelings like I do*?" I whispered. "You mean you still have feelings for me?"

"Don't be stupid, Reesy," he answered reproachfully. "I was too deep into you. I told you, I've never felt about anybody the way I do about you. I can't just leave you hanging in the wind."

Tears dropped from my eyes onto his hands.

"Besides . . . your girl's out on the open seas with her new husband. Who were you going to turn to for moral support?"

"Hmmph," I chuckled. "I guess in my case, it would be more like *immoral* support."

Dandre laughed. It was not a hearty laugh. In fact, it seemed almost a little pained.

"You said it, not me."

I laughed softly along with him.

"So Julian says your boy is definitely backing out of investing in the show."

"He's *not* my boy, Dandre. Please don't call him that."

"My bad," he said. "Figure of speech."

I nodded.

"Those articles he planted messed things up for everybody here," I said.

"You know, I could really hurt him up for what he tried to do to you," he offered. "I mean, the blackmail and all. I don't appreciate that shit, despite the other situation."

"Naw," I said, shaking my head. "Just leave it alone. I'll handle it on my own."

He pursed his lips together and looked away.

Neither of us said anything for a minute.

"So listen," Dandre finally said in a low voice. "I've got an idea."

"So run your mouth," I sighed. "I could use some ideas right now."

"Well, you know I got a li'l bit a paper, right?"

I chuckled.

"Yeah. I'd say so. Just a li'l bit, mind you. Not much to speak of."

"Exactly. And I invest well. Have been for years. So I got some more sitting around that could be put to real good use. Plus my pops has got a shitload of paper that he don't know what the hell to do with, and a buncha doctor friends at Howard who would probably love to get in on something like this."

I was beginning to feel where he was going. A smile of surprise was forming on my lips.

"Keep talking," I said. "You're making sense so far."

"So I say we put together a syndicate of investors and back this thang ourselves. We don't need no German money. *Black Barry's Pie* could be a shining example of black dollars in action."

I was grinning now.

"So what do you think?" he asked foolishly, still waiting for my opinion.

I flung my arms around his neck.

"Oh, Dandre, that would be perfect!!!"

He hugged me tightly, close to his chest. It felt good to be pressed up against him again.

To my surprise, though, he pried my arms free and moved himself away from me.

"So you like my suggestion?" he said, staring at me with an unreadable expression. "You think it could work?"

"Money's money," I replied, disarmed and confused. "Ain't no venue gonna say no if you got the cash to make the move. And we've got a solid rep now."

"A'ight then!!" he exclaimed, leaning forward. "I say let's do this!"

I searched his face.

"Dandre, swear to me you're not playing some kind of nasty, cruel trick to get me back for hurting you."

He looked directly into my face.

"I swear to you, I'm not playing with you, Teresa Snowden."

I looked at him long and hard. He seemed pretty genuine.

"But, *um,* I do wanna add something else," he said, clearing his throat.

"What's that?" I asked hopefully.

He leaned back in his chair and gave me a look that was firm and solid.

"I need for you to realize that this is *just* a business deal. I care about your career. You're extremely talented, and there's no reason that you shouldn't have your shot at Broadway."

I sat there, listening to him. A ball of lead dropped into my belly.

"I see my investment as a *win-win* kinda thing. The show's already popular. The people are gonna come."

I took a deep breath. Wanting to know. Not wanting to know.

"So what are you saying?"

Dandre let out a heavy, somber sigh.

"I'm saying that this is strictly business. And that's *it*. There can never be anything romantic between us again. That bridge has been burned. I can't *ever* revisit those feelings for you."

My insides turned to sawdust. My gut wrenched at his every word.

I tried to keep a straight face.

"How can you say that?" I whispered. "I said I was sorry. I realize now how much I love you. I never expected to love you, Dandre. But I do."

I reached out for him, but he leaned away, holding his palm out in a gesture for me to stop.

"Don't do this, Reesy," he implored softly, shaking his head. "Don't do it. Please, let's not do or say anything where either of us will feel like our dignity's been compromised. I think we've both had enough of that."

"You can't mean what you're saying," I half-whispered, half-whined. "I *know* you. You still love me. I know that you do."

"I didn't say I didn't," he replied. "I *do* still love you. But if you really knew me, you'd also understand that when I say I can't go back, I mean just that. When it comes to you and me, I can't *ever* entertain it again."

"Why not?!!" I woefully demanded.

"Reesy, I'm a man. When I saw you at your house . . ."

His breathing seemed strained.

". . . *Shit!!* I don't even want to conjure up the image. I really can't even talk about this."

"*No!!*" I entreated, leaning in toward him. "Tell me, please. I need to know."

Dandre's eyes were dark and hurt.

"Reesy, when I saw you standing there with that man . . . *naked* . . . a big part of me just died. Right there in your house. I can't ever get that part of me back again. *Ever.* Do you realize that?"

"I'm sorry," I whined, reaching out for him.

"No," he snapped, holding up his hand again. "It's too late for sorry, and that's not the reason why I came here to begin with."

I leaned back in my chair. Dandre kept talking.

"I'm saddened at the fact that I believed in something that was never really there. I hate to think that a part of me that was once very trusting and very much alive will never be that way again."

I began to cry. I couldn't help it. It wasn't what I wanted to do, but I couldn't stop myself.

"Reesy," he whispered, "I didn't say any of this to make you cry. I came here for something good, not for something bad."

"How could you not expect me to cry about this?"

"The time for either of us to cry has passed. It serves us no purpose to do it now. Let's just take care of business, and get this show back on the road."

I sat there whimpering. I looked away, refusing to beg him to give me another chance.

What was scary was that I *considered* begging him. I mean, that shit actually flitted through my mind for a minute.

Now, ain't *that* a blip?

Reesy, *of all people,* begging a nigga not to go!!

"So are you down with me on this investment thing?" he asked.

I nodded, still looking away.

"All right," he said, standing. "Well, I'm going to go talk to Gordon. Where can I find him around here?"

"He's probably in his office," I struggled, still looking off. "It's just down the hall."

"Cool! We're gonna get this thing rolling again. And we're gonna make a lotta money doing it!"

"Mmmm-hmmm," I mumbled, doing my best to straighten my face before I let him see it.

"Well, I'm outta here. I'll let you know how things go with Gordon, okay?"

"Okay."

I heard him moving toward the door.

I still didn't turn around.

"Reesy," he called.

"Yep."

"Turn around."

"Uh-uh."

"All right, then. You gon' be okay?"

"I'll be just fine," I replied, my voice artificially firm.

"Okay," he sighed. "Just remember, no matter what, I've always got your back. You may have hurt me, but like I said, I still care for you. And this is your dream. I want to help you make it come true."

I sat there, totally confused. I was moved by the fact that he had my back. I was devastated by the fact that I would no longer have his front.

I couldn't let him see how I was feeling. As I sat there, I did everything within my power to keep my emotions under control.

"I appreciate what you're doing," I managed.

"Well, see ya later," he said.

"Peace out," I chirped.

He closed the door behind him.

When I heard it click, I collapsed on my dressing table and sobbed hysterically.

By late that evening, Dandre had talked to Gordon and Julian, and things were once again in motion to relocate *Black Barry's Pie.*

Everybody's dreams were back on track.

Including mine, I suppose.

Dandre had swept into my life like a nightmare at Burch, and now, in matter of minutes, turned my dreams of Broadway into a reality.

I should have been happy.

Instead, I was so miserable, I was barely able to breathe.

ALLOW ME TO EXPOSE MY COLON

The show went on, as usual, only now Dandre was heavily involved.

Actually, I didn't see him very much around the theater. He was more involved from a financial standpoint, and dealt with Gordon and his partner more than anyone else.

When Helmut realized that *Black Barry's Pie* and Reesy Snowden were going to move on despite his threats, he backed off. He called me at home a few times, apologizing for being so hotheaded. He said that he had fallen for me and was driven by resentment to retaliate in some way.

Fuck *that*. He was trying to mess with my life.

I don't play that, I don't care *who* you are.

What was I talking about? What made what Helmut did to me any different from what I had done to Dandre?

I had to think about that, long and hard.

As unforgiving as Dandre was to me, I had been just as unforgiving of Helmut.

Looking at it in those terms made it easier to understand the position Dandre had taken.

That still didn't stop me from loving him, though. What we'd shared was special and real on a whole lot of levels.

What had happened between me and Helmut couldn't even compare.

Every now and then, Dandre stopped by after the show to say hi to me, and sometimes he called me at night just to give me words of praise and encouragement.

Other than that, I didn't see very much of him at all.

I don't know what he was doing with his evenings, but he wasn't spending them coming to the theater to see me like he used to do.

Misty and Rick were still out on the high seas. Probably lying up on the isle of Crete basking in the sun. They'd been gone now for almost a week and a half.

It'd be two and a half weeks before she'd even be back.

I'll bet she was so happy. I'll bet her life was so complete.

In the meantime, other than how things were going with the play, my life was as raggedy as a shredded pair of drawers.

I wasn't going out with anyone or doing anything after things fell apart with Dandre. I just went to rehearsal every day, showed up for the play every night and for matinees, and then took my ass home.

I wasn't even calling Grandma Tyler as much as I used to. I needed the moral support, but didn't feel like having the conversation that had to take place in order for me to get it.

Most nights, I just came home. I delayed going to bed as long as possible, because I'd been having terrible nightmares about Dandre with other women.

Famous, beautiful women.

The dreams taunted me, and arrived, like clockwork, within minutes after I drifted off to sleep.

So, to avoid that, I usually just stayed up and watched TV, or I got on my computer. While I was on, I'd always have my Maxwell playing in the CD-ROM.

Maxwell was my one consolation. I wrapped myself up in his music and did my damnedest to let him sing away my pain.

Sometimes I surfed the net and hung out in chat rooms. Black Voices and Net Noir on America Online were my favorite places. I'd go there, checking out what people had to say, listening in the background to the crazy conversations as they scrolled across the screen.

A few brothers tried to pop into my world, sending me instant messages wanting to know about my interests and if I liked having hot butt-naked sex until the break of dawn.

After experiencing *that* a few times, I just blocked the instant message feature on my system. I wasn't interested in getting my rap on with anybody. Hooking up with someone else was the *last* thing on my mind.

And I *certainly* wasn't interested in cybersex, to say the least. What *was* on my mind was Dandre. *All* the time.

One night, while I was on-line, I typed in his full name and did a member search to see if he had an AOL screen address. I was really just playing when I did it. Even though Dandre had a computer, he was certainly not the Internet type.

But guess what?

He *did* have a screen name.

It was *AMackNoMor.*

I looked at the profile.

It read:

> *Member Name:* Dandre Hilliard
> *Location:* New York City
> *Date of Birth:* Nunna . . .
> *Marital Status:* Single, But Officially Off the Market
> *Occupation:* Whatever I Damn Well Choose
> *Hobbies:* Pleasing my woman . . . If you saw her, you'd know why. Enjoying my life.
> *Quote:* "When I'm sad, she comes to me. With a thousand smiles she gives to me free."

The quote was the giveaway that it was him. It was from one of his favorite songs. "Little Wing" by Jimi Hendrix.

Obviously, he hadn't updated his profile since our breakup.

I sat there staring at the computer screen, eyes welling up, a big lump in my throat.

I never knew he even surfed the net enough to have an on-line membership. I guess there were a lot of things about Dandre I still had yet to learn.

Things that I'd never ever get a chance to learn.

I signed off the computer and crawled my ass to bed.

I was determined not to cry myself to sleep.

After all, I was Reesy Snowden. I didn't do the crying thing. Not for *no* man, and *no*body.

I kept chanting that to myself as I stared up at the ceiling in the darkness, the tears cutting paths down the sides of my face.

I woke up the next morning, fresh from an awful dream about Dandre announcing to me that he was now dating Robin Givens, with a bright idea.

I was going to write him a letter. Rather, send him some e-mail.

It was a way for me to express to him how I really felt, without the burden of having him interrupt me, or give me some look that would make me change my mind about what I was saying.

E-mail was easy. I could just drop my heart into it. I mean, really put myself out there, and send it on its merry way. Computers always made communicating safer. Perhaps he'd feel more comfortable talking to me in cyberspace anyway.

The cool thing about having America Online was that if the person you sent e-mail to was a member, you could check the status of when they received the mail. You could even send mail *return receipt*. That way, you'd get an e-mail informing you of exactly when the person read your mail.

I dashed over to my computer and wiggled the mouse.

The screensaver kicked off and my desktop appeared. I double-clicked America Online and signed on.

First thing I did was check my e-mail. Not that I would have any. The only person who ever wrote me was Misty, and she was gone.

I just kinda pathetically hoped that perhaps me and Dandre were cosmically feeling each other, and maybe he'd done a search for my screen name and dropped me a line.

(By the way, my screen name is *PnutButr*. That was my stage name when I was an exotic dancer. I liked it, and thought it worked well for cyberspace. But it also explained why I got so many instant messages about having hot butt-naked sex. With a name like that, comments about licking were inevitable.)

I looked at the little icon of the mailbox on my computer. The words underneath it screamed out my answer.

You Have No Mail.

Yeah. Story of my life.

I clicked on the little icon to compose mail, typed in Dandre's screen name, and tried to begin.

I didn't know how I would start, but once I did, I knew it would all just flow from there.

And I wasn't going to edit what I said. I was going to tell him I loved him, and why I acted the way I did. I'd talk about how I'd fallen for him in spite of any other intentions I may have had.

I'd spit it all out, in writing, for him to see it for himself.

I took a deep breath, and typed *Dear Dandre.*

An hour later, when I finished, my eyes were wet with tears.

That night, after the show, I signed on to AOL to see if he had gotten it.

I had some new mail, but it wasn't from him. It was the return receipt, showing me that he had read the mail at 10:15 P.M. that night.

That was cool. It was now 10:45 P.M. More than likely, he would be calling me up before the night was through.

I felt infinitely better. I was so glad that I'd decided to communicate with him that way. At least it was insurance that I was heard.

Being heard, and understood, was what mattered to me more than anything else.

I signed off the computer, flipped on the TV, and channel surfed, waiting for him to call.

Dandre was a very fair person. He was always willing to give an individual the benefit of the doubt.

I watched the news, *Mad TV,* and parts of *Saturday Night Live* and *South Park.*

I laughed at Cartman's stupid antics, and wondered what ridiculous way they'd find to kill Kenny this week.

I was happy. I'd be hearing from my baby any minute now.

The fact that I was laughing was good. Things were on their way to being right with the world.

• • •

When I woke up, it was morning.

My face was crusty, the TV was still on, and the sun was shining through my living-room windows.

I got up from the couch and checked my e-mail again.

Nothing.

I yawned and stretched, making my way back to the bedroom.

I realized something. For once, I hadn't had a bad dream about Dandre with another woman.

I smiled. That was *definitely* a good sign.

He'd call me before the day was out. I was being too hasty. What I needed to do was give him some time to think. After all, he was entitled to that much, wasn't he?

Of course he is, I thought, as I climbed into bed and drifted off to sleep.

I was mortified.

It was exactly a week since I'd sent Dandre the e-mail, and *still* I hadn't heard from him.

No phone call, no visit, no showing up at the Nexus to talk to me. No e-mail response, no acknowledgment. No *NOTHING*.

He could have at least e-mailed me back and said *Bitch, leave me alone.*

*Some*thing.

I had been checking my e-mail frantically, every morning and every night, looking for some kind of sign from him.

Not nary a peep.

I felt like a stone cold *fool* for putting myself and my emotions out there, for him to read, laugh at, print out, show to his buddies, or *God forbid,* some *other* chick.

(I didn't take the ridiculing thang too well.)

I wanted to kick myself for being stupid enough to leave a freaking paper trail directly to my heart.

My first instinct was to want to cry. But no way was I going to indulge *that* emotion again.

All I could do was just belly up. The e-mail was out there. He had it. Wasn't nuthin' I could do to change that.

All I could do was just go on with my life.

As if it never happened. As if I'd never sent it.

It was Saturday. I'd just awakened from a dream where he and Lela Rochon were having wild sex in a dark hall. He saw me staring, but just grinned and kept on bucking.

No way could I go to work today, not feeling the way that I felt. I decided to play hooky from *Black Barry's Pie.*

(Tamara could have her pitiful moment in the sun. See if I freaking cared.)

Gordon wasn't too happy about it when I called him up, but he knew how hard I worked, so he was totally accommodating.

I was tired and dragging and humiliated, but I was not going to let that get to me. This day was going to be all about *me.* I needed to spend a day just doing things to pamper myself.

I sat down, thinking, and came up with a master plan. I made a quick phone call. I already had an appointment set up for the afternoon, but I called to see if I could push it back a little.

I took a nice long, hot shower, threw on some jeans and a sweatshirt, tossed some things into a bag, and headed out into the streets.

It was early. Only about 7 A.M.

First, I went and had my braids redone at one of those African braid shops on 125th Street. The ones where you can barely get out of your damn car without the African women accosting you, begging, "Hair braided? Hair braided?"

It only took the woman four hours to do what typically took eight to ten hours back home in Florida, even in Atlanta.

The braids were so tight, my eyes were slanted. I wouldn't need them done again for at least another month.

Those African women were *nots* to be messed with.

After that, I headed over to my appointment. The one I had called and had pushed back. I had set it up a couple of weeks before. It was something I had long been wanting to do for myself.

Julian had a friend, a woman named Mina, who did spa treatments out of her brownstone in Park Slope in Brooklyn. She stayed booked up, but had called me a while back about a Saturday cancellation that she'd be able to fit me in.

What was cool about Mina was that she only took care of one customer a day.

Hell, I see why. She charged enough for it.

So I rode over to Brooklyn after I got my braids done, and let her give me a total body pampering.

I got my nails done (manicure and pedicure), my body waxed, a full massage, my brows plucked, a mud treatment—the whole shebang.

She even had this soothing aromatherapy candle burning in the room and played a CD of the ocean washing up on the shore. All this to relax me.

The scented candle was fine. But I brought my own CD. I asked her if I could have it played instead of hers.

She, of course, said yes.

(What else was she going to say? I was paying her behind $250 for the visit. I was going all out to treat myself that day.)

Can you guess what CD I gave her to play?

I'll bet you can.

I *know* what relaxes me. I wasn't even about to mess around when it came to *that*.

I was in heaven, lying facedown on the cushy massage table, a heated pad on my naked back, with a blanket thrown over it to cover me. My man Maxy was crooning to me strong.

I drifted off to sleep, totally relaxed and stress-free for the moment.

For once, it was a restful dream.

When I woke up, I was totally at peace.

When I walked out of Mina's place at dusk, I had a spring in my step, my head was clear, and I was once again the proud, cocky bitch I'd always been.

It was time to slay again.

I was feeling a little ripe.

I hopped in the Boxster and headed over to the Dean Street Cafe. It should be jumping tonight.

Might as well stay in Brooklyn since I was already there.

The Dean Street Cafe was a popular spot that was always thick with people, deep into the wee hours of the night. The food was great, and the atmosphere was pretty cool, even if it was a bit tight in there at times, what with all the people there.

I rode by. The parking was ridiculous. People were parked all up and down the street. There was no room to spare.

I drove by the restaurant slowly, looking through the window. As usual, the crowd was thick. Much too thick for me to want to contend with at the time.

I thought of another spot and whipped the car around. A place where the food was always good, and a sistah was bound to see a fine brother or five, hanging out with his boys, just getting his grub on.

I hopped back on Atlantic, zipped down the avenue a little ways, and found an empty meter in front of the restaurant.

I peeked inside.

True to form, I saw some cuties at various tables. Some were with women, some were not. And the crowd wasn't so thick that I couldn't deal.

I checked myself out in the rearview mirror.

My braids were kickin', and I was looking and feeling totally *hooked*. I had on a short leopard slip dress with my patent leather go-go boots. On my legs, I wore a pair of funky black hose. *Nuthin' but net*. My perfectly toned thighs were exposed for all the world to see.

The weather was a little brisk, but not too cold, so I had a light wool jacket, black, thrown over my shoulders, just to get me inside. Then it would immediately come off.

I'd brought the clothes with me to change into at Mina's. Just in case I felt in the mood to go out afterward.

I was glad I'd brought them. A sistah was feeling pretty darn good.

And, as I stepped out of the car and walked into Cafe Brawta, from the way the brothers' heads snapped in my direction, they were glad I'd brought them, too.

Cafe Brawta was a cool Jamaican restaurant that was one of the trendiest spots in Brooklyn.

The food was *da bomb*. Oversized decorative plates filled with healthy, delicious dishes like curried coconut shrimp with rice and peas and cabbage, jerk chicken, oxtails, and vegetarian fare. There was ginger beer, sorrell, sea moss, and an amazingly fresh fruit punch with honey in it. One sip, and it blew your mind.

There were no carbonated beverages to be found.

Nothing but pure, all-natural, good-ass eating.

I pretended to ignore all the fine brothers at first. I noticed some of the sistahs who were there with their men giving me strange looks.

"Welcome to Cafe Brawta," the bright-faced waitress greeted. "Will you be dining in, or ordering takeout?"

"I'm dining in, thank you," I answered sweetly.

"Are you meeting someone here?"

"No, I'm not," I said in a singsongy voice. "All I need is a table for one."

She gave the room a quick survey, then led me over to a table near the back, by the window.

It was right next to a table with two very attractive brothers.

I smiled my most saccharine smile, gave a quick hi, and flipped my braids back as I passed.

I noticed both their eyes in my direction as I slid into my chair.

They were waiting to see if my dress was going to ride up.

I could tell. I'd seen *that* look a million times before.

"Do you need a minute with the menu?" the waitress asked.

"No. I know what I want. Let me have the buttered shrimp with rice and peas and cabbage. And a glass of fruit punch."

She scribbled away.

"Will that be all?"

"Yes. Thank you."

She hurried off, leaving me to look around the room, starting first with the two brothers to my immediate left.

They both nodded. I quickly scanned their left hands to see if they were married, not that that was a true indicator. Brothers were always taking off their rings when they went out to hang.

Besides, they could be, as Dandre's profile said, *Single, But Officially Off the Market.*

I quickly pushed the thought of Dandre out of my head.

I didn't see any ring outlines on their fingers.

Well, there were at least two for me to pick from, for starters.

I glanced around the room. There were more brothers together at a table near the bathroom. Four of them. Hip-hop hard-cores, or at least they were trying to be, with bubble jackets (even though it was no way *near* cold enough for them yet) and skullies.

"'Zup, sexy," one of them said.

He was a cutie with a round brown face and a goatee. He looked *real* young. I wondered *how* young.

I wondered what was too young for me to mess with. I'd been out of true circulation for so long, hanging around with Dandre, that I'd forgotten my own parameters.

If he was at least twenty-three, then maybe I'd hit it. If he was any younger, I'd just have to walk away.

"Wuzzup," I nodded back.

Just as I was cheesing at him, a couple came in through the front door.

I saw them out of the corner of my eye, and I could tell that the brother was cute. I turned, full-face, to look in their direction.

He *was* cute.

He was *beyond* cute.

He was fine as *hell.* Just the kinda fine I liked.

My jaw was wide open in utter surprise.

It was *Dandre.*

Every hair on my body was standing on end.

The woman who was with him was beautiful. She was light brown with a very short haircut. She was practically bald. But her face was so pretty, she didn't even need hair.

She looked like a supermodel.

In fact, I think she was. I had a copy of *Essence* magazine at home with that very same woman smack-dab on the cover.

My chest began to heave a little as I sat at the table, unsure of what to do.

Actually, I was *not* unsure. I knew *exactly* what I *wanted* to do.

I wanted to go *off* on his ass, right there in Cafe Brawta.

The *nerve* of him, being out on the town with some bitch other than me!!!

That's why his ass wasn't answering my e-mail!!!!

They didn't see me because I was sitting back there in the corner. But it's not like Cafe Brawta was all that big. All they had to do was turn their faces just half an inch, and I'd be right there in plain view, big as day.

Dandre leaned close to her and whispered something in her ear. His hand was on her arm.

I felt acid boiling in my belly and rising up to my throat.

The woman threw her head back and giggled, like what he'd just said was the funniest fucking thing in the whole wide world.

She touched him back.

I was so full of steam, if it shot out of my behind, I would have taken off like a rocket.

I wished I had a gun. An *Uzi*. I could have shot that bitch right there on the spot and left her pulpy ass spinning in a bloody messy heap.

Stop it, Reesy, I said to myself. *It's not her fault. Don't get mad at the woman. Get mad at the man.*

Bump *that*!!!!

I wanted to *KILL* that bitch for being out with my man!!!!

Besides, he had probably showed her my e-mail. She probably knew all about my ridiculous, pitiful letter asking him to reconsider.

The waitress spoke to them for a moment, then began to lead them my way.

Dandre saw me instantly.

His face turned into stone.

I couldn't read his expression, but from the way my temples were throbbing, I knew damn well that he could read mine.

The waitress seated them at a table one over from me. The supermodel grabbed her seat first, leaving Dandre the chair that was directly facing me.

I glared at him. He looked at me blankly, then smiled and turned his attention to the *Essence* girl as she leaned forward to ask him something.

The waitress came back with my fruit punch and food.

"Excuse me," I heard Dandre say to his date, nodding in my direction. "I see someone I know. Let me go speak to her for a minute."

She turned her head and looked back at me. Her eyes narrowed a little, as if she was trying to qualify who the hell I was. I saw her lip curl into a smile.

She *did* know about my e-mail!!!!

Before he could get up and come over to me, I rose from my chair. When he saw me getting up, he sat back down.

I opened my wallet and quietly placed a wad of money on the table. I drank a quick sip of the fruit punch and walked away from the table, past him and Miss *Essence* without a word and right out of the restaurant.

By the time I got into the car, my blood was on full boil.

How could he *do* that to me? How could he just go out with another chick and be all pushed up with her like that? Apparently, what'd we had meant nothing to him for real. He had just moved on.

From one coochie to the next.

And what the hell was he doing in Cafe Brawta to begin with? What kind of ironic shit was *that*?

Dandre and I had never been to the restaurant together.

Besides, he lived all the way on the Upper West Side. He usually went to restaurants in Manhattan, claiming he wasn't feeling Brooklyn the way everybody else was these days.

Then, what that *hell* was he doing there? Tonight?

What's even wilder is that he'd never taken *me* to Cafe Brawta. I'd found out about the place on my own, one afternoon, in a quest for some good Jamaican food. Dandre knew I liked West Indian cuisine, but he had never once mentioned this joint to me.

And I *know* he had to notice the Boxster when he pulled up at the curb. The evil bastard probably rolled up to the restaurant, knowing I was in there, just to drive home his point.

(Of course, I knew that was a lie as I thought it. Dandre wasn't one to try to lord something over you. When he left you alone, he left you alone.)

Lording was *my* specialty. I was the queen of vengeance.

And look at where it had gotten me. Behind the wheel of a fancy car, all alone, with shitload of egg on my face.

What in the world ever made me send that e-mail his way?!

As I cranked up the car and went to drive off, I noticed there was a full moon in the sky.

That explained it.

Full moons were my thang. One way or another. Whenever

there was a full moon, which, obviously, was every month, something really weird and ironic always happened to me.

Always.

Without fail.

The type of weird varied. It could be something wonderful, wild, and exciting.

Conversely, it could be something so fucked up, it defied description.

Any way you look at it, irony was always involved.

Well, I guess tonight was my night for irony. And there's no need to guess which kind of weird *this* moon turned out to be.

I pulled away from the curb, heading down Atlantic, whipping a right turn at the light on Boerum Place just before it turned red, and zipping my pitiful behind toward the Brooklyn Bridge.

I don't even remember the drive uptown on the FDR. All I remember is pulling up in front of the building, being grateful that it was the weekend and the fact that I didn't have to deal with Mayor Giuliani's fucked-up alternate-side parking law, and going upstairs to my crib.

I went from front door to sleep in less than four minutes. I didn't even turn on any lights. I glided through the living room into my bedroom, along the way peeling out of my apparently-not-sexy-enough dress, kicking off my shoes, and flinging my purse down.

I slid under the covers. I pulled them tightly over my head and around my body so that no manner of light could possibly manage to get in. Secure in the darkness, I squeezed my eyes shut.

I wanted to block out the world and any thoughts of Dandre, like he'd apparently done of me. Forever.

Who needed his sorry ass anyway?

I knew the answer, as I felt myself drifting off to sleep.

I did, that's who.

I was awakened by the constant ringing of my buzzer.

I pulled the covers from over my head and glanced at the clock.

It was only 1 A.M. I was surprised at how early it was. I thought I'd been out much longer than that.

I was actually happy to be awake. I'd been having another one of those dreams.

This time, Dandre was banging Salt-n-Pepa. That's right, the *entire* group, *including* Spinderella.

That, to me, was taking it just a bit *too* far.

Perhaps if I'd slept a little longer, I would have gotten to the part where Treach from Naughty by Nature, Pepa's man, kicked Dandre's natural black ass.

That would have made the dream worthwhile, I think.

I dragged up, naked, from the bed. I blindly reached for my robe off the back of the door and slipped it on.

I rubbed my eyes. My braids were hanging all over my face. I felt like I had been asleep for a hundred years.

"Who?" I muttered, my throat scratchy.

"It's me, Reesy," the deep, familiar voice bellowed. "C'mon, buzz me in."

"What do you want?" I asked plainly.

This was so weird. I was neither happy nor angry that he'd come by. I was so tired, my emotions hadn't kicked in at all to register anything.

"I wanna talk to you. Open the door."

I pressed the buzzer.

I didn't know why. I didn't see why not.

I was standing there with the door cracked when he came up.

I didn't know what I looked like.

I didn't care.

Dandre was looking good, but what else was new?

My heart, usually prone to leaping at his sight, stayed perfectly still. I didn't know what he wanted, or why.

I was just plain numb. The night, and that damn Salt-n-Pepa scene, had been far too much for me.

He stopped in the doorway and studied my face.

"You look tired. Did I wake you?"

"Come in and shut the door behind you," I said, and walked away.

I went over to the couch and sat down. Dandre came over and sat next to me. There was about a foot of space between us.

Which was fine with me. The last thing I needed was to be crowded right now.

"Why didn't you give me a chance to come over and talk to you?" he asked.

"I wasn't in the mood."

"Oh."

"Besides," I added, "you've had plenty of chances to talk to me. You obviously weren't in too much of a rush to do it."

He looked down at the floor as he rubbed his chin.

"You're talking about your e-mail."

"What e-mail?" I denied.

"Oh, *please*, Reesy," he scoffed. "C'mon now. Don't go *there*."

I got up from the couch. He reached for my hand to try to stay me.

I glanced at his hand on my hand. My natural reaction was to resist and put up some sort of fight. I wasn't in the mood.

So I sat back down.

"Come closer," he said. "What you doin' way over there?"

"Please. I don't think that's appropriate for us anymore. Isn't that what you said?"

"Reesy, I read your e-mail."

"I know you did. You read it seven days ago. And never bothered to respond."

Dandre sighed.

"I didn't know how to."

I leaned my head back against the pillows, too tired to even have the conversation.

"Do you mind if we just leave this whole thing alone?" I asked. "I got your point. I know where you stand. I know where *I* stand. Let's just leave this whole thing alone and let the bullshit go. Cool? I'm much too tired to even talk about it anymore."

He placed his hand on my forehead.

"You feel warm," he said.

I gently took his hand off my face.

"I'm fine. I just woke up from a bad dream."

"Aw, sweetie," he cooed, and moved a little closer.

"Dandre," I said flatly. "Please . . . *don't*."

"All right. I'm sorry. But I need for you to understand something."

I exhaled heavily, closing my eyes.

"And what is that?"

"You didn't see what you think you saw tonight."

I smirked. Here we go with *this* shit. The oldest lie in the book.

"Doesn't matter. You owe me no explanations, so please, don't offer any."

"That woman was Tiana. She's an old friend. We used to date a long time ago."

I raised my finger tiredly.

"I told you. I *don't* wanna know."

"Please, Reesy. Just hear me out."

I sat up, opening my eyes.

"No, Dandre, I need for you to just hear *me*. I am *sooo* tired of loving you. Tired. I'm tired of baring my soul, and acting like a gotdam fool for a man who knows exactly how I feel and still doesn't give a shit to respond to it."

He was quiet, watching my mouth.

"I needed to see tonight, whether I wanted to or not. I needed some closure. Something to make me move on. The fact that you didn't answer my e-mail helped. Seeing you with another woman tonight did the total trick."

I raised up from the couch again.

"Now, if you don't mind . . . I am so tired, it's not funny. I'm gonna go back to bed and lay down. Let yourself out, okay? I'm not tryna be rude, I'm just exhausted. That's all. I appreciate you coming by, trying to explain things to me."

Before he could respond, I went into the bedroom and climbed back into my bed. I closed my eyes as soon as I lay down. Salt-n-Pepa could show up with Dandre all they wanted. I didn't give a damn what they did with him now.

Isn't that amazing? Without knowing it, in just one night, I had gotten to the point where I didn't care. It's funny, how one revelation can make you have a whole change of heart.

Dandre came in behind me and sat down on the edge of the bed.

I had my back to him.

"I went out with Tiana tonight to talk about you," he said.

I didn't open my eyes. Sleep was calling me, but I could still hear him clearly as his words floated through my fading consciousness.

"When I got your e-mail, my first instinct was to delete it. Reesy, you don't understand how much pain I've gone through over this thing with you."

Sleep was dragging me under with both hands.

"Remember I told you about my moms? And how much my pops loved her?"

I was completely unresponsive.

"Remember I told you that she was my standard? Well, when I met you, you met those standards. You were the total woman, lover and friend for me. Imagine how I felt to learn that all that was a game for you."

I was entering dream mode. Dandre was walking toward me through a misty fog.

"It was like something in me just died when it happened. My heart just packed up shop and took off."

I didn't know which one of him was speaking to me. The real one or the dream.

My body shook weirdly. It shook so that I opened my eyes for real.

"*Whaaa . . . ?*"

"Sweetie, please," Dandre whispered. He'd been shaking me gently to get me to wake up. "I need for you to hear me, okay? Talking to you like this isn't easy for me."

"I told you I was tired," I complained.

He very deliberately sat me up in the bed.

"I know. But I just need for you to hear me on this one issue."

I sighed heavily, rubbed my eyes, and leaned back against the pillow. His face was pained and intense.

"Speak," I said blankly.

Dandre sighed, looked down at the floor, then looked up at me.

"I heard everything you said to me in your e-mail. Loud and clear. And I felt it. I really did."

I said nothing.

"Reesy, I know you still love me. I really do. I need you to understand that I do get that message. And you know I still love you as well. You can't just turn something like that off, no matter what you do."

I studied his movements. He was rubbing his right hand against his right pant leg nervously.

"But you gotta realize how hard this is for me. I wanna be with you. I wanted that from the very beginning. But how do I ever trust you again?"

"You learn to forgive," I whispered.

"That's easier said than done. You weren't so willing to forgive me for what happened at Burch."

Guess he had me there. I chewed at the inside of my bottom lip.

"I can't tell you how many times I read your e-mail last week," he said.

"Then why didn't you give me some kind of sign to let me know you got it?" I asked. "You could have just said *Step off, bitch,* or something. Or did you get a sick thrill out of knowing you were torturing me?"

"I didn't know what to do. I was too confused to do anything."

"I'll bet," I muttered. "That's why you were out with ol' girl tonight. Laughing and touching each other on the arm and shit."

"I told you, Tiana and I went to talk about you. She's always been a great sounding board. Especially when Rick's not around."

"I used to be your sounding board," I said.

"You used to be a lot of things for me," Dandre replied.

"So what did Miss Tiana say?" I asked with sarcasm.

"She told me I should let my anger go and talk to you. Find a way to move past all of this. Something I already knew, but wanted another perspective on."

I was thoroughly surprised.

"She told you that?"

"Uh-huh."

"But if she had told you to drop me, you woulda dropped me, wouldn't you?"

"Nope," he answered. "I was coming back anyway. The feelings were too strong."

He locked his gaze onto mine.

"And as time passed, I was missing you more instead of less, so I knew that something had to give."

My insides went soft and my left cheek twitched. I didn't know what to say to him in response, but I felt like a cloud had just been lifted from my life.

He moved his face closer to mine. My eyes grew large with surprise.

"Stop bucking your eyes like that," he chuckled.

"What are you doing?" I dumbly asked.

"I'd like to kiss you, if you'll let me."

"Sorry. You caught me off guard."

"Didn't mean to."

He drew nearer to me, scooting closer on the bed, his lips a mere millimeter away from my own. I could feel his breath coursing over my mouth.

I closed my eyes, waiting.

He pressed his lips to mine and lingered there. He ran his tongue along the outline of my mouth, then parted my lips and explored inside.

I felt like I was going to die. I'd been wanting him to do that for so long, it was like pure paradise.

We kissed like that for maybe five minutes or more. Our eyes closed, gently exploring each other. Dandre's hand was caressing my face. My arms were thrown around him, pulling him tighter and closer to me.

After a few more kisses, he pulled away. He peered intensely into my face, searching my eyes for a hint of something.

He exhaled.

"All right," he mumbled. "I guess I feel safe enough to do this now."

"Do what?" I whispered.

"*Sssssssssshhhh!!*" he admonished. "Just let me talk, all right. This is hard enough as it is."

He reached into his pants pocket. "Let me show you something."

He pulled out a little purple velvet box.

"I've had this thing so long now, it ain't even funny," he chuckled.

"What is it?" I asked, looking at the funny-shaped box.

My heart was racing wildly.

"This is one of the things I talked to Tiana about."

He played around with the box in his hands.

It was shaped like a trapezoid. With Dandre, Lord only knows what it could have contained.

He took a deep breath, then let it out slow.

"You know, I bought this three days after we first hooked up. I showed it to Rick and he laughed me off. He told me I was jumping the gun in a *biiiiiiiiiig* way. Bruh scared me. Made me think that maybe I was a bit on the rush."

Now he was making me nervous. I didn't dare to hope.

Okay, maybe I *did* dare to hope.

"So *what* is it?" I repeated nervously.

He solemnly flipped the lid and looked into my eyes.

It was a very, very, *very* large, very sparkly, marquis-shaped diamond solitaire.

I gasped, in utter shock.

"Dandre . . . ," I whispered.

I stared searchingly into his eyes. He was all seriousness and calm.

I reached for the ring and went to put it on my finger. He stayed my hand.

"I've waited a long time to do that. Can I please have the honors?"

I giggled.

"Yeah. Sorry. Go ahead."

I handed him the ring.

With that, Dandre suddenly got dramatic on me.

He bent down on one knee and held my hand.

I sat in the bed, staring at him with disbelief. My eyes must have looked like plates, I was stretching them so damn big.

"Are you sure you wanna be down there like that?" I asked.

"Reesy, please . . ."

I shut up. I'd never expected to see this day, let alone expected it to happen with Dandre.

"Teresa Snowden . . . ," he began, ". . . despite everything that happened between us, I want you to know that I do love you. Really. No matter how I may act sometimes."

I chewed my bottom lip furiously. My nerves were running wild as I listened to him talk.

"If you can forgive me for what I did to you at Burch, I can put aside what you did to me. You think we can do that?"

I nodded foolishly, my lips pressed together.

"You have to answer out loud," he insisted. "We have to make this serious and official."

"Yes, Dandre," I replied obediently. "I can forgive you, if you can forgive me."

He pursed his lips together to keep from laughing.

"Okay. All right. *Here goes...,*" he said.

He cleared his throat.

"Teresa Snowden, would you do me the honor of being my wife?"

I paused, rolling my eyes up casually in the air, considering.

"You gon' cheat on me?" I asked.

"You've got your nerve!!" he laughed.

"This ain't about my nerve," I replied. "You gon' cheat on me or not?"

"Never," he answered seriously without missing a beat.

I pressed my lips together again.

"Then . . . I think you better call Tyrone."

"What?!"

I chuckled.

"My *daddy*!! We better get on the phone and call up my folks. Looks like their overgrown daughter done caught herself a husband."

"Say the words," he replied. "Remember, we have to make it official."

"Okay," I sighed. "Yes, Dandre LeRon Hilliard. I would love to be your wife."

Dandre's left eyebrow flew up.

"How you know my middle name?" he asked. "I don't know yours."

"Don't you worry 'bout that," I laughed. "That just goes to show you, don't be tryna slip nuthin' past me. You never know *what* I know and *how* I know it."

"All right, baby girl. That's a bet."

Dandre slid the ring onto my finger. Then he got up from the floor, sat on the edge of the bed again, put his arms around me, and pulled me close to him.

We kissed tenderly for what seemed like an eternity.

When we broke free, I leaned my face close against his ear.

"I was praying that you would let me in again," I whispered. "You've been a godsend to me. I don't ever want to let you go."

He held me tighter.

"I just hope you remember that forty years from now, when you're all complacent and cranky, walking 'round the crib with a mouthful of attitude and a head full of gray braids."

I laughed.

"I'll have dreads by then," I replied.

"Oh, goodness! I better start bracing myself now, then. My angry black wife. Somebody turn off the lights and call the law!"

"Silly," I whispered, leaning in to kiss him.

We sat like that for a few minutes, just laughing and holding each other, varying our positions and kissing.

When we finally made love, it was a symphony.

A moment of music that even Maxwell couldn't top.

YOU DA BEST, DADA

We were riding up the highway, on our way to Martha's Vineyard.

Misty and Rick had been back for weeks, and were obviously on honeymoon part two.

Dandre and I hadn't seen them since their return. But we had other things to address.

We were in the Z, the sunroof was open, and the wind was blowing wildly through my braids.

Dandre was behind the wheel, navigating the traffic like the pro that he was.

Erykah Badu's live CD was pouring out of the speakers.

I'd brought nine CDs with me. *Mood music,* I liked to call it. Music to think by. Music to love by. Music to make memories with.

I'd brought all three of Maxwell's joints (. . . What you think, I'm stupid? I ain't going *nowhere* without my boy by my side!), Sweetback, the soundtrack to *Love Jones* (mostly because Maxwell sang on both—ha! you betta act like you know!), and D'Angelo and Erykah's first and second albums.

"Ye Yo," Erykah's jam that I loved to sing so much (Dandre was now calling me his *ye yo*) was playing.

According to Miss Badu in the song, *ye ye,* from which she got *ye yo* I guess, was a Swahili term for mother.

Dandre had no idea how significant the title was.

"So . . . you ready to do this?" he asked.

"So . . . you ready to have me do it?" I replied.

I had my dark shades on and my feet were on the dash. I was cold-chillin' like a villain.

"I *think* I'm ready," he laughed. "Be patient with me, though. I told you, I've never had anybody do this with me before."

"I'll be cool," I promised.

We were going to spend some time at his crib by the beach.

I had taken off another couple of days from the show. Tamara was getting plenty of chances to act as my stand-in. (I didn't care. No threat there.)

Dandre and I had a quiet, romantic weekend planned. But, more importantly, we were going to sit out by the ocean, side by side. The two of us together. And we were going to contemplate the sea.

It was his private thing that he'd done for years and had never shared with anyone.

But I wasn't even sweatin' it. I didn't know what my man was so nervous about. As far as *I* was concerned, he and I had already contemplated the sea.

I'd seen it long ago in a dream. It was almost perfect. Except for the part where we'd talked about Helmut. This time, I knew, as the foam washed over our feet at the water's edge, we wouldn't be talking about Helmut at all.

No way.

This time, the dream would be absolutely unmarred. Helmut would be the last thing on our minds that afternoon.

What we *would* be talking about was this seed in my belly.

The one we'd planted the night he proposed.

I hadn't taken a pregnancy test or anything, so I didn't have any true proof that I was with child. After all, it had only been a few weeks.

But, in my heart, I knew it. I'd never been more positive about anything before, other than my love for Dandre.

A girl knows her body and when she's going through a change. Whether it's real or intuitive.

"What you over there grinnin' at?" Dandre asked, smiling at me.

"I'm not grinnin'," I snapped briskly.

"You're grinnin', black woman. Skinnin' like a Cheshire cat."

"What*ever*."

"Uh-huh," he laughed. "*Whatever* is right!"

"I'm just thinkin'," I said. "Can't a girl just think for a minute?"

"Well," he replied, "save some of that thinkin' for the sea."

I took off my shades and glanced over at him.

"Oh, trust me," I assured him, "I am. You just make sure you're ready for some of these thoughts I'm gonna drop."

"Lay it on me, *ye yo*. A brother's ready for *anything* you got."

I smiled to myself. He wasn't ready. *No way* was he ready for *this*.

I wasn't even sure if *I* was ready.

As a matter of fact, I couldn't believe I was even falling into the whole fairy tale bit that I wasn't sure I ever really believed to begin with. That whole *girl-meets-boy, girl-falls-for-boy, girl-gets-married, girl-gets-pregnant* (well, maybe not necessarily in that order), *girl-lives-happily-ever-after* thang.

Reesy gets rescued by a man and rides off into the sunset.

The end.

Uh-uh. I don't *think* so.

It was too easy. It was too trite.

It was so . . . *not me.*

Even though I'd had Tyrone and Tyrene as examples of marital bliss with a twist, I was still too much of a skeptic to fall for *that* old bit.

Suddenly, out of nowhere, I felt a little apprehensive.

I cut my eyes over at Dandre again.

Sure, he was sitting over there smiling *now.* But what would his expression be as he sat behind the wheel this time next year? Or next season? Hell, a *week* from now?

Would I even be in the car?

My heart did a little *thunk-a-thunk* of fear mixed with dread.

As I sat there, I slowly began to freak.

I mean, how could I be sitting there planning anything with him in the first place? *My* ass was so volatile, how the heck could I expect to be able to deal with *him?*

Half the time, I didn't know how *I* was going to be from one day to the next.

On top of that, it's not like he and I had a sane relationship. It was a roller-coaster ride that had been founded on vengeance, deception, and sex.

I cut my eyes over at him again, my hand upon my belly.

Shit. I loved him so.

I let out a heavy sigh and stuck out my bottom lip.

"Stop worrying about things that you can't control. I'm not going anywhere, girl."

My heart stopped on a dime.

"What?!!"

"You heard me," he said softly, putting his hand on my leg. "Stop worrying about the future. The future will take care of itself. Let's just do this thing day by day. That's all we can do. Take it day by day, and minute by minute. *Ye yo, ye yo.*"

My mouth curled up into a smirk.

"You make me sick," I mumbled.

He rubbed my leg soothingly.

"Oh yeah? Why is that?"

" 'Cause . . . you think you know me! Your ass don't *know* me. You don't know nuthin' *about* me!"

"If you say so," he chuckled.

"I *know* so!" I snapped.

"A'ight, baby, whatever you say. But let's put it this way . . . I know enough."

I couldn't help but smile, so I chewed on my bottom lip to keep it from showing.

I rubbed my stomach, my hand trying to feel for the bud of a baby within.

I was still a little scared. Okay . . . a *lot* scared. This baby would affect my career and introduce a whole 'nother person into my life, on top of me dealing with this marriage thang.

It meant that I was *really* going to have to be responsible now. Responsible for how I did *everything*. Not just ripping and running and doing whatever I wanted, whenever I wanted to do it.

I couldn't just act any old kind of way, either. There were a lot of changes I was going to have to make, to be the kind of parent I knew my child deserved to have.

"Guess what?" I blurted.

"What's that, babe?"

"I'm going to stop cursing."

"Oh *really?*" he chuckled. "And what brought about *this* drastic decision?"

"You say that like I curse all the time!" I snapped. "Like I'm addicted to it or something!"

"Well . . ."

"*Fuck you,* Dandre!"

He burst out laughing. I couldn't help but laugh at it, too.

"That's all right, sweetie," he said in a patronizing voice while patting my knee. "I'll work with you on it. We'll hold each other's hands and quit this cussin' thang together, okay?"

"Bite me," I quipped.

"Don't get mad, 'toine," he teased.

I cut my eyes at him.

How could I be mad at him? The good part of it all was that I knew Dandre would definitely step up to the plate, even *after* I told him about the baby. And he'd be happy to be there with me. Lock, stock, baby, curse words, and all.

I suddenly had another thought.

"Hey."

"Uh-huh."

"Are we riding off into the sunset?" I asked.

Dandre laughed.

"Yeah. I guess you could kinda say we are."

I nodded slowly, chewing on my bottom lip again.

"So . . . who saved who?"

"What?" he asked, glancing over at me. "Saved *who* from *what?*"

"You know what I mean!" I said with exasperation. "The man is always saving the woman at the end. Here we are, in your white Z. You may as well be the knight on a white horse. This shit is as hokey as it gets."

"Well . . . you weren't a damsel in distress, if that's what you mean. I'm surprised you even said yes to marrying me. You act like you don't need nuthin' from nobody."

I stared ahead at the road, still chewing on my lip.

"So you don't consider yourself as my savior or anything?" I finally asked, looking over at him.

"*Hell no!* Save *you?* Woman, *please!* You can fight your own battles and slay your own dragons! You don't need me for *jack!*"

He grew quiet for a moment.

"Come to think about it," he said curiously, "why *are* you with me? What can I do for you that you can't do for yourself?"

"*Exactly!*" I exclaimed. "You can't do *anything* for me that I can't do for my damn self!"

Dandre smiled.

"All right, Miss Bad Ass. I guess you *told* me."

"Don't forget that."

"Sheesh . . . ," he laughed, "how can I? But I want you to always be aware of one thing."

"What's that?" I asked, cutting my eyes at him suspiciously.

"Just remember . . . I don't need you, either. It's not like I'm some punk-ass negro. I was mackin' before your triflin' behind came along."

Dandre was staring at me as he said this.

Both my eyebrows shot up at once and my lips balled up.

He burst out laughing and stared back out at the road, delighted at the reaction he'd gotten.

"See there?" he said. "Don't feel so good when people just slam you with insensitive remarks, does it?"

I said nothing. I just sat there sucking on my bottom lip, sulking.

We rode along in silence for a few miles, both of us staring out into the horizon.

My hand was still on my belly. His hand was still on my leg. He moved it a little in a rubbing motion.

"I'm with you because I love you," I mumbled reluctantly. "I've never really loved anyone like this before."

Dandre said nothing. He just let me talk.

"And you give me a lot of things. You give me love. You give me comfort . . . security . . . nurturing."

He was still silent.

"And every now and then, you slang it real good, too."

"Hmph!" he chuckled softly. "Glad to be of service."

"I *want* to share my life with you," I said. "I'm not doing it because you're saving me or anything. I'm doing it because I *want* to be here."

"Are you talking to me or yourself?" he asked.

"Both of us, I guess."

"Well, I ain't mad at cha."

We were both quiet again, as the miles rolled away beneath us.

"So I guess we kinda saved each other, huh?" I offered.

I looked over at him, waiting for a response.

"Yeah," he nodded. "I guess you could say that. But actually, neither one of us was in any real distress."

"Right," I agreed.

He rubbed my leg as he made a humming noise under his breath.

"I've got an idea," he said. "Why don't we say we're just riding off into the sunset because we want to. Just because it's there."

I grinned.

"I like that."

"Good," he said, leaning over to kiss me on the cheek. "I like it, too. I don't think we could have picked a prettier sunset to ride off into."

"Word."

He took his hand off my knee and took my hand from my belly. He clasped it tightly in his.

We sat there like that, rolling on the road, feeling the hum of the car buzzing up simultaneously through our bodies.

Symmetry in motion.

Separate, but in sync.

This thang might work, I thought. *If I roll with it, it might come together just fine.*

At least I could say with a fair amount of certainty that he was putting in the same amount of juice that I was giving.

And, as far as I was concerned, that was all that mattered.

Ye yo. Ye yo.